I0748476

The Renegade Campaign

A Novel

JAMES FABER

Salem-Danvers Village Press
HAELLSTADFTSS PRESS

Published by HAELLSTADFTSS PRESS, an imprint of Salem-Danvers Village Press, which is a division of Organ Group Corporation

First Edition; Hardcover

Subversion Series Book 3

Publication note:
This work is a creation of fiction. Any events, places, and or people in this book are fictitious, even if they might seem real. This book might be based on and contain real people but any and all events that take place are fictitious and have been made up. Any person indicated in this work of fiction is clearly an idea of the author. Nothing represented in this work of fiction is real, even though actual things might seem real. The publisher nor the author, or anybody affiliated with them are responsible for anything that occurs. This means that you may not file any legal action against us for something that occurs or occurred in your life.

Cover Images by Trafa and JGolby © 2019

City destroyed by war & Mysterious Woman

Cover Text and Design by James Faber © 2019

ISBN 10: 9780998431185
ISBN 13: 0-9984311-8-4

The Renegade Campaign

A NOVEL

James Faber

DEDICATION

This book is dedicated to those who support the ideologies of socialism, communism, and Marxism, because without you this book wouldn't be possible, but keep an open mind since a decrease in government regulations and taxes can help America prosper to its fullest extent making it possible for the American people and society to thrive at its best.

ONE

I

In the deep confines of a political disaster, there is some hope for the rest of the world that something indeed will happen that will lead to the desired promise of hope and change, as people around the world are watching people drowning in floods and burning in fires around the giant cesspool of American politics, all the while forests are burning down making trees disappear, that wild animals are roaming free and terrorizing the hell out of everyone and everything, and several groups of environmental terrorists who to target next in their vengeful act of criticizing people that eat meat and every other animal.

As the worlds watches the deadly events happening in America there is just concern about what will happen next, as buildings start mysteriously turning to dust and rubble.

There is a change that some people will hope that will lead to the first female president in the history of the United States of America.

It is certainly not far-fetched but that will have to remain to be seen, only as a hope for the future which has yet to come, due to nothing more than craziness, misinformation, and chaos, causing anarchy and destruction everywhere.

But California is just under attack, with no help in sight as the men and women of the fire department try to put out severe flames that don't want to stop because of the never-ending battle between activists and government about preventing them to begin with.

There is a day for all this.

That day is the day when it will be time to lead a political revolution against the elite political class.

That day is when the people rise against the corrupt politicians of Washington DC.

That day is when the populists and the people rise up in order to tell those corrupt politicians and lobbyists that their time is up.

That day will be when people take to the streets by protesting the corrupted elite and political class.

That day is when chaos is in full swing and where the masses will demand change.

That day is today!

Fast forward to the past before this happened!

There were all types of commotion going on in the minds of the political elites.

It was just revolutionary at what happened where forest fires did not matter at all, because everything changed for the better, as the world started to watch in despair their financial and personal security risk is in a greater peril than it was once before.

News reports start appearing on air saying Russian criminals have hacked credit card data with the help and blessing of rogue intelligence agencies around the world.

Analysts and pundits suggested it was the work of people who had nothing better to do but then just a week later it was just more and more in a never-ending situation, to the point that these were people that wanted to ruin the lives of innocent people.

An imminent news report indicated the successful hack of credit card and other financial information from a major discount retailer, and the first traces of evidence led to Russia and China with the help of organized crime in an all too familiar way.

But this was just the beginning, a devastating blow to the security and safety of America.

The world was watching and they were scared.

It was just a panic attack and created adrenaline that has never been seen before.

People have been let down.

The consequences have set in and now there is just a surprise waiting for everyone.

Time passed by and people just forgot about everything until there was just chaos and anarchy yet again.

"What's going on," asked an IT staffer in a panicked voice?

"There is something desperately wrong with our computer network," stated another IT staffer for the National United Peoples' Traditionalist Labor Workers Party Committee.

"What's just happened to our security network," said one other panicked IT staffer?

"Oh no, someone or something has just shut down our security network," said a fourth IT staffer.

"Quickly, we must tell the leadership of the NUPTLWP, or else we'll be doomed, said the first IT staffer.

Rushing down the hallway to the central security monitoring center of the NUPTLWP Committee, chairwomen Stephanie Donavan-Candy told everyone to stay calm.

"We must not hesitate or else those bastards of the Central Administration Party will say we cannot defend our networks against hackers," said Donavan-Candy.

"But who, because if we contact the Central Bureau of Domestic Investigations, they might try to pin the blame on us, so we must get an outside who will vouch for us but will also try to mislead the public so that we won't be blamed," said Donavan-Candy.

"I know who we can get; we can contact Tri-National Security Defense, because they are former CBDI officials who we have hired before, and members of their families are even on our payroll," stated Donavan-Candy once again.

As everyone stood aghast, the entire team stood steadfast, and Donavan-Candy stated, "In a week's time we shall hold a press conference in order to tell what happened to us."

Exactly one week has passed since the investigation has begun into what happened to the computer networks of the NUPTLWP.

Already, the Tri-National Security Defense investigation has gathered information into who could have hacked or infiltrated the security networks at the NUPTLWP because of possible digital fingerprints.

So far the investigation has pointed out that Russian agent might be responsible for everything and reports have already leaked out to the public. There is one problem though. It has not been confirmed Russia is behind the alleged cyber-attack.

Instead, it has been indicated that the leadership of the NUPTLWP because Donavan-Candy has already stated she intends to hold a press conference in a few moments of time.

Around 11:59 am Eastern Time, Donavan-Candy held her intended press conference in regards to what might have happened.

"Hello everyone!

As you know my name is Stephanie Donavan-Candy, the chairwoman of the National United Peoples' Traditionalist Labor Workers Party.

About a week ago, there was a cyber-attack launched against the computer systems network of the NUPTLWP Committee.

We have not identified the people or group behind it but we suspect it is the Russian government because of their disdain for our political party and the political process.

We have every intention to believe that the Russians do not support our campaign to help elect the first female President of the United States of America.

They want us to live in a time that promotes racism, misogyny, sexism, and xenophobia in a way that has never been seen before.

We know that our indication of who tried to launch a cyber-attack us will receive doubt because we haven't had the time to fully investigate.

We have hired Tri-National Security Defense a week ago today. And today, we can report that their initial investigation has revealed possible evidence that Russia was behind the cyber-attack.

How do they know this?

Well, Tri-National Security Defense has indicated electronic evidence of ransomware, spyware, malware, and specific IP addresses that can be only from Russia.

The evidence so far indicates it is Russia who is the only entity behind the alleged cyber-attack.

As I have stated before in previous press conferences, this type of activity is not to be tolerated.

We will not let the Russians get away with this because it is an attack against us and an attack against America.

It is an attack against our democracy and an attack on women.

We have previous evidence that the Russian government is helping the Central Administration Party to get their nominee elected.

As for the cyber-attack, we believe this evidence is revealing and will lead us to the truth about why the Russians are trying to attack our democracy.

We will not need to contact the Central Bureau of Domestic Investigations because we believe our contractor will be able to handle everything. I will be taking some questions now."

Hi, this is John Smith from Cyber Action News DC, "Chairwoman Donavan-Candy, why did you not contact the Central Bureau of Domestic Investigations to examine your computer network?"

Well John, the people and experts at Tri-National Security Defense are all retired CBDI agents and with their previous knowledge of working for the CBDI will aid in the investigation.

Hello, I'm Carina Alexander for American Systems Broadcasting Network Channel 7 News, "You said you and your organization believe Russia is helping the Central Administration Party to elect their candidate so that he can become the next President of the United States of America, so what is your evidence of this?"

Well Carina, It is well-known that the Central Administration Party is very Pro-Russian, so it wouldn't be a surprise that they would get the Russian government to help them win the election. It is a fact that they have always had a friendly relationship with the Russians.

"What you have said is potentially false and misleading, as there is no evidence or indication that the Central Administration is pro-Russian, because you have no evidence, and instead you are again trying to make this about politics, so why do you keep on doing this," asked Carina Alexander of American Systems Broadcasting Network Channel 7 News.

"Are there any other questions, no, then ok," asked Donavan-Candy of the National United Peoples' Traditionalist Labor Workers Party?

Meanwhile, back in 2005, Katrina Maribelle is back from her trip of an alternate dimension of Earth. A mild summer day, it is still different in the town of Winslow, South Dakota. There are people but not as busy, but the day is still young and everybody is in church. It is still early in the morning but church starts early here at sunrise. But, there is a problem that is still unknown from a certain point of view.

Quickly, Katrina races back to her house with her friend from the alternate dimension. She sees blazes of bright orange flames and there is deep black smoke coming from everywhere.

The timing could not be worse. She just got back from an alternate dimension and the same could be happening here.

Perhaps this is just a dream but it is not yet known what is happening.

As Katrina watches she just stops to see what is happening. She still does not know if it is just her imagination or someone wants her attention. Silently, while calmly moving forward, Katrina bends down to see what looks like a flyer asking about a reward for a missing dog. This could be a message or even a trap, but there is no certainty if it is something meant to spread propaganda. Time will eventually reveal itself to the explanation of this event. It must be explained in a way that will expose what is currently happening.

Katrina takes the flyer, folds it up, and places it in her black trench coat double-breasted jacket.

Across the street, she notices something very strange that feels like déjà vu. It kinds of resembles what happened in the alternate dimension she visited.

Then, out of nowhere, men dressed in all black with what looks to also be ski masks appear, and they start racing back to the place where Katrina is looking.

Suddenly, there was a large pounding, like the sound of thunder ringing in the aftermath after it starts.

There is no other reason that could explain this because it sounded as if though buildings started to collapse under the weight of their foundations.

There is no known explanation if anyone even survived because it was like as if a loud crash of an airplane caused destruction of everything.

Nothing could be revealed but then there are no signs of the men dressed all in black with ski masks.

It seems as though they have vanished again just like before.

Could anyone explain the reason?

Well, no, because there is no reason for any of this.

Then, there was what felt like an aftershock of the ground shaking in response to the loud crash that sounded like thunder or an airplane.

Katrina waited there and stood still, not being affected by what was happening. It could all be a warning or something useful.

It is just a reminder of everything of the past but there seems to be something new.

Then, another loud but terrifying aftershock of the ground trembling took place again.

It all seems all too familiar and sinister. But there is just something wrong and it won't happen overnight.

There is just this sinking feeling in the mind of this déjà vu because of the things that are happening now in Winslow, South Dakota.

All of a sudden, everything all around Katrina goes up in bright red and blue flames with the presence of thick black smoke spreading to every corner.

Katrina is safe and puts on a gas mask.

Trees all around are up in flames with bright orange flames billowing from leaves and branches.

Houses are filled with very thick black and white smoke that resembles fog or even smog.

People can be heard screaming and there is just no way to escape.

The roads are beginning to tremble again but this time harsher and harsher with the force of cracking.

Sidewalks are now the only safe place to be on and it seems the fires are spreading to the grass because it is now burning bright red and orange with some showing of white smoke.

Everything is just up in flames and it is just a lost cause.

There is no way that people in trapped buildings can escape now because it is just too late.

Quickly, Katrina finds her prisoner from the alternate dimension, but she is nowhere to be found.

The prisoner has disappeared and maybe that is just a coincidence or she just knew about these fires.

Now with no one in sight, there is just misery and death.

There is just the sound of people screaming with anguish and sadness because they are afraid.

This is all too common but very mysterious.

Temperatures are not even high enough to cause a fire and the cold breeze should not even cause flames and smoke to appear.

There is just no explanation for this to happen unless it is an electrical fire, but that doesn't even make sense.

Fires and flames just don't spread like this from building to building in a matter of seconds of they are different buildings.

Trees just don't catch on fire in a matter of seconds all at the same time.

This is just a strange event and it seems like the new normal.

At least the road trembling seems to be normal while the grass catching on fire is due to falling leaves and branches.

Everything else is just strange or it is just something that is somehow an act of God.

But now, there is a new threat that seems more dangerous than any other thing that has appeared.

It is the appearance that the sky is no longer its natural color of blue.

It is the appearance that something dark is blocking the natural color of the sky with some type of pollution.

It is the appearance that this pollution was caused by the sudden thick smoke from these unnatural fires.

It is the appearance of smog and it is extremely thick with a known consistency of primordial ooze but it was more than that.

It felt like a very thick fog that was too hard to be penetrated.

But then a thick orange haze appeared making it worse, as now this was from the flames and that was just the beginning of the end.

II

Rushing past everything as fast as possible, Katrina ran in order to escape the flames and smoke of the fires.

Fleeing like the speed of light, she quickly disappeared in a flash of bright white light with the presence of a sonic boom.

With that, there was no trace of Katrina in sight.

She was gone forever and would not know where she was headed.

It could be something of her imagination but soon time will tell, and eventually Katrina will find herself some place new.

For the time being it is just all conjecture and it too shall be revealed.

Then, a bright flash of white light appears in a dark alley with the sound of a quick sonic boom.

Some figure appears and walks out with what looks like a smirk on their face.

The bright flash of white light suddenly disappears.

There appears to be a person there but so far they could be hiding in the shadows.

Someone somewhere is up to something and it won't be long until it is found out.

Suddenly, a shadow appears from the dark alley and then the person is revealed to be Katrina in her black trench coat jacket showing no sign of emotions.

It just seems like a normal and regular day for her as usual in the mindset of an explorer.

Unfazed, Katrina moves forwards and refuses to look back behind her or that soon will lead to a chaotic mess that will create more trouble.

Upon leaving the dark alley, Katrina spots a bench in a very empty and barren place.

She sits down and closes her eyes for a few minutes in order to think about stuff.

And then she opens her eyes and sees trees, grass, and a city full of people around her doing what they normally do.

And then a newspaper appears on top of her lap.

The date on the newspaper indicates it is June 15, 2015 and the lead story is about famous software and real estate developer billionaire Carlton Chris Winters officially declaring his candidacy from the day before to run for President of the United States of America.

The story doubts Carlton Winters will become the next President because they think he does not have a chance, believing that Cynthia Norwell Anderson, who declared her candidacy for the National United Peoples' Traditionalist Labor Workers Party on April 11, 2015, has the upper hand.

Katrina does not think much of the lead story and decides she needs a place to stay but she does not know where she is.

Katrina looks at the newspaper again and sees the city is indicated as Washington DC and then decides to look at the travel section to see if there are any good nearby hotels.

She notices that Carlton Winters has recently opened his hotel the day before and that certain rooms are for sale.

Knowing that her parents own a home in DC, Katrina goes to the affluent neighborhood of Massachusetts Avenue NW so that she can get some money from her room when she lives there in the summer months during school breaks while her parents live there most of the year because of their work.

Passing by the trees and sidewalk, Katrina walks calmly to her second home in a matter of twenty minutes.

She reaches the front door and does not know if she has a spare key but checks one of her pockets and feels what looks to be an old black and silver skeleton key.

She puts the key in the doorknob and then turns it, revealing it to work and unlock the door, in which the door pushes in forward.

Closing the door behind her, Katrina sees there is nothing but complete darkness with a lack of lighting even if there are lamps and lights attached to the walls of the interior.

This house is nothing like her house in Winslow, South Dakota where she lives with a maid, butler, and house servants most of the time. Sure, her parents do live with Katrina in Winslow, South Dakota for some days out of the year, but since her parents have a department of defense and homeland security contract, it is easier for her parents to live in DC, notwithstanding their past careers as news reporters and fighting in the second world war.

Katrina walks past a straight corridor and remembers to turn left and then right to reach her room.

She turns the knob left and her room opens in front of her.

Katrina recalls the code to her safe and enters it correctly with all three lights turning green to reveal it is ready to be opened by turning the lever to the right then to the left.

Not knowing how much cash she needs, she takes twenty-five bundles of five million dollars and places it in a solid black briefcase.

Karina quickly closes the safe, walks out of her room and shuts it, and then locks the front door.

Taking the scenic route to the hotel, Katrina walks pass many trees.

After realizing the hotel is just a few blocks away, Katrina comes to an abrupt halt and enters the white revolving doors of an old government post office building.

She goes to the front desk and asks about the rooms available for sale.

Katrina sees the front desk person dial a number and asks if Carlton Winters is available for a meeting with a new and potential buyer of the penthouse on the thirty-seventh floor.

The front desk person is told soon in a few minutes.

"So, Carlton Winters will be down shortly, and will discuss the sale with you," said the front desk person.

"Will there be anyone else that will be part of this meeting," asked Katrina?

"Yes, possibly the personal attorney of Carlton Winters, so you can sign your potential contract if you decide to buy the penthouse for the asking price or a negotiated deal, but in the meantime please take a seat in the lobby while you wait" said the front desk person to Katrina.

A few minutes passed, and the elevator doors opened, revealing a tall heavy-set man in a dark black suit standing next to a moderate person of average weight and height.

Carlton Winters went to the front desk with his personal attorney, Harrison Nicholas.

"Good afternoon Mr. Winters and Mr. Nicholas, if you follow me, I will take you to your potential buyer of the penthouse in this hotel," said the front desk person.

"Here she is, the person who wants to buy the penthouse," said the front desk person.

"So, what is the reason you want to buy the penthouse on the thirty-seventh floor," asked Mr. Winters.

"Well, I need a place of my own while I am here, even if I have another house near Embassy Row, because I just want a place of my own and not always rely on my parents in the future," said Katrina.

"Hmm, a women who wants to be independent, ok I will take that," said Mr. Winters.

"Well, I have been through a lot the past few weeks and I know what it takes, and plus I want to sprout my wings and live my dream," said Katrina to Mr. Winters.

"So, you are focused and you have an idea what you want to do in life; I like that, because it shows you have potential," said Mr. Winters.

"Right now, my current residence is in Winslow, South Dakota, in my parent's house, but they live here because of their jobs, and that house in South Dakota is always maintained by hired staff," said Katrina.

"Okay, so the current price on the penthouse is about $75 million but we can work out a deal with a mortgage or loan company if you need help paying," said Mr. Winters.

"No special deal is needed because I can pay you in cash now," said Katrina to Mr. Winters.

Katrina opens up her briefcase and takes out fifteen bundles of five million dollars.

"Here you go, here is $75 million," said Katrina.

"Well then, I can have a contract drawn up in a few hours so you can complete your first homeowner's transaction," said Mr. Winters.

"Where do you want to sign your contract to buy the penthouse," asked Mr. Nicholas.

"We can sign it at my parent's place at 202 Massachusetts Avenue NW," said Katrina.

"Okay then, we will see you then, but until that I will need to count all the money you handed me, and if it falls short I will tell you at your parent's house when you sign the contract," said Mr. Winters.

"In the meantime, I will be back at my parent's house waiting for both of you to complete my purchase, and since I don't have a job here I might want to help you with your campaign so you can win," said Katrina.

"That will be excellent, but just tell me when you are ready and I can put you on as a fulltime staff member," said Mr. Winters to Katrina.

With that, Katrina went back to her parent's house near Embassy Row waiting to sign the contract and possibly asking about a job to join the presidential campaign of Carlton Winters.

It could be that all of this a set up intended to destroy the political career of Carlton Winters since he has never run for office for before, but that is never unusual, as usually someone will always attempt to destroy the opposing political campaigns.

It is surely one of the greatest rights of democracy by deciding the most appropriate person for political office.

It will always be like that because of the freedom and rights granted with unlimited freedom of speech.

Of course people will object to that, such as the opponent of Carlton Winters.

It will only be a matter of time until the inevitable happens.

Later that day, Carlton Winters and his personal arrived at Katrina's parents' house.

"Good afternoon, Miss. Maribelle, shall we get to you signing your contract for you to buy the penthouse," asked Mr. Nicholas?

"Of course we should," replied Katrina.

"Okay then, feel free to look over the contract and sign, date, and initial on each page after you have read it, and feel free to ask any questions" said Mr. Nicholas.

Katrina looked over each page and signed, date, and initialed her name at the bottom of each page.

She found it very interesting about how short it was, since it was only five pages long.

But it went into detail about what was expected of her and how to live.

That was certainly strange since it mentioned no consequences, probably because it was a purchase agreement and not a lease.

Anyways, it was a done deal, and Katrina was now the proud owner of a new penthouse.

"Good day, Miss Maribelle, you are now the proud new owner of the penthouse at my recently opened hotel," said Mr. Winters.

"What about the money, do I still owe anything," asked Katrina to Mr. Winters.

"You are fine, you do not owe me anymore money, since it was all paid in full," said Mr. Winters.

"Thank you, I will move in shortly, and I am considering joining your political campaign," said Katrina.

"Okay, I might just happen to bump into you at the hotel so that no one suspects a thing," said Mr. Winters.

"Farewell, until we meet again," said Katrina to Mr. Winters and Mr. Nicholas.

With that, Mr. Nicholas handed Katrina an all access key card to her room, as it was the penthouse, but it was an all access key because of her importance of buying the penthouse.

A few minutes later, Mr. Winters and Mr. Nicholas left, wishing Katrina a good day.

It wouldn't be long now but time will tell if there is anything else to do.

Katrina, on the other hand, had some thinking to do in regards to her now completed purchase.

Should she move in now or later, and why?

It would be shortly that something bad might happen, so she must be secured somewhere else, or it is only just rumors and gossip.

In the height of this possible deception happening, there is one clear thing Katrina must do first before she moves into the penthouse.

She must secure her parent's house in Washington DC.

The beginning has yet to begun and it is still in the interest of everyone else to collude with each other in order to win the campaign at all costs.

As Katrina decides her fate, she knows what she must do, and she has a plan of achieving it in order to make sure everything goes her way so nothing bad will ever happen to her.

Katrina can see it now, the time it needs to happen, and how it must happen in order for her plan to be achieved.

So, there is a dilemma of what to do next, and in that sense that will be at the crosshairs of society during a very unpleasant time.

A few hours later, Katrina has finished securing her parent's house and is heading towards her new penthouse.

No one saw what she did but no one even knows anything anymore.

Arriving a short time later, a girl hooded in a black and red cape is seen entering Carlton Winters newly recent hotel with a brown suede briefcase and a trench coat.

This scene seems all too familiar but she looks and then briefly smiles at the front desk person and then continues to walk forward in a professional yet convincing manner.

Arriving at the elevator, Katrina enters and pushes the "P" for penthouse on the floor level selection panel.

And then something else happens but just the speed of how fast the elevator is going.

It zooms all the way to the penthouse in a matter of just one minute.

Opening up before her, Katrina can see just an entire corridor but she is looking in the wrong direction.

The elevator doors open behind her as well and she can see some type of light behind her so she turns around.

Right in front of her is her new penthouse, filled with all types of amenities, more than one bedroom, multiple bathrooms, several walk-in closets, a full-size kitchen, a dining area, a spa, an entertainment area, and a living room.

And before she gets enough of it, Katrina discovers a gorgeous view from a wide but gorgeous balcony.

Katrina takes off her cape and trench coat and reveals a gorgeous black laced dress beneath it and then leaves her room.

III

Out of nowhere, Katrina bumps into Carlton Winters, and she accepts a job offer as a paid grassroots community adviser, after both bumped into each other in the hotel for a prescheduled unscheduled meeting for some mysterious event. But this is not an ordinary position, as Katrina will be in charge of going undercover and Carlton Winters knew this was what Katrina wanted because of a recent background investigation that was conducted on her family.

So, what to do next!

Katrina thinks for a minute and starts to get an idea of how to go about this idea.

She decides she will embed herself in the Anderson campaign at a cost to spy on her boss's opponent to learn what she is doing so that the Carlton Winters Presidential Campaign can always have the upper hand and know everything.

And besides that, that is in her job description anyways, but Mr. Winters explained to Katrina only one copy of her job description exists and that Katrina was the only one who has access to it.

In reality, Katrina is a campaign spy that will infiltrate the Anderson Presidential Campaign, but on paper she is a paid grassroots community adviser, which simply means she will advise Carlton Winters on anything she finds out in the field. That is simply the perfect cover for any spy to have.

But Katrina knows she must disguise herself so that no one will find out her secret.

She must wear a mask, cut her hair, or put on heavy makeup so that the Anderson campaign doesn't find out anything.

So, she sets it as a goal but reminds herself to also embed herself to infiltrate any other political campaign not associated with Carlton Winters.

Katrina wants to spy on any and all opponents of the Carlton Winters Presidential Campaign because it is her job and she wants to gain useful information to help Carlton Winters to win and become President of the United States of America.

It is a task that Katrina is up to and willing to accept.

IV

Looking forward to infiltrate the Anderson campaign, Katrina goes to a local coffee shop to spot out political supporters of the Anderson campaign so that she can ask those supporters certain questions and to maybe ask to become a volunteer or staffer to the Anderson campaign.

It is not like it will immediately work but Katrina will just have to just go with it. Maybe it will work because the majority of Washington DC supports the politics of the Anderson campaign except for a few people.

This might work after all, as no one even knows who Katrina is, as when she does live in DC it is only for a very short time.

It is highly unlikely she will get spotted but there is always a chance for something. It is just too late to abort the mission, as Katrina must move on with it in order to move forward, and that is what she is going to do so she can succeed.

It will probably be boring scouting out for supporters of the Anderson campaign but it is worth it for Katrina because she needs to infiltrate it for a short time.

Katrina orders a plain dark coffee with no sugar or crème, because she likes her coffee dark to taste the fresh aroma of the plump and freshly ground coffee beans.

She waits and that is all that must be done, and she knows this is common for political supporters to have meetings at local restaurants and businesses to recruit more supporters and to explain the policies of the candidate.

Then, out of nowhere, a group of people show up in what seems to be wearing campaign apparel that supports the Anderson campaign.

It is a large group of around fifteen people and they are all seated immediately.

"Hello, Mr. Charles and guests, how may I help you today," asked a waitress?

"Oh, just give us our usual, what we usually eat," said Mr. Charles to the waitress.

"Fine with me then, six cheeseburgers with fries, five organic green salads with grilled chicken, two veggie burgers, and two grilled chicken sandwiches with avocado and mushrooms," said the waitress.

"Oh, and for drinks, five regular sodas, six diet sodas, three iced teas, and one glass of water with lemon," said Mr. Charles.

"Fine with me," said the waitress.

The waitress went to go get the drinks and then headed back to the podium to wait for more guests.

Meanwhile, Katrina is anxiously waiting to make contact with the members of the Anderson campaign so she can begin her mission.

And then it happened for some strange reason or another, that the plan has been put into motion.

Let's hope that the supporters or members of the Anderson campaign will buy the stunt put forward by Katrina or else all hope has been lost.

But surely, no one can be that naïve, but you will never know in this world, as people can tend to believe anything they want to because the information can be regarded as genuine and authentic.

So the members or supporters of the Anderson campaign might believe everything that Katrina might say to them.

And it was just like that:

"Hello, I overheard you are with the Anderson presidential campaign, and I am interested in maybe volunteering or joining her campaign because I believe in what she stands for.

Right now we have a problem with the current political climate; the other political party denies the existence of science and claim there is no such thing as climate change because they believe the world is not warming.

The other political party does not want to reduce greenhouse gases or carbon emissions because they believe it can never cause pollution to the Earth's atmosphere.

Instead, they say that it is fine to use coal and fossil fuels because the people are used to it. And that is very troubling because they do not want to promote and move gradually towards green energy such as solar panels and wind turbines.

No because they rather pollute the atmosphere with deadly toxins that can cause cancer and respiratory problems.

The thing that makes everything worse however is that we have a gun violence problem because the other political party supports military assault weapons in the hands of civilians.

I believe that only the military should have access to those types of weapons because the military needs to defeat the enemy; and the other side of the spectrum doesn't even want to address the issue.

Whenever there is a mass shooting the other side just says thoughts and prayers, which does not even fix a thing.

We need gun reform now and we need to limit the type of weapons a person can have and the number of bullets that it can shoot, because having more than ten bullets in a magazine can cause a person to go on a shooting rampage that can lead to innocent people dying.

There is also a problem with our current tax system because the wealthy aren't paying their fair share of taxes.

The rich need to pay more in taxes, like 75% of their annual income, so that we can help provide a better future for Americans.

We need to raise taxes on the wealthiest Americans because they hardly pay taxes at all and America needs to prosper.

We must make sure the tax loopholes are closed for Wall Street and the corporate atmosphere, because they tend to cheat the American people.

But that is still not the end of the problems with the other side, as they do not support debt-free college.

The other side believes college is a privilege and that not everybody needs to attend, but the more serious problem is that they believe if a person decides to attend college then they should pay for it.

To me, college is a right and all people who live here in America should graduate debt-free.

I believe that college should be free because education is necessary now in order to get a good-paying job.

And besides, we need to fix the current educational system because too many college graduates have too much debt to pay and they can't get a good job, forcing them to go into bankruptcy.

As an American, I also believe in health care being a universal right.

We are the only country in the world that doesn't provide free health care to people in need.

Currently, the insurance companies and hospitals are dictating the terms of what people should pay, and it is outrageous because the insurance companies and hospitals are charging patients too much money.

We must make sure that health care is free for everyone so that anyone that needs medical help does not go into bankruptcy.

We must make sure that people have enough to live on and that is why people need to make a minimum wage at least of $15.00 per hour, so people can afford the things that they need and to pay all of their bills.

People shouldn't be homeless, but I would support a $20.00 per hour minimum wage because it can provide for a better future.

There is nothing wrong with that because everyone needs to be treated equally, including minorities and people of other racial and ethnic backgrounds.

Right now there is the problem of white privilege and toxic masculinity, as too many minorities are getting in trouble for doing nothing wrong while white people are getting off on major crimes.

Too many white men are also beating up on people and on women because they believe they are more powerful than women and believe they are always right because they have more experience because of just saying so.

As I woman, no one should accept violence and aggression from any man, because people deserve to be treated fairly and equally with respect.

But as a woman, I believe the government should not outlaw abortion, because people need abortions, because sometimes a woman can be raped.

As a woman, the government shouldn't limit access to my body, because they do not know what is best for me.

The other political party has decided to launch a war on women's health care, because they want to regulate our bodies.

We must stop this now. We must reform our criminal justice system because people are not receiving fair sentences.

Judges and prosecutors are deciding the cases against minorities in a discriminatory and illegal manner because white people are receiving less harsh sentences than people of other racial or ethnic backgrounds.

We must reform this now because it is a problem.

People have the right to be treated with respect and dignity and that is how it must be."

With that, Mr. Charles handed Katrina a card, and told her to meet them at the next campaign meeting, which was on the back of the card so she doesn't need to ask.

"Thank you for your time, I won't disappoint, because we need a better future, and the other side only wants to set progress backwards," said Katrina.

It was surely a surprise that Katrina said what she said to Mr. Charles and his guests, but she never actually believes in any of that because Katrina is just trying to infiltrate the Anderson campaign in order to learn tactics, strategies, and political information that might also devastate the Anderson campaign so that the Winters campaign can win in the end.

And surely, what she said to Mr. Charles and his guests convinced them that she fully supports the Anderson campaign, so now Katrina can just infiltrate it.

She fooled them all.

That was the best strategy to convince everyone.

Surely, saying stuff you don't believe in while showing passion makes it all convincing and no one will ever know the truth.

On the back of the card, the address of the next meeting was at a local park next to an independent pizzeria.

The meeting date was the next morning around 10. So now, Katrina has to decide if she will attend, but it is too late for that, as she has already cozied up to the most important senior officials of the Anderson campaign.

She decides that she will attend otherwise they will suspect something is wrong. Now she must decide what she will wear in order to infiltrate the

Anderson campaign.

Time shall face the inevitable task that something might show up in the last minutes of campaign, that a certain surprise might actually hurt the Anderson campaign because there was a traitor on the inside for which is a betrayal to the party itself.

That time could be now because of Katrina and how she presented herself but it is more likely to occur within the last few weeks to the last few days of the presidential campaign.

When time itself it is ready, there will be a surprise for the world to revel in, but until then, Katrina will just have to set everything in action.

It is no surprise that the Anderson campaign believed what Katrina said to them, but Katrina is just using the usual talking points while also asserting emotions while expressing beliefs in a very believable manner that she doesn't even believe in.

Surely, all of those senior campaign staffers believed they gained a valuable friend or asset in helping to get the first women elected as the president.

But if Cynthia Norwell Anderson is not elected president, then something sinister might happen to the rest of the country and the world.

It is just as simple as that but that is here to say otherwise.

In the mind of some, there is just the case of everything that might be heard and said.

That is just how it goes and that is how it must be, but the course of action is now.

The country will panic.

The people will riot in the streets.

It will be a nightmare for everyone to experience.

Soon, the extremists will wake up and start throwing projectiles at innocent people and buildings.

Extremism will take over everything.

Nobody will be able to control it.

There will be stand down orders and the extremists won't comply with any orders.

It will be just an angry mob rising up against the people who support freedom, liberty, and the pursuit of happiness.

They who rise up will be considered the new normal.

And they shall call themselves the resistance because they are against the constitution.

People will get hurt on the streets, at their homes, and at their place of work.

Fires will be the norm of everyday living.

There will be mass violence everywhere and no one will be able to stop it.

The resistance will claim responsibility and will say it is necessary to use such tactics because the law and constitution favors discrimination and inequality.

The police won't respond.

And soon, they shall be elected to the halls of legislatures around the world, trying to overturn history and heritage.

They will form new committees and organizations.

They will become the majority in the legislatures.

They will overturn the constitution and create laws that support a police and surveillance state.

And every day, their supporters will celebrate in the streets, starting fires, and causing chaos.

It will surely be something to watch.

Yet, this will not happen overnight, as it will take time, because after a few years in office, people will decide to vent and will try to take it out on the person who they thought should have not won the presidential election two years ago.

The members of the opposing political party who call themselves the resistance will only campaign and fear, hoping the people and the world will listen to their propaganda and lies, because they claim that government can help fix everything.

The people will never surrender their freedoms and liberty though, as they will try to defeat the resistance, because the resistance will only move to further divide the country and the world because the resistance wants to turn everything backwards, where government controls everything.

If that ever happens, the resistance will be in power and people can be arrested for any kind of reason, even for hurt feelings.

It is a place that doesn't need to exist because it will result in a very scary situation, where people will fear the worst will only happen to them.

It is like an anger waiting dormantly and will only show itself after enough anger builds up to the point that they can't handle and control the problem no more.

But that is years away, even if they already start to chant in the streets about taking away freedoms and liberty because they say it leads to marginalization of women and minorities.

The resistance will make up anything just to get into power.

And it is sad because of what the world has become.

Thankfully, the resistance has not fully risen up yet to that kind of level, because it is still manageable and only a prediction of sorts.

Indeed, that is not all the resistance would try to do, because in their minds they will demand justice for everyone, but when they mean everyone they actually mean for everyone but white people.

And they say they are not racist or discriminatory towards anyone.

The resistance will constantly say they are tolerant of all people, but that will be a lie, because if and when they gain political power they will abuse it.

A centralized review board will review all actions of everyone.

Minorities and women will always have an advantage.

White people will automatically be considered the enemy of the people and of the government.

All houses will be wired with secret spy cameras connected to all electronic devices.

Hurt feelings will result in criminal prosecution.

These things will happen if the resistance gains power in the government, but it will happen either way, even if Anderson wins and then becomes president. So it doesn't matter.

It never mattered.

The whole situation was why it even became an issue.

And then there will be a bunch of youths patrolling the streets to arrest people for no reason.

The whole country will change.

And it will turn to violence, aggression, and chaos.

The end will be near and it will turn to the only thing that matters the most: pandering and procrastination.

V

The next day arrived, and Katrina was just getting ready to go to the meeting to see what she could find out.

Wearing a sexy but slim blue dress, Katrina was ready to leave in order to go to the park.

After a few minutes, she left, and arrived at the park a short time later.

Mr. Charles was already at the park waiting for the rest of his party.

Katrina sat down, and shortly thereafter, the rest of the people arrived.

The meeting began.

"Hello all, I just like to say we are welcoming a new member to the Anderson campaign, and now since it is her first day on the campaign as a junior staff member, she can introduce herself and expand on what she has said yesterday so we can better respond to the crisis in America now, so please give her a welcoming hand," said Mr. Charles.

"*Hello everyone, my name is Katrina, and I just want to expand on what I said yesterday.*

I feel like America is at a crossroads now more than ever because we have many people who constantly harass women.

We have people who don't believe the law should apply to them.

We have politicians who lie and cheat and don't believe in change and reform.

There is constant racism, xenophobia, misogyny, Islamophobia, and discrimination from the other political party.

They do not own up to it and they actually encourage it because they want the American public to be afraid.

We live in a great country but there is a lack of justice and equality.

We must end it now so that the younger people can be treated fairly with respect.

We must make sure no one is discriminated against and that innocent minorities and black people don't get arrested for their skin color.

We must make white privilege a thing of the past and to further help the working-class Americans so they can receive a fair paycheck that doesn't result in living on paycheck to paycheck.

We must make sure immigrants are treated with respect and be treated the same as Americans.

We must end income inequality.

We need to act on global warming because of the rising sea levels and the other political party is refusing to do anything.

We need to do just that."

Katrina was finished talking.

Everyone started to clap and cheer because they all liked what she said.

"Now, we need to go over our plan to get out the vote, possibly setting up a grass roots campaign so we will have a greater chance of winning," said Mr. Charles.

Then there was the next thing to happen.

"Okay, I am going to give all of you, minus Katrina, a sheet of paper with names and addresses so you can knock on doors," said Mr. Charles.

"The meeting is adjourned," said Mr. Charles.

Everyone got up and left, but Katrina stayed to view the scenery, as did Mr. Charles.

"You know, you might have fooled them but not me, because I know you are working as a campaign spy for the Carlton Winters presidential campaign, and I also know that you are a very wealthy person who recently bought the penthouse at the new hotel, but I also know that you believe in nothing that you say as you are trying to infiltrate the Anderson campaign, yet I too am a campaign spy who is working for the Winters campaign and spying on the Anderson campaign, so your secret is safe with me, and I hope to see you soon," said Mr. Charles to Katrina.

With that, there was nothing else to say, and Mr. Charles and Katrina departed the park to go somewhere.

Meanwhile, the other members of the Anderson campaign started to knock on the doors written on the paper.

All were either independents or members of the National United Peoples' Traditionalist Labor Workers Party who have previously voted for members of the United Labor movement once before or who are leaning towards it.

And given that the official name of the political party is too long, party leaders have adopted the shortened name of United Labourists, just because it presents a clear agenda, by trying to help the working class families and not the rich.

It surely sounds familiar, but identifying as a United Labourist will bring in more people as the people will better pivot themselves to accepting what the party has to offer.

It will be enshrined in the minds of the people because they won't have to keep saying such a long and complicated name, as sometimes it is hard to remember and forget.

So, the thing is now to have an idea of what to do next.

The members of the Anderson campaign knocked on each door to see if they would support Anderson as the first female president of the United States of America.

That is because they want to make sure they have enough votes by the first caucuses or primaries that begin early next year.

It will be a tough battle to climb but Cynthia Norwell Anderson is hoping that the second time around will give her the win.

Time has come and gone, and it is already past one o'clock in the afternoon.

It is time to go home and rest, but the campaign workers go to eat lunch, as they have finished the first half of their quotas and have found that the people whose doors they knock on will overwhelming support and vote for Anderson as president.

Meanwhile, Katrina is back at home, trying to make her next move on further infiltrating the Anderson campaign, but now she has help.

But she does not know whether to trust the other fourteen campaign workers because they seem to be diehard United Labourists and actually believe in what she actually said.

Katrina and Mr. Charles don't believe in all of that propaganda and nonsense, even if Katrina said it.

The whole point of Katrina's spiel was to get accepted into the Anderson campaign so that she could infiltrate it, and so far it has worked.

Now, back at home, Katrina decides to rest for a while.

It is just in the nick of time that this happens.

All by herself, there is nothing left to do today, but to clear the mind of what to do next. It is just that time again to relax.

That is the situation at hand here.

There is just the time for everything because it is just how it seems to be in some places.

This might be something for the times of the indication of the rest of society.

But everything will take time and patience.

This is going to be one long campaign season and Katrina is just getting started.

A few hours later and Katrina wakes up from her slumber, not knowing what to do next, but seeing she is in the nude she decides to take a shower to refresh herself.

There is nothing like a lukewarm shower in the afternoon with water and soap running down your entire body.

It is a certain tingling sensation that excites the body waiting for more, and the experience is such a pleasurable memory in all forms.

All wet from the shower, Katrina grabs a towel and carefully lifts her right leg first to dry between her thighs and then repeats it with her left leg. The experience feels her with glee and pleasure.

Katrina dries off the rest of her succulent yet sweet and sexy body and grabs something to put on before someone sees her, which is unlikely. Seeing there is not much to do, Katrina turns on the television to see what is happening.

Katrina has already cozied up to the Anderson campaign and has been accepted as a diehard supporter as well, but Mr. Charles knows she's not because he works for the Carlton Winters campaign as well.

But that doesn't mean she hasn't successfully infiltrated the Anderson campaign, because she has already has, since she was very believable to the supporters and campaign staffers of the Anderson campaign.

The timing was all too good.

VI

With three days left until Christmas, there is little time to waste, because the Iowa Caucuses are just around the corner, with a little more than a month away until February 1, 2016.

The timing must be exactly right and there is little time to waste, because around the corner, campaigning will pick up speed in the New Year.

The campaigns have slowed down because it is time to be with family and friends, and campaigning should begin shortly after the first of January.

There is just little time to spare and it is at the behest of society. Everything must be done precisely and that is about to change for the worst event yet to arrive.

Katrina and Mr. Charles are busy spying on the Anderson campaign so they can better help the Carlton Winters campaign succeed.

It isn't that it is great but this needs to happen in order to defeat the opposition.

There is nothing wrong with having a staffer of an opposing campaign embedded within the campaign from another campaign. It is perfectly normal and happens all the time.

The only reason it is considered bad is when the news media finds out and that only results in such press coverage if people want to request government and campaign records of candidates just because it is public record.

Otherwise, it will never really get reported, because no one even cares about it.

Anyway, it is almost that time of year again, and Katrina must prepare herself for Christmas Eve.

There is little doubt about the Anderson campaign, as it is the favorite to win the general election, but that might not be exactly true because no one can be sure of flaws existing.

And that is when hell will turn loose and open up to show the world.

To Katrina, this is nothing new.

It's probably rather welcoming.

But at times there is something that might happen to the rest of the world that might not be fair.

Surely, something is up to gain some sort of extension.

And that brings it all back to the doomsday scenario of the so-called resistance and its members.

Hopefully, nothing will change.

But, with that, there is time.

So, the theory is what will happen next.

But the resistance has one goal in mind, to control all branches of government.

They will try hard at all costs.

Bombs will be planted.

Property will be destroyed.

People will be targeted and harassed because of their beliefs and values.

The country will become more divided because of the goals of one political party.

But it won't just be the extreme fanatics.

It will also be the moderates who will join the resistance as well.

They will demand change.

They will demand men be stripped of their jobs and positions.

They will demand that it be required to force women to serve on the board of directors on businesses.

They will demand a maximum wage.

They will demand a minimum wage.

Their policies will destroy the basic livelihood of society and it will surely attract the attention of the Central Administration Party.

Everything will be up in chaos if the resistance wins. They will control every part of the government and will try to make everything illegal.

They say it is for the common good but they really want to decide what is what and what is wrong because they think they know what's best.

But that is such a flawed strategy.

It consists of stupidity.

It is plain ignorance.

It is a waste of tax payer's money.

And that will only be the beginning.

Innocent people will be arrested.

Crimes will be through the roof because new and unjust laws will be invented to arrest the people who question the unjust laws.

The resistance wants to silence the people.

They exist solely to make sure nothing good happens because they want to control everything.

It is just something that is meant to be the end of the new beginning.

VII

It is the night of the first presidential primary in the 2016 general election to decide who will become the next President of the United States of America.

The Iowa Caucuses are here and people are going to submit their votes in a matter of a few hours.

All 1,681 precincts are getting ready to prepare for the madness ahead for people to convince other people who to vote for.

It is surely one of the more interesting primaries, since every vote cast is still counted by hand.

You literally have people from each political party sitting in different rooms or sometimes just standing up because there are no tables and chairs.

The process is different for the Central Administration Party and the United Labourists.

United Labourists use a proportional system of deciding who will become a chosen delegate for the candidate selected while the Central Administration Party uses some type of proportional system as well but in a different manner.

There is nothing wrong with this process but it can be quite difficult convincing other people who to vote for, as some people still might not want to be convinced.

That is the same thing as the true form of democracy but it exists in a society that some say is not how it should work.

At the least, it is about time that people need to take a stand and decide who they will nominate.

It is nearly 7 o'clock in the evening, and the voting is just about to begin.

The voters are taking their seats at their assigned voting locations and seats.

With almost 700 caucusing locations for the Central Administration Party and about 1,150 caucusing locations for the United Labourists, this is surely going to be a huge yet important night for America.

It will have a true and lasting impact of all of society.

It is about a minute until voting begins, and a person starts to speak in each of the caucusing locations about the proper rules and procedures of how to caucus and what happens after.

Katrina is waiting with Mr. Charles at the campaign headquarters of Carlton Winters. There is much to do but all that can be done is to wait.

And now it begins.

People are sitting around tables to convince other people to vote for their candidate.

There is much noise everywhere.

The only thing to wait for is for the results.

Members of the Central Administration Party or CAP for short who are known as Centralists talk amongst their group at each table to discuss the importance of the candidates that they will vote for and what they will do to help the country succeed.

Each person at the table already knows who they are going to vote for but they talk amongst each other to get each other's view of why they are voting that way and what is important to them.

It is just meant to promote democracy and transparency about politics.

It might be the reason why it is more of a democratic process for the Centralists rather than the United Labourists because of the process about selecting the person to be the party nominee.

At the same time, the United Labourists are choosing who they want as their nominee and the delegates for the party conventions.

There is more chaos in this process because you have these people who can't seem to make up their mind.

They don't know who they are going to vote for and this can make things more complex and complicated, as members who support other candidates of the United Labourists will try and to convince those people to vote for their candidate.

And then you have those people who will vote for a United Labourist candidate who will probably suspend their campaign after the initial results come in.

But this process of caucusing is trying to persuade the undecided votes, and that will result in more chaos because this will usually resort in propaganda and lies from the beginning.

It is usually a few people at each table who can't make up their minds and when they finally make up their mind they will only vote for the candidate who really can't keep their promises because Congress might block it.

So, either way for the United Labourists, the major candidates are lying to them about what they will be able to accomplish.

With nearly just minutes left, members from both major political parties and the undecided voters write down the name of the candidate who they would like to see as the next President of the United States of America on a blank piece of paper.

In precinct 156, a lady dressed in a bright red dress with spaghetti straps walks around the room to see if people are ready to line up.

The experience can't be any more than exhilarating and people can't wait until the results are announced for some reason or another. It is the thing that keeps on giving.

"Live from national election headquarters in DC, this is Roman Anthony Andrews from National Media News Network, and I am here tonight with our usual guests and political pundits to report on the live results coming in from Iowa," said Roman Anthony Andrews.

"The time is now 8 o'clock at night and all polling stations have closed in the state of Iowa, and live results of the votes are currently being tallied to see who will win and who might end their campaign tonight; it is an exciting time tonight, let's go to reporter Ryan Margherita in the state of Iowa where he is seeing firsthand the votes being tallied" said Roman Anthony Andrews to his panel of guests and pundits.

"As the precinct staff is counting the ballots they are dividing them into separate piles for each candidate so there will be no confusion, and from this early information we are being told that the Anderson campaign is ahead of the Elias Dominic campaign for the United Labourists," said Ryan Margherita.

"What about the other lesser known candidates for the United Labourists," asked Roman Anthony Andrews?

"Well, Roman, I just heard that the Carter Oliver campaign has just announced that Carter Oliver will suspend his presidential campaign," said Ryan Margherita.

"Some very surprising news of the night; we already have our first defeat; and we can confirm as of now that former governor Carter Oliver of Maryland has just now told us that he is indeed ending his campaign for president, which is some very sad news to report here tonight," said Roman Anthony Andrews to the panel of guests and pundits.

"What this means is no one wants to vote for a skinny white man because they don't believe he is diverse enough to be the next President of the United States of America," said Terrell Dominique, the former Ocean policy adviser to the United Labourists.

"No, I believe you are getting it all wrong, because no one wants to vote for someone by the name of Carter Oliver because they much prefer a woman as president since it is regarded as a gender issue; you have people on the far left and left who only wants to vote for Cynthia Anderson because she is a woman and nothing else, and they are not even voting on policy issues because they are just voting for her based on her gender," said former Centralist Rhode Island speaker of the house Bradley Lucas.

"Hold on now, we are going to a Centralist precinct, where Jeremy Dustin Scott will give us a live update of what is going on there right now with the tallying of the votes," said Roman Anthony Andrews.

"Jeremy, what is happening over there right now," asked Roman Anthony Andrews?

"Well, Roman, it seems the voting has ended and they are about done tallying all of the ballots," said Jeremy Dustin Scott.

"Do we know yet who has won this particular voting location," asked Roman Anthony Andrews?

"Well, so far Centralist candidate Carlton Winters has a slight lead of about 15 votes, but expect that to change with the counting of additional votes; Uh, but wait, I am getting confirmation that the tallying of the votes have been completed and the Centralist senator from Texas Francisco 'Alan' Alvarez," said Jeremy Dustin Scott.

"We are also learning that other precincts and voting locations in Iowa have declared Alvarez the winner as well," said Jeremy Dustin Scott to Roman Anthony Andrews.

"Okay, stand by Jeremy, because we are going to make our projections soon, but right now it is time for another commercial break." said Roman Anthony Andrews.

"We are back from our commercial break, and we are going to make our first projections; we are projecting that the Centralist senator from the state of Texas, Alan Alvarez is going to win the Iowa caucuses beating billionaire businessman Carlton Winters; this is surely an upsetting night for the Carlton Winters campaign," said Roman Anthony Andrews.

"We are now going to our national political correspondent Aaron Campbellson to see what is going on with the United Labourist precincts," said Roman Anthony Andrews.

"Roman, what we are seeing here right now is that the Anderson campaign is barely up by a quarter of a percentage point, which means the independent senator from Vermont who calls himself a true United Labourist is showing that he is indeed a very competitive challenger," said Aaron Campbellson.

"So Aaron, what would it take for the Elias Dominic campaign to win an upset victory over the Anderson campaign," asked Roman Anthony Andrews?

"Well, Roman, the Elias Dominic campaign will need to gain additional votes in the suburbs and in the major cities; and if that doesn't happen then the independent senator from Vermont will face his first lost in the presidential primaries," said Aaron Campbellson.

"Please stand by, as we are going to make another major projection of the night for the Iowa caucuses; we are projecting that Cynthia Norwell Anderson will win the Iowa caucuses for the United Labourists with just half of a percentage point," said Roman Anthony Anderson.

"Right now, the two candidates who promised change are not going to win and that shows that America is not ready for that," said Terrell Dominique.

"But there is still the New Hampshire primaries, which might be the only hope for many of the candidates on both sides, but right now tonight it is the end for at least one of the United Labourist candidates," said Roman Anthony Andrews.

"Yes, indeed, as Carter Oliver has already told us that he is suspending his campaign for the presidency," said Aaron Campbellson.

"After the New Hampshire Primaries on February 9, we plan on seeing more candidates suspending their campaigns because they have failed to meet the required threshold that they wanted so dearly," said Roman Anthony Andrews.

"And of course, we must not forget about the speeches that the candidates will give tonight, because surely they will be reassuring to the supporters of each of the candidate's base," said Aaron Campbellson.

"Right now we are waiting for the candidates to speak at rallies about their wins and losses, and will surely be a spectacle with people cheering and booing because of the news," said Roman Anthony Andrews.

"There are several campaigns that are on life support, and they must decide now or after the New Hampshire primaries to see if they are going to suspend their campaign or keep on going until the end," said Aaron Campbellson.

"This is surely a tragic defeat for Carlton Winters, but he wasn't intended to come in at second place; Carlton Winters actually over performed in the Iowa caucuses, so we will see what will happen with him," said Roman Anthony Andrews.

"Since Elias Dominic lost by a razor thin margin, I guess you will see him saying that there is potential so don't give up because we will win some and we will lose some, so don't give up because this is only the beginning and there is still a lot of ground to cover," said Aaron Campbellson.

"Yes, indeed he will, but we are getting word now that Alan Alvarez is speaking right now in front of his supporters, so standby and let us listen in to see what he has to say," said Roman Anthony Andrews.

"*Tonight is a good night.*

Our campaign showed it could win when nobody else thought we could. It's great to be in Iowa.

Tonight, the state of Iowa has given our conservative grass roots campaign the chance to beat the elites and establishment in DC.

Tonight, we stand up to all of the career politicians in DC and all of America that career politicians will not defeat us anytime soon.

Tonight is a night when we cheer for the hope of our society that things soon shall change and get better.

Tonight is a night that shows we can defeat even the toughest opponents.

Iowa has made it clear tonight that they want change after eight years of the Barrington Hashim Martin, after he and his United Labourist party have dragged down and nearly wrecked the economy with his destructive policies of constant regulations.

Tonight is a night that demonstrates unity that the American people want and demand change because they have been burdened with high taxes, unconstitutional laws that demand you buy health insurance or buy a fine, and targeting conservatives for tax purposes because of political beliefs.

Tonight is a night that we remember the chance that the Americans are sending a message to all of the elites in DC.

Tonight's victory wouldn't be complete with the nearly fifteen thousand campaign volunteers who helped us gain support in the great state of Iowa.

Tonight is a victory for the Judea Christian values and beliefs that this country was founded on and it demonstrates that you can't hinder religion in a place like America.

Our victory tonight shows that people are uniting with us to help take back the country.

It shows us that the Reagan Labourists, the evangelicals, and the freedomers are supporting our campaign to win the presidency because they want to see the country grow and prosper again.

The American people tonight want to see an end to this agenda put forward by the Martin administration and his cronies from the United Labourists.

It shows us tonight that you are with us and you want to stop socialism, communism, and Marxism.

I thank you tonight for our victory because you are showing that the elites in DC that change will be here soon.

We are here tonight because of you.

I want to thank George Henry of the Religion for Hope Foundation, Scott Isaccs of the National Society for Family and Religion, John Lincolnshire and his national syndicated radio show, and Vance Goodson my campaign adviser.

Tonight you have demonstrated that you give America hope for the rest of the country and the world.

We will continue to move forward.

A vote for me will mean an end to the end of sanctuary states and sanctuary cities.

A vote for me will mean you will hold the United Labourists to account.

A vote for me means our border will be protected so that illegal immigrants can't take advantage of America anymore.

We will stop radical terrorists like the members of the Victory World Front.

We will send our military to destroy them all to a pulp. We will defeat these radical Islamic terrorists if you vote for me.

We will repeal MartinCare, because no one should be forced to pay health insurance and then be fined a penalty.

We will stop the United Labourists from destroying the very values put forth by the constitution.

We will uphold the second amendment and all other rights granted under the bill of rights and the constitution.

A vote for me tonight and for every other election means that you want the true originalist intent of the constitution to be interpreted as it was originally written.

It means you want to maintain the original intention of the constitution and do not want to veer away from its true meaning.

It means you support our country and the way it was founded and that you know that our rights are granted from a divine God and not from people in government.

We will preserve this nation for our children and grandchildren because they will face the real world soon.

Right now, it looks like that the United Labourists are neck and neck because you have two people who want to give away everything for free and the voters couldn't make up their minds who they were going to vote for because they wanted to know who will give them more free stuff.

Right now, it seems that the Anderson campaign is going to win in a narrow margin victory."

I look forward to debating her in the debates. Friends, tonight is not just a victory for us, it is a victory for freedom, liberty, and the pursuit of happiness.

And if you voted for someone else, we welcome you hear tonight to join our campaign so you can support us to take back the White House.

God Bless! Thank you for supporting our campaign to take back the White House!

Goodbye and goodnight!

We will see all of you soon."

"Some very choice words there from Alan Alvarez, the Centralist senator from Texas, who is hoping to become the next President of the United States of America," said Roman Anthony Andrews.

"It shows us that the junior senator from Texas is defiant to the end and is mischaracterizing MartinCare because his supporters do not want to help the poor and needy; it shows us that tonight that the people who voted for Alan Alvarez are racists and misogynists because of their hatred for everything about the Anderson campaign, and it shows us tonight that the traditional conservative Central Administration Party wants to turn back progress by making health insurance less affordable; it finally shows us that the Centralists do not believe in hope and change for the Americans, as they want to take everything back," said Terrell Dominique.

"I think tonight shows us that the billionaire didn't win even if he used his money, but I do think that people do want change because they didn't like what the Martin administration do to the country, since they saw his administration as a threat to democracy," said Chief Political Correspondent Gina Tucker.

"I believe tonight that the Carlton Winters campaign fell short of the vote because the voters preferred Alan Alvarez's message," said Aaron Campbellson.

"Hold on, I believe Carlton Winters is just about to come to the lectern to give a speech in Iowa about his loss; let's listen in," said Roman Anthony Andrews.

"Thank you, Thank you!

I love all of you people.

Everyone told me in the beginning not to go to Iowa to campaign because they said it would be too crowded and that I didn't have a chance of making it into the top ten.

Well, tonight we came in second place, but first I will like to congratulate Alan Alvarez for his great win, my wife, my campaign volunteers and staff, and my family.

I have no idea what is going on with the United Labourists but it seems the Anderson campaign is ahead of the Dominic campaign because I guess more people are voting for her because she is a woman.

And I don't think much about her or Elias Dominic, but I think they are wrong for America because they will bankrupt the government due to their policies and plans they want to implement.

I don't know about them but I plan on being in New Hampshire by tomorrow evening so we can get out the votes.

We will win the candidacy to become the presidential nominee for the Central Administration Party.

We continue to gain support every day and we will win the

nomination and then the presidency to take America back so that she can prosper again.

Thank you again and goodnight Iowa for all of your support, and I will see you tomorrow."

"Well, Carlton Winters just conceded to the Texas senator, Alan Alvarez, but he seems optimistic," said Roman Anthony Andrews.

"Now, let us go back to the Iowa caucuses for the race between Cynthia Norwell Anderson and Elias Dominic," said Roman Anthony Andrews.

"Hi Roman, it seems that now we have to take back our early projection about Anderson winning the Iowa caucuses, because now the race is neck and neck, as Elias Dominic is trailing Cynthia Norwell Anderson by a few hundred votes," said Stephen Mazton.

"It seems like this indeed will be a very long night for the United Labourists and the fight for the nomination," said Roman Anthony Andrews.

"Roman, I'm getting confirmation now that all precincts are now fully reporting, so we can indeed call the race for Cynthia Norwell Anderson, but we are now hearing that Anderson will give a victory speech, so let's listen in," said Aaron Campbellson.

"*Hello! What a great victory for America tonight!*

You have given hope that America needs us more than ever.

It was an incredible honor to campaign with all of you here tonight to promote the case and the change we need for America as well as from the United Labourists.

It was a pleasure for all of you who came out to help me in order to win.

I am very grateful for all of you here tonight for what you did to help me.

It isn't that frequent that someone like me with extensive experience and a proven record is able to win this very important contest.

I have a proven track record of getting things done.

It is important here tonight that we have a Progressive United Labourist like me who can provide what America wants because I know we can fix what we didn't finish.

I believe that education can be provided for everyone free of charge, no matter the disadvantages that some people might have.

I believe we can combat climate change and promote green energy to get rid of the fossil fuels contributing to global warming.

I will fight for your healthcare and will make sure MartinCare is moved to the next step, by providing free healthcare to all.

I believe we can stand up to the gun-rights' lobby to demand common-sense gun reform that will restrict guns and magazines.

I know I and the United Labourists have the best idea to run this country but we need to all be united in the end.

We must not let the Central Administration Party win because their campaign and policies are bad for the future of America.

They are seeking to divide us because of their divisive rhetoric. We must not let them win.

Our vision is clear: to help make sure America succeeds at its greatest hours and to help people to secure jobs so they have a better life.

We must have a minimum wage so that people don't go into debt and we must make sure college is free for all because students go into debt without getting good-paying jobs.

I have a vision to help all of you, and with help from you and the United Labourists, we can succeed at making this happen.

But first, we need to win the nomination for the United Labourists so that I can be the nominee for the party in order to provide for that vision. And then we will win the presidency.

Only then can we get the vision of America that we want to see.

Goodnight and God Bless America, to all of you tonight!

Thank you Iowa for helping us to support a better vision for America!

Let's win the nomination so we can win the presidency!

Thank you again, Iowa, and God Bless!"

"Okay, what a speech that was," said Roman Anthony Andrews!

It resembles the kind of change that we need in this country and how she wants to accomplish it," said Terrell Dominique.

"Hold on, I believe Elias Dominic is about to give a speech about his loss in Iowa to former secretary of state Cynthia Norwell Anderson, so let's listen in to what he has to say," said Roman Anthony Andrews.

"Hello Iowa! Thank you!

It was nine months that our campaign went to Iowa and we weren't really organized.

Now, nine months later, you have helped us succeed in the future.

I believe at the end of the night we will have at least half of all of the delegates in the great state of Iowa.

I would like to congratulate former secretary of state Cynthia Norwell Anderson on her win tonight, even if we only trail her by a few hundred votes.

Tonight, we are sending a very powerful message to all of the establishment Centralists and the establishment United Labourists that we are going to put up a fight because America is in need of new change.

We are sending a message here tonight that it is time for all of the corrupt and elite politicians on both sides of the aisle that they need to retire.

We must send a message that we won't stand for their shenanigans anymore and that we are demanding change so that the people of America can have a better future.

We must tell the corrupt elite that by next year, they won't be in office any longer.

We must demand that the corrupt Citizens United decision be overturned because it only promotes the interests of the wealthy elite.

Many men and women help us to protect the vote and they are not the wealthy billionaires.

I am glad for all of your support who helped me. Our campaign doesn't represent Wall Street, the billionaires, or the wealthy elite.

We don't want their money.

We only want your support because you are the backbone of the economy.

You are the grassroots of America.

Our average donation was twenty-five dollars and none of that came from the top 1 %.

It is not fair for the wealthy elite to own the majority of America when they don't even help anyone.

We must stop this rigged economy so it works for the working class.

America represents family and not the wealthy elite.

So, we are going to demand change once and for all in order to demand an economy that promotes the working class family unit because you are the backbone of America, not the wealthy elite who have stolen billions of dollars from you over the years.

And yes, I will make sure the minimum wage goes up to $15.00 per hour because people need to make a living wage in order to live and survive and to pay off their debts in order to avoid bankruptcy.

This change is radical and good because it will help you and the American public but not the wealthy elite, because they should suffer from their actions.

I promise you also women will be paid more than men because they deserve it.

And I guarantee that I will help you with your college education.

I will make sure that your public education will be free at any public college because you deserve to be debt free.

And we will do it by implementing a speculation and revenue tax on Wall Street for each cent of profit they make because they are misusing your money and you deserve a good college education without being owned by these big banks and loan companies that hold you hostage.

But we must fix this problem of too many minorities of being sent to jail or prison, because in this country too many people of color are being disproportionately and inappropriately sent to jail for civil infractions.

We must stop this and send a clear message to the private prisons that under my administration we will cancel their contracts because they are not helping society, as they are part of the problem with this country.

Too many African-Americans and Latinos are ending up in jail and I am promising to provide them with jobs.

Yet again, I am declaring that climate change is real and it is harming our environment because too many cities and states are suffering from bad air and water.

We must get away from the fossil fuels so we can have a cleaner and brighter future so that we can provide for clean air and water.

There is only one candidate on the other side who is funded by the wealthy elite and that must stop.

I am saying here today that I believe in health insurance for all and that it should be free for all.

We must provide Medicare to all free of charge in America because I believe health care is a right and not a privilege.

People have a right to be taken care of and treated with respect when they are seeking medical treatment for an illness.

We must change this country for how it operates and treats the people.

I am promising you all a political revolution and tonight this is the start of that political revolution.

Tonight is the start of the new beginning because tonight we are demanding change.

We are going to win in Hampshire and the wealthy elite won't like that.

We will win and we will get things done.

Thank you and goodnight Iowa!"

"Wow, that was surely a very excited crowd, who showed their support to a person challenging the establishing favorite," said Roman Anthony Andrews.

"You see Elias Dominic literally behind by just a few hundred votes and he and his supporters still seem excited, as they believe he and them have the energy to keep on campaign, since they see tonight only as a minor setback and that they are going to win some and lose them," said Terrell Dominique.

"And now prepare for our post-election coverage here on National Media News Network," said Roman Anthony Andrews.

VIII

Before long, the first presidential primary of the 2016 general election was in the history books.

Katrina is with Mr. Charles watching the post-election coverage and strategizing to see what they will do next to help the Carlton Winters campaign to win.

It could consist of attending rallies of both major candidates running as United Labourists and even some candidates running as Centralists.

But the New Hampshire primary is just a week away, so time must be spent well.

There is just little time to spare.

The campaign season is in full swing and nothing is going to stop it.

With the fresh loss in his mind after senator Alan Alvarez defeated him in the Iowa caucuses, Carlton Winters knows he needs to change his campaign strategy, so this time he is planning to hold several campaign rallies leading up to election day in the state of New Hampshire so that it will be fresh in the minds of his supporters and for the undecided voters.

If he loses New Hampshire, then Carlton Winters might need to reassess his campaign.

But Carlton Winters has already made a presence for himself in New Hampshire, as he held at least ten campaign rallies in the state leading up to the Iowa caucuses instead of campaigning in Iowa.

It was probably his way of saying New Hampshire is more of a competitive state than Iowa, but he needed to decide if he was going to campaign in Iowa, New Hampshire, or both, since he does not want to waste his time and come up short in the end.

Already, the Carlton Winters campaign is picking up tremendous speed, and people are flocking to see him.

Several thousand have already been to one of his campaign rallies but more want to get in.

And, as he continues to campaign, more people are listening to his message about normal working Americans succeeding in life.

This just shows you that the campaign is growing by the day and that the people are realizing that Carlton Winters is right about what is happening in America and what needs to happen in America so it can become more prosperous in order to help the economy and to make sure that people can succeed as well.

That is the point he is trying to make and it seems to be working.

"It's settled then, I will do eight more campaign rallies over the next six days so I can grow my support in New Hampshire," said Carlson Winters to his senior campaign staff.

"Sir, you are already up by double digits in the state of New Hampshire, but that is not the problem, because the problem will be where and when to hold these events since your supporters are growing by the hours," said Mr. Charles.

"Well, we will release a press statement saying the first of those rallies since the Iowa caucuses will be held tonight, and I expect that tickets will be immediately sold out," said Mr. Carlton Winters.

"That is fine with me but I would need to know the exact location for the event tonight so I can schedule it with event organizers so the people will know," said Mr. Charles.

"Ok, it will be in the city of Manchester and it will take place at the Citizens Arena downtown," said Carlton Winters to Mr. Charles.

It was settled then; Carlton Winters will start holding these non-stop massive rallies until the eve of the general election; and he surely will get much support as possible in order to receive the most votes from the old Electoral College.

It was a sure thing that this might just work, as each and every day Carlton Winters is increasing his polling numbers for the favorite candidate in the Central Administration Party.

But the real question is if Carlton Winters can face off against the establishment favorite Cynthia Norwell Anderson of the United Labourists.

It would be a sure thing that Cynthia Norwell Anderson would win the general election and become the first female president of America, only because that is how the media wants to play it with their biased polls.

But, it is all about timing.

IX

"This is Roman Anthony Andrews from National Media News Network, and we just got new polling data that shows Carlton Winters up by five points in the state of New Hampshire, and we are also just learning that later tonight that the Carlton Winters campaign will hold a massive rally in Manchester, in which people are already lining up," said Roman Anthony Andrews.

"Straight off from a political loss in Iowa, Carlton Winters is making sure he wins New Hampshire," said Aaron Campbellson.

"If I am correct in my analysis, I believe Carlton Winters never even campaigned in Iowa at all, because he said in an interview with some other network that Iowa didn't matter because he believes the voting process there is idiotic," said Terrell Dominique.

"It's interesting to see that Carlton Winters will only visit one state over the other because of the voting process, and usually all of these candidates visit both states so they could win over the voters there, and that seems to make Carlton Winters some type of outlier, since he doesn't care about a particular state," said Aaron Campbellson.

"That certainly makes Carlton Winters look like an outlier, but since he is putting all of his energy into campaigning for New Hampshire rather than with Iowa, maybe he will just win the state," said Roman Anthony Andrews.

"Never in the history of presidential politics has a presidential candidate ignored one primary over the other, and that is the cause for alarm because it is important to campaign in all states, unless it is one of those one-party states that have a lack of voters who support that candidate's political party," said Terrell Dominique.

"But it is also important that Carlton Winters is nervous after he just lost to the Texas Senator Alan Alvarez, who is a force to be reckoned with because both have similar-sounding messages but are saying it in a different way, but it will depend on the people," said Roman Anthony Andrews.

"After his campaign blitz in New Hampshire, it is possible that Carlton Winters will focus on Super Tuesday, in a way that will be massive and unexpected," said Terrell Dominique.

"You can expect Carlton Winters to win the majority of the states on Super Tuesday while Texas senator Alan Alvarez might win a few that night, but it all depends on the message, and so far we don't know who has a higher edge in the Central Administration Party," said Aaron Campbellson.

"The problem though is Carlton Winters himself, as people might think he is very divisive because of what he says to people who do not say nice things to him; and if his critics calls him out then he will say that they are wrong and have always been wrong for America but also that he will say that those who criticize him are just a bunch of losers," said Terrell Dominique.

An exact dilemma to deal with is how the tide will turn but there is no knowing who will win New Hampshire.

But Carlton Winters is spending more of his time in New Hampshire than any other candidate running for president.

It seems he has a ground game in New Hampshire but not in the state of Iowa.

The only reason why Alan Alvarez won was because of his ground game, as Carlton Winters campaign in the state of Iowa hardly existed to begin with.

That is simply something to recognize and it is partly due to convincing people.

There is however a threat to be reckoned with.

And his name is Texas senator Alan Alvarez who says he is the only true conservative who will cut government spending.

The senator from Texas views big government as a waste of taxpayer's money because he believes the more you give to the government then the more they will spend.

The senator believes that DC does indeed have a spending problem and he is willing to cut government spending in order to decrease the federal deficit and the government debt, as they are just too much to handle in a time when every dollar counts.

But the question is about whether the plan will work, as Carlton Winters has a similar plan but is saying it a different way.

There is just no time to waste and it will be a matter of time until time will tell who will win over the voters.

This is a cause for action of getting out the votes in the best possible outcome.

People might not care but it is the way it must be.

It is the type of situation that is just a part of life.

Before long, all of this will be over.

Nothing will be left and then people will mainly decide over two candidates with very different views and values of America, except in which that some people will vote for a third party candidate because they do not like either of them because of their overall messages.

Sure, there is a chance that anyone can win in the general election, but so far it is such a crowded field for the Central Administration Party that no one will know who will win the nomination.

But for the United Labourists, it is a sure thing that Cynthia Norwell Anderson will eventually become the nominee, but she still has to fend off Elias Dominic because he is a force to be reckoned with, as his crowds are huge like Carlton Winters.

That is just the competitive nature of presidential politics, but it is all about winning and the ground game to gain more supporters.

It's all about making sure a solid base of supporters is built so that once they become a supporter they will always remain a supporter.

This is nothing new but it shouldn't surprise anyone that the candidates need to build up their base in order to win.

The base is all that matters and the test of time shall prove that when there is a case to undermine the legitimacy of the presidential election only when the correct nominee doesn't win because if someone else wins then the legitimacy might be called into question.

And this will be a case of hypocrisy because the party that doesn't win will complain that their opponent in the beginning of the campaign wouldn't comply, but now that same person who called out their opponent will cry wolf.

It is all about timing.

X

Later that day, it is almost time for the rally. It wouldn't be a surprise if not everyone could get into the building, because Carlton Winters seems to have a growing number of supporters who believe he is the correct person to lead the country because of what he says.

It isn't just that but it is also his message about building the country back up where it was before the current presidential administration took over back in 2009.

No, the young senator from Chicago who would later become the president of the United States of America has repeatedly apologized for what America does and he has repeatedly divided the country because of his crazy and unethical attacks against innocent tax-paying Americans.

He has repeatedly announced when he will leave the Middle East as well as announcing when the enemy will face their untimely demise.

Of course, all of this has its setbacks, because the enemy will be far away before they are ever defeated, thanks to a public announcement.

No, the Barrington Martin administration will feel like fools if they don't get the outcome they want in Cynthia Norwell Anderson, since Martin himself wants Anderson to keep his legacy in place.

It is just the case of another situation abound.

"Reporting live from downtown Manchester, New Hampshire at the Citizens Arena, this is Jeremy Dustin Scott from National Media News Network.

I am here today reporting live from the campaign rally for Carlton Winters and there must be hundreds of people waiting in line to hear the presidential candidate.

The rally is set to begin around one hour from now and the line is only growing.

It seems there is massive support for the billionaire businessman who has built an empire in the software and the real estate development industries.

Right now, it is certain that not all will get in, and it seems that the arena is going to be standing room only.

Roman, after I arrived at the event location I went inside to see the size of the crowd.

And from the size of it, it looked enormous, as half of it was already filled up and this resembles the growing support for Carlton Winters.

There seems to be thousands upon thousands of people already waiting in the arena waiting for Carlton Winters to give his speech.

Roman, back to you!"

And then, there it was.

There were only a few minutes left until the rally would begin, and there was already a member of the delegation getting ready to introduce Carlton Winters.

The media was everywhere, parked in their vans, and under their big white tents.

People were still outside and that included many supporters of Carlton Winters who couldn't get in because the building reached maximum capacity.

So, overflow was opened, and it consisted of standing room only because the overflow was just the hallways leading to the inside of the arena, but they still had televisions so they could see the crowd cheering as well as seeing Carlton Winters speaking to his supporters.

But that too was maxed out, and so everyone else had to watch in the parking lot where the media vans were all located.

It was a good thing though there were speakers and a large glass screen connected to the outside of the building just in case this scenario occurred.

It was an uplink connected to where Carlton Winters would speak inside with wires connected to an outside area in a secure area so that no one could damage anything.

There must be about hundreds of supporters outside but there is still enough room for all of them to move around without bumping into each other when there is much support for a person such as Carlton Winters.

Nothing can stop this movement and it will only be the beginning.

The media was already inside the building but some members were stationed outside because there were already too many members of the media inside.

It kind of felt like it was an attack on the first amendment but that wasn't the case at all, as these were reporters who would interview any of the supporters of Carlton Winters.

And also, someone had to control all of the timings for any commercial breaks, correspondents, and reporters, so if no one controlled the control panel, then television wouldn't exist, which will in all effect mean the lack of a live feed from inside the Citizens Arena.

It would be the same exact problem people have with society.

That seems to be what is happening here because it looks like chaos in the arena right now, as the supporters are all waiting for Carlton Winters to speak at his campaign rally in Manchester, New Hampshire in the Citizens Arena because they believe what he says.

If it is anything like his other speeches, it will be quite long of an event, and there could be protestors inside who will try to create some form of distraction or another because they don't like Carlton Winters or his message at all because they believe he is a fascist.

But surely, it is all about change and promising to bring back America to its rightful place in the world, and people are just tired of what Barrington Martin did to the country by promoting his radical agenda of social justice and tyranny over the rule and laws of America that violates the constitution every day of the year.

It was just a sad day for all of America when someone who champions the redistribution of wealth to other people who have not earned it.

That is just government theft of wealth and Carlton Winters will make sure that it will never happen if and when he is elected to president of the

United States of America.

There will be no radical Marxist or socialist ideology here under a Carlton Winters presidency.

No, because there will be free-market capitalism and a reduction in regulations everywhere.

It will not only help the country but it will help Americans succeed and to save more money.

It is the right choice and it is now.

Carlton Winters just arrived on stage and he is about to give his speech to his enthusiastic crowd of this thousands of supporters.

It is just what needs to happen and that is the way it must be.

And that is the case of the indication when there are two different sides of politics.

That is the time and it is now and forever.

Carlton Winters started to speak and the crowd was in fascination of just seeing him.

It was surely a spectacle that will never be forgotten until the day they die.

"Wow!

What a crowd!

This is only the beginning of a beautiful process that will transform America back to its true roots of defending itself from enemies abroad.

I will make sure that the enemy is defeated abroad.

We will have a policy that promotes America first before anything else.

For too many years, America has suffered at the hands of the Martin administration, with his refusal to stand with Israel and his constant complaints of what is wrong with America.

His administration has wrecked the very ideology of what it means to be an American, but if he criticizes the greatest country in the world, then he will gain more support, because our enemies and even some of our so-called allies believe that America is the cause of all of the world's problems.

Let me tell you something.

They are dead wrong. America stands for freedom, liberty, civil rights, freedom of speech, freedom of religion, and the pursuit of happiness.

Those other countries might give you a warning for saying something true or even worse they might threaten or even actually jail you for stating a fact.

That is not what freedom is supposed to be. Freedom is supposed to promote difference of opinion without the threat of imprisonment.

Those countries that do that have lost their way of life but I can already see that happening here in America.

You see, those liberals and progressives of the United Labourists are attempting to do the same to this country here if they get their way.

The United Labourists believe that free speech should be limited because they believe only what they agree with should be considered free speech.

If you say something that is in disagreement with the United Labourists, then they might say that you should be thrown in jail.

It is simple really, because they believe only their views, beliefs, and opinions should be tolerated and that everything else represents a form of hate and discrimination.

You see, they say we are the fascists due to what we believe in. But actually, the United Labourists are the fascists, since they continually try to silence the views, beliefs, and opinions they disagree with by protesting or rioting through political violence.

They are the real fascists because they want to silence everything they disagree with.

It is their choice but if you have a different opinion, view, or belief on an issue, then they will try to violently attack you.

Their view is that socialism, communism, and Marxism will lead to a better society because it limits what people can do because it is a form of big government that supports a police state with constant surveillance.

Well, let me tell you something.

Their view of America is wrong because they don't believe in the values and beliefs that America was founded on.

They easily become offended because of what you say and they believe America is racist as hell.

But we won't let them prevent us from presenting our message, because we will be united against them by having a message of unity and prosperity for everyone.

But that isn't the only real problem we face from a tough opposition.

We face the constant attacks from terrorism.

The Victory World Front is currently encouraging a world-wide attack against major U.S. cities such as New York, Chicago, Boston, Miami, Austin, Dallas, Chicago, Houston, Los Angeles, Philadelphia, Phoenix, and San Diego to name a few.

They want to see America burn because the Victory World Front sees us as the infidels because they believe in an ideology that promotes terrorism.

The Victory World Front promotes a vision that they want innocent people to die.

They want to blow up buildings and people just to state their opinion. It is such a sad day in America when the United Labourists support terrorism over Americans.

I will make sure the Victory World Front is defeated when I am elected president.

I will end their wrath in the Middle East and around the world.

I will make sure to bomb all of their oil fields because they don't deserve a penny because every penny or dollar they make goes to support terrorism.

We must take back our country and we will.

We will not listen to any foreign body such as the Global Federation of United Nations because they do not get to tell us what to do.

Those unelected bureaucrats believe they know what is best but repeatedly under the Martin administration, the president has allowed the Global Federation of United Nations to replace United States law with their laws.

Ladies and gentlemen here tonight, that is simply unacceptable and wrong, because our laws are superior to any of their laws, because their laws do not hold up to our constitution.

The Global Federation of United Nations is hijacking our country and they will not get away with it.

As your president, I will pull out of the bad Paris Climate Deal, because it is a violation of the constitution of our great constitution since it was never ratified by the Senate, but it is also a bad deal for America since we have to pay the majority of the money to their climate fund for the bad decisions of other countries.

They do not get to tell us what we can't and can do because their law is not US law.

As Americans we believe in democracy and our constitution.

The United Labourists do not have the same view, as they believe it is crucial and necessary for the Global Federation of United Nations to decide what is necessary and what is bad for America.

The United Labourists want to give up the governing power of the United States government to a third party.

This is not only wrong but it is also unconstitutional, as it undermines the very principle of America as a country.

And yet the United Labourists say that the second amendment does not matter because they do not want anyone to have access to weapons unless it is them or the military.

The United Labourists even attack the police for having weapons because they believe no one should be shot if there is a threat facing someone.

It is all about power for them.

The United Labourists have degraded our military under the Martin administration and has forced mandatory health care against our will and forced it under our throats.

It is their very intention and goal to hurt the middle class and to destroy the economy for all.

But they constantly say that they are the voice of the middle class and that we are the voice of the millionaires and billionaires of all of society.

But that is not true.

The millionaires and billionaires actually support the United Labourists, as many of them are part of the coastal elite of America.

They do not want to admit this but they constantly get outside help by the liberal and progressives in Hollywood.

The Hollywood elite give the United Labourists outside money so they can cheat or promote some type of propaganda, and no one actually calls them out.

Now, under the Martin administration, one of my first goals will be to get rid of all regulations that are harmful to business.

I plan on getting out of the bad Paris Climate deal that was signed.

I plan on promoting border security and stopping these terrorists in the Middle East.

We must have a prosperous economy so that the middle class can grow.

We must make sure no one takes advantage of the United States of America.

Ladies and gentlemen, our country is being taken advantage of and America is seen as the laughing stock of the world.

The United Labourists are refusing to protect the border, as they believe borders do not belong in a free democracy.

They believe everyone should be entitled to the American dream, even if they crossed illegally over the border and have no intentions of following the law.

The United Labourists are actually helping illegal immigrants by breaking into the United States of America and no one is stopping them.

The United Labourists are supporting something unheard of in history because they rather help illegal immigrants rather than Americans such as you and me.

Let me tell you something about these illegal immigrants.

They are not vaccinated and they carry the threat of disease and viruses.

They do not care about the law and many of them are criminals who want to bring drugs into our country.

They are saying they need asylum but they openly admit they want jobs in America.

And yet, when one of those illegal immigrants murders an innocent person in our country, the United Labourists says it is a tragic event but they still say that a society with open borders is still necessary.

The United Labourists never learn and they do it because of their views and beliefs in society.

As your president, I will stop this open border policy and I will make sure a border wall is built so we can stop these illegal immigrants.

We can do more if I am elected president, because America is failing now, and we need to get back to number one in the world.

Our economy has been underperforming because of all of these burdensome regulations have caused a collapse.

Before Barrington Martin, our economy was prosperous, but since he has been in power he has given power to radical social justice warriors who do not believe in law and justice at all.

Well, today I am telling you that I am the candidate for law and order, and I will protect all Americans and make sure that all laws are enforced to the fullest extent.

We must have an America that promotes Americans and America over foreign entities and we must do it soon before it is too late.

It needs to be now.

There comes a time when the people will rise up against their oppressive government, and we must rise up to tell the government that their days are numbered, because when I get elected as president I will dismantle their entire agenda.

Folks, there might not be another chance like this to take our country back.

If I am not elected as your next president then America will continue to fall.

This chance might not come again.

So, this is the most important election in your life, because it could be the decision that could lead to economic prosperity or it would lead to the downfall of a once great nation.

As I stand here today, I am rejecting money from the interests and lobbyists because they do not represent America.

Those lobbyists and interests represent the millionaires and billionaires of the elite.

It is only important that I accept political contributions from the people who actually represent America.

Those people are you.

The current average donation is about fifty dollars.

I know I am the wealthiest person running for president but I am counting on you to get me elected as your next president.

I know I am funding my own campaign because I don't need the money from those interest groups and lobbyists giving me outside money from unknown and dark sources.

Folks, you need to vote next Tuesday for me if you want America to regain her prosperity.

Thank you and God bless America and all of you patriots here in New Hampshire!"

The speech was quite long and it happened to be one of his greatest speeches ever.

Carlton Winters was certain to win and it would be made sure he won because of his massive rallies.

It was just the thing America needs, a true leader who knows what he's doing.

A time of change is needed and that is now.

XI

It is election night in the state of New Hampshire, and hope is hinging on who would win.

Will it be the billionaire businessman or the up-and-coming senator from Texas who wants to change everything from the inside out?

That is the question that needs to be answered.

People and pundits are anxiously waiting for the results and it is just so painstakingly long.

Will this be an all-nighter or will the country learn immediately?

There is no telling what will happen and when the race will be called, but either way, people will hear a victory speech from the other side for some reason or another.

The polls have barely closed but there are still some open in other parts of the state.

No one can make a projection until all precincts have closed, and that might take a while because people are still lining up to vote one way or another.

But since New Hampshire is such a small state, it should be an early night for all parties involved.

There could still be that scenario that causes an automatic recount but that rarely happens in a case like this.

The possibility that will happen is slim but the media should be prepared to stay up all night in any political race.

It is now half past seven, but there is still thirty minutes to go until the final polls close.

Some results are already in but the rest will take some time due to certain restrictions put into place.

There is just a certain decorum this process must follow so that nothing bad happens.

It is without a doubt the most exciting but important thing an American can do. People in New Hampshire will decide who they want to be their nominee for president for both parties.

The time is now 8 o'clock and all polling stations have officially closed.

"This is Roman Anthony Andrews from National Media News Network, and right now we are anxiously awaiting results from the New Hampshire Presidential Preference Primaries. The polls have all closed and right now we are waiting who will win on both sides of the aisle. Once we get a steady amount of votes we can make our projections. Right now, let's go to Aaron Campbellson to see what he can tell us tonight."

"Okay Roman, what we are seeing is a steady amount of votes coming in but we will still need to wait; this could be an all-nighter or it could be declared within an hour or so; right now it looks to be the latter, as the votes are being tallied fast by the precincts; so we might be looking to declare winners within the next half hour or so," said Aaron Campbellson to Roman Anthony Andrews.

"Aaron and panel, I have been notified that we can make a projection of who has won the New Hampshire primaries, and we are ready to declare the winners on this historic night," said Roman Anthony Andrews.

"We can project that billionaire businessman Carlton Winters will be declared the winner for the Centralists; we can also project that Elias Dominic be declared the winner for the United Labourists; these are much needed wins for both candidates, and soon we will hear speeches," said Roman Anthony Andrews.

"What we see here tonight is the fight against the establishment; tonight we saw the establishment getting defeated because the people got tired of the same old agenda going on in DC; they want to see change and they believe Carlton Winters and Elias Dominic are the best two people who can battle it out in the general elections; but tonight represents a time in

America where the people decided the two extremes will need to battle it out to further better the country; history has decided it is time for the old group of people to retire; tonight, this shows us that from now on the people are in charge and they do not want the large interests and lobbyists to control DC anymore, because tonight is a time of change," said Terrell Dominique to Roman Anthony Andrews.

"I believe Elias Dominic is just about to give his victory speech, so let's listen in" said Aaron Campbellson.

"*Thank you New Hampshire!*

Shortly before I got on stage, former secretary of state Anderson spoke on the phone with me to congratulate me on my win in this great state.

I would like to thank my great campaign staff for their ground game in the Granite State.

Tonight, we are setting a new precedent by telling the wealthy campaign donors that their days are now numbered.

We began this campaign nine months ago with no staff and money.

But tonight this is a record-breaking voter turnout because we fought against the establishment.

We won tonight because of your excitement and enthusiasm. Tonight, because of what you did here tonight, that will happen all across this country.

Tonight we serve notice to the political and economic class of people we will no longer accept a corrupt finance campaign system and a rigged economy where everything goes back to the one percent.

I would like to thank my opponent again for her vigorous and hard campaign against me.

We must make sure that the conservative Centralists not win the presidency because last time it led to an economic downfall.

We will not allow tax cuts to the wealthy, education, or social security.

We will not allow a political party back into the White House who opposes climate change and denies science.

The people want real change and not from the establishment in power.

We must fix our campaign finance system because it is too corrupt and needs to stop the oligarchy.

We will not allow that to continue.

I am overwhelmed from our campaign because of what we did.

We are the only campaign that didn't accept money from the big donors.

The average donation was about twenty-eight dollars.

Tonight, I am going to hold a fundraiser here right now all across America.

Please help us to raise the funds that we need to continue our fight.

That is our fundraiser.

Now, we are going to help the economy by increasing the minimum wage to fifteen dollars an hour.

We are going to make pay equity possible for women.

We are going to make public colleges and universities free for all. Too many people have debt and they need help.

We are going to impose a tax on Wall Street speculation.

We need to stop their illegal behavior.

This means ending the disgrace of ending the disproportionate amount of people in jail.

Too many African-Americans and Hispanics are in jail and this needs to end.

We need to recognize the reality of climate change being caused by humans.

We must transition away from fossil fuels and move towards renewable energy.

Now, I have been criticized from every direction but we are thinking big to end this status quo.

We have a problem.

Every other country guarantees healthcare and that what needs to happen.

We can and must do better than MartinCare and we can provide this free to all.

We must end copays and deductions because that is bad for Americans.

Health care must be free for all.

And when we arrive at the White House, the pharmaceutical industry will no longer control our drug prices.

My health care for all plan will save you billions of dollars per year and will lead to a better country.

As I have said before, we must not be the policeman of the world, and we must destroy the Victory World Front.

But it must be done in a way that doesn't harm our military in the front lines.

We must provide a pathway for citizenships for any immigrants who have crossed the border.

We must provide safety for all people no matter their views and beliefs.

We must let people decide what they want to do.

My friends, we must tell the wealthy elite that they will start paying their fair share of taxes.

Together, we will fight for change and for a new hope.

This is the beginning of a political revolution and it will bring everyone to support us.

Good night New Hampshire and see you soon in South Carolina."

"I believe Carlton Winters is just about to give his victory speech in his big win over Texas senator Alan Alvarez, so let's listen in," said Roman Anthony Andrews.

"Hello New Hampshire!

Wow!

What a win tonight!

Thank you New Hampshire!

Tonight we made history.

Tonight you went against the elite from DC.

Tonight marks a new night in history because we say no more to those powerful lobbyists and interests in DC.

We will no longer accept their usual demands of deciding what needs to be done.

Tonight is the beginning we are going to take back our country.

Now, tonight is indeed a very large victory and it is only the beginning.

I would first like to thank my parents and my brother who are watching over me.

I want to thank my sister, who is a judge.

I also want to thank my wife who has to deal with the biased media every day of this campaign.

I would like to also thank my wonderful and beautiful daughter and her husband who have worked tirelessly to get us to this point.

I would like to also thank my campaign manager Anthony Kowalczyk.

Without him this wouldn't be possible.

Lastly, I would like to thank all of the candidates who ran a campaign here.

But I would like to thank my campaign manager because he made it possible to get out the vote for us thanks to him leading a very effective ground game.

Now, we might not have won last week, but we won this week, and I believe we will continue to win every week.

Some of these candidates that I face ran a very hard and excellent campaign and I would like to thank them for all of their hard work they tried to accomplish.

I want to tell you all that I have heard Elias Dominic's speech before I took the stage and let me tell you I didn't think much of it because what he said.

Let me tell you something about him.

He wants to sell out our country to foreign powers.

He believes in the Global Federation of United Nations and their anti-Israel policy.

He has no clue what America wants and need.

I promise you we are going to defeat China and all of those other countries who want to cheat us.

We will hire the best business people to take on those countries and we are going to make sure that never happens again.

I don't know what Elias is up to but I will make sure no one cheats us again.

Right now we have very bad deals because the people negotiating them for our side are purposely making it bad for us and giving the countries a better deal.

This is the best part of self-funding a campaign because the special interests do not support us.

I will promise you we are going to protect our border and veterans.

We have a problem with criminal migrants who don't follow the rule of law.

We have a drug problem on the southern border, where the cartels control the flow of people illegally flowing into our country.

We will end this drug problem on the border and I will make sure there is a border wall is built to better secure our border to stop the flow of drugs and illegal immigrants.

We need to take our country back. I will make sure MartinCare is repealed and replaced so that no one is forced to buy something they don't want again.

We will get rid of this crazy and ridiculous Natural Foundation plan and we will move forward with local school boards setting the curriculum instead of having the government making the educational guidelines.

Education is a local and state issue and no one should mandate some ridiculous plans that teach children that history is bad and that math be solved in a manner that doesn't make sense at all.

We must bring back control back to the local and state levels because this Natural Foundation plan is just put forward by leftists and their special interests that have nothing better to do.

We are also going to protect our second amendment because we need that type of protection for our people.

You see states like California that violate the second amendment all the time and restrict gun rights, and then you see countries like France where the only people that have the guns are the criminals and terrorists.

You see, the only people who don't listen to the laws are the criminals and terrorists, but in places like California or France it now seems illegal to protect yourself from those criminals and terrorists.

I will promise you that I will restore order and I will be the best jobs president there ever was.

Don't believe those jobs numbers because they do not include everyone who gave up on the economy.

The real rate is about thirty percent because of the people who gave up on finding a job.

We will make our country so strong.

We can't win on trade.

We are going to defeat the Victory World Front and we are going to win.

We are going to win so much that you are going to get tired of it.

We are going to the state of South Carolina and are going to win there too.

Thank you and good night people of New Hampshire!"

"Such enthusiastic speeches by the two winners of the night, and it seem to be just beginning," said Roman Anthony Andrews.

It seems like everything has just begun.

TWO

I

Super Tuesday has now arrived, and the excitement is extremely enthusiastic. People who have never voted before will vote for the first time and people who haven't voted in years will vote for a candidate who they believe will be important for the country than ever before.

It is that very excitement that will lead to chaos and destruction.

Now all that needs to happen is for the people to cast the votes and for them to be tallied by the precincts and certified by the state.

It is a tiring process but people will just have to wait to see what happens next.

With the arrival of March 1, 2016, there is a new hope for all of humanity because of what is at stake.

But for the past month, Katrina has been busy gathering information from within the Anderson campaign in order to provide the Carlton Winters campaign with better information so that Carlton Winters can win the general election.

With eleven states on the fence, this is by far the most important night in presidential primaries for selecting delegates who will vote for the presumed nominee of both parties.

Not only is it important for the election process but it is also important because of the amount of delegates to be proportioned to the winners and losers of the night.

With 661 delegates available for the Centralists candidates and about 865 available for the United Labourists, tonight is certainly a big night for all to see and watch because it will decide who will continue and who will decide to suspend their campaign to seek the presidency, one of the most prestigious offices a person can hold in the world.

There is just little time to lose and with states closing their polling locations at different times, people should get out the vote so they can use one of their most cherished rights or privileges of democracy.

Once in line, people will be able to vote, even if they enter into their polling place minutes before closing time.

There is always a chance a voter will be allowed to vote, if the polling location has already closed, but no new people can line up to vote.

Alabama, Georgia, Vermont, and Virginia all close at 7 o'clock and then the votes will continue to roll in through the night.

Massachusetts, Oklahoma, and Tennessee all close at 8 o'clock and the votes will continue to be reported throughout the night.

Texas closes most of their polling locations at 8 o'clock, but since a few close at 9 o'clock, votes won't be reported until then, but then they will continue to roll in throughout the night.

Arkansas will close their polling locations around half past 8 o'clock and then the votes will be counted and reported throughout the night.

Minnesota will start their caucuses around 8 o'clock, and then the votes should gradually roll in throughout the night.

Alaska is the last of those eleven states to report, since their polling locations will close at midnight and it might be a while for votes to be counted.

Of course, all times are reported in Eastern Time, so the people who are waiting to vote or who are watching the results to come in should be respectful of that, since, the states are located in different time zones, and that could hold up some of the data.

There might be a chance this could help the campaign season but it will be determined by the delegates.

Whoever wins big tonight will probably be the nominee for their political party in the general election in November.

And there could be claims of corruption, wealthy donors, and the powerful elite and establishment deciding the outcome tonight.

That will only take place if it doesn't go the way of certain candidates.

It is surely a way to fire up the base of that candidate's supporters.

But then they said that there is election rigging by the people in charge but then deny the existence of voter fraud.

That should sound the alarm but tonight is the case of who will be able to win in November, because the person who wins big tonight will gain the most momentum to defeat all opponents.

It is just how democracy works in America, while it could be seen as unfair to many people; that is just how it works in order to make sure the wrong person doesn't get elected in the end.

Sure, people will complain, but if they never voted, then they don't really have the right to complain because they never actually exercised their right to vote if they were eligible.

And then, there will be something that will lead to chaos after tonight, which is the case for all to listen to democracy.

No one can ever deny democracy in America but if it is denied it shall always be at the behest of corrupt politicians who passed some sort of ballot harvesting legislation and then having it signed into law, which in the end will make it legal to count votes after the deadline has passed.

And sure, that same law will only benefit the candidates or nominees of one political party, which is the political party who proposed the legislation in the first place to begin with.

But tonight, no one should think about that, because that might only occur if the general election does not turn out how it is supposed to, at least according to one specific political party.

Sure, that will mean that if a candidate or nominee legally wins a political race they might not actually be the declared winner, since the political candidate of the other political party who lost the election will probably win in the end because the politicians who passed the legislation will simply bring in more uncounted ballots that they stored away in a mysterious location.

It sounds illegal but it is not if it is part of a law.

Yet, tonight is not about that type of law, because tonight is about selecting the future president of the United States of America.

Tonight is the day that people will vote in several states.

It isn't the first election.

And it won't be the last.

Super Tuesday is about getting out the vote in as many states as possible in order to maximize voting.

Tonight will be a very long night and it will become part of the history books for people to read and learn about.

Nothing is more important than voting.

No one can ever take the vote away from anyone and that should be how it stays for always.

It is just a part of life and how it needs to be or there will be chaos.

For every day that is mentioned, it will just be the same for all to hear.

Timing is essential.

And the people will decide who will continue and who will end their campaign tonight.

It is essential for freedom and democracy to work.

II

It is election night in America for several states. Polling places in Alabama, Georgia, Vermont, and Virginia have now closed and the time is now 7 o'clock.

Now it is time to wait for all of the votes to be tallied and roll in throughout the night.

There might be some surprises here tonight but no one actually cares about that unless they are desperate to win, which might be certain presidential candidates.

That will surely spark a firestorm of some kind or another but it is without a doubt something interesting concerning the process of selecting presidents.

It must be the most convoluted and strange yet confusing process that exists in the world but no other country has this same type of process because America is unique in which that the founding of the country was done in such a way in order to prevent the corrupt and illegal practices of other countries.

But someone politicians of a certain political party try to get around that because they like to disregard the law of rule and the constitution, as they want to make up their own laws in which it doesn't apply to other people.

From the very point of existence, these elections tonight are part of freedom, liberty, democracy, and the pursuit of happiness.

Other countries pale in comparison because they only use a popular voting system, like is what is used to select members of the House of Representatives, Senators, and members of state legislatures, city council, and county commission.

No, the presidential elections are different in order to make sure the crazy people don't get elected but only the best, so there will be a true leader who could lead the greatest country in the world.

But people don't really believe in that anymore because people with a certain political ideology identify and engage in identity politics in which they criticize and use propaganda against people who they disagree with politically.

It is just about life and it is meant to destroy the very fabric about America and that is what something is going to become if they don't stop their extremist behavior of saying that everything and everyone is racist and sexist.

But there is resolve and that will be decided tonight.

Results are slowly coming in and it looks like neck and neck races in all states that have now closed their polling places.

It is now half past seven and Alabama has seemed to have declared a victor for their presidential primaries.

Carlton Winters and Cynthia Norwell Anderson have won the state of Alabama, beating their opponents by double digit leads.

Within minutes of declaring a winner, Georgia, Vermont, and Virginia have now all predicted a winner as well.

"Carlton Winters has won the states of Georgia, Vermont, and Virginia for the Centralists by double digit leads, and by some cases he has pulverized his opponent, the senator from Texas Alan Alvarez," said Roman Anthony Andrews.

"Meanwhile, we are waiting for more live results from states that will close soon," said Roman Anthony Andrews.

"This just in, we can project that Vermont senator Elias Dominic has won his state of Vermont for the United Labourists, while Cynthia Norwell

Anderson has won Georgia and Virginia for the United Labourists," says Roman Anthony Andrews.

"So now, it appears Carlton Winters has won 4 primaries, Cynthia Norwell Anderson has won 3 elections, and Elias Dominic has won 1 election tonight on Super Tuesday," said Roman Anthony Andrews.

So far the night is young, but there are still about seven additional primaries that need to have declared winners before everything can get back to normal again.

"The time is now 8 o'clock and polling places in the states of Massachusetts, Oklahoma, and Tennessee have all closed, but we are still waiting for Texas since some of their polls will close within the next hour or so, but let's go to Aaron Campbellson who is currently waiting at the magic panel," said Roman Anthony Andrews.

"Yes, Roman, we can report the race in Massachusetts is nearly neck and neck between Anderson and Dominic, so right now it's too close to call," said Aaron Campbellson.

"Okay, I believe we can project a winner for Massachusetts, Oklahoma, and Tennessee on the Centralist side; we can now project that Carlton Winters has won the states of Massachusetts and Tennessee and that Alan Alvarez has won his first of the night with the state of Oklahoma," said Roman Anthony Andrews.

"We can also now declare that Elias Dominic is projected to win the state of Oklahoma and Cynthia Norwell Anderson has won the state of Tennessee for the United Labourists, but we are still waiting for the state of Massachusetts since that race is still too close to call," said Roman Anthony Andrews to his panel of guests.

The night is getting older but there are still more results rolling in, so people should stay tuned.

The time is now a quarter past nine o'clock and results are now coming in live from the states of Texas, Arkansas, and Minnesota.

"Right now the only race that seems neck and neck is the state of Arkansas for the Centralists, but now I am getting confirmation that Carlton Winters has just narrowly defeated Alan Alvarez in that state by two percentage points," said Roman Anthony Andrews.

"We can also project now that the senator from Texas Alan Alvarez has won his state of Texas by double digits, as this was expected all along and would be a disappointment if he didn't win," said Roman Anthony Andrews.

"We now have enough information to declare the senator from Florida, Felipe Juan Alonso, the winner of Minnesota for the Centralists, but so far that is his only win in any of the presidential primaries all season," said Roman Anthony Andrews.

"Okay, it seems that this could be Felipe Juan Alvarez's only win tonight and for the rest of the campaign season, but at least he won a primary in a state that might not even matter," said Aaron Campbellson.

"Hold on, we can now project that Anderson has won the states of Texas and Arkansas by double digits, and now the state of Massachusetts in a razor thin margin for the United Labourists, while Elias Dominic has won the state of Minnesota in a very easy contest," said Roman Anthony Andrews.

"Now we only have to wait for the state of Alaska, but I'm just receiving some news that we forgot to include the state of Colorado because it seems the United Labourists is holding their primary tonight as well, and it seems we have enough votes and information to declare Elias Dominic the winner, so now the only race tonight to be called is Alaska," said Roman Anthony Andrews.

And it seems everything is going as planned, but with just one state left, it might just take a while, but the United Labourists are not holding a primary in Alaska tonight, since that is only the Centralists, and this might be an easy night after all but no one actually knows who will win in a state that receives cold weather all year long.

Before long, there will be a call for the race in Alaska, and that might be sooner or later, but hopefully the race will be called before the next day in Alaska, and that should benefit all who live there.

"Hold on for a projection, we can now declare in a narrow win for himself tonight, that the senator from Texas, Alan Alvarez, has won the state of Alaska by just two percentage points," said Roman Anthony Andrews to his panel.

And now there are just the victory and concession speeches to see who will continue and who will move on.

It will be a long night and morning ahead.

III

"Good morning, if you are just tuning in, today is the day after Super Tuesday, if you are tuning in from the east coast, but let's get to the historic wins of yesterday, however, before that, we will now go live to the campaign headquarters of Carlton Winters in which he will give a victory speech about his several wins of the night yesterday," said Roman Anthony Andrews to people just tuning in to the Super Tuesday coverage.

"Wow!

What a night!

Because of all of you tonight, you made it so that my presidential campaign can advance to the next stage.

I really do appreciate what you all did to get me and you here tonight at this historic stage of a presidential campaign.

This wouldn't be possible without any of you.

So, I say thank you all who have voted for me, and thank you all that helped me to get here tonight.

You guys are really making this into a new movement and a political revolution.

First, I would like to congratulate Alan on winning his state of Texas because he worked really hard on it and I would have been surprised if he lost his own home state, since that would tell you he probably wasn't very well liked.

But I am congratulating Alan for his hard work tonight because he deserves to win his home state and I would also be surprised if I won the state of Texas because I don't really have any association with the state.

So far, it has been a great night, and I believe we have won seven of the eleven presidential primaries of the night, and that seems to be a great accomplishment.

I did watch Cynthia's speech and I have to say she is talking about the same nonsense as always, because she and the rest of the United Labourists still believes that America is divided and broken because of us and you, because she believes that conservative Centralists like me and you do not want to seek progress but to instead turn back history and make it harder for everyone to live and work.

Well, let me say something about what progress truly means according to United Labourists.

Progress is just another way of saying we want to bring you back to the dark ages but to also instill and implement heavy regulation on everything and everyone by deciding what you can and cannot do in life.

Essentially, to them progress means a way of restricting your civil rights, your freedom, your liberty, and your pursuit of happiness because they want to control your life.

And then they will attempt to make it illegal if you speak up against their tactics, as they believe in government control of everything.

My plan for all of you is not that.

My plan is to let you enjoy your freedoms, your individual liberties, your civil rights, and your pursuit of happiness.

From day one of my administration, I will seek out Congress to pass tax reform so that taxes can be reduced dramatically, because no one really wants to pay all of their hard-earned money to the government.

If you worked for your money you deserve to keep most of it, and I will tell Congress to lower taxes for all in America significantly.

My opponents on the other side though believe that high taxes are necessary because it funds wasteful programs and that it is fair for the government to take your money without asking.

And by that, they will drastically raise taxes and probably impose a wealth tax because they claim they hate the rich but they are supported mostly by the rich and elites across the coasts.

I believe I heard Elias saying he wants to increase the top tax bracket to 95%.

Now if you are like me, you will agree that no one should pay that much in taxes, because it takes away from what they earned through hard work.

No, my plan will reduce tax rates to just three brackets: the first being 9%, the second being 12%, and the third being 15%.

Now, anyone who is making 15,000 or less as an individual or 30,000 as a couple will not be taxed at all.

But, if you have children and are single the first 25,000 will be tax free while the first 50,000 for married couples will also be tax free.

And from there, people making 25,000 and up who are single will pay a tax rate of just 9% while married couples who are making above 50,000 will pay that same 9% rate.

The 9% tax rate will max out at 124,999 for single people and 249,999 for married couples.

The tax rate of 12% will begin at 125,000 for single people and will max out at 249,999, while the same tax rate of 12% will begin at 250,000 for married couples and will max out at 499,999 for married couples.

The tax rate of 15% will begin at 250,000 and single people who make anything above will still continue to pay this rate.

For married couples, anything 500,000 and above will result in a 15% tax rate.

Now, I am not done there yet, because I will make sure businesses benefit as well.

And for me that includes both small and large, so that all businesses pay their fair share.

I am proposing a 13% flat business tax on all businesses because we need to be competitive with the rest of the world, especially with small businesses, because small businesses are family-owned and usually that is the life of the economy.

However, my opponents on the other side don't believe in this and actually want to raise taxes, because they believe the rich should pay more in taxes. Well, let me tell you something.

The rich already pay 88% of all taxes in this country we call America, but the people over at the United Labourists don't want to acknowledge this because they are just greedy for money, since they support socialist and Marxist ideology along with wasteful spending.

Most of the middle-class doesn't pay taxes because they either fall below the poverty line or they are barely making enough above the poverty line that will result in poverty.

We need to fix this problem and I will promise you that.

But, we must also repeal MartinCare and then replace it with something better that doesn't impose mandatory insurance on people.

You know, if people can't afford something, they shouldn't be forced to pay a fine, because here in America you are able to pick and choose what you like.

And MartinCare has significantly increased the costs of health insurance for all but the United Labourists do not want to admit to that because they support a policy or law that forces something down your throats.

And if you don't purchase it you will have to pay a fine to the federal government.

That is absolutely ridiculous and it is a violation of our great constitution as well.

I will propose a health care policy that makes it optional for people and businesses to purchase health insurance for them or their employees. And I will make sure everyone can afford health insurance by making sure any health insurance policy will qualify for coverage.

But I will make it so that I promise everyone can purchase health insurance, even if you have a preexisting condition.

My opponents however want to make it free to all and to keep the individual mandate, but if it is free to all, then the individual mandate actually goes away, and then everyone will be able to have free health insurance coverage.

But, there is a catch.

The catch is that it will cost over fifty trillion over the next ten years, and if a law like that gets approve, it will essentially bankrupt America, and soon Britain might try to invade us again because we have no money.

Yet, my opponents on the other side of the aisle says it is affordable, because there will be a tax on Wall Street speculation, a tax on gambling, and a tax on everything else that can think of.

Elias Dominic even admits that he will raise taxes on the middle-class to pay for healthcare for all.

Is that a plan you want?

I think not, because it has the ability to bankrupt us during a very vulnerable phase during our existence as a country.

My opponents on the other side that taxes will pay for this, but in reality, new taxes will only cover fifteen percent of the programs they propose.

The new taxes will instead go mostly to current programs already in existence.

We need a tax system that will make our economy prosperous and more competitive again and I will help get you that when I get into office.

But reducing the taxes is just the beginning.

We have a problem on the southern border that the United Labourists want to simply ignore because they believe in open borders and illegal immigrants.

It is of their belief that America is a racist and sexist country while also saying that any illegal immigrant should be able to vote and become a citizen, simply because they crossed into our country illegally.

And many of those illegal immigrants come here with deadly diseases and criminal pasts. Some of them are also members of the drug cartels in Mexico, and they aim to bring more illegal and deadly drugs to our country.

The drug cartels also smuggle people across the border for a fee and you have many of these illegal immigrants who admit they are already breaking the law by paying a known smuggler to sneak them into our country.

We must end this now before it becomes deadlier.

The United Labourists are failing to protect and secure our border and do not care if an innocent American is killed because they believe in not asking about their past.

Yes, that is right; those so-called United Labourists do not want to acknowledge that many of those illegal immigrants who cross our southern border illegal are actually criminals from other countries.

But the worst part about their plan is that they want to give asylum to all of those illegal immigrants and those illegal immigrants are even trying to apply for asylum based on a lie.

However, they only want jobs in America and are saying they are escaping gang violence and economic hardship.

Well, that is not actually a legitimate claim of asylum, because we have gang violence and economic hardship here in America as well, and you don't see Americans going to poorer countries to declare asylum.

No, because there will always be economic hardship and gang violence everywhere, but the United Labourists don't care about that and does not want to admit that, because all they see is that these illegal immigrants will vote for them in the future.

And we won't stop there, because we will continue to build our wall to stop the flow of drugs into our country and to stop illegal immigrants from coming in.

We want a safe and secure America that treats everyone with respect.

We will make sure the second amendment is not violated because those United Labourists believe only the military should have access to guns and that people should not have the right to self-defense.

I will make sure terrorist groups such as the Victory World Front are defeated so that our country and interests can be safe here and abroad for Americans to live and work.

If you support the United Labourists you will just hear more of the same, but they will reduce the military and the enemy will win.

I will promise you tonight that I plan on removing America from the bad Paris Climate Deal agreed upon by the Martin administration, and that we won't let foreign powers decide our laws.

I will make sure that the Natural Foundation Plan is replaced with school choice and education be turned back over to the school boards and states.

We must bring America back to a state of prosperity and opportunity so that everyone can succeed in the future and have a better life.

And I will promise you all of that because we need to take our country back.

Thank you and good night!

I will see you all soon.

God Bless and Good Night!"

With that, Carlton Winters gave one of his most successful campaign victory speeches in days, and it was all because of his supporters.

"Let us now turn to analysis, but before that, what can we interpret from what has happened tonight," asked Roman Anthony Andrews?

IV

It is the Wednesday after Super Tuesday, and the campaign season is in full swing.

The candidates aren't taking any chances and soon there will be more dropping out because they know they cannot make it.

Something is about to change that will cause panic everywhere and that will result in the collapse of society.

But hey, that is too early to tell, and it shall be at the behest of the voters to decide what will happen next in a tight constraint of unusual circumstances.

The goal is to get the most delegates in order to be nominated as the presidential nominee to represent that political party in the upcoming general election.

And then, once that candidate receives the minimum number of delegates, that person shall be nominated at the party convention for their associated political party.

But soon it will be time for that to occur, so both the United Labourists and the Centralists need to get behind someone that will be the best to win the general election or else there will be chaos.

Thankfully, the voters seem to have gotten behind Carlton Winters for the Centralists and it looks like they are getting behind Cynthia Norwell Anderson for the United Labourists.

But there can always be a late bloomer who comes up from behind, such as Elias Dominic, because people are really starting to like his message about getting free stuff at the expense of others and themselves.

On the other side, it seems unlikely for Alan Alvarez to take the lead because the voters simply prefer the simplicity of what Carlton Winters is saying because he describes it so very well that it makes it easier for all the issues to be understood.

It seems there is still much needed effort to get behind a candidate for both political parties, because the party conventions are less than five months away, and that is not enough time to delay unity.

There needs to be someone who has the energy and stamina to get out the vote and campaign in the much needed swing states to win the Electoral College and this person needs to make sure it is nonstop campaign because any breaks will cause potential votes to be missed.

As a rule of thumb, there will always be a candidate who is lazy, and that will cause a lack of enthusiasm, so it will be up to the voters and supporters to persuade the potential voters who might be missing out on what the candidates have to offer.

With that, there must be a strain on voters and the campaign staff because of the tough work that is required of them to get out the vote.

But before any of that happens, there is a second Super Tuesday on March 15, which is about two weeks away from about yesterday, but this time it is just five states: Florida, Illinois, Missouri, North Carolina, and Ohio.

This second Super Tuesday will hopefully narrow the field of the much crowded field of candidates running for the Central Administration Party for the presidential nomination.

And it will be here soon so there will be some heavy campaigning to do.

Meanwhile, Katrina has been busy infiltrating the Anderson campaign by passing along specific information to the Carlton Winters campaign by copying certain documents that might present weaknesses to the United Labourists.

And the Anderson campaign or the United Labourists are not even aware of anything, because they believe Katrina is a staunch and heavy supporter of the policies of the United Labourists.

So, it will be a shock to them if they ever found out.

The goal to begin with for Katrina to find out information about the Anderson campaign and Anderson herself and to report back to her boss Carlton Winters, and then later on during the campaign season, there will be a press conference if the media ever finds out about this information if there is a freedom of information act requested.

And that will surely rile Anderson and her campaign because they would be caught off guard if any of this information is ordered to be released by a federal judge, and then in turn the Carlton Winters campaign will use that information to attack what Cynthia Norwell Anderson did.

It is as simple as that but they won't even notice any misplaced documents because they would already be stored where they are supposed to be filed.

But no one actually cares about that, so it is just a theory of what might happen.

And then, without a doubt, there will be nothing left but panic and chaos throughout the Anderson campaign.

People will be blaming other people and then there will be people fired as campaign staff or being replaced with more effective people such as fixers who promise to do illegal things in exchange for money and the pay for play schemes.

It is nothing new but it does happen in order to get an edge on the opponent.

That will be the best of all to consider nothing but distasteful discourse.

But nothing will be worse than an October surprise.

There is excitement in the air today.

It is just another time to vote because today is March 15, 2016, the second Super Tuesday of the month of March and possibly the last of the 2016 presidential campaign season.

And it will hopefully determine who will continue and who will suspend.

Tonight will decide the fate of who might win the general election and who will face off against each other.

"Live from National Media News Network, this is Roman Anthony Andrews, on the second Super Tuesday of this month, and hopefully we will get a better picture of who might become the presumptive nominee for their political party; we have reporters live in all five states reporting the results live and a group of panelists who will discuss the outcome of tonight's elections and what it will mean for the future of America; the first polls close in about an hour but we will be here for you so don't change the channel if you want to watch the results live; and now to Aaron Campbellson where he will join us at the magic panel."

"Good evening Roman, the time is currently 6 o'clock, and we still have one hour until the first polls close in Florida, but we will have to wait until one hour later because the panhandle closes at 8 o'clock and are located in the central time zone; so let's take a look at our magic panel; we have no idea if the senator from Florida is going to win his home state, and if he loses it to Carlton Winters, it is likely he will suspend his campaign and drop out of the race, because he believes the person that wins Florida will become the nominee for the Central Administration Party; so, his supporters might be sad but tonight there should be more unity around a particular candidate; but let's look at the scenarios in play here; currently, Carlton Winters is leading the pack with over twice as many delegates as Alan Alvarez, and it will take a miracle for Alan Alvarez to make that up, so he would have to win all five elections tonight or just Florida to have a chance; and then you have the senator from Florida, who has only won one election so far this campaign season, and it will be a travesty if he can't win his own state, but we will keep an eye on him tonight because he says internal polls have him up by a few points over Carlton Winters and Alan Alvarez, yet he is trying to get anyone to vote for Alan Alvarez over Carlton Winters; and now we can turn to the other side; right now this is just a race between Cynthia Norwell Anderson and Elias Dominic, and we will see tonight who has the stronger message; Roman, tonight will be a historic night, no matter who wins or loses, because of the money spent," said Aaron Campbellson to Roman Anthony Andrews.

"If you are just joining us now, all Florida voting locations have officially closed, and we are still waiting for live results from Ohio, North Carolina, Missouri, and Illinois; they should be coming in soon, but we are currently watching the very crucial state of Florida to see which Centralist candidate wins because that could make the difference between continuing and suspending a presidential campaign, so we will have to wait and see what happens," said Roman Anthony Andrews.

"Roman, we can report now that Carlton Winters has a substantial lead of about twenty points in the state of Florida, and it looks like the senator from Florida, Felipe Juan Alonso, is going to fall short of winning, so we should be hearing a concession speech soon enough," said Aaron Campbellson.

"Aaron, panel, hold on, I believe senator Alonso is speaking at his campaign headquarters in Florida now, so let's listen in," said Roman Anthony Andrews.

"In America, people have a greater chance of living than other countries because we offer the freedom of religion, the freedom of liberty, the freedom of speech, the freedom of individual rights, the freedom of saying and doing what you want to do, and the pursuit of happiness.

You see this great country that we live in, America, gives people the right to live as how you want to, and we acknowledge that our rights come from God and not some government official or government that persecutes their people and restricts necessary freedoms, civil rights, and liberty.

We are a nation of laws and not a banana republic.

Today, on this day, my mother was able to cast a ballot for me, her son, because in America we allow the process of people to participate in democracy.

We are not a country such as Cuba or Venezuela that allow dictators and tyrannical rulers do decide our faith.

No, because we allow the people, not the government, to dictate the official terms of who will be voted into power.

But I have to disappoint you all tonight.

It might not have been in God's intended plan, but I am suspending my campaign tonight in the great state of Florida.

Tonight has been a great night, but even though I am suspending my campaign for president, I will still like all of you to have hope, because the Centralists have the opportunity to take back the White House back from the United Labourists, and this could be the last chance to save America.

I never thought I would make it this far in this campaign, but since I was able to make it to this stage, I don't see a viable path anymore, and the people have spoken.

We must make sure America still remains a special place and we are very hopeful because we are the descendants of men and women who were destined for more.

We can disagree on policy but let's now allow fear to get the better of us.

So, in closing, let's make sure America is and always remain the special place that it was intended to be, because of our great heritage."

"You just heard from Felipe Juan Alonso and he has just gave his concession speech in Florida suspending his campaign because he no longer sees a viable path, but he knew he had no path to victory once the numbers in Florida were released, as Carlton Winters had too large of a lead," said Roman Anthony Andrews.

"The time is now exactly 9 o'clock, and we can now make a major prediction in the state of Ohio; okay, we can now project that Ohio governor Jonathan Evanston will win his home state of Ohio and will deny Carlton Winters those 66 delegates," said Roman Anthony Andrews.

"Yeah, Roman, it seems Carlton Winters has lost Ohio, but it is no surprise that the governor has won his own home state, because Jonathan Evanston does have support in Ohio but not like the lack of support in Florida for Alonso, and right now the Evanston campaign think they might have a chance, but let's see about that in the future," said Aaron Campbellson.

"I believe Jonathan Evanston is giving his victory speech, so let's listen in," said Roman Anthony Andrews.

"*Yes we can!*

It is about America and you better believe that.

It's about the USA. First, I want to say when you leave your family to campaign for president, there is a toll taken, and it gets hard at times.

I would like to thank the hard work put forward by Florida senator Alonso who has put in a hard effort this campaign season.

You know, things were bad, and Ohio was hanging in the balance, and I said you don't understand the people who live and work in Ohio.

See, in Ohio, we led the country in reducing taxes and Ohio is currently out of debt.

Most of my family has not graduated from high school or college.

You want your children to have a better life than you did because our children are the future.

We need to forget the politics, the polls, the pollsters, because I represent you and no one else.

I know these problems and I know when it is time to cut the red tape.

So tonight, I can say that I will continue my campaign.

I want to tell you that I am here to fight and I want to remind you that I will never take the low road to become president.

We have many challenges and in the first 100 days we have an obligation to get our agenda put forward.

The lord has made everything here tonight special because we are just here in a moment of time.

Your job is to help the people and your family to succeed.

We must change the world by being neighborly to everyone.

The spirit of America rests in the people and not with us, but you elect people like me to get things done.

But we must do better.

We must have a purpose in life that allows us to get things done.

Well, guess what?

I am going to Philadelphia tomorrow to continue my campaign.

And all I can say is thank you.

But I will say tonight is we are going all the way to Cleveland, Ohio to secure the Centralist nomination.

I want to thank my parents for helping me understand that party affiliation does not matter and that you can vote for anyone you want.

We still have one more trip here in Ohio and then I will defeat Cynthia Norwell Anderson and will become President of the United States of America.

God Bless America and God Bless the great state of Ohio!"

"If you are currently tuning in, that was Jonathan Evanston, who just attacked Carlton Winters, and it seems he believes he is going to win, but that does not seem likely," said Roman Anthony Andrews.

"Roman, it seems very unlikely that Jonathan Evanston will win the Centralist nomination, because Carlton Winters has such a huge lead over anyone else, and it will take a miracle at the convention to have him elected as the nominee, so I don't see him becoming the Centralist nominee anytime soon, but I also believe that his campaign is on a lifeline but because he won Ohio he survived another day of campaigning," said Aaron Campbellson.

"Okay, I believe the senator from Texas, Alan Alvarez, is about to speak, so let's listen in," said Roman Anthony Andrews.

"Thank you Texas!

It is a great night and we continue to gain delegates as we move forward.

Let me just say one thing about one of my opponents.

You know, Felipe is a friend of mine, and ran a strong campaign of his family escaping a Cuban dictatorship.

His effort sparked millions and has encouraged many people because of his positive campaign.

To all those who voted for Felipe, you are welcome here tonight and I hope you will join us tonight.

You know, there are only two campaigns that can win: mine and the campaign of Carlton Winters.

Let me tell you here tonight that I am the only one who can defeat Carlton Winters because I have single-handedly defeated him 9 times.

I can promise you a greater America.

As president, I will turn around the stagnation of the Martin-Anderson economy.

And it is easy to say to make America more prosperous, but our message here tonight is to make America better than ever before.

If I am elected president, I will promise we will repeal every word of MartinCare; we will move toward a flat tax towards corporations and the people; we will make sure that the economy is not overly regulated.

We will stop amnesty, stop welfare benefits, and secure the border so we can stop the wasteful spending.

Too many politicians have special interests controlling them and then those who buy that influence because of their goals.

We will repeal job-killing regulation.

There have been far too many politicians on both sides who have benefitted the rich, and that is not who we are.

I will not compromise your second amendment and every justice I appoint to the Supreme Court will uphold the constitution and bill of rights as they were originally written.

I will not apologize to the world and I will defeat the enemy. I will rip up this Iranian nuclear deal.

Over seven years, Barrington Martin has weakened this country, and it will take me only a few short minutes to get America back on track.

I will help the economy and will stop this regulation.

Once again, we stand together; we can have a new morning together.

Now is the time for people on all sides to unite behind us.

God Bless America and see you all tomorrow!"

"What a defiant speech against Carlton Winters, and he believes he is the best choice over Carlton Winters, and tonight we know both candidates seek to take away people's health insurance," said Terrell Dominique.

"It is for that reason why the people are in hysteria," said Gina

Tucker.

"And, that is possible that America will be more divided tonight," said Roman Anthony Andrews.

"Yeah, tonight represents unity and division, and to decide if we will elect a white racist or the first female presidential nominee to a major political party," said Terrell Dominique.

"Stand by, I believe Cynthia Norwell Anderson is about to speak, so let's listen in," said Roman Anthony Andrews.

"*Thank you so much!*

You know, we are still waiting for final results in Illinois, we believe we can make it so we can win them all tonight.

We will add to our delegate lead and are moving closer to the United Labourist nomination in July and to winning the presidential election in November.

And I want to congratulate Senator Elias Dominic for his vigorous campaign against us.

We are breaking down borders and moving towards more equality.

We still need your support so please join us.

We can't do any of this without you.

Tonight is clearer than ever because the next president will start making decision that will help or harm people in America.

And I know that Martin fought hard with his decision.

So our next president needs to keep us safe and keep us together.

But the other side does not have a solution because he wants to divide us even further.

Whenever you here a presidential candidate saying they will deport 12 million innocent immigrants, banning all Muslims from entering our great country, and building a border wall, you know there is a problem in America because we as a nation have become too divided as a people.

When he embraces torture it makes him look weak and wrong.

We will not build a border because we need to break them down.

This isn't just about Carlton Winters because every one of us needs to do our part.

We have a problem with the young people who are currently

struggling with student debt.

There are problems with retirement.

We must fight for the future of all people in America.

We need equal pay and the people have waited long enough.

If we work together and respect each other, we can get things done.

So, we must unite, because it is important to make America a country that promotes the family.

It is for everyone, and we must stop the gun violence.

It is for those who are forgotten.

We can unite together and we shall win.

Thank you very much tonight, Ohio!"

"That was surely an attack against Carlton Winters and his campaign, and you could hear it in her voice," said Roman Anthony Andrews.

"Now, I believe the nomination is closing for Elias Dominic, but he still has a chance of winning the Superdelegates," but that is still unlikely to happen," said Aaron Campbellson.

"Hold on, I believe we are now hearing from Carlton Winters about tonight's election wins, so let's listen in to what he has to say," said Roman Anthony Andrews.

"Thank you!

Thank you very much everybody!

This was a great night we had tonight.

They just announced we won North Carolina and so far I don't know if we won Illinois or not but I do know that we are up by many points and it seems impossible for anyone to overtake our lead.

I think they will have to announce it soon because we are so far ahead that no one has a chance to catch up.

Florida though was such an amazing win tonight for us all.

You know, NMNN put out a poll saying we have no chance of winning, and that is just pathetic, because they simply don't understand math and statistics, since they don't acknowledge my support.

They always try to poll too many United Labourists and independents that align with the United Labourists.

"From the very beginning, the media never liked our campaign to begin with, because they knew we had a good chance of winning the elections throughout the campaign season.

They knew that my message of supporting America and Americans as a number one goal would win but they kept on trying to spread propaganda about me and my supporters.

But we won't let that get to us.

My message is stronger than ever and once I win we will have change.

These companies will no longer leave our great country and open up their headquarters in Europe, because once I become president, I will make a promise to you that they will want to come back. Because I will make sure the tax system is reformed.

There is no chance I will allow corporate inversions, as we need that money.

But we can fix this.

Too many companies are leaving our country because we have too high of a rate of taxes.

"They are just leaving our country to get their money because our tax system is broken."

We need to make sure that this stops. And we need to unite our party because we have a chance to make our country great again.

Our theme when we started was about trade and borders.

I was leading in the polls from the very beginning but people said I will never win or run for president.

Some say we like the deals being made, by giving 150 billion to the terrorist state of Iran in cash and by negotiating a nuclear treaty.

Let me tell you something.

We do not make any good deals anymore.

We get taken advantage of during all of our deals when we negotiate with other countries.

I believe that is intentionally done in order to appease our enemies.

You see, whenever we negotiate, we never object to anything.

And currently, the Martin administration allows our negotiators to be stepped on intentionally by the other countries because the team that negotiates for America does not want America to get a great deal like the other countries involve.

That is not right.

I will change that when I take the oath of office.

You see, we don't win anymore.

Our borders are not protected.

Our military is weak.

Our veterans aren't taken care of anymore.

And it's really a shame, because the people want it to be fixed, but instead these United Labourists and special interests get in the way and try to make it impossible to change.

And then we had the terrible Paris climate deal a while back, and that was just terrible, because America was blamed for everything and would be forced to pay for the problems of other countries.

We would have to pay for everything while every other country would be getting everything for free.

And the Martin administration says we must apologize to what America has done to the world.

Well, from day one, that will no longer happen, because I will take the United States out of this bad Paris climate deal.

I won't let unelected bureaucrats decide what we as a country can and cannot do, because they do not understand our constitution, since our constitution supersedes any foreign power, because we as America are sovereign, and that makes government responsible towards Americans and not some foreign power.

This campaign has given me a new chance and meaning about America.

We need protection.

We are going to have some great trade deals.

Over the next few months or so, I will be going to lots of places to campaign.

We are going to win and I believe it will be great.

We will make our military strong again because we hardly win anymore.

We have so many losses that the enemy laughs at us.

I will make sure we will always win.

We don't win on trade.

Any country that deals with us takes advantage of us.

We will win on trade again and will become rich so we can have prosperity again.

We just have to wait for one more state.

But to win Florida by such a large margin, it means our message is working.

And I would like to congratulate Florida Senator Alonso for a great run in the state of Florida.

But I have been attacked so negatively during the campaign season because of my wealth and my message for the American people, because my opponents on the other side know that they won't win against me.

And really, they say that I am connected to all of those executives, but it is them who are because those executives and people on Wall Street always donate large amounts of money to the United Labourists for some reason or another.

So, it was the worst negative campaign against any presidential candidate in the history of our existence.

Again, I would just like to say thank you to everyone who ran.

It has been a tough run with the vicious reporters and the constant attacks but we are going to move forward.

We are going to win.

And we will move on to November.

Thank you everybody and I will see you soon!"

"If you are just tuning in, Carlton Winters has just finished his victory speech, but not before he directly attacked our network," said Roman Anthony Andrews.

"We can also project that Carlton Winters will win the state of Florida as he has said, but also the states of Illinois, Missouri, and North Carolina, but now let's go to former Martin administration adviser Terrell Dominique," said Roman Anthony Andrews.

"What you have just saw here tonight is a man who is attacking a free press; he is attacking us because he does not like facts or the truth; he is just a person who wants to say whatever he wants, and if people start to believe that, then we should all be afraid; America is in trouble now and it needs a true leader such as Cynthia Norwell Anderson, because she has the experience to get us into the twenty-first century and through tough messes; so to all of his supporters, I hope you don't get bamboozled, and let's hope you will open your eyes to a true leader," said Terrell Dominique.

"Now, we turn to Aaron Campbellson, who is at the magic panel," said Roman Anthony Andrews.

"Roman, it seems the math just isn't there for Jonathan Evanston to win the Centralist nomination because he is so far behind that it will take a miracle at the convention, but also not many people like his message because he is viewed as having too much of a moderate view; and it may be that him being too moderate will make him lose and then potentially drop out of the race soon; the only two people who have a chance are either Carlton Winters or Alan Alvarez, but the latter still needs to win many states in order to have the full support of the party; right now it seems to just be a two-person race between Carlton Winters and Alan Alvarez in the Central Administration Party; for the United Labourists, it is still possible for Elias Dominic to win, but he would have to win the major states plus most or all of the Superdelegates at the nomination convention, and that might be hard to do because the Superdelegates really like Cynthia Norwell Anderson due to her being the establishment candidate; for now it seems that Carlton Winters is leading for the Centralists and Cynthia Norwell Anderson is leading for the United Labourists, and back to you Roman," said Aaron Campbellson.

"Hold on, I believe we have a major projection coming up very shortly, so don't change the channel," said Roman Anthony Andrews.

"We can now project that Cynthia Norwell Anderson will win all five states of Illinois, Florida, North Carolina, Missouri, and Ohio; that is surely a very big win and a disappointment for the supporters of Elias Dominic, so it seems that the Dominic campaign will have to make a tough decision very soon or he will risk embarrassment," said Roman Anthony Andrews.

"Roman, by the end of the night, the total delegate count will be 621 for Carlton Winters, 396 for Alan Alvarez, 138 for Jonathan Evanston, 168 for Felipe Alonso, 800 for Elias Dominic, and 1,561 for Cynthia Norwell Anderson, but Roman it is also important to know that Superdelegates are already included in the total delegate count for both the Anderson and the Dominic campaigns," said Aaron Campbellson.

"Right now the race seems close, but that might end pretty soon due to a lack of states, as there are not a whole lot more, so if Alan Alvarez does not win all of the remaining states anytime soon it would be impossible for him to win the presidential nomination for the Centralists, and that means Carlton Winters will officially become the nominee for the Centralists, which will cause some headaches in the party itself," said Roman Anthony Andrews to the panel.

"It seems that Alan Alvarez is running out of time because he hasn't won many elections since Super Tuesday, but there is still hope since there are still the late March to mid-April primaries as well as the Acela primary and some other races that have yet to take place, so there is still some time left but the math isn't looking that good, and Carlton Winters could clinch the nomination for the Centralists between now and then, so let's see what happens," said Aaron Campbellson.

VI

Today is just the beginning of the chaos to start a race of epic and utter proportions.

It should be the beginning of the end for some candidates and then the confirmation shall occur.

And people will start to panic before something bad occurs. It seems the people are already in a panic against a Carlton Winters nomination, but none could be worse than a nomination for an establishment candidate such as Cynthia Norwell Anderson, because if she wins the nomination then populism will not win.

"Breaking now, this is Roman Anthony Andrews, and we can project that Carlton Winters has won the territory of American Samoa."

It begins now and it is part of something new.

"This just in, Carlton Winters has won the state of Arizona," said Roman Anthony Andrews.

"We can now report that Alan Alvarez has won the state of Utah," said Roman Anthony Andrews.

"Reporting live now, we can project that Carlton Winters has won the state of North Dakota," said Roman Anthony Andrews.

The races kept on being declared, win after win, but there would be no knowing of what will happen.

"The state of Wisconsin goes for Alan Alvarez," said Roman Anthony Andrews.

"The senator from Texas, Alan Alvarez, has won the state of Colorado," said Roman Anthony Andrews.

It was just one win after another and Alan Alvarez thought he had some very good momentum, but then maybe he was just lucky, or it could also be he would actually win the Centralist nomination. Time would tell and that is the people.

"Tonight, we can project that Alan Alvarez has won the state of Wyoming," said Roman Anthony Andrews.

There remains only one state that could decide the nominee of the Central Administration Party, and that is the home state of Carlton Winters, so there might be something big that happens soon.

There is just the case of who will win and why it will take such a course of action.

"Tonight is the most important race for Carlton Winters because if he doesn't win his home state of New York, then Alan Alvarez could still have a chance of winning," said Roman Anthony Andrews.

"Get ready for a big projection now; okay, we can now project that Carlton Winters has won his home state of New York, giving him 89 out of 95 delegates; it seems this is a major upset but it probably went the way it did because Alan Alvarez criticized New York values, and surely the people of New York didn't like that so they voted for Carlton Winters, and this result just made it harder for the senator from Texas, so let's go to the magic panel now," said Roman Anthony Andrews.

"We can now report that as of tonight on April 19, 2016, that it is mathematically impossible for Alan Alvarez to clinch the nomination as the presidential nominee for the Central Administration Party, but there are still several primaries to go, so we will continue to watch those results," said

Aaron Campbellson.

VII

Tonight could be a make it or break it for certain candidates, but time will tell if anyone drops out of a presidential race.

"Live from our Washington DC headquarters, this is Roman Anthony Andrews of National Media News Network, and tonight will determine who might be the favorite to win the Centralist nomination for president, so please stay tune because we have a panel with policy experts and pundits; tonight is the Acela primary along the northeastern corridor."

"Polls are still open and we will report the results live, so please stay tuned to us, because we have the most up to date information available that no one else has," said Roman Anthony Andrews.

There is an unlikely chance that Alan Alvarez will win, because he doesn't have the votes or the supporters, but Carlton Winters has yet to be declared the nominee for his party, so there is still some waiting to do.

"Live from DC, we are waiting for the polls to close in the Acela primary," said Roman Anthony Andrews.

"We expect there to be a vigorous campaign after tonight in order to finally declare a winner on either side," said Roman Anthony Andrews.

"The five states of Pennsylvania, Delaware, Maryland, Connecticut, and Rhode Island all close at 8 o'clock eastern time, and so far our exit polls and polling data are supporting an Anderson and Winters's victory," said Roman Anthony Andrews.

"The time is now 8 o'clock and we can now project that Carlton Winters has won the states of Maryland, Connecticut, and Pennsylvania; we can make this projection because of the data we are receiving from the exit polls and preliminary results, and we can turn now to Aaron Campbellson at the magic panel," said Roman Anthony Andrews.

"Roman, so far tonight it seems Carlton Winters is so far ahead of Alan Alvarez and Jonathan Evanston that no one is able to beat him, and that will be a problem for both Alan Alvarez and Jonathan Evanston because there is just no more support for them anymore; and if we continue to see this pattern we will see that Carlton Winters will become the presumptive nominee of the Centralists; Roman, back to you," said Aaron Campbellson.

"Okay, stand by for another big projection; we can now project that

Carlton Winters has won the state of Rhode Island," said Roman Anthony Andrews.

"And now we can project that Carlton Winters has won the state of Delaware clinching all five contests of the night for the Centralists, while we can project that Cynthia Norwell Anderson has won the state of Delaware for the United Labourists; so it seems that this is not good news for any of their opponents anytime soon," said Roman Anthony Andrews.

"Stand by for another major prediction; we can now project that Cynthia Norwell Anderson has won the state of Pennsylvania for the United Labourists, a major defeat for Elias Dominic," said Roman Anthony Andrews.

"This just in, we can now project that Elias Dominic has won his first state of the night, Rhode Island, but it won't yield him many delegates because Rhode Island is just a small state, but this was probably expected to happen," said Roman Anthony Andrews.

"But now, we can project that Cynthia Norwell Anderson has won the state of Connecticut for the United Labourists, and we can now project that Anderson has also won the state of Maryland, so get ready to hear some speeches tonight from the candidates, and I believe Elias Dominic is about to speak, so let's listen in," said Roman Anthony Andrews.

"*Hello West Virginia!*

Thank you!

Such an extraordinary turnout here tonight!

First, I would like to thank Bob Deavein and Harry Unidom for their speeches tonight.

But I would like to thank all of you for being here tonight celebrating our win in the progressive state of Rhode Island.

This wouldn't be possible without all of your support.

I would like to thank each and every one of you because together we have started a political revolution that has caused the corrupt 1% and Wall Street to panic.

This campaign is not just about electing a president but about transforming a nation and to cause a political revolution and you my friends are the revolutionaries.

Let me tell you a little secret.

The fight that we have begun is not that easy because of the corrupt campaign finance laws supported by the elite and wealthy donors from Wall Street.

When we began this campaign we had no money and were up against the wealthy establishment who said we never had a chance.

We were called a fringe campaign because of the political elite who don't want to see us win.

When we started out we were only polling about 2% in the national polls and were 75 points behind Cynthia Norwell Anderson.

Well, a lot has changed since then. We have now won 16 primaries and caucuses since we have launched this campaign.

With your help we can win here in the great state of West Virginia.

We have won over 1,200 delegates to take to the United Labourist National Convention and we will win more with your help next week.

Now, the national polls have us several points up against Carlton Winters, and that is good news for our revolution.

Almost every national and state poll has us beating Carlton Winters by 15 to 20 points more so than Cynthia Norwell Anderson because we have the independents supporting our campaign.

And I will tell you why we will win.

We will win because in the general election everyone can vote.

But in New York over 3 million independents couldn't vote because they were not registered as members of the United Labourists.

We will win because we are supporting the truth and we believe the process should allow anyone to vote in a primary, regardless of their political affiliation.

The truth will make us win.

Unfortunately, our media does not want you to see the truth because of their interests to the corporate elite.

So let me give you a few examples of what the media does not want you to know.

I traveled all around the country.

I went to Flint, Michigan and I feel for the children there, because they have been poisoned by lead in the water, and the current government isn't doing anything to fix it.

I have been to Detroit, Michigan, and I have seen firsthand at how bad the public school system is there, as the children there are suffering because it is on the verge of financial collapse.

Again, the current government there in Michigan is not funding our schools probably.

I also know that addiction is a major problem here in West Virginia but I want to let everyone know that I won't forget about it because it is my number one priority.

We have to stop the drug companies and the doctors from putting high prices on drugs.

We need drug prices to be reduced because people can't afford them and they are resorting to buying and selling drugs on the streets because they can't afford to buy their medication.

But the people have become so addicted to the drugs that they can't live without it.

So, we need to tell those drug companies to stop forcing extremely dangerous and strong drugs upon people, because those doctors have caused an epidemic by prescribing heavily addictive medication to people who can't handle it.

We are considered to be the wealthiest country in the world but it seems we still have problems in 2016.

We still have the highest youth unemployment in the world.

We have school systems that are collapsing financially.

We have problems with our infrastructure.

That is one far too many problems and the richest country in the world should not have any problems at all.

But we have these special interests in the forms of billionaire and Wall Street who don't care about you at all.

They only care about their big pay checks.

The greatest nations in the world are not judged by the wealthy elite or how many rich people exist.

No, the greatest nations in the world are judged by how it treats the weakest, poorest, and the most vulnerable people who live there.

As a great nation we have to treat everyone with equal respect and not just the wealthy elite.

We must acknowledge that the most vulnerable and the weakest of us tend to have a lack of money and that problem should not exist today.

People should be paid a living wage so they don't suffer.

I will promise you that I will demand Congress to institute a minimum wage of at least $15.00 per hour, which is around $600 a week, $2,400 a month, or $28,800 a year.

And that should be significantly more than you make now, but then you still have bills to pay.

So, I would support a minimum wage of at least $20.00 per hour, which is around $800 a week, $3,200 a month, or $38,000 per year.

That might not seem much but it is much more than many of you are making now.

With that extra money you can afford the things you need and might want.

You can now pay off your bills and not live from paycheck to paycheck anymore.

With a better minimum wage you won't feel constrained.

We must send a message to the wealthy elite and the greedy corporations that the current minimum wage makes it unfordable to live in America.

We must tell them that we will stand up to poverty and that everyone should have a home.

By voting for me I can promise you that I will stand up to the wealthy elite, the special interests, the Wall Street financiers, and the political elite by demanding Congress pass a new piece of legislation to mandate a living wage, because our people deserve better than living on the streets and under bridges.

We need to have a society that promotes equality instead of inequality.

Right here in the state of West Virginia we have an unemployment rate of about 55%, and that is such a shame, because qualified people can't find any work.

It is such a shame that people here in West Virginia are considered some of the poorest in the nation.

We must fix this problem because everywhere you go you find the same problem.

You always see the rich not taking care of the poor or the weakest class of people.

Now, being poor is not about just trying to afford a new flat screen television, because being poor also means whether you are going to die at an early age or live to see your grandchildren have children and then watch them mature.

If you look at people in other states such as Virginia or New York, you will notice that the majority of people die around the age of 85 compared to many counties in West Virginia in which many people die around their early fifties.

You see, the problem is the cost of health insurance is too much money, and people are not going to the hospital to get treated.

Instead, the people just die at home, because they know that they can't afford the hospital bill and they find health insurance coverage to be too much as well.

It is about the cost of living in a country.

And while we passed what was known as MartinCare, that law is not enough.

We must put the health insurance companies on notice that their product is making people die because it costs way too much to purchase.

With me as your president, I will push for universal healthcare for all, because everyone deserves the right to free healthcare without getting into any debt at all.

By giving the people access to free healthcare, the people would never have to worry again if they are going to live or die.

I believe healthcare is a basic human right because you deserve to be treated with respect.

But then they will say it is impossible to pay for or it would cost too much money.

Well, we will and can prove them wrong, because this shall all be paid for by imposing a tax on Wall Street.

We will impose a tax on speculation because every time some person speculates they earn money, but these people usually don't care about you or me because they grow corrupt with greed and want all of the money in the world for them.

We must stop it.

This campaign is making everyone to think outside of the box because this is truly a political revolution that no one on the right or the establishment wants to fight because they know they will lose and face defeat.

Our message is equality to all people but that won't work unless we fix this rigged economy.

We must fight for a better future in order to ensure our children, grandchildren, and future family members are able to afford it.

You have some of the wealthiest families in the world living here and they employ millions of people throughout their corporations, but they fail to pay them a living wage.

And now, with technology existing and taking over the workforce, people are being replaced by machines, because they are too greedy to pay people money.

They rather hire less people because they know it will improve their profits.

We will put them on notice and when I get into office I will make sure that never happens again.

We must stand up to these rich corporations. And then you have these terrible trade agreements such as the North American Free Trade Agreement or NAFTA, which hurts our employees because it doesn't help our economy, since it was written by corporate America.

We must tell corporate America to get out of our trade deals, because all that benefits are the special interests, the wealthy elite, and the political class.

But we won't stop there, because we will get rid of student debt.

For far too long, we have allowed students to go into debt.

Well, I believe that needs to end, because I believe no student should beholden to student loan companies.

I believe access to college is a human right and that all that wants to attend a public institution should be able to for free because no one needs to pay off large amounts of debt when they graduate.

And for all of you who have student debts, well, I will make sure that they are forgiven, because you need to grow and or support your family.

And having too much student debt will make it too difficult to live because every paycheck will go to your loans.

I will make sure everyone has the access to public education.

If there was enough money to bail out the largest banks in America, then there is enough money to make college free for all at public institutions.

We can pay for it all because this is surely a new political revolution.

We can hold Wall Street accountable and we can make sure America is better.

But we must address the threat of climate change, because it is caused by human activity.

And I am disheartened that none of my opponents from the Central Administration Party believe in the issue of climate change.

We must address this problem soon because if we don't then the world will suffer a major setback of rising water.

We must stop the big oil companies and hold them accountable and promote renewable energy such as solar and wind power.

If you think about it we can actually achieve it because we are the wealthiest and greatest country in the world.

We can afford anything because we are America.

So, West Virginia, I hope you will join me in supporting this new revolution."

"Such a fiery and defiant speech given by the United Labourist Elias Dominic, and it surely has fired up his base," said Roman Anthony Andrews.

"Now, we are still waiting for two more speeches," said Roman Anthony Andrews.

"I believe Carlton Winters is just about to walk up to the podium to speak, so let's listen in," said Roman Anthony Andrews.

"*I asked them how they would pivot out of this mess and well they said not to worry about it.*

Well, I guess they knew what they were doing all along because they were professional politicians.

But tonight is for you folks here and who are watching live from home that has supported this campaign since day one.

It is also for all new supporters who have jumped on board after your first or second choices had to drop out.

I know that for some or even many of you that I wasn't your first choice but I would just like to welcome you to our campaign.

I would like to thank you all of you who are here tonight and to all who have followed us.

Without you this wouldn't be possible.

Because tonight has become a bigger win than I ever thought was possible.

Tonight we have won all five states and they are saying that I got over two-thirds of the votes.

I loved when the pundits says that I never had a chance but I don't know what they think now.

I guess they still attack me because they don't want me to win because they have already decided that my opponent on the other side has already won the general election and it's not even November yet.

So we have already proved them wrong because I am winning all the time.

And I guess you could say we are winning because of the failing campaigns but let me tell you something.

Last night something strange occurred, because I saw many campaigns get together to try to see what they could do so insert a white knight candidate so I wouldn't continue to win as I am now.

That shows you weakness and they don't want you to see economic prosperity. I guess you could say it is collusion, but in business, whenever you collude with other businesses, you get arrested or sent to jail and then face a trial, because they say price fixing is bad or something.

But when there is collusion in politics, well, I guess it isn't illegal, because it is only seen a meet up with people to discuss the future of politics.

But anyway I do believe it sends a weak signal and the Central Administration Party doesn't really need that because we as a party need to stand united and to support the nominee.

So, I will be in Indiana soon, in order to further our wins across the country.

We have millions and millions of more votes and supporters than Alan Alvarez, but I wish him well, because he ran one of the toughest campaigns against me.

And we have millions upon millions of more votes than Jonathan Evanston, who has only won one state, and I really don't know why he is still here, but I guess he thinks he can snatch the nomination from me at the convention in July, which I don't believe is possible.

You could also say that Alan Alvarez, Felipe Alonso, and former New

Jersey governor Steven Sestance won more delegates than Jonathan Evanston, and that just tells you that everyone except for Evanston knows when their time is up to suspend their campaign.

But we will continue until the last vote of the last primary is counted. And by then we should win the nomination in July in Evanston's state of Ohio.

That should be something to watch and we will see if he shows up. If he doesn't, well, then we already knew that, because he was the only candidate who won't give up.

I mean, when you read about Alan Alvarez, you could agree with him, but he is really just using people in order to get their votes.

And I don't believe anyone likes that.

So I do consider myself to be the presumptive nominee and it looks like I am going to win the primaries in the states of California and Indiana.

I am up by a margin that no one can overtake me.

We should be doing well in Indiana because I don't want our companies to leave for Mexico where products are not as good as they are here.

If you think about it, this campaign season began with about 17 people, and now we have about maybe 3 left, 1 of which shouldn't be here because he really has no chance, and the other one who just wants to be the moral compass.

So, you look at the numbers now, and each time there was a primary, you had people drop out, because they knew they couldn't win any delegates.

The magic number is 1,237, and we are much closer to that number than anyone else.

Look, when I began this campaign, everybody thought I had no chance of winning, and they placed me at 17, but now I am always winning and I expect to win the remaining contests.

The reason why is because of my message.

I guess people understand me better because I say it like it is.

And you hear the news give me problems.

But I do have support from many people.

We still have problems though.

Students go to good schools hoping to get good jobs but when they graduate they can't find any job at all and they graduate deep in debt.

So there's a problem and we need to fix that.

I will promise you that I will improve the economy by cutting taxes and getting rid of burdensome regulations.

We need jobs for everyone, including the young people, because no one wants to remain in debt for the rest of their lives.

People want to prosper. And we are going to fix the issue of China and North Korea.

If you look at my opponents on the other side all they talk about is socialism, but they are funded by Wall Street, because most of them are United Labourists themselves.

And they don't really believe in legal immigration or a secure border, but I want to say that I will make sure criminals and drugs will never make it across the border anymore because I will build a wall to protect our country.

Anyways, I believe the people have spoken and are ready.

Ladies and gentlemen, thank you, very much tonight for the wins tonight.

I really appreciate it."

"If you are just tuning in, Carlton Winters has just finished giving his campaign victory speech, and we are still waiting for Cynthia Norwell Anderson to give her speech," said Roman Anthony Andrews.

"Okay, I do believe she is giving her speech now, so let's listen in to see what she has to say about her wins tonight," said Roman Anthony Andrews.

"*Thank you!*

Thank you so very much!

Wow, what a crowd!

Thank you so very much, Pennsylvania!

What a great night tonight was!

I want to thank you all.

I want to thank every single one of you.

Since day one of my campaign you have supported me and a time for change.

I really appreciate your support.

Wow, such enthusiasm tonight!

Thank you so very much!

Well, I would just like to thank all of you again for helping us get this far.

And I want to thank each of you who voted for me here in Pennsylvania and across Delaware, Maryland, Rhode Island, and Connecticut.

Tonight, everyone should be happy, because of how hard they worked to get out the vote.

It was surely an amazing night because of your help.

And with your continued help and support we can go to Philadelphia in July to win the nomination because we have the most pledged delegates of this campaign season for the United Labourists, and I believe we are the only campaign that can win in July at the convention.

We shall unify our party together and we shall stand strong against the Centralists because they are wrong for America.

We need you to keep volunteering so we can get our message out to the voters.

I know there are barriers but our nation is great and whatever the other candidates say don't believe them.

We can build America without any hatred from the other side of the aisle.

I believe we can achieve greatness and we can do anything if we just set our minds to it.

I believe in creating better jobs for all of America and I believe these opportunities will provide for the better of the country.

We can help lift up people with the some progressive ideology as Franklin Delano Roosevelt did.

And we can agree that climate change is a real threat caused by humans so we must act now by moving away from fossil fuels.

We must better educate our children. We must stop Wall Street from harming our society.

We can stand together and help each other move America into the 21st century in order to treat women with respect and to provide for equality with a living wage.

The other side wants to ban the Muslims because they feel threatened and we say that kind of hatred and discrimination is unaccepted.

With your help we can take this campaign to the next phase: to win the nomination in July and then to win the presidency in November.

We need equal rights for women and we need to make sure that those Centralists never take away women's healthcare, because it is their right to decide what to do with their bodies.

So, I would just like to say if you are a United Labourist, an Independent, or a thoughtful Centralist thinking about your future, I believe you can see that the approach from the other side is the wrong way, because we can do better than that.

And I want you all to imagine this was tomorrow because we can tear down walls instead of building them, where everyone can be invited.

There will be equality for all to see and live. We have a hope and future for everyone in America but my opponents on the other side believe in divisive rhetoric and hatred in which there is constant discrimination against minorities and women.

We are hopeful that children will succeed in the future by building better schools throughout our neighborhoods.

And we can guarantee that no student will graduate with debt because public institutions of higher education will be free for all to attend.

We will get through this.

We must learn to be strong and to help each other be better.

We need strong bonds to stop this divisive rhetoric and hatred.

We must be better than them.

Our declaration of independence and constitution were just signed a few blocks away from here, and ever since then we have faced an uncertain future.

Well, I want to make sure that no more uncertainty happens, because we will move our country forward, and we will be proud.

So go register to vote if you haven't already and volunteer.

Thank you all so very much and I will see you all at the convention in July!"

"If you are just tuning in, Cynthia Norwell Anderson has just gave her victory speech for the night in Philadelphia, and we can expect soon that she could be declared the presumptive nominee in just days or weeks," said

Roman Anthony Andrews.

"Now, we can focus on the Indiana primary and the future of who will remain," said Aaron Campbellson.

"Thank you all who have been tuning in for our live coverage and have a good night, so we will see you all tomorrow here soon again, and remember we are the best name in news," said Roman Anthony Andrews.

VIII

Tonight was a big night and it helped dwindle down the choices of who might win.

Well, then something happened.

"This is Roman Anthony Andrews, and we have confirmed that tomorrow morning Alan Alvarez will officially name former CEO of Sloan-Oxford Dana Genucci as his running mate for Vice President, so let's go to Aaron Campbellson.

"Roman, this sounds like Alan Alvarez is naming a woman as his running mate because he believes it will help him take away delegates from Carlton Winters; this is very unusual because Alan Alvarez has no chance of winning the Centralist nomination for president; but we will say what other people say," said Aaron Campbellson.

"Very unusual indeed, and we will see how his critics and the voters respond to him selecting a running mate, but now the focus is on the state of Indiana and beyond," said Roman Anthony Andrews.

"Welcome to our coverage of the Indiana Primary; Today is Tuesday, May 3, 2016, and we will be updating you every minute of the hour with live results; tonight could be the decider of who will remain and who will drop out in the near future; and this is Roman Anthony Andrews reporting live from DC, so let's go to the magic panel," said Roman Anthony Andrews.

"Hello Roman, tonight might finally determine who will be considered the presumptive nominee for the Centralists, but we might still have to wait maybe a month to see the presumptive nominee for the United Labourists will be; but keep in mind that there is no chance of Alan Alvarez and Jonathan Evanston of getting enough delegates unless Carlton Winters decides to drop out; so tonight we will be looking at the important counties for Carlton Winters, Cynthia Norwell Anderson, and Elias Dominic need to do well in, and back to you Roman," said Aaron Campbellson.

"Okay, be prepared for a projection soon; the time is now exactly 7 o'clock, and we can now confirm and project that Carlton Winters will win the state of Indiana, but it is still close to call to declare a winner in the race between Cynthia Norwell Anderson and Elias Dominic," said Roman Anthony Andrews.

"It is a victorious night here for Carlton Winters, and no one will ever stop him from going down," said Gina Tucker.

"Now all we need to wait for are the victory and concession speeches tonight, and we will see what each one has to say," said Roman Anthony Andrews.

"Wait, we are receiving word that Elias Dominic is giving a speech of some kind, so let's listen in to what he is saying," said Roman Anthony Andrews.

"*Hello Indiana!*

No matter what happens tonight we will continue to have momentum.

We are doing this for the future of America.

We need to stop the corrupt Wall Street financiers from targeting people with loans and debt.

We need to fix our education and healthcare system.

Most of all, we need to have equality in the workforce and make sure people are paid a living wage.

This wouldn't be possible without you.

We will go on because we don't want the establishment to win.

Hold on a minute because some of my advisors need to tell me something.

Okay, well, I believe all of you here are going to like this news.

I have just been informed that we have won the great state of Indiana.

The Anderson campaign said we would not win and her supporters said we had no chance of winning another primary.

Well, tonight, we proved them wrong.

Tonight, we will gain more delegates and we will go to the convention in July.

We will not stop now.

We are going to California, Oregon, and Washington, and I believe we have a good chance of winning in California because the people demand action.

And that is the way it is.

We don't want someone like Carlton Winters because he will turn all of progress made by the Martin administration and past presidents backwards into oblivion.

We have a message that will win because the people know what we stand for and need.

They are tired of the corrupt campaign finance laws and the Super PACs controlled by the billionaires.

We must stop Wall Street from doing their misdeeds.

I believe healthcare is a human right and we need to make sure everyone is protected.

We indeed have a path to victory but it is a narrow path, in order to win the pledged delegates.

We will make a case to many of the Super-delegates that they vote for us because the world has changed and because the polls show us beating Carlton Winters.

And many of these Super delegates were pledged to Cynthia Norwell Anderson before she ever committed to run, and I believe that is unfair.

I believe we can win in California because we have a great ground game and because the people there support our agenda more than Anderson.

We feel like today's victory will lead to a stronger campaign.

We might not have a Super PAC like Anderson has, but we have grassroots, so we are not going to spend over $100 million on campaign advertisements.

We will decide where to place our ads.

We have engaged many people and they are willing to vote for me because of my message.

You see, Centralists win when voter turnout is low, and United Labourists win when voter turnout is high.

We believe we have the support to win and that will be great for the United Labourists.

So, I will see you all tomorrow as we move forward."

"We can now go to the Alan Alvarez campaign, as he is just about to speak about his future," said Roman Anthony Andrews.

"Thank you every one for being here tonight!

We have gotten so many more delegates than some other campaigns did during this process.

And during this process, it had shown me that no matter what, you will always have full support from your supporters.

We saw a movement grow while the pundits and media said we never had a chance.

Well, we proved them wrong again.

Over five million people donated an average of just $60.

It was your grassroots support that helped us get off the ground and to proceed with our campaign.

That is what our campaign was about.

I would just like to thank the volunteers who helped me with my campaign for their countless hours, and to my family, and to Dana who has been a fabulous running mate.

But from the beginning, I have always said I will always continue my campaign, as long as there is a viable path forward.

But with a heavy heart, I will just like to say that I have to suspend my campaign for president effectively tonight, and that might be sad news tonight, but we can all move forward.

I believe God has a better plan for me and that I guess he never intended for me to become the nominee for the Centralists.

Now, don't get discouraged, since there is time to think about it. But for me there is no viable path to the nomination.

Carlton Winters will be the nominee and hopefully when the general election is held in November he will win.

But we must remember not to use this heated rhetoric and we must always be respectful of others.

We must have unity and stand for something.

But this doesn't mean I will end my campaign to support liberty, because we need to hold government and the bureaucrats accountable to the people.

We must make sure people are not falsely targeted by government agencies.

We need to stop the establishment from deciding our fate.

We owe it to our founders because they knew that our rights come from God and not from government or politicians.

We have to stand strong and we will succeed.

Together we shall restore what America was and what America was founded on.

Together, we will help stop this government waste and we will not stop under the government is held to their actions.

We will stand together and we will not be purged from the history books.

We can unite and we will fight for your freedom and liberty.

But we must move forward.

Thank you all tonight for being here."

"That was Alan Alvarez saying he was officially suspending his campaign to seek the presidential nomination for the Centralists, and now let's turn to Carlton Winters, because he is about to speak," said Roman Anthony Andrews.

"*Thank you very much!*

Well, first off I want to thank my family, my parents who are watching over me, and my grandparents, but I just want to thank my entire family.

The people of Indiana have been incredible.

But not too long ago the media said I had no chance of winning and said I was about 20 points down.

I went there and campaigned a lot and the people heard my message.

And you know we had a tremendous victory tonight.

We have to learn to win again.

We lose with everything.

We are not going to lose again because we are going to win again.

When I got home tonight I knew we were going to win and the media knew it right away.

But all the time I see these negative ads against me.

They only have false information in them and all of them are funded by left-wing propagandists.

They spend too much money against me. And now we are going to

West Virginia to get the miners back to work.

Let me tell you something about Cynthia Norwell Anderson.

She told the truth because she doesn't believe in coal.

Well, we shouldn't allow that because the miners deserve better than that.

She wants to put many people out of unemployment because she prefers solar and wind power over a much needed commodity.

And let me tell you something, we are going to defeat former secretary of state Anderson in November.

She supports NAFTA, open borders, free healthcare, and all of that nonsense that supports too much government spending.

Well, we won't allow that to happen.

We are going to change everything and stop these companies from going to other countries.

And if they are going to a different country, well, they will face very serious consequences.

We must support our local and state economies and not some country that devalues their currency.

I have worked all my life but I have seen bad deals and good deals. But let me tell you something.

I do not know if Alan Alvarez likes me but he was one tough competitor.

He faced a hard decision.

I want to keep all of my 16 other opponents involved because I believe we can win.

I believe we need to do it.

We have 21 trillion due soon and it might go up even more with the recently passed budget.

We are going to have great relationships with other countries.

In this building I have the largest bank from China as a tenant.

But we must not rely on them for our products.

We need to take out the Victory World Front.

We need to have better trade deals. And we need to help our veterans more so they don't face many problems.

We can do it. A recent Hessen poll came out the other day showing that we are defeating Anderson by several points and that sure sound like something the media doesn't want to support because it doesn't fit their narrative.

We are going to help America.

We are going to do great with the Hispanics and the Blacks.

We will provide jobs to people and we are going to grow the economy.

We are going to win.

I would just like to thank the National Centralist Administration Committee and the chairperson there Perance Flintri.

It isn't an easy job and he is doing a great job leading it to help our campaign.

I also want to thank my staff, Anthony, Gary, and Faith for helping me.

Again, this has been a very tremendous evening and I owe it all to you people.

This movement wouldn't be possible without you and we can win in November with your help.

I would also like to thank Alan Alvarez and what he did tonight.

Because you know what he said tonight was not easy.

He is right.

We do need unity, because without unity we would allow the United Labourists to win, and I know none of you want that to happen.

So we need unity and we are getting there.

We owe it to the Central Administration Party.

And you wouldn't believe it from the media.

They now say they want to get on our team because of our movement.

They say don't worry about it I told them they attacked me.

But I want to thank everyone.

I would like to thank the evangelicals.

We are going to say Merry Christmas again.

We will stop this political correctness.

Again, I want to congratulate Alan Alvarez, my wife, my staff, and everyone who have been here from the beginning.

Our theme is to make America prosperous again so that we can win.

With your help we can win and we will win big in the month of November.

Again, Thank You!"

"Such optimism and contempt for his party, but he believes he has the unity to move forward," said Roman Anthony Andrews.

"Well, it seems with Alvarez dropping out Evanston will also drop out, and it seems we are now learning that he will suspend his campaign tomorrow but we have yet to confirm that information, yet it seems Carlton Winters will become the presumptive nominee for the Central Administration Party," said Roman Anthony Andrews.

"Breaking news, it is Wednesday, May 4, 2016, and we can now confirm that Jonathan Evanston will announce he will suspend his campaign to seek the presidential nomination of the Central Administration Party, so we can now confirm that Carlton Winters has become the presumptive nominee of the Central Administration Party because there was no viable path to victory for Evanston," said Roman Anthony Andrews.

And now all hope rests on unity.

IX

There is now a little more than a month to go before the two major political parties hold their nominating conventions.

It will be an exciting and hopeful event but there is something to provide for.

"Breaking now, we are reporting tonight on June 6, 2016, that the former secretary of state, Cynthia Norwell Anderson, has officially clinched enough delegates to win the nomination for the United Labourists, and this makes her the presumptive nominee, but we still have more races tomorrow," said Roman Anthony Andrews.

"Tonight is the night dreaded for the Dominic campaign because it will ultimately confirm or deny Cynthia Norwell Anderson clinching the presidential nomination for the United Labourists, but we must move forward to see what lies ahead for both political parties," said Roman Anthony Andrews.

"The time is now 7 o'clock and we are waiting live for results from the states of New Jersey, South Dakota, Montana, North Dakota, California, and New Mexico, but first let's go to Aaron Campbellson who is at the magic panel," said Roman Anthony Andrews.

"Good evening Roman, the first state to close is New Jersey at 8:00 pm Eastern Time, followed by the states of South Dakota and New Mexico at 9:00 pm Eastern Time, then the state of Montana at 10:00 pm Eastern Time, and lastly followed by the pair of states of California and North Dakota at 11:00 pm Eastern Time; but Roman, it is important to note that we might still not know tonight of who wins these six races because some states take longer to count than others, so we should know in a few weeks who has won; yet there are states that Elias Dominic want to perform well in but he might not because they could be closed to the independent voters," said Aaron Campbellson.

There seems to be an uncertain advantage over all of this nonsense that is going on here.

It could be that people campaign for two years but the American public want to understand and get to know a future politician before voting for them, and this is certainly to gain trust.

But that is not the same as in other countries.

Everywhere else there are limits to how many days a person can campaign along with any political advertisements.

It is not the same in other countries because they are not America.

They are countries that try to restrict freedom and truth that ends up resulting in betraying their own people.

And that isn't to say that something is better but it is almost time to report the results.

"The results are starting to come in from the state of New Jersey, and so far it looks like Cynthia Norwell Anderson is ahead by a very large margin about twice the percentage as Elias Dominic and that will certainly be very disappointing to him," said Aaron Campbellson.

"We can now announce who will win the state of New Jersey; okay, we can project that Cynthia Norwell Anderson has won the state of New Jersey for the United Labourists and that Carlton Winters has won the state of New Jersey for the Centralists," said Roman Anthony Andrews.

"We still have less than an hour left until the next polls close so we will update you with much needed information from the magic panel as needed," said Roman Anthony Andrews.

"Roman, let's look at the reason Anderson won New Jersey; the reason why Anderson won the state of New Jersey is because in the majority of the counties she performed so well that Dominic didn't have a chance; this could be due to Anderson being declared the presumptive nominee or it could be the people of New Jersey liking her message; but the reason why she is winning the state of New Jersey is because she performed well in all counties except for two: Sussex and Warren, in which Dominic won those two places; but the big picture here tonight is that the United Labourists have decided to unite for Anderson for the best of the party," said Aaron Campbellson.

"Okay, it seems we are getting in new information, so let's see what is happening in the state of North Dakota," said Roman Anthony Andrews.

"Yes Roman, it seems the Centralists are not holding an election tonight here in the state of North Dakota because they already held a party convention earlier in the campaign season around April, but the problem here tonight for the United Labourists is trying to convince people to vote for their candidate, and it seems that there is an argument about why voters should support Dominic over Anderson and vice versa," said Justin Jeremy Scott.

"Okay, let's go to the magic panel with Aaron Campbellson to look at the voting in North Dakota," said Roman Anthony Andrews.

"Since North Dakota is a caucus state, the voters might prefer Elias Dominic, because, well, North Dakota has many rural communities, and there tends to be more people who support his message there; it seems the people of North Dakota might vote for Dominic because they want to be recognized by the government, and while the official poverty rate might still fall below the national average it is nonetheless still high around almost 11%, and those voters might just vote for Dominic since he says he will stop the wealthy elite," said Aaron Campbellson.

"So, what does that mean, could you explain it to our viewers what that might mean," asked Roman Anthony Andrews to Aaron Campbellson?
"Yes, so for the people who are in that 11% range of poverty, well they might feel like there are no jobs for them; they will feel left out of the economy; and then some of them will demonize the corporations and businesses because they feel as though that all they care about is money and greed; so

you will see they believe they have an unfair disadvantage because no one cares about them; and in that instance, if you have these same people who are always in poverty and can never escape it, well they will become dependent on government; the people in constant poverty will now live on government handouts such as welfare in addition to their low-paying jobs, but their low-paying jobs will force them to go on government welfare; however, there would be some people who will want to escape government welfare because they know it is only temporary and not a permanent fix, and then you have the other people who are so dependent on government welfare that they never want to give it up because they want the free money; and for those people who never want to give up the government welfare, they won't try to seek better paying jobs, because they believe it is their money even if they never earn it," said Aaron Campbellson.

"So, it is just a feeling about being left out or not being included in the economy," asked Roman Anthony Andrews?

"Yes, that is exactly right, and it is because of that situation that could result in Elias Dominic winning the state of North Dakota," said Aaron Campbellson.

"Now, what about the other side of the political spectrum, how do the Centralists fare in the elections in North Dakota," asked Roman Anthony Andrews to Aaron Campbellson?

"Since North Dakota is a state where many rural communities exist, and most of the counties are rural, the people rely upon farming and other types of agriculture; but North Dakota tends to be genuinely more right-leaning and conservative in nature, meaning they are more business friendly due to their belief in family values and business, yet also because they tend to always promote the value of hard work; so this would mean the majority of the people would vote for a candidate to nominee such as Carlton Winters because he supports the farming and agricultural industries and both the people of North Dakota and Carlton Winters know the values of hard work," said Aaron Campbellson to Roman Anthony Andrews.

"Hold on, we are just getting word that Carlton Winters is speaking to a crowd of supporters in New York, so let's listen in to what he has to say," said Roman Anthony Andrews.

"*Tonight, we finish a very historic night, and now we are moving towards the nominating convention and winning back the White House in November.*

My agenda has been the most conservative since Ronald Reagan and I will promise you we will prosper again.

Our campaign received the most votes in any primary combined in the history of this country.

And I will promise you real change that will help you and not that mantra of hope and change from the Martin administration.

I will give you real change and it will help the economy, reduce your taxes, and will build a border to protect our country from criminals and illegal immigrants.

We will protect our veterans and rebuild the military again. We will prosper like we never before did.

I know and understand that I must carry the mantel and I promise you that I will fulfill my duties as your nominee and as your next president of the United States of America.

You will be proud of this movement.

Recent polls have us above Cynthia Norwell Anderson and they continue to grow but just keep in mind of the fake news.

To any of you who supported Elias Dominic but were left out because of the Super-delegates, you are welcome to vote for us.

We are going to have the jobs.

I will never ever back down from my promises if I am forced to defend something.

I am going to be your champion and I will never back down.

Every election year politicians promise change but they fail to deliver.

I beat a rigged system by winning but I couldn't say the same for Elias Dominic.

We can't fix this rigged system by counting on the politicians who have created it.

We must campaign strongly like I did and go against the establishment.

The last thing we need in the White House is Cynthia Norwell Anderson because that will just be an extension of the Martin administration disaster.

We love our country.

Every American worker deserves to have the same rights, protections, and privileges, but the people in power say we can't change.

We are going to change it and we are going to put America back to work.

We are going to take care of everybody.

We are going to make you safe and prosperous and you the American people will be put first again.

Ladies and gentlemen, we will make America great and prosperous again, like it used to be.

Thank you!"

"If you are just tuning in, Carlton Winters has just finished giving his victory speech of the night, and he looks very optimistic about winning the presidency in November," said Roman Anthony Andrews.

"Please stand by for a projection; okay, we can now project that Cynthia Norwell Anderson has won the states of South Dakota and New Mexico for the United Labourists and that Carlton Winters has won the states of South Dakota and New Mexico for the Centralists; again, both of the two presumptive nominees have won these two states," said Roman Anthony Andrews.

"The time is now 10:00 pm and we can make another projection of who will win; we can project that Elias Dominic will win his first state of the night of Montana, but we can also project that Carlton Winters has won the state of Montana as well," said Roman Anthony Andrews.

"Okay, I am just hearing we will be hearing from all three campaigns shortly about what they will do next, so we will hear what they have to say, and there might be some more surprises," said Roman Anthony Andrews.

"But, we are now anxiously waiting for the results in California and North Dakota, and those results will arrive in the next hour, so please stay tuned, but this might go into the early morning of tomorrow," said Roman Anthony Andrews.

"We are just receiving word that Cynthia Norwell Anderson is in the middle of giving her victory speech, so let's listen in to what she has to say," said Roman Anthony Andrews.

"It might be hard to see tonight but we are all sitting under a real glass ceiling tonight.

Now, we won't break this glass ceiling tonight but I just want to tell you how glad I am.

I can't be happier to tell you that a woman will finally become the official nominee for president of the United States of a major political party.

That is one huge milestone and we will make it to the city of Philadelphia and win the nomination there for the United Labourists where we will envision a plan for the future and the next generation of Americans to survive.

We will do this and we will be elected to the White House.

See you in Philadelphia and God Bless!"

"Okay, we just got the Anderson campaign just in time before she finished her speech; she sounds very optimistic about her future and she did use a metaphor of some kind to describe her campaign; the idea of the glass ceiling being present should make sense because she might be using that at the nominating convention and even at the watch party during the November general election; overall she was proud," said Roman Anthony Andrews.

"So we wait for the Elias Dominic campaign and I believe he will give his speech soon; okay, I believe he is in the middle of it right now, so let's listen in to see what he has to say," said Roman Anthony Andrews.

"I want to thank you of you for being here tonight.

I want to thank all of the volunteers here in the state of California here tonight.

Thank you for all of your hospitality.

Over a year ago when we started we were considered a fringe campaign.

We have won my big numbers the votes of young people because they understand they are the future of America.

I am optimistic of the future of our country.

We have a vision for America that the young people understand.

And we will take it all over America.

We must change our destiny so we will have a better America and to provide for our children and the next generation.

Our young people understand that you must fight for social justice, environmental justice, and economic justice.

We must fight for the future of our country so it will still exist and not disappear because of decisions made by the corrupt elite.

This is not just about just defeating Carlton Winters.

This is about promoting change to help everyone succeed.

So, next Tuesday we will continue this fight to the last primary in America in Washington DC.

We will fight hard to win the primary in DC.

And we will take this fight of social, environmental, and economic justice to Philadelphia in order to fight the corrupt establishment.

We will fight for our movement.

Thank you!"

"That was Elias Dominic, who said he was not going to give up, and was going to fight for delegates until the end, but right now we have the projections for California and North Dakota, so please stay tuned if you want to see live results," said Roman Anthony Andrews.

"Okay, we can now project that Elias Dominic has won the state of North Dakota for the United Labourists and Cynthia Norwell Anderson has won the state of California for the United Labourists; and with no competition, Carlton Winters has won the states of California and North Dakota in an expected win," said Roman Anthony Andrews.

"Tonight we have the results soon in the last primary of the year for the presidential election; we will be bringing you those results as soon as we can determine who is going to win the United Labourist primary in DC; be prepared for a projection," said Roman Anthony Andrews.

"We can now project that Cynthia Norwell Anderson will easily win the Washington DC primary for the United Labourists, and this basically seals the nomination for her in late July at the United Labourist nominating convention," said Roman Anthony Andrews.

"Right now we are hearing that Elias Dominic will put out some sort of statement or message regarding the future of his campaign for president, and we will provide it to you live when he announces the next steps of what he will do," said Roman Anthony Andrews.

"So please stay tuned for any future announcement and good night," said Roman Anthony Andrews.

There was just something left to do and no one could figure it out but it will be likely that Elias Dominic will support Cynthia Norwell Anderson's bid for president now, which could upset many of his supporters, yet no one knows what will happen at the nomination convention.

It could be that Elias Dominic holds on to his delegates because he despises the establishment and the political elite.

But he could also give away his delegates to Cynthia Norwell Anderson and that could result in his supporters being betrayed by him.

There is no clear solution here but the primary campaign season is over and it is now time to begin campaigning for the general election that will take place in November.

Something will indeed happen but it could be a surprise to all.

It might be an October surprise or something that isn't true at all.

It could be that a campaign official will end up in trouble or will lead to the demise of something bad.

It could be good or it could be the end of something in the midst of an unknown mystery, but there is no known person or thing that could ever describe something to the ends of the earth.

Time will tell when it will be revealed.

Until then it is only a conspiracy theory.

There is only time and nothing else.

THREE

I

Today is March 24, 2016, and foreign policy adviser of energy Alexander Christopoulos has a meeting with Andres Zerafa about having a future meeting with Russian president Dmitri Leninov.

Alexander is getting ready for the meeting and does not know what to expect.

This could be some sort of trick to undermine a political campaign. It could be the end of the career politicians.

It could be the end of a political dynasty.

Today is the day that could feel regretful.

It won't last forever but there is always the center of attention in who actually benefits from this information, if any information is revealed to anyone.

"Hello, Mr. Christopoulos, I'm glad you could make it to today's meeting," said Andres Zerafa.

"I am told you have connections to Dmitri Leninov, the president of Russia," said Alexander Christopoulos.

"Yes, that is right, I do have connections to the president of Russia," said Andres Zerafa.

"How would I get into contact with them so I could try to help the Carlton Winters campaign," asked Alexander Christopoulos.

"We can discuss that at a later date, but first let me introduce you to Katrina Maribelle, who is a niece to the president of Russia," said Andres Zerafa.

"What type of information would we be addressing," asked Alexander Christopoulos?

"The information would involve helping the campaign of Carlton Winters, but you should receive a text telling you where and when to meet me," said Andres Zerafa.

"Will it be potentially harmful or just dirt on the Anderson campaign," asked Alexander Christopoulos?

"It could be both, but until then, we shall meet again; Goodbye Mr. Alexander Christopoulos," said Andres Zerafa.

With that, both men left the meeting place, while Katrina spends some time in the city of London to enjoy the atmosphere.

This event could lead to something more drastic and significant that might change the life of Alexander Christopoulos forever, and it could haunt him because he never even heard of Andres Zerafa until someone introduced him to him during a meeting last month.

This could be a trap and he probably won't know it until there is a lack of evidence to support the claim.

It isn't the first time that an expert would be fooled into believing false information and a bunch of lies, because that is exactly how espionage works.

The goal would be to trick someone into believing something.

Let alone, there is the example of Katrina Maribelle, as Alexander Christopoulos has never even heard of or met her before.

And beside that fact, Katrina is a senior adviser to Carlton Winters himself, which makes something look sinister, or it could be an elaborate fraud.

It could just be that Katrina could be trying to help the foreign policy demands of Alexander Christopoulos.

This could just be a giant trick and trap set by people who do not want to see Carlton Winters as the next president of the United States of America.

It could be a trap set by members of a deep state organized in order to support the establishment so no change will ever come to Washington DC.

Surely, there are forces within the federal bureaucracy who do not want to see freedom and liberty prosper because they want to make sure democracy and the constitution do not get to see the light of day.

It is all too common and they think they can get away with it but they could be having some grand problems.

As a result, there could be some issues ahead.

At a beach in Spain, Katrina relaxes until she has to leave for New York tomorrow.

But there is something there is just the kind of people in this world.

It all matters and it will in the next several weeks.

There is just this sense of craziness everywhere, so there is time to think over all of this chaos and anarchy.

It wouldn't be the same without the people who have always tried to trick the innocent but it will lead to misinformation all over the world in order to spread propaganda.

That is just the information that people will listen to because they don't know any better.

For that, it is all about getting to the bottom of it and that remains to be seen because there will always be those people who do not need to understand anything.

That is just the case about the solution of nothing.

For all purposes a liar could believe he is not a liar and that is just insane and probably believable.

Because they have a heightened sense of one's self that they believe everything they say.

That will just be the downfall of society as we know it.

II

Yesterday, on April 25, 2016, Alexander Christopoulos received a text from Andres Zerafa to meet him for breakfast at the Cornwell London hotel on Sheffield Street.

"Hello again Mr. Christopoulos, I have some good information for you; I have dirt on the Anderson campaign that will hurt her chances of winning, but specifically I have that information in the form of thousands of emails; I can give you this for a price but it needs to be good in order to release it to you," said Andres Zerafa.

"What does this information involve," asked Alexander Christopoulos?

"It exists only of emails that say Cynthia Norwell Anderson is intentionally breaking the law," said Andres Zerafa.

"Let me think about it and I will send you a message if I need those emails," said Alexander Christopoulos.

With that, both men paid for their separate bills and they left to go back their separate ways.

To Alexander, it all sounded too suspicious because he had no real information to go on and he didn't really know if this so-called professor was lying or telling the truth.

It could all be an elaborate hoax in order to frame an innocent person. But there could be another thing that is elaborated on.

Several days have passed since that breakfast meeting but now it is May 10, 2016, and Alexander Christopoulos has found out that the top-ranking Australian diplomat, William Thomas Thompson is drinking at a local bar on Wellington Street across from Huntington Street in the south side of London.

"Hello, I just want to tell you that I am from the Carlton Winters campaign and that I would just like to say that I have information that the Russians have dirt on Cynthia Norwell Anderson; here's to us knowing the truth, but you should contact Andres Zerafa," said Alexander Christopoulos.

With that, Alexander left but there is nothing left to know of what will happen.

There have been some suspicious reports about scams going on here in order to make a quick buck or so.

But there is just something to it that might not be in order.

It could be that the information is not true or it could be true and there is indeed something there.

III

And then something happened on the future of Elias Dominic's campaign.

"We are getting brand new reaction from the campaign of Elias Dominic, and we are learning he will now endorse the presumptive nominee Cynthia Norwell Anderson in the hopes of preventing Carlton Winters from winning the presidency, and we will update you with more information as it comes in," said Roman Anthony Andrews.

"We are learning that Elias Dominic is just about to speak at an event in Portsmouth, New Hampshire to endorse Cynthia Norwell Anderson as the presumptive nominee for the United Labourists, so let's listen in to what he will say," said Roman Anthony Andrews.

"*Hello, Hello!*

Thank you all for being here today.

First, I would like to thank all of the 13 million people who have voted for me throughout the United Labourist presidential primaries.

Without you we wouldn't have started this movement.

So, thank you all for helping me getting my campaign off the ground and launching a political revolution, because you told the political elite and Wall Street you won't stand for corruption and greed any longer.

I would also like to say thank you New Hampshire for being my first win of the presidential primaries.

You were our great first victory.

And I would also like to say a special thanks to the state of Vermont since the day I started out as a mayor, then a congressman, and finally a senator.

I would like to thank Vermont for supporting me and my family for the years that I have represented the state at a local level and now at a federal level.

Your support is why we started this political revolution.

I would also like to say thank you to the hundreds and thousands of campaign volunteers and staff who helped get out the vote and to campaign for me.

You folks helped get out the people to vote in a grass roots campaign.

You showed us that we could get a national campaign going when everybody else said we will never win any primaries.

Together, we have all started this political revolution to transform America, and the revolution continues to this day.

We shall take the government back from the 1% and we will put them on notice by telling them that their days are numbered.

We will tell the political and wealthy elite they will no longer take advantage of Americans.

We shall continue to fight for a representative government that gives everything back to the American people.

We will fight for a better future and will succeed.

We will fight for a government based on social, economic, racial, and environmental justice so we can make sure equality exists for all.

I am very proud of the campaign we have run here in the great state of New Hampshire.

All of you here today have helped me win my first great victory and I thank you for that because it was the start of this political revolution.

Together, our campaign has won over 1,900 delegates and 22 states, and that will be presented at the National Convention for the United Labourists later this month.

That was far more than we thought we could win. But that is still enough needed for the nomination.

Secretary Anderson is going to the convention with more than 389 delegates than us and has the support of additional super delegates than we do.

Secretary Anderson has won the nominating process for the United Labourists.

And today I congratulate her here today for her historic victory of being the first woman to be nominated for president of a major political party in the United States of America.

And I do intend to do whatever it takes to make her the next president of the United States of America.

But I am not here today to talk about the past because I want to address what we can get done in the future.

The future will be determined at whatever happens on November 8th in voting booths across our great nation.

I am here today because I want to address my clear support of Cynthia Norwell Anderson and why I am endorsing her for the next president of the United States of America.

Over the past year, I have had the extraordinary advantage of speaking to almost 2 million Americans across my cross-country tour to become president.

I have encountered many people in small communities across America who has asked me that the government doesn't care about them.

And this just proves it isn't about me, Anderson, or Carlton Winters for any purposes.

It is about helping the American people so they can succeed, prosper, and not fall victim to the wealthy elite.

This campaign is about helping the American people and addressing the crises that happens every day.

And as we continue this political revolution, there is no doubt in my mind that Cynthia Norwell Anderson is by far the best candidate who can get those things done.

It can be very easy to forget though that the Centralists want us to forget what occurred over 7 years ago when Barrington Martin got into office.

That was surely a historic day in America when the first African-American became president of the United States of America.

And as a result of the greed and corruption from the political and wealthy elite as well as Wall Street, we have seen the most tragic outcome to our economy since the Great Depression.

It is all due to the banks intentionally lying to the people of America. About 850,000 people a month were losing their jobs thanks to the greed of Wall Street and the people in charge, and there was no recourse.

We were running up a record-breaking deficit and our economy was on the verge of a financial collapse that could have bankrupted our country.

However, we have gotten very far since the last seven years, and I would just like to thank President Martin for his role in fixing our economy and standing up to Wall Street.

And I will just like to thank vice president Walter Bryant Ross for helping America to succeed as a better country.

But this election isn't just about that.

This election is also about the millions of women who don't get equal pay.

This election is about the millions of other workers who don't get the opportunity of making a living wage.

This election is about the little guy making enough money to get by.

It is an election for the millions of people who fall behind because of the Wall Street financiers and the wealthy and political elite.

Cynthia Norwell Anderson understands that issue and she can get it done without any problem.

She understands that we need to fix our economy because it is rigged towards the 1% and that needs to change.

She understands if you are working a 40-hour work week that you should not be living in poverty.

She believes we need to make the minimum wage a living wage so people have enough money to live on.

And she believes in creating millions of jobs by rebuilding our crumbling infrastructure, such as our streets, roads, and bridges.

But her opponent, Carlton Winters, does not believe in that.

Carlton Winters believes that each state should decide the fate of the minimum wage and that it should be eliminated if possible because he says it isn't right.

If Carlton Winters is elected, there will never be any type of increase in the federal minimum wage, because he is part of the elite class of billionaires.

We must stand against him and to better our society for the future.

Who do you want on the Supreme Court?

We need justices who will overturn the decision of Citizens United to show them that we won't stand for dark money and corrupt campaign finance laws.

If Carlton Winters is elected he will protect Citizens United and we must not let that happen.

We must not allow the billionaire class dictating how they can buy elections with their money.

We must limit their influence on politicians.

And we must make sure the Supreme Court protects a woman's right to choose and to healthcare.

Who will defend the LGBT community?

Carlton Winters sure won't.

Who will defend the rights of workers and the needs of minorities everywhere?

Who will protect our immigrants and the ability of the federal government to protect our sacred environment?

Carlton Winters will not protect any of those issues.

This campaign is also about access to universal healthcare because healthcare is a human right not a privilege.

And we must reduce the number of people in our country who are uninsured.

Cynthia Norwell Anderson wants people to have the choice of a public option in which people can decide to pay for their insurance or they can get it free of charge.

But Carlton Winters opposes such an option because he supports the greed of Wall Street.

She wants to see people have better access to low-cost prescriptions and to cut out the middleman.

She wants to see more healthcare and mental health practitioners going into struggling neighborhoods to help the less fortunate.

In New Hampshire, just like in Vermont, we have this problem of the opiate epidemic, and we must tell the drug companies to stop it with the targeting to vulnerable Americans, and Cynthia Norwell Anderson understands that so we have to improve our mental health institutions in order to prevent a relapse.

She understands we must have and develop stronger programs to reduce the drug addiction problem.

She wants to help the people.

We need to expand community health and improve how we treat people.

We don't need a president who doesn't believe in universal access to healthcare.

We need a president who won't take away health insurance away from millions of people.

We also must increase the manufacturing of generic prescription medication.

These drug companies should not be making billions of dollars off of us because they don't care about us or the lives that we live.

They only care about greed and their profit margins.

We must stand up to them.

We must stop their greed and make sure that income inequality is a thing of the past.

Cynthia Norwell Anderson understands and knows all of that.

And she knows we must help our middle class and people in poverty to succeed.

She understands we must fix this economic problem of why the rich become richer and the poor become poorer.

She has a plan to stop this from happening.

We need to tax the wealthy elite and the Wall Street financiers so they will pay their fair share of taxes to the government.

She knows that they don't give a penny to help pay down the debt, to pay taxes, and to help fund the government.

She wants them to acknowledge their role in harming the economy and rigging it.

She believes in a fair tax code for all and believes it is necessary for the wealthiest to pay more.

But my friends, Carlton Winters does not believe in a fair tax code, because he believes corporations and the wealthy elite should pay fewer taxes.

That is just plain wrong and it will never happen in a progressive America, because the wealthy will pay for their crimes and problems they have caused this country.

The reckless economic policies of Carlton Winters will not only bankrupt America but they will also cause income inequality, an increase in our national debt, and force many students to take out college loans.

Cynthia Norwell Anderson believes we need to reduce college debt as much as possible so that students don't have to face years of finding ways to survive and live in America.

Her plan is to make public college affordable and free for all so that no one will ever suffer economic consequences.

No one should beholden to the big banks and loan companies to pay for college.

No, because we believe that college should be free to all that want to attend in order to advance their career or to get a good job to make a living.

It is just common sense.

And we also need to make sure that our society here in America is good for future generations.

We need to acknowledge the threat of climate change and how small communities are threatened by floods and droughts.

We must acknowledge that hurricanes, tornadoes, and thunderstorms are now stronger because of the human effect from climate change.

We must acknowledge science and that climate change is real and that humans and carbon emissions are the primary causes.

And we must acknowledge it is a threat to our national security because we need clean air and water.

We need to move away from the fossil fuel industry and tell them they must stop what they are doing and force them to pay steep fines for polluting our air and water.

Cynthia Norwell Anderson believes in all of that and she will fight for you.

But sadly, Carlton Winters, like most of the conservative Centralists, do not believe in climate change.

They believe in an America that promotes the fossil fuel industry, they do not acknowledge the threat from climate change, and they deny the existence of science.

No, they have a basic misunderstanding of everything.

She believes in universal access to healthcare because no one should have to pay steep fees to the greedy insurance companies.

She believes in protecting DACA recipients because they deserve to be protected.

We need a leader like her because she knows what to do in tense and difficult situations.

Ladies and gentlemen, I am happy to have Cynthia Norwell Anderson here today, and I fully endorse her for the next president of the United States of America.

Let's give her a warm welcome."

"Okay, you have just heard from Elias Dominic, who has now fully endorsed Cynthia Norwell Anderson for president of the United States of America; and she is speaking now so let's listen in to what she has to say from this endorsement," said Roman Anthony Andrews.

"Hello, New Hampshire!

Wow! What a crowd!

It is so great to be here today in the state of New Hampshire.

Thank you so much. I have to say it is a great privilege to stand here today next to Senator Dominic from the great progressive state of Vermont.

And I can't tell you how exciting this election season has been so far. Because together we are stronger and can do great things to help make sure America is better for generations yet to come.

I would just like to thank Elias for all of his hard work he has achieved during his time as mayor, congressman, and now a Senator.

He has worked so hard to achieve his accomplishments.

And now we can stand here today knowing we are united.

Thank you Elias for your years of fighting injustice all across America!

Thank you for fighting the systematic racism that harms our institutions and plagues our country with discrimination!

We must reform our criminal justice system because too many minorities are caught up in it and because we must stop arresting people based on their skin color because they could look suspicious.

We must have community involvement so law enforcement and neighborhoods can work together.

We need our economy to work for everyone and not just a few people at the top. And we can do all of this with your help and support.

My campaign has been calling to end racial profiling, disparities in sentencing, mass incarceration, the school-to-prison pipeline, and to encourage better employment opportunities to everyone.

We can end all of those problems and then help them to receive better jobs.

And of course we need to make sure gun violence and these mass shootings never happen again.

We must limit high capacity magazines and the types of weapons people can purchase.

No one but the military should own weapons of war.

These weapons are slaughtering innocent people and children because the gun lobby does not want to do anything about it.

Well I am going to stand up to the gun lobby when I become president.

I will tell them that you don't control America.

I will tell Congress to pass a gun law restricting the types of guns people can purchase, because people don't need these assault weapons.

They don't need anything that fires more than one bullet at a time.

We have to change as a society.

And we need to stop this mass carnage.

But friends, that is not the end.

We must decrease inequality because it is just too high and people are suffering.

Women are not treated with respect.

Women are not paid fairly.

Women are not treated the same as men.

And that must end because it will when I become president.

We must make sure people are paid a living wage.

People have bills to pay.

They have children.

Some might need to pay off student loans, mortgages, credit card companies, and aspects of daily living.

We need an economy that will work for all Americans.

As president I will support good-paying jobs, I will not decrease the minimum wage because I will make sure it is increased, I will promote the use of clean energy by making sure we move away from fossil fuels and coal, I will combat climate change, and I will make sure working families are protected.

I will make sure we never negotiate anymore bad trade deals that are bad for America and her people.

We are going to make college debt-free so no one has to suffer anymore and for those who are paying off loans we will help you.

You want good-paying jobs because that is the American dream. And for anyone or any family making $155,000 or less, well your tuition will be free of charge for anyone in your family who wants to attend to get a college *degree.*

Of course, this will only apply to public colleges and public universities, but you won't have to pay for anything because we will make sure it is debt-free.

But that is not all because we will also make it affordable for all students who attend public colleges and public universities with respect to living expenses, books, supplies, and food.

We want to make sure there is no financial burden so you can focus on getting your degree.

And we are going to make sure companies don't get the chance to move overseas because of taxes.

We will punish those companies with higher taxes who try to move overseas and if they don't want to come back here to America.

They are not paying their fair share of taxes and they need to face the consequences from the American people.

We will focus on making sure our financial industry is protected so that banks and investors can no longer take advantage of us.

And we will make sure the super-rich on Wall Street and the corporations pay their fair share in taxes.

They need to help the American people and not hurt it.

This is why people see the tax code as rigged because it is riddled with too many loopholes, scams, and special breaks that make it so that millionaires and billionaires pay fewer taxes due to advantages afforded to them by all the special interests.

We need to stop that and make sure they pay higher taxes because they can afford it.

But if you compare that with my opponent's plan, Carlton Winters, you will notice he wants to lower taxes for the rich and wealthy as well as for all of the corporations who make too much money.

The independent analysts say it will add more than $30 trillion to our already exploding debt.

His plan is not even feasible and will bankrupt America to a greater extent.

But I will tell you I won't let that happen if I become president.

And lastly, we will make sure social security is funded throughout its existence so that people don't have to worry about their future.

But I will also make sure women receive equal pay as men.

But here is another radical idea.

We are going to get rid of Citizens United and I will make sure I only appoint justices to the Supreme Court who will get rid of that terrible campaign finance decision made by the Centralists.

Together we can to this and achieve anything.

So, I am asking all of you to support my campaign, because together we can win this election and we can make history.

Thank you so very much!"

"If you are just tuning in, that was Cynthia Norwell Anderson, who has just accepted Elias Dominic's full endorsement for the presumptive nominee for the United Labourists to seek the presidency of the United States of America," said Roman Anthony Andrews.

IV

Today is the first night of the Centralist Administration Committee nominating convention and no one is more stressed than Perance Flintri, the chairperson of the CAC.

It would be filled with fanfare and excitement for all to watch.

But there will be protests and possibly riots by those pesky people who call themselves anti-fascists.

It will just be the case that has to stand till time.

And then there will be the protests about nominating the presumptive nominee because some feel he isn't morally qualified to lead.

At least that is made clear.

But it could be made clearer or it is just about how he views the world.

There will be a test of courage and strength to see if the leadership in charge of the CAC can lead the party to unity.

There is a test to see if the delegates will rally behind their presumptive nominee.

There will be a test to see if the entire Central Administration Party can unite to support and honor one candidate for president, because the other choice will lead the country into chaos and destruction by imposing high taxes and socialist tactics upon the weak and poor, while also claiming that it is important to impose a goal of targeting the innocent because that will be the claim being made by the communists and Marxists.

Of course, the communists, Marxists, and even the socialists will use an agenda that harms the poor and weak, because they think their plans will actually hurt the rich.

The choice is either between capitalism and a society in which corruption exists via socialist, communist, and Marxist tactics during the 2016 presidential election.

And that is why the opposing sides will say you should vote for their side. It is just not the same way but this is why there is a convention.

It matters mostly to the base and to gain potential supporters but there must be unity so everyone is always in agreement.

There must be a way to demonstrate a passion for the issues.

There must be a vision of how to lead the greatest nation in the world.

And there must be excitement so that people will be enthusiastic to vote in the general election.

It is all a reason why there must be unity because there will be chaos if no one agrees with each other in the coming days.

It will be at that time when the people will decide if they want to see order or a time of uncivility.

That is what everyone must agree upon in order to proceed.

"Welcome to the 2016 National Centralist Administration Committee nominating convention here in the great city of Cleveland in the great state of Ohio, and I personally welcome all of you here today and for the next week to experience our great hospitality, so without hesitation I would like to say thank you to all of you and the Central Administration Party for hosting their nominating convention here in Cleveland, Ohio," said Alfred Frederick the United Labourist mayor of Cleveland, Ohio.

"Please welcome the chairperson of the Centralist Administration Committee, Perance Flintri, as he now officially opens the 2016 National Centralist Administration Committee nominating convention," said the announcer.

"This convention shall come to order.

Welcome everyone to the 2016 National Centralist Administration

Committee nominating convention; but before we begin let us take this time to give our condolences to the fallen police officers of Baton Rouge, Louisiana, Dallas, Texas, and elsewhere because we appreciate what they do in order to protect us from crime and violence by putting their lives at risk and in danger when they try to protect everyday people.

I would also like to say thank you to all of those who have put their lives at risk for protecting our country abroad because without you there will be more danger and threats of national security around the world.

So if you wouldn't mind, please join me in a moment of silence.

Thank you!

Please stand for the presentation of the colors, so let's give them a warm welcome.

Please remain standing for the pledge of allegiance, the national anthem, and the invocation.

Ladies and gentlemen, the chair has an important announcement to make before we commence with today's schedule and events because of time constraints.

As the rules are described in the order of business, the chair will like to put all of the delegates and alternate delegates on notice that there must be written satisfactory support for each state in order to nominate the candidate.

This confirmation is needed in order to ensure we follow the set rules established by the committee.

The chair would also like to remind the delegates they must notify with any evidence concerning changes to the names of the candidate for the president and vice president and report it to the chair within one day before the roll call of the delegates begin for the states.

This is in accordance with our rules from previous conventions and our modern practice of motions and orders.

I would also just like to remind all of our alternates and guests that business on the floor is limited to the delegates.

So, it is extremely important for all of the guests and alternate delegates in the gallery to remain silent during the voice votes to remain assured that chair can hear the appropriate people and numbers from the states of who voted for who so that such information can be recorded and registered with the committee to be certified at convention.

But now let me say the following.

As declared by the National Centralist Administration Committee in 2012, there shall be a convention in 2016 that the opening shall begin no earlier than 9:00 am and no later than 9:00 pm at night for the first day.

The stated rules have been adopted by unanimous vote.

And now we rule on the motion to proceed with business.

And that shall begin later today around 6:00 pm in the evening.

Thank you every one and we will see you all here later tonight, so please enjoy Cleveland."

With that the convention to nominate Carlton Winters as the official presidential nominee of the Central Administration Party has begun and it will be the first time a non-politician will be nominated to be the president of the United States of America.

No one knows how it will begin and how it will end but it surely will be a spectacle for everyone to watch and criticize if there is something to see.

It is the time of opportunity that the country gets back on track to save our future.

There was something to set towards a bright future.

It would be the opportunity to win back the White House at a most crucial time in history when a radical socialist named Barrington Martin put enemies before the American people.

It is a time in history when our military was the smallest since the end of the Second World War.

It is a time in our history when we need to rebuild our economy because we are only growing at an average rate of 1.3% per year.

That is just unacceptable in our time when people need to work.

There is a desire for the American dream so that people can succeed to be prosperous.

It is a time when people fight for change because they demand an end to socialism, an end to communism, and an end to Marxism.

It is a time when people demand dictators and despots to resign or be executed for the safety and well-being of the people.

It is necessary that this process play out right and correctly so that nothing can ever cause the right of the wrong in hysteria.

That is just what needs to take place.

V

Katrina was waiting in her office at the convention venue for the events to begin.

It would surely be an exciting night and week of events and speakers but there would be have to be something done.

Everything was already planned out but it could change at the last minute due to delays or even cancellations.

There could be an unexpected situation that could occur and that might create some sort of chaos.

It might only be the beginning but it will be worth it.

There is just something that isn't part of the logic that holds the cards.

It is just how it is.

Suddenly, it was the afternoon of the first day of the convention, and there was already chaos on the convention floor.

A crowd of Never Winters people started protesting on the convention floor saying that want to change the rules.

The Never Winters group is so opposed to Carlton Winters that they want to try to sabotage his nomination.

It was a sad day in the Central Administration Party because there was supposed to be unity and this is not how anyone would want to start a process of nominating a person to the highest office in the land.

It is a case study of why there must be transparency towards an open forum. But these Never Winters people wanted to make one last stand before anything further happened.

It was a case brought to the news media that there was chaos in the party and that the United Labourists would be using that to incite falsehoods and propaganda.

So the opposing sides would be trying to use everything to their advantage in order to make a point by saying Carlton Winters and the Centralists are unfit to lead because there is chaos and a lack of party unity.

But that is only the beginning of a political campaign to target chaos.

And now, the Never Winters people have brought it to the attention of the rules committee, making it certain that they would be listened to and not to be ignored.

They certainly believed it would work but there was something wrong with their plan.

It wasn't foolproof.

It was a case in which they were so outraged at the rules that they sought change in which they believed was democracy by standing up to the man in a time of need and change.

It was just a classic for the rest of the people to watch.

The Anti-Winters people had no choice but to shout to get the attention of the rules committee because they didn't want the delegates to be bounded to Carlton Winters.

It was a sure sign that only a certain amount of people wanted to make their voice heard that they are against Carlton Winters so they align themselves as either Never Winters or Anti Winters.

Their explanation was that they wanted delegates to vote their conscience because they saw Carlton Winters as a person who had no morals because of what he said.

It was their last ditch effort in order to take the nomination away from what they saw as an immoral person that could be elected the next president of the United States of America.

It could work but they knew it would fail.

And then as the Anti-Winters people shouted to make their case they got drowned out by the Pro Winters people in a case of retribution.

It was a case of trying to stop the chaos. But as the Anti Winters people waited their proposal was voted down.

It was seen as a sigh of relief to the Pro-Winters people while the other side continued shouting.

And then it was unanimous that the rules committee passed by voice votes a rules package that the Anti-Winters people did not like.

Delegates who supported Alan Alvarez were outrage at the rules being adopted and they sought to have it overturned but soon three states withdrew their petition.

It was a case that has been seen everywhere as the people demand action.

But their action failed and was defeated again, so they did not succeed.

It was a time for a new beginning and that shall begin soon for the better of the people.

The evening has arrived and it is just about to begin.

It will be a time for all to watch.

It could be exciting to watch and there is just about that reasoning to take a chance.

The first speaker is about to speak and he is a fierce supporter of Carlton Winters.

Something could be better but it is just a time of why there must be unity.

The first speaker gives his benediction about why Carlton Winters must win.

And it is surely a strange one at that because he praises Carlton Winters while being political.

It was the first benediction ever to be seen as political and fiery but it indeed was a crowd pleaser.

Something was just as planned and it was part of the new century.

It was a case to promote unity for the people.

It would help the people succeed so they could support one person in November.

But the part the media will criticize the most is how he said Cynthia Norwell Anderson is the enemy of the people.

They would see that as frightening and a case of sexism.

They surely would try to target the people because of their agenda.

And then it happened, the speech was over in a matter of minutes, and everybody cheered about what they saw as a great beginning to uniting the party to bring everyone together.

It was a transformation of beliefs and the speakers each gave their speeches about what they expected America to become and what they saw as a great America.

The first few speakers have already spoken and it is so far an eventful night marked with unity and not like with chaos as earlier in the afternoon.

It would surely lead to a more united front towards the end.

As the event continued, it was now time for the second headliner to speak, a lieutenant-general by the name of Vincent McLoughlin, who is fed up at the corrupt Anderson political machine.

"What an enthusiastic crowd!

How exciting! Tonight I am here for all of you.

I am here determined to tell you that Carlton Winters is the only true and right choice for the next president of the United States of America because we need to stop the corrupt United Labourists from controlling our lives.

We need to tell those United Labourists that their agenda will bring chaos and harm to the world.

We need to tell them that they are not right for democracy or the future of our country because they want to undermine the rule of law and the constitution.

They fail to see that they are wrong because they believe government knows better.

So I say to all of you tonight, WAKE UP AMERICA, or you will forever be doomed by spiraling into constant debt because of wasteful spending.

Folks, I am here tonight to tell you Carlton Winters is the best choice for president because of his demonstrated leadership.

The other side's presumptive nominee likes to say stuff but politicians who call themselves United Labourists shower our enemies with cash, they cower to the goals of the terrorists, and they do not show strength toward leadership.

Instead, they try to restrict what the military can do to the enemy. But the enemy has one goal in mind, to kill many innocent people as possible while trying to spread their message of hate and terrorism across everywhere, yet the United Labourists seem to not get this.

They keep on supporting the terrorists and hostile nations that support terrorism.

They give them ransom to release our captured soldiers.

They allow terrorists to be released from Guantanamo Bay because they believe terrorists should be welcome to live in our great country of America.

Well, they are wrong.

We here in America need to make sure our freedom and liberty stay intact.

We value our liberty and freedom in this great country of ours because our founders knew that our rights originated from God and that it is him and only him who can judge everything.

We believe our freedom and liberty is greater than anything else because it is.

Our freedom and liberty represents something rather exceptional.

Other countries might say that they have freedom and liberty but they do not have a bill of rights.

So, what do they do when they don't like what you say?

They silence you.

That is right; you heard me correctly.

America is an exceptional country because we are the greatest nation in the world and no other nation can ever substitute that, because we see how far we become.

Folks, our American exceptionalism is being threatened by the goals and agenda of the United Labourists, because they want to continue their radical plan after Barrington Martin leaves office.

They want to put the interests of Wall Street, lobbyists, activist groups, and the enemy before the interests of the American people.

They want to put the interests of illegal immigrants over American citizens and valid green card holders.

They rather see America fall than succeed.

Ladies and gentlemen, when Carlton Winters becomes the next president of the United States of America, we shall begin a new American century in order to fix the problems caused by the previous presidents who were in office.

We will correct the bad policy changes from George 'Percy' Anderson and Barrington Hashim Martin, and we will never look back because those two people have been responsible for a lack of business growth and starving the middle class with their overzealous policies of big government.

We will say no to the radical policies of President Martin and his radical agenda because they have wreaked havoc on the American people by limiting the economy.

And we can do this because we finally have a true and courageous leader who can get things done.

We have that person and his name is Carlton Winters.

We have a leader in Carlton Winters who chooses to say as he sees it because we are at a crossroads now.

We have to stand up to all of this political correctness because it is ruining our society and the rest of the world.

It is causing people to hide and has a mob mentality.

Those people who identify as politically correct believe you don't have the right to free speech.

They believe anything you say that they disagree with is considered to be hate speech.

They say they are tolerant but then they do not want to hear the views of other people.

The politically correct wants to suppress your freedom of speech.

They want to control and say what you do.

They want to limit what you can eat and what you can wear.

They don't want you to celebrate the holidays of other cultures.

And most of all, they have a taste for socialism, communism, and Marxism, which they view is good for America because America is too greedy, racist, sexist, Islamaphobic, misogynistic, and homophobic.

They constantly label you names if you don't agree with their views. And if you are hosting an event on college campuses, they will start to protest and then riot because they don't want to have people with different political views on campus.

The politically correct is the problem and we will not allow them to win.

We will stop with this political correctness when Carlton Winters is elected as the next president of the United States of America.

We will finally have a country that is back to its original roots of the constitution and we will make sure only pro-life justices are appointed to the Supreme Court.

We will make sure that only strict constructionists and textualists are appointed to the courts.

We need to follow judicial review not judicial activism.

We need to make sure these radical United Labourist judges are outnumbered so we can finally win again.

We have a duty to lead our country back to greatness and to help the common man.

Ladies and gentlemen, we have that person, and he is ready to give you change and hope that you have never seen before.

We are tired of these empty speeches by President Martin and we are tired of his apology tour.

We are tired of his rhetoric that pushes America to the back of the line making America to have the weakest and smallest military before the beginning of the Second World War.

We cannot have that anymore or else the terrorists will take advantage of us.

We cannot allow the United Labourists to hold and make the controlling decisions because that will lead to disaster.

And this is same case with the presidential nominee on the other side. Cynthia Norwell Anderson believes if you release terrorists then that will end the war but releasing terrorists is no way to protect Americans.

It will instead make the United Labourists sympathetic to terrorists.

And then we have this present administration that does not support the Kurds.

The Martin administration instead supports tyrants and radical Islamic clerics.

All of these actions supported by the Martin administration are failed policies because they do nothing to help or secure America.

We must act with integrity.

We must make sure our national security comes first before any other country.

We must acknowledge the threat from our southern border because the United Labourists sure don't since they want to let everyone in.

America is one of the safest countries in the world and we have the best that people can achieve.

Our decisions must always be decisive and not show empathy to our enemies.

We must take seriously that our enemies could have weapons of mass destruction and that they might use them to attack us or our allies.

We must be prepared to fight and not back down.

Folks, Cynthia Norwell Anderson, just like Barrington Martin, are failed politicians with failed policies that will never work because they will turn America into a socialist-Marxist nightmare.

We must make sure that they are never granted their wish list because it would lead to the collapse of our great economy.

We must have a true leader like Carlton Winters that has the proven business experience that can get things done.

We need a fresh face in Washington DC to lead our country.

We had enough of the same old politicians who do nothing.

You know, I repeatedly called on Cynthia Norwell Anderson to drop out of the race, because she does not put our national security first.

She puts the interests of Iran, the European Union, the globalist elite, and terrorists before our country.

That's right, LOCK HER UP!

She should be locked up because of her crimes of intentionally deleting emails and using an illegal server to skirt the FOIA laws.

LOCK HER UP!

LOCK HER UP!

LOCK HER UP!

Yes, I will keep saying it, because she is careless with our national security.

Look, she admitted to having a personal server locked away in some bathroom in of all places.

And then we also learn that she or another person deleted classified emails.

Folks, that is not something we want in a leader to lead the free world.

We want someone that promotes law and order.

We need a person who isn't careless and reckless with classified information.

LOCK HER UP!

LOCK HER UP!

LOCK HER UP!

And you know we always say that?

Because we believe she broke the law intentionally and if you or I did a fraction of what she did we will be in jail right now.

There is just a double standard because there are two tiers of justice here it appears.

We can't have that in our great country anymore.

Her carelessness will get innocent people killed and it already has in Benghazi.

Let me be clear, America is an exceptional country, because we are the greatest country in the world.

We have the capability to do anything if we achieve it.

Remember, our country was built upon Judeo-Christian values, but the United Labourists want you to know religion is bad.

Just remember we don't mandate a specific religion, but we as a country believe in the Judeo-Christian values because it promotes peace and openness and it also allows us to forgive.

We do not allow religion to dictate our laws but the United Labourists want to transform America's judicial system promoting Sharia law, and that goes directly against our constitution.

We cannot allow these radical United Labourists lead our country anymore.

So we need to remember these sacrifices put forth who have gone before us and we must remember that America is a unique place.

We must remember there is a time and place for everything but it is our mindset of achieving the impossible that is most important.

We must hold true to these values and we must not allow anyone to say otherwise.

We must not have fear because we have all of the needed faith to accomplish anything we conquer.

We are America.

And we are the future of the Republic.

We have a way of life that no other country can surpass and we have some of the best people in the world.

But before I close, let me just say this, Exceptionalism is and will always remain a part of America because of our innovations to adapt and change.

As a country, we have everything to be happy about, because we began as an experiment over 200 years ago to fight against a tyrannical empire.

We need true leadership.

We need someone who can execute peace through strength.

We need a person who will stop apologizing to the rest of the world for what America has done.

We need to stand strong against the enemy.

We need a person who will not broadcast our plans to our enemies and competitors.

The people of America must wake up.

You must not sit this election out.

This could be the last chance to save our great country.

So, please, get out of your houses or apartments and vote for Carlton Winters as your next president of the United States of America.

God Bless the United States of America!

Thank you all tonight!"

It was a rousing speech filled with people cheering as it gave hope to everyone that change will be coming soon to the White House.

It was a case that could rally the base and bring in other people to support the election of Carlton Winters.

But the night just went on and the last three speakers spoke that were left. Before anyone knew it was the next day and that is the day that matters most.

The second day of the convention arrived and today is the day when Carlton Winters is officially nominated to be the presidential nominee of the Central Administration Party.

It is still early in the day so no one knows what will happen next. People will just have to wait and see.

The evening arrived and everyone was waiting for the festivities to begin.

And so, the people waited for the night's events to begin.

"Delegates, ladies and gentlemen, please take your seats and give a warm welcome back to the chair, Perance Flintri," said the announcer.

"This convention shall come to order.

Good Afternoon!

Welcome to the second day of the convention.

Let us commence with the presentation of the colors, pledge of allegiance, and the national anthem.

Okay, please give a warm welcome to the permanent chair of the convention, Mr. Daniel Shea of Wisconsin."

"Hello!

It's great to be here today.

If you don't know me allow me to introduce myself as Daniel Shea the permanent chair of the convention.

So, let's get to business.

But before we begin let me just remind all delegates of the provisions of the rules in which you must follow to nominate a candidate to be the president of the United States.

The rules require that each candidate nominated for president of the United States of America have sufficient support prior to the presentation of the candidate's name for nomination.

The chair wishes to say this requirement has been met but let me remind you all that it is customary for non-delegates to give speeches on behalf of the candidates nominated and to report the number of delegates for each person to be nominated.

So let's begin the roll call of the states. But let it be known that it is approved for the state of New York to go out of order in regards to roll call and the announcing of the delegates."

"Ladies and gentlemen, please welcome the assistant secretary in charge of roll call Mark Chris and the secretary of roll call Donna Sebastian," said the announcer.

"Alabama, with 50 bound delegates in the following manner, awards 36 for Carlton Winters, 13 for Alvarez, and 1 for Alonso," said Donna Sebastian.

"The great state of Alabama, with 50 pledged delegates, awards 36 for Carlton Winters, 13 for Alvarez, and 1 for Alonso," said the delegate from the state of Alabama.

"In accordance with the rules of the convention, the state of Alabama awards 36 Carlton Winters, 13 Alvarez, and 1 Alonso," said Mark Chris.

"Alaska, with 28 pledged delegates, is awarded to Carlton Winters," said Donna Sebastian.

"Alaska, with 28 delegates, proudly vote the way we did, with 12 votes for Alvarez, 11 votes for Carlton Winters, and 5 votes for Alonso, and we proudly support the nominee Carlton Winters of New York," said the delegate from Alaska.

"In accordance with the rules of this convention, 28 votes are awarded to Carlton Winters," said Mark Chris.

"American Samoa, with 9 pledged delegates, is awarded to Carlton Winters," said Donna Sebastian.

"The territory of American Samoa awards all of its 9 delegates to Carlton Winters," said the delegate from American Samoa.

"In accordance with the rules of this convention, all 9 votes are awarded to Carlton Winters," said Mark Chris.

"Arizona, with 58 pledged delegates, goes to Carlton Winters," said Donna Sebastian.

"The hottest state in the country, Arizona, proudly announces that all 58 votes go to Carlton Winters," said the delegate from Arizona.

"In accordance with the rules of this convention, all 9 votes are awarded to Carlton Winters," said Mark Chris.

"Arkansas, 40 bound delegates for the following candidates, awards 16 votes for Carlton Winters," said Donna Sebastian.

"Arkansas, with a booming economy and fishing industry cast 40 votes, with 15 for Alvarez and 25 for the next president of the United States of America, Carlton Winters," said Greg Flanagan.

"In accordance with the rules of this convention, 25 votes for Carlton Winters and 15 votes for Alvarez," said Mark Chris.

"California, 172 delegates to be awarded, goes to the following people: 172 for Carlton Winters," said Donna Sebastian.

"Mr. Chairman, I am happy to announce that 100% we support the nominee and that all 172 votes are going to the nominee, Carlton Winters, the next president of the United States of America," said the delegate from the state of California.

"In accordance with the rules of this convention, all 172 votes are awarded to Carlton Winters," said Mark Chris.

"Colorado, 37 delegates," said Donna Sebastian.

"Madam Chair, the centennial state votes 31 for Alan Alvarez, 2 votes being abstained, and 4 votes for the next president of the United States of America, Carlton Winters," said the delegate from Colorado.

"In accordance with the rules of this convention, 4 votes for Carlton Winters, 31 for Alvarez, and 2 votes being abstained," said Mark Chris.

"Connecticut, 28 delegates awarded in the following manner, 28 Carlton Winters," said Donna Sebastian.

"The great state of Connecticut, where nuclear submarines are built, and where women always win, is casting all 28 delegates for the next president of the United States of America, Carlton Winters," said the delegate from the state of Connecticut.

"In accordance with the rules of this convention, all 28 votes are awarded to Carlton Winters," said Mark Chris.

"Delaware, 16 delegates for the following bound delegates, 16 Carlton Winters," said Donna Sebastian.

"Delaware, the first state to ratify the constitution, announces it awards its 16 votes for Carlton Winters, the next president of the United States of America," said the delegate from Delaware.

"In accordance with the rules of this convention, all 16 votes are awarded to Carlton Winters," said Mark Chris.

"District of Columbia, with 19 bound delegates with the following bound delegates, 19 for Carlton Winters," said Donna Sebastian.

"Madam Chair, Mr. Chairman, the District of Columbia, the capital of the greatest country in the world, are duty bound to cast 10 votes for Senator Alonso and 9 votes for governor Evanston," said the delegate from the District of Columbia.

"In accordance with the rules of this convention, all 19 votes are awarded to Carlton Winters," said Mark Chris.

"Florida, with a total of 99 bound delegates, 99 Carlton Winters," said Donna Sebastian.

"I am proud to lead the delegation of Florida, with its beautiful and vibrant beaches and home to the Florida Keys, we are honored to cast all of our 99 votes for the next president of the United States of America, Carlton Winters," said the delegate from the state of Florida.

"In accordance with the rules of this convention, all 99 votes are awarded to Carlton Winters," said Mark Chris.

"Georgia, with 76 bound delegates, votes the following way, 42 Carlton Winters," said Donna Sebastian.

"Madam Secretary, on behalf of the peach state and the Georgia Central Administration Party, with the number one state for growing new business, I stand here proud today with support from our great governor, that we cast 16 votes for Senator Alonso, 18 votes for Senator Alvarez, and we proudly cast 42 votes for the next president of the United States of America, Carlton Winters," said the delegate from Georgia.

"In accordance with the rules of this convention, 42 votes are awarded to Carlton Winters, 18 votes for Alvarez, and 16 votes for Alonso," said Mark Chris.

"Guam, with 9 delegates," said Donna Sebastian.

"We, the delegates of Guam, pledges its 9 delegates to Carlton Winters, the next president of the United States of America," said the delegate from Guam.

"In accordance with the rules of this convention, all 9 delegates are awarded to Carlton Winters," said Mark Chris.

"Hawaii, 19 bound delegates cast in the following manner, 11 Carlton Winters," said Donna Sebastian.

"Aloha, from the great state of Hawaii, with our beautiful tropical island paradise and beaches, the best place to vacation and fish, and home to luxury and many tourists, we proudly cast 7 votes for Alan Alvarez, 1 for Senator Alonso, and 11 for the next president of the United States of America Carlton Winters," said the delegate from the state of Hawaii.

"In accordance with the rules of this convention, 11 votes are awarded to Carlton Winters, 7 for Alvarez, and 1 for Alonso," said Mark Chris.

"Idaho, 32 bound delegates in the following manner, 12 Carlton Winters," said Donna Sebastian.

"Madam Secretary, we are the most conservative Centralist state in the country as well as our famous potatoes, and we are proud to cast 20 votes for Alan Alvarez and 12 votes for Carlton Winters, the next president of the United States of America," said the delegate from Idaho.

"In accordance with the rules of this convention, 12 votes Carlton Winters and 70 votes Alvarez; uh, let's do that again; in accordance with the rules of this convention, 12 votes are awarded to Carlton Winters and 20 for

Alan Alvarez," said Mark Chris.

"Illinois, 69 bound delegates in the following manner, 54 Carlton Winters, 9 for Alvarez, and 6 for Evanston," said Donna Sebastian.

"I am a very proud citizen of the state of Illinois and I am here today to cast 6 delegates for governor Evanston, 9 for Senator Alan Alvarez, and 54 delegates for Carlton Winters the next president of the United States of America," said the delegate from the state of Illinois.

"In accordance with the rules of this convention, 54 votes are awarded for Carlton Winters, 9 for Alvarez, and 6 for Evanston," said Mark Chris.

"Indiana, with 57 bound delegates cast in the following manner, 57 for Carlton Winters," said Donna Sebastian.

"Madam Secretary, we are the Hoosier State and home to a surplus of jobs under the great leadership of our next vice president of the United States of America, Timothy Simon, the governor of our great state, and we are glad to award all 57 votes to the next president of the United States of America, Carlton Winters," said the delegate from Indiana.

"In accordance with the rules of this convention, all 57 delegates are awarded to Carlton Winters," said Mark Chris.

"Iowa, 30 bound delegates allocated to the following candidates, 30 Carlton Winters," said Donna Sebastian.

"Thank you Madam Secretary; I am the former secretary of state of Iowa, the home of the longest-serving governor, and I am proud to announce the delegation of Iowa casts all 30 of its votes towards Carlton Winters, the next president of the United States of America," said the delegate from the state of Iowa.

"In accordance with the rules of this convention, all 30 delegates are awarded to Carlton Winters," said Mark Chris.

"Kansas, 40 bound delegates awarded to the following candidates in the following manner, 9 Carlton Winters, 24 Alvarez, 6 Alonso, and 1 Evanston," said Donna Sebastian.

"Madam Secretary, home of the greatest fans of the current World Baseball Series champions, we cast 9 votes for Carlton Winters the next president of the United States of America, 24 votes for Alvarez, 6 votes for Alonso, and 1 for Evanston," said the delegate from Kansas.

"In accordance with the rules of this convention, 9 delegates for

Carlton Winters, 24 delegates for Alvarez, 6 delegates for Alonso, and 1 vote for Evanston," said Mark Chris.

"Kentucky, 46 delegates with the following bound delegates, 17 for Carlton Winters," said Donna Sebastian.

"Mr. Chairman, I am from the bluegrass state of the commonwealth of Kentucky, home to the great bluegrass music and where people still believe in God and support our great military, and we are proudly casting 7 votes for governor Evanston, 7 for Senator Alonso, 15 for Senator Alvarez, and 17 for the next president of the United States of America, Carlton Winters," said the delegate from Kansas.

In accordance with the rules of this convention, 17 delegates Carlton Winters, 7 delegates Alonso, 7 votes Evanston, and 15 votes Alvarez," said Mark Chris.

"Louisiana, 46 delegates with the following bound delegates, 18 Carlton Winters," said Donna Sebastian.

"The great state of Louisiana, with 46 delegates, cast 15 votes for Alvarez and 31 votes for the next president of the United States of America Carlton Winters," said the delegate from Louisiana.

"In accordance with the rules of this convention, 31 delegates are awarded to Carlton Winters and 15 delegates awarded for Alvarez," said Mark Chris.

"Maine, 23 delegates with the following bound delegates for the following nominee, 9 Carlton Winters," said Donna Sebastian.

"Madam Secretary, the great state of Maine, home to only one remaining federally-elected United Labourist official, and the place of the rugged coasts, is proud to cast 12 votes for Senator Alvarez, 9 votes for Carlton Winters, and 2 votes for governor Evanston," said the delegate from the state of Maine.

"In accordance with the rules of this convention, 9 delegates are awarded to Carlton Winters, 12 delegates Alvarez, and 2 votes Evanston," said Mark Chris.

"Maryland, 38 delegates," said Donna Sebastian.

"Madam Secretary, Maryland, home of the oldest state capital in the United States of America, proudly casts all 38 votes for the next president of the United States of America, Carlton Winters," said the delegate from the state of Maryland.

"In accordance with the rules of this convention, all 38 delegates are awarded to Carlton Winters," said Mark Chris.

"Massachusetts, 42 delegates with the following bound delegates for the following candidates, 22 Carlton Winters, 4 Alvarez, 8 Alonso, and 8 Evanston," said Donna Sebastian.

"Madam Secretary, the state that outperformed every other state in the nation, casts 4 delegates for Alonso, 8 delegates for Evanston, 8 delegates for Alonso, and they said we were the bluest state but we are officially casting 22 delegates for Carlton Winters the next president of the United States of America," said the delegate from Massachusetts.

"In accordance with the rules of this convention, 22 delegates are awarded to Carlton Winters, 4 delegates for Alvarez, 8 delegates for Alonso, and 8 delegates for Evanston," said Mark Chris.

"Michigan, 59 delegates with the following bound delegates for the following candidates, 25 Carlton Winters," said Donna Sebastian.

"Madam Secretary, we wish to announce Michigan passes," said the delegate from Michigan.

"Michigan passes," said Donna Sebastian.

"Minnesota, 38 delegates with the following bound delegates for the following candidates, 8 Carlton Winters," said Donna Sebastian.

"Madam Secretary, on behalf of the great state of Minnesota, the state with the longest drought of casting delegates for a Centralist president, I am pleased to announce we are casting 17 votes for Senator Alonso, 13 votes for Senator Alvarez, and 8 votes for the next president of the United States of America, Carlton Winters," said the delegate from Minnesota.

"In accordance with the rules of this convention, 8 votes are awarded to Carlton Winters, 17 votes for Alonso, and 13 votes for Alvarez," said Mark Chris.

"Mississippi, 40 delegates with the following bound delegates for the following candidates, 25 Carlton Winters and 15 for Alvarez," said Donna Sebastian.

"Madam Secretary, the birthplace of music, the state of Mississippi, will cast 15 votes for Senator Alvarez and 25 votes for Carlton Winters, the next president of the United States of America," said the delegate from the state of Mississippi.

"In accordance with the rules of this convention, 25 delegates are awarded to Carlton Winters and 15 to Alvarez," said Mark Chris.

"Missouri, 52 delegates with the following bound delegates for the following candidates, 37 Carlton Winters," said Donna Sebastian.

"Madam Secretary, Missouri, the birthplace of talk radio, Missouri, birthplace of ragtime music, Missouri, the home of a great conservative Centralist Senator, Missouri casts 11 votes for Alvarez and 41 votes for the next president of the United States of America Carlton Winters," said the delegate from Missouri.

"In accordance with the rules of this convention, 41 delegates are awarded to Carlton Winters and 11 for Alvarez," said Mark Chris.

"Montana, 27 delegates with the following bound delegates for the following candidates, 27 Carlton Winters," said Donna Sebastian.

"Madam Secretary, we the delegates of the state of Montana proudly cast all 27 votes for Carlton Winters," the next president of the United States of America," said the delegate from Montana.

"In accordance with the rules of this convention, 27 delegates are awarded to Carlton Winters," said Mark Chris.

"Nebraska, 36 delegates with the following bound delegates for the following candidates, 36 Carlton Winters," said Donna Sebastian.

"Madam Secretary, the state that offers the good life with great opportunities, the number one beef producing state in the country, Nebraska proudly casts their 36 bound delegates for Carlton Winters, the next president of the United States of America," said the delegate from Nebraska.

"In accordance with the rules of this convention, 36 delegates are awarded to Carlton Winters," said Mark Chris.

"Nevada, 30 delegates with the following bound delegates for the following candidates, 14 Carlton Winters, 6 Alvarez, 7 Alonso, 1 Evanston, and 2 Doyle," said Donna Sebastian.

"Madam Chairman, the state of Nevada, where green lives matter, Nevada the desert oasis, Nevada proudly casts 1 vote governor Evanston, 6 votes Senator Alvarez, 7 votes Senator Alonso, and 16 votes for the next president of the United States of America, Carlton Winters," said the delegate from the state of Nevada.

"In accordance with the rules of this convention, 14 delegates are awarded to Carlton Winters, 6 delegates for Alvarez, 7 delegates Alonso, 1 delegate Evanston, and 2 delegates Doyle," said Mark Chris.

"New Hampshire, 23 delegates with the following bound delegates for the following candidates, 11 Carlton Winters," said Donna Sebastian.

"Madam Secretary, my name is Anthony Kowalczyk, a proud supporter of Carlton Winters and his former campaign manager, and I represent the people from the great state of New Hampshire, the state that delivered the first victory to Carlton Winters, and it is my pleasure to read the cast votes tonight for the candidates: 2 votes for Senator Alonso, 3 votes for former Florida governor Douglas Oswald 'DON' Noland, 3 votes for Senator Alan Alvarez, 4 votes for governor Evanston, and 11 votes for my personal friend and the next president of the United States of America, Carlton Winters," said the delegate from New Hampshire.

"In accordance with the rules of this convention, 11 delegates are awarded to Carlton Winters, 2 delegates Alonso, 3 delegates Noland, 3 votes Alvarez, and 4 delegates Evanston," said Mark Chris.

"New Jersey, 51 delegates with the following bound delegates for the following candidates, 51 Carlton Winters," said Donna Sebastian.

"Madam Secretary, I am the son of Steven Sestance, the governor of the state of New Jersey, and the Garden State is pleased to announce that its 51 delegates will be cast for Carlton Winters, the next president of the United States of America," said the delegate from New Jersey.

"In accordance with the rules of this convention, 51 delegates are awarded to Carlton Winters," said Mark Chris.

"New Mexico, 24 delegates with the following bound delegates for the following candidates, 24 Carlton Winters," said Donna Sebastian.

"Madam Secretary, I am a committed conservative Centralist from the great state of New Mexico where we have the first female Hispanic governor and a diverse background, and I am pleased to report that the state of New Mexico is proudly casting their 24 delegates to the next president of the United States of America, Carlton Winters," said the delegate from the state of New Mexico.

"In accordance with the rules of this convention, 24 delegates are awarded to Carlton Winters," said Mark Chris.

"New York, 95 delegates, with the following bound delegates for the following candidates, 89 Carlton Winters and 6 Evanston," said Donna Sebastian.

"Madam Secretary, New York, the Empire State and the home of

Carlton Winters, passes," said the delegate from New York.

"New York passes," said Donna Sebastian.

"North Carolina, 72 delegates, with the following bound delegates for the following candidates, 29 Carlton Winters, 27 Alvarez, 6 Alonso, 9 Evanston, and 1 Doyle," said Donna Sebastian.

"Madam Secretary, North Carolina, home of the largest military bases in the world, North Carolina, one of the fastest growing state economies, North Carolina proudly casts its 72 votes as follows: 1 Dr. Samuel Doyle, 6 Senator Felipe Juan Alonso, 9 for Ohio governor Jonathan Evanston, 27 for Senator Alan Alvarez, and we are proudly casting 29 votes for Carlton Winters, the next president of the United States of America," said the delegate from the state of North Carolina.

"In accordance with the rules of this convention, 29 delegates are awarded to Carlton Winters, 27 delegates Alvarez, 6 delegates Alonso, 9 delegates Evanston, and 1 delegate Doyle," said Mark Chris.

"North Dakota, 28 delegates," said Donna Sebastian.

"Madam Secretary, North Dakota, the only state that is getting younger, is pleased to announce 1 delegate for Doyle, 6 delegates for Alvarez, and 21 delegates for Carlton Winters the next president of the United States of America," said the delegate from North Dakota.

"In accordance with the rules of this convention, 21 delegates are awarded to Carlton Winters, 1 delegate Doyle, and six delegates Alvarez," said Mark Chris.

"Northern Mariana Islands, 9 delegates with the following bound delegates for the following candidates, 9 Carlton Winters," said Donna Sebastian.

"Madam Secretary, Northern Mariana Islands, a place where it is always summer, and is the most conservative Centralist island in the world, proudly casts all of its 9 delegates for the next president of the United States of America, Carlton Winters," said the delegate from the Northern Mariana Islands.

"In accordance with the rules of this convention, 9 delegates are awarded to Carlton Winters," said Mark Chris.

"Ohio, 66 delegates," said Donna Sebastian.

"Welcome to Cleveland the home of winners, welcome to Ohio the host of the National Centralist convention, Ohio proudly announces that it casts all of its 66 votes for Governor Jonathan Evanston," said the delegate from the state of Ohio.

"In accordance with the rules of this convention, 66 delegates are awarded to Evanston," said Mark Chris.

"Oklahoma, 43 delegates, with the following bound delegates for the following candidates, 13 Carlton Winters," said Donna Sebastian.

"Good evening, I am the chairwoman of the Oklahoma Centralists, Oklahoma, the second home to the speaker of the House and his wife, Oklahoma, the state with Centralist supermajorities in both chambers of the state legislature, Oklahoma, the state that produces the energy we rely on, and Oklahoma is proudly pleased to cast 19 delegates for Senator Alvarez and 24 delegates for Carlton Winters the next president of the United States of America," said the delegate from Oklahoma.

"In accordance with the rules of this convention, 24 delegates are awarded to Carlton Winters and 19 delegates are awarded to Alvarez," said Mark Chris.

"Oregon, 28 delegates, with the following bound delegates for the following candidates, 18 Carlton Winters," said Donna Sebastian.

"Madam Secretary, Oregon, the most beautiful state with abundant forests, Oregon, ground zero in the fight against corruption from United Labourists, Oregon proudly announces it casts 5 delegates for Alvarez and 23 delegates for Carlton Winters the next president of the United States of America," said the delegate from Oregon.

"In accordance with the rules of this convention, 23 delegates are awarded to Carlton Winters and 5 delegates Alvarez," said Mark Chris.

"Pennsylvania, 71 delegates, with the following bound delegates for the following candidates, 17 Carlton Winters," said Donna Sebastian.

"Madam Secretary, I'm the chairman of the Centralist Administration Party of Pennsylvania, the Keystone State, and Pennsylvania defers to the great state of New York," said the delegate from Pennsylvania.

"New York, 95 delegates, with the following bound delegates for the following candidates, 89 Carlton Winters and 6 Evanston," said Donna Sebastian.

"Madam Secretary, New York, the Empire State, proud to be the home of Carlton Winters, and proud that we were the first state to cast a majority of our primary votes for Carlton Winters, proud that he won the majority of the votes in 61 out of 62 counties and more than 63% of the vote, and proud that we have one of his sons who is a delegate here today, Howard Carlton Winters Jr.," said the delegate from New York.

"Thank you very much, Joe, thank you very much family; thank you Daniella, Brandon, and Ashley; thank you to all of our great supporters in the great state of New York, even if some of the places aren't even conservative at all; we have such tremendous support here and now we will put the state of New York into play; now, I have the tremendous and most incredible honor of putting my father over the top; and now the delegation from New York proudly casts 89 delegates for my father Carlton Winters and the other 6 delegates for Evanston; congratulations father, we love you," said Carlton Winters Jr. to everyone.

Everyone cheers as Carlton Winters has officially received the required 1,237 delegates to become the official presidential nominee of the Central Administration Party.

"In accordance with the rules of this convention, 6 delegates are awarded to Evanston and 89 delegates are awarded to Carlton Winters," said Mark Chris.

Celebratory music plays, as the giant LED screen lights up with OVER THE TOP and fireworks in order to celebrate Carlton Winters officially becoming the presidential nominee for the Central Administration Party with 1,267 votes.

"Puerto Rico, 23 delegates, with the following bound delegates for the following candidates, 23 Felipe Juan Alonso," said Donna Sebastian.

"Madam Secretary, the territory of Puerto Rico, an island of wonderful beaches and a leader in tourism, announces that we cast our 23 delegates for Senator Felipe Juan Alonso, in accordance with the binding laws of Puerto Rico," said the delegate from Puerto Rico.

"In accordance with the rules of this convention, 23 delegates are awarded to Felipe Juan Alonso," said Mark Chris.

"Rhode Island, 19 delegates, with the following bound delegates for the following candidates, 12 Carlton Winters, 2 Alvarez, and 5 Evanston," said Donna Sebastian.

"Madam Secretary, I am the chairman of the Centralist Party of Rhode Island, and we cast 2 delegates for Alvarez, 5 delegates for Evanston, and 12 delegates for the next president of the United States of America,

Carlton Winters," said the delegate from Rhode Island.

"In accordance with the rules of this convention, 12 delegates are awarded to Carlton Winters, 2 delegates for Alvarez, and 5 delegates for Evanston," said Mark Chris.

"South Carolina, 50 delegates, with the following bound delegates for the following candidates, 50 Carlton Winters," said Donna Sebastian.

"Madam Chairwoman, I am the chairman of the Centralist Party of South Carolina, the Palmetto State, and the birthplace of Barbeque, and South Carolina, home to great travel destinations such as Charleston and Myrtle Beach, and South Carolina is pleased to proudly cast all of its 50 delegates to Carlton Winters, the next president of the United States of America," said the delegate from South Carolina.

"In accordance with the rules of this convention, 50 delegates are awarded to Carlton Winters," said Mark Chris.

"South Dakota, 29 delegates, with the following bound delegates for the following candidates, 29 Carlton Winters," said Donna Sebastian.

"Madam Secretary, the great state of South Dakota, home to the great monument of Mount Rushmore, proudly nominate Carlton Winters for the presidential nominee of the Central Administration Party, by awarding him with all 29 delegates," said the delegate from South Dakota.

"In accordance with the rules of this convention, 29 delegates are awarded to Carlton Winters," said Mark Chris.

"Tennessee, 58 delegates, with the following bound delegates for the following candidates, 33 Carlton Winters, 16 Alvarez, and 9 Alonso," said Donna Sebastian.

"Madam Secretary, the volunteer state, the state with no state income tax, the state with a surplus and a balanced budget, the state of Tennessee proudly casts its votes: 16 for Texas Senator Alan Alvarez, 9 votes for Alonso, and 33 votes for the next president of the United States of America, Carlton Winters," said the delegate from Tennessee.

"In accordance with the rules of this convention, 33 delegates are awarded to Carlton Winters, 16 delegates to Alvarez, and 9 delegates to Alonso," said Mark Chris.

"Texas, 155 delegates, with the following bound delegates for the following candidates, 104 Alvarez, 48 Carlton Winters, and 3 Alonso," said Donna Sebastian.

"Madam Secretary, Mr. Chairman, I am here on behalf of my great friend and one of the most conservative Centralist governors in America, Robert Richard, and as the lieutenant-governor of the greatest job producing state in America and the 10th largest economy in the world, and where no United Labourist has won statewide since 1988, I am proud to report our votes: for Felipe Juan Alonso 3, for our great conservative friend and the great son of Texas Alan Alvarez 104 delegates, and for the next president of the United States of America who will receive a concession phone call from a lady named Cynthia Norwell Anderson who repeatedly broke the law and then lied about it, Carlton Winters 48 delegates," said the delegate from the state of Texas.

"In accordance with the rules of this convention, 48 delegates are awarded to Carlton Winters, 104 delegates Alvarez, and 3 delegates for Alonso," said Mark Chris.

"U.S. Virgin Islands, 9 delegates," said Donna Sebastian.

"Madam Secretary, from the delegation of the U.S. Virgin Islands, an island territory of tropical paradise, we proudly cast 8 delegates for Carlton Winters, the gentleman from the state of New York, and with the blessing, let's make America and the Caribbean prosper again," said the delegate from the U.S. Virgin Islands.

"In accordance with the rules of this convention, 8 delegates are awarded to Carlton Winters and one abstention," said Mark Chris.

"Utah, 40 delegates, with the following bound delegates for the following candidates, 40 Carlton Winters," said Donna Sebastian.

"Madam Secretary, the state that has its priorities straight, the state that supports God, family, and our country, the state with number one in the country with economic growth and in job creation, Utah proudly casts all of its 40 votes for Carlton Winters, the next president of the United States of America," said the delegate from Utah.

"In accordance with the rules of this convention, 40 delegates are awarded to Carlton Winters," said Mark Chris.

"Vermont, 16 delegates, with the following bound delegates for the following candidates, 8 Carlton Winters," said Donna Sebastian.

"Thank you very much Madam Secretary, Vermont, home of Calvin Coolidge, the 30th president of the United States of America, who was nominated in Cleveland back in 1924, Vermont, home to one of the best cheese producers in the world, and Vermont, the state known for one of the best producers of maple syrup in the world, and Vermont proudly casts 1 delegate for Jonathan Evanston, 2 delegates for Kentucky Senator Kevin Keith, and 13 delegates for Carlton Winters," said the delegate from the state of Vermont.

"In accordance with the rules of this convention, 13 delegates are awarded to Carlton Winters, 1 delegate Evanston, and 2 delegates Keith," said Mark Chris.

"Virginia, 49 delegates, with the following bound delegates for the following candidates, 17 Carlton Winters, 8 Alvarez, 16 Alonso, 5 Evanston, and 3 Doyle," said Donna Sebastian.

"Namaste, Mr. Chairman, Virginia, the home to Jamestown, and the place where the dominion of England began and endured, and Virginia, home to opportunities, and I proudly cast the votes on behalf of the delegation of Virginia: 3 votes for Doyle, 5 votes for Evanston, 8 votes for Alvarez, 16 votes for Alonso, and 17 votes for our next president of the United States of America, Carlton Winters," said the delegate from Virginia.

"In accordance with the rules of this convention, 17 delegates are awarded to Carlton Winters, 8 delegates Alvarez, 16 delegates Alonso, 5 delegates Evanston, and 3 delegates Doyle," said Mark Chris.

"Washington, 44 delegates, with the following bound delegates for the following candidates, 44 Carlton Winters," said Donna Sebastian.

"Madam Secretary, from the Ever Green State, the state of Washington, and the home to the National Christmas Tree, and we are now happy to cast 44 votes for the future 45th president of the United States of America, Carlton Winters," said the delegate from Washington.

"In accordance with the rules of this convention, 44 delegates are awarded to Carlton Winters," said Mark Chris.

"West Virginia, 34 delegates," said Donna Sebastian.

"Madam Secretary, I am proud to hold up the hat of a coal miner, and in West Virginia we have been pillaged by the current administration of Barrington Martin; and his presumptive corrupt successor, Cynthia Norwell Anderson, wants to put our industry out of business, and it's time we bring back our coal mining industry because the Martin administration devastated our industry by over 10,000 coal miners losing their jobs; so now I say we proudly cast our 34 delegates for Carlton Winters," said the delegate from the state of West Virginia.

"In accordance with the rules of this convention, 34 delegates are awarded to Carlton Winters," said Mark Chris.

"Wisconsin, 42 delegates, with the following bound delegates for the following candidates, 6 Carlton Winters and 36 Alvarez," said Donna Sebastian.

"Madam Chairwoman, we are happy to introduce to you the only governor who has won a recall election, Taylor Patrick, the governor of the great state of Wisconsin," said Perance Flintri and Daniel Shea.

"Madam Chairwoman, Wisconsin, the number one producer of cheese in the country and the number one state where United Labourists tried to use corrupt means of money and special interests in order to get rid of me, is a proud state, and we proudly cast 36 votes for the Alvarez and 6 votes for the next president of the United States of America, Carlton Winters," said Taylor Patrick.

"In accordance with the rules of this convention, 6 delegates are awarded to Carlton Winters and 36 delegates are awarded to Alvarez," said Mark Chris.

"Wyoming, 29 delegates, with the following bound delegates for the following candidates, 1 Carlton Winters, 23 Alvarez, 1 Alonso," said Donna Sebastian.

"Madam Secretary, Mr. Chairman, we are the delegation from the great state of Wyoming, the number one producer of low-sulfur coal, we have a $1.9 billion surplus and no corporate or individual income tax, so we proudly cast its votes in the following manner: 1 vote for Senator Alonso, 2 votes for governor Evanston, 23 votes for the great Senator from Texas Alan Alvarez, and 3 votes for Carlton Winters the next president of the United States of America and the only person who can defeat the corrupt Cynthia Norwell Anderson," said the delegate from Wyoming.

"In accordance with the rules of this convention, 3 delegates are awarded to Carlton Winters, 23 delegates to Alvarez, 1 delegate Alonso, and 1 delegates Evanston," said Mark Chris.

"Michigan, 59 delegates, with the following bound delegates," said Donna Sebastian.

"Madam Secretary, I am Ramona Robertson Thompson, the chairwoman of the Michigan Centralists, and we are the home of former president Gerald Ford, and we proudly cast 2 votes for the governor of Ohio, 6 votes for Senator Alvarez, and 51 votes for the next president of the United States of America Carlton Winters," said the delegate from Michigan.

"In accordance with the rules of this convention, 51 delegates are awarded to Carlton Winters, 2 votes Evanston, and 6 delegates Alvarez," said Mark Chris.

"Pennsylvania, 71 delegates, with the following bound delegates for the following candidates, 17 Carlton Winters," said Donna Sebastian.

"Pennsylvania, the home of 13 Centralist Congressmen, the state that will determine the winner of the 20 electoral votes on November 8, we cast 1 delegate for the Senator from Texas Alan Alvarez and 70 delegates for Carlton Winters, the next president of the United States of America," said the delegate from the state of Pennsylvania.

"In accordance with the rules of this convention, 70 delegates are awarded to Carlton Winters and 1 delegate is awarded to Alvarez," said Mark Chris.

"Ladies and gentlemen, please welcome speaker Daniel Shea," said the announcer.

"Does any state wish to cast its vote or change its vote," said Daniel Shea?

"I am speaking on behalf of the delegation of Alaska because we were never told the secretary will misreport our votes," said the delegate from Alaska.

"Is the gentleman asking to recount the votes," asked Daniel Shea?

"Yes," said the delegate from Alaska.

"Okay, staff members of the National Centralist Administration Committee will supervise the recount of all delegates," said Daniel Shea to the delegates.

Music plays in the background and the party leadership along with the secretary and her staff discuss the rules.

"Well, that failed," said Daniel Shea to Perance Flintri.

"Okay, the speaker will yield to the chair of the NCAC to explain the rules," said Daniel Shea.

"Okay, this is a rule that really only affects four states; First of all, the states and territories are all bound by the 1,682 delegates and the secretary is mandated to read the bound votes, but the gentleman from the state of Alaska is correct, in which it applies to the rules, procedures, and bylaws of the Alaskan Central Administration Party, yet when a candidate drops out and there is only one candidate is left, then the delegates are required to be reallocated to the remaining candidate," said Perance Flintri.

"Okay everybody, have a great night," said Daniel Shea.

"The votes from the state of Alaska shall be recorded 28 delegates Carlton Winters due to the rules," said Daniel Shea.

"The chair is now required and prepared to announce the results for anyone who received delegates: 1,725 Carlton Winters, 475 Alvarez, 120 Evanston, 114 Alonso, 7 Doyle, 3 Noland, and 2 Keith; and the chair votes that receiving a majority of the delegates required that Carlton Winters becomes the Centralist nominee for president for the Central Administration Party; and his escort committee shall consist of his children," said Daniel Shea.

The roll call was officially completed and certified by the permanent chair of the convention, Daniel Shea, and Carlton Winters officially became the presidential nominee of the Central Administration Party.

The speakers of the second night of the convention started giving their speeches one-by-one, and it was soon time for Carlton Winters Jr. to give his headline speech.

"Please welcome Carlton Winters Jr. to the stage," said the announcer to the audience.

"Thank you!

Good evening!

My name is Carlton Winters Jr., the eldest son of my father, Carlton Winters.

Thank you!

I am the father of three young children.

Tonight I want to discuss the country we live in, America, and how you can help us as a nation succeed.

As you might already know, this is the most important election possibly in your life time, and that could be for several reasons.

But think for it for a minute or so.

Could you see yourself living in Venezuela, where everything is collapsing, or could you see yourself in North Korea, where people are starved to death?

If you would say no, then you are in luck, because right now we live in the greatest country in the world.

We do not have the problem of a dictator or despots but our image of America is not shared by the United Labourists and their far-left groups who want to develop something more sinister.

The goal of the United Labourists and their far-left fringe groups are to divide America as a whole.

They support communism.

They support socialism.

They support Marxism.

The United Labourists and their far-left fringe groups want to take away your wealth and redistribute it to the poor.

And they don't believe the middle-class, upper-class, or working-class Americans should exist.

Instead, they want to transform all of America into a single social class.

They want you and us to share our wealth with everybody because they say that is equality.

Well, that is not right.

We don't need that here in America.

We work hard to make our money and the government does not have the right to take it away from us just because they want everyone to make the same amount of money.

No, because that is called communism, and in a communist state they want to have a classless society, where everyone is of equal value.

They want to take away the right to own property so that the government will own it.

And they believe anyone who makes money from any business is the enemy.

Believe me, communism is bad, and you don't want to live in such conditions.

We live in a great country that allows us to achieve success and to seek the American dream.

We have been told for too long that the growth of our GDP won't go above 1.5% because they say it is just the new normal.

We have been told that everything is better this way and that the economy is at its best since before the Great Depression.

We have been told that there is nothing wrong with America but something wrong with business.

Well, if you believe that, then you must be clueless, because it is not business there is a problem, as it is the problem with government policies.

The problem we face here today is that the United Labourists have ignored our problems for far too long.

We can't provide a better future for our society if the United Labourists keep ignoring our safety.

We must have the funding to succeed but the United Labourists don't want to help us due to their beliefs.

Instead, they rather support illegal immigration and an open border society.

The United Labourists do not want to fix anything.

It is just another plight on America.

Look, my father taught me about investments and business from a very early age, and I know when a deal can be good or bad. But today, that is not the case, as parents no longer believe their children will be safe because of financial stability and leftist ideology.

Listen, this is a once in a lifetime election, because you will either get growth and success or a continuation of the Martin policies.

And I will tell you how my father will lead as the next president of the United States of America.

My father will lead America into a financial success.

We will always win.

And I saw that firsthand when I was in his office.

I saw time and time again the deals he negotiated with other businesses and countries.

I saw how everything was approached.

He never hid behind some giant desk.

No, he was always out in the open helping Americans.

He always helped people as he saw fit.

My father saw the talent in the people and promoted them to positions be believe they would succeed in.

My father had a sense of trying to understand the problem from the perspective of a common American.

And today he is still succeeding.

Today, my father helped thousands of people reach their full potential.

He created real jobs not something promised by government.

My father understands the problem of everyday Americans living from paycheck-to-paycheck, as he saw it firsthand with people trying to survive.

My father does not bow down to the special interests like the United Labourists.

He says it like it sees it.

And for years, no one has understood the problems Americans face, until now.

We have this problem with political correctness in which too many United Labourists believe in the ideology of political correctness.

And this ideology has caused many of the American people to be ignored.

With this ideology, the United Labourists have caused business into financial collapse and into financial ruin.

With this ideology, the United Labourists have caused our economy to collapse.

With this ideology, the United Labourists have given us a bad immigration system filled with many loopholes.

With this ideology, we have failed to address any issue facing the American people.

We have seen Americans suffering with MartinCare.

We have seen Americans suffering from the government because of terrible policies that bully people and organizations of a certain political party. We have a problem and it is that of the United Labourists.

Today is a historic day, because it is the first time in history when a non-politician officially became a presidential nominee for a major political party.

Today marks the day of change.

We are going to elect a president who has a record of getting things done.

We are going to elect someone who can help bring back our economy and to stop this problem of illegal immigration.

We will fix our border and will do amazing things.

And when you elect my father as the next president in November, we can do all of that and more, and we will.

Thank you!

God Bless!"

Carlton Winters Jr. gave an optimistic speech about what his father can and will do as president.

And the people applauded and cheered because they liked his message of bringing back the America they knew.

It was a very exciting speech because of what could happen next.

And it certainly helped the people to be more optimistic that they will have a better future.

It is about that for which everything is about.

The night's events continued but before long it was time to wrap up because the last speaker spoke for the night, and there were still two more nights of fun and excitement.

There was just more optimism in what will come next. It could offer help to the rest of Americans so that no one will be left behind.

And it will be at the expense of no one.

Today is the third day of the Centralist Administration Committee nominating convention and there is much more to wait for.

The lineup for tonight will feature great speakers who support the nomination of Carlton Winters.

The defeated senator from Texas, Alan Alvarez, will speak tonight, but it is stated that he will take a punch at Carlton Winters, which could be political suicide.

But it is a good thing Alan Alvarez is not a headliner, but if he was, then his speech would probably have to be revised.

And you bet your ass off that Alan Alvarez will be booed at for what he says.

It is expected only because he will probably trash the nominee.

Nothing could help Alan Alvarez.

But Katrina is waiting in her office in the convention venue, coordinating the week's events, because she was in charge of everything for Carlton Winters regarding the convention itself.

And it is only the beginning.

However, the big event of the night will be that of Timothy Simon, the vice presidential nominee of the Central Administration Party.

It is sure to excite everyone and it will help secure the win in November.

Before long, the third night was already well underway, and it was now time for Alan Alvarez to give his surprise speech.

"*Thank you, and god bless to all of you here tonight in our time of need to take back control from the bad policies and laws of the United Labourists.*

My wife Emily and I are happy to be here tonight in Cleveland and we both believe America and the Central Administration Party can make a comeback in order to break away from the control and the bad policies of the United Labourists.

We believe it can be done.

Tonight, I would like to congratulate Carlton Winters for winning the presidential nomination for our party last night.

But like each of you here, I want to see the values restored in America that were lost during these past seven and a half years so that we can lead again.

I want to see our values to prevail in November.

Because the truth is, we can't afford to continue on this road pursued by the United Labourists and their special interests.

We need common sense so that the American people can prosper.

Now, I know this week can be quite exciting, because conventions can be fun, but we must not let the hatred of the United Labourists divide us in any manner.

We must help each other and not resort to hate.

We must not resort to using divisive rhetoric that inflames the people.

We have a real chance of taking our country back but we must make sure it is not at the expense of others being taken advantage of.

Look, we have protesters and rioters who want to destroy our message and America, and they are here today.

These people don't believe in the founding values of America as we do.

They want communism.

They want socialism.

They want Marxism.

And they support big government.

We have a problem in society when one political party wants to take away your freedom of speech and the right to defend yourself.

We need to make sure freedom is protected.

We are a country that cares about individual rights, freedom, liberty, and the pursuit of happiness.

As Americans, we should be proud of how far we have become, and we should reject the political establishment.

We should reject the bad policies of the United Labourists.

We should reject the bad policies of the political establishment.

We should understand that the United Labourists want to hurt and harm everyday Americans like you and me, because they want to impose high taxes, they want you to fund their wasteful programs, and they want you to listen to their propaganda.

We are at a crossroads because times are changing.

We can win if you join in today.

For once, we need to stand up to the open border people, and we need an immigration system that won't harm America.

We need an immigration system that doesn't support or endorse illegal immigration.

We need an immigration system that doesn't support the Victory World Front or any other terrorists.

We need an immigration system that protects America so that her people can be safe.

And we have the chance to do all of that, if you help us.

We can succeed if you want to protect America.

We have the people who can get us there and we will.

We need a courageous leader who will tell the political elites that we demand and mean change.

When we mean freedom we mean it.

Look, my father escaped Cuba with only a few hundred dollars in his pockets, because he saw Fidel Castro as a very evil man.

My father did not like the economic situation in Cuba.

He saw the walls crumbling down and that everything would get worse.

My father knew his rights were being infringed upon and he had a choice to make.

He either could stay in a corrupt state ruled by a dictator or he could choose freedom by coming to America.

Well, my father decided to go to America to experience the freedom, and ever since then he always succeeded in life.

Look, you can't succeed in countries like Cuba or Venezuela, because they will limit what you can do and how much you can make.

The only winner is the government.

So, everybody should appreciate what we have here in America, because freedom is our greatest asset.

God bless everyone here tonight!"

The speech was quite surprising, to say the least, but it was a speech of unity.

But there were times when the audience booed at Alvarez because they thought he was taking aim at Carlton Winters.

It was the thing that could kill his political career and that is what the media would say.

And it would be a time of chaos, according to the media.

They will claim Alan Alvarez has committed political suicide and has ruined his chances of reelection in 2018 and beyond.

They will claim it would be too difficult for him to recover for what he did at the convention to Carlton Winters.

They will claim that he is dead in the water and that he has no political future anymore.

Well, it has yet to be seen, but the media will probably say that Alan

Alvarez is toast.

And there is a time for everything but Katrina must move things forward so the convention will end smoothly.

It isn't run by itself, as that would be a disaster.

But artificial intelligence would mess everything up and no one will be happy.

And there was more speculation about what would happen next.

It could be catastrophic or it could be beneficial.

Whatever it is there will be someone to blame for everything else and that is how it's always is.

Before long, the third night of the convention is almost over, but not before one of the most important speakers tonight.

It won't be a full eventful night until Timothy Simon speaks to the audience.

"Ladies and gentlemen, please welcome to the stage Timothy Simon, the vice presidential nominee for the Central Administration Party," said the announcer.

"*Mr. Chairman, Madam Secretary, delegates and alternates, family and friends, and guests, thank you for being here tonight.*

I appreciate your support very much.

And on behalf of all Americans, I accept the vice presidential nomination for the Central Administration Party to be the next vice president of our great country, the United States of America.

I would also like to thank speaker of the house Daniel Shea.

And he knows I like short introductions, so thank you very much Daniel.

Now, let's get to the actual speech.

I am quite new to this campaign.

I never imagined being here at this moment in time.

I thought I would be home in the state of Indiana.

But I appreciate that I was chosen to be the vice presidential nominee of the greatest political party in the world.

But then days ago I was with Carlton Winters in New York, after he defeated 16 excellent and well-qualified candidates.

It is such an honor to be nominated to one of the highest offices in the land and alongside Carlton Winters, who has achieved the American dream.

We live in a very fortunate country where a person can start a small business in order to succeed in life.

We don't control the lives of people like the governments of China, Cuba, or Venezuela, because we believe in something called the freedom of speech, and we never try to silence our people here.

We believe in freedom of religion and the right to bear arms in order to defend your life.

We believe in the freedom of the press and we believe it is wrong to put journalists in jail because a despotic leader doesn't like what people say about them.

We believe in the right of a speedy trial determined by our peers and not some show trial.

We acknowledge that America isn't a perfect country but it is one of the greatest countries in the world that offers freedom, liberty, and the pursuit of happiness.

And we acknowledge that America is the greatest country to live in because our founders knew that our rights are derived from God and not some government or bureaucrat.

But in order to keep America the greatest country in the world we must make sure people are safe and that they can succeed.

When I first became involved in politics, I was a member of the United Labourists, until that one day when I heard the optimism from the great Ronald Reagan, because I learned you needed to earn something before you could claim it, so it would be fair to the rest of Americans.

And that is still true today.

You need to work hard for it and not always rely on the government to give you everything.

But, that is old news.

Over 32 years ago, I married the girl of my dreams, my high school sweetheart, my wife Patricia.

And we are happy to be the parents of two great children in the world.

Today, the most important title I have is that of a dad.

Nevertheless, if you know anything about the Hoosier state, Indiana, you will know we will be putting up a fight to win.

And on November 8, we will win and Carlton Winters will become the 45th president of the United States of America.

We need a fighter who will never back down from his promises.

We need new people in Washington who will get things done and will not bow down to the special interests.

We need to make sure that everybody is able to live and thrive in a prosperous economy and society.

We can do all of that and more and we will get things done when Carlton Winters becomes the next president of the United States of America on January 20, 2017.

We will win on November 8 because we are addressing the issues and problems that are plaguing the economy.

We will fix the immigration system.

We will make sure our borders are secure in order to keep out illegal immigrants, the criminals, and the members of the drug cartels.

We will prioritize border security so that drugs are kept out.

We have a drug problem and an epidemic in many states, and part of that has to do with an unsecured border.

So, we will prosecute anyone that brings drugs across the border illegally with the intent to sell and distribute because we don't need any bad people here.

We will improve our economy.

We will make sure that those burdensome regulations imposed by the Martin administration and the United Labourists are outright repealed and abolished from the federal code of our great country.

We will reduce taxes for everyone because people should not pay the government all their money they worked hard for.

We will implement a fair tax for our small businesses and any corporation that does business in America, because we need to compete with the rest of the world.

We have the highest corporate income tax in the entire world and it is unfair to the small businesses, since the large corporations move overseas to get a better income tax rate.

We will have a flat corporate income tax and that shall be fair to all businesses.

We will bring back the coal miners.

We will make sure the MartinCare law is repealed and replaced with something that doesn't force something down your throats.

We will rebuild our military again so we won't be at our weakest since the Second World War

We shall win and we can do it.

Ladies and gentlemen, Cynthia Norwell Anderson would just be a third term of Martin, and she will continue the reckless policies of his bad administration.

We won't let that happen because our message is greater.

It is our time to unite the party so that America can become prosperous like it used to be.

We have the best person to guide us.

We need someone like Carlton Winters to lead us out of this mess.

We need a leader with a proven record.

We need someone to fix our weak borders.

We need someone to bring back our economy and make it stronger like it once was.

We need to make sure everything is prosperous for the American people again.

That person is Carlton Winters.

And if you vote in November and we win, I will have the great privilege of being your vice president of the United States of America.

I will not waiver and will always support our president, Carlton Winters.

My fellow Americans, my parents ran a successful oil and gas station company, and they knew what it took to succeed.

They learned from their mistakes and today it still exists.

My story is about the American dream.

And if my parents who immigrated here could achieve the American dream with hardly anything in their pockets, then you can succeed too.

Tonight I stand here and tell you that we can achieve anything and you can help us win.

But if the United Labourists win in November you won't see anything positive happening, because they will continue with their reckless policies."

Together, we can achieve anything.

But we must make the right choice.

We have a successful businessman by the name of Carlton Winters that actually knows about how to operate a business and then we have a person by the name of Cynthia Norwell Anderson who has been involved in government all her life.

And that outcome will determine the future of our country.

But the best choice for the job is Carlton Winters because he actually will bring America back.

Thank you and god bless everyone."

With that the third night of the convention concluded and soon all cheered for the great and optimistic speech.

All remains to be seen at what will happen tomorrow.

It could be optimistic or it could be dark.

But the media will sure turn facts into fiction because that is all they do and it will only work against them.

And so, there is just a remainder of time to think about.

Tonight is the last day of the convention and everything looks optimistic.

Everyone who was scheduled to give a speech already gave it, and now it is time for the most important person of the week to give his speech and to accept the president nomination of the Central Administration Party, Carlton Winters.

"Please welcome to the stage, Carlton Winters," said the announcer to the audience.

"Thank you, thank you all for the incredible support.

Friends, delegates, alternates, family and friends, and members of the audience who have come here today and this past week, I appreciate what you have done for me over the past year.

Therefore, I humbly and gladly accept the presidential nomination to the presidency of the United States of America.

Who would have thought that over 13 months ago we would have gone this far into the campaign?

We had 16 other very talented candidates who could have been the nominee, but the entire party united to support me, because you all saw that I was the right choice.

You believed in my message that we need to make this country prosperous again.

You believed in my message about securing the homeland so it can be safe again.

You believed that I could get things done because I say things like they are.

And, I will honor your commitment to support me.

I will promise to get things done when I get to Washington so I can fix the mess created by the United Labourists.

Together, we can take back the White House, so we can achieve great things once again.

Folks, the time of this convention comes at a great crisis in our time, as our military isn't succeeding in the world, we are losing to other countries who are taking advantage of us, and we are constantly apologizing for what America stands for.

And even more, there are attacks on our police.

There is terrorism in our cities, and the Victory World Front is getting stronger by the day.

Our borders are being invaded by people who do not care about are laws. Left-wing groups are trying to usurp our very constitution, because they believe it is outdated.

And the United Labourists are doing nothing to stop it.

They are not doing anything to grasp these problems, and any politician who fails to call upon to address these issues or fix them are not fit to govern.

We must take a stand and be united against what the United Labourists stand for and to fix our government before it goes into chaos.

Ladies and gentlemen, tonight is a moment of celebration, and then tomorrow we go up against a corrupt political machine.

When we win on November 8, everything will change, beginning on January 20, 2017.

We will not bow down to those special interests.

We will take back our country.

We will make sure everyone is protected.

On January 20, 2017, we will restore order back to America by restoring safety everywhere.

For too long, crime and violence has plagued our cities and towns all across America, and the United Labourists have not down anything about it to reduce or even prevent it.

Instead, they welcome criminals from other countries with open arms who illegally cross the border rather than giving the support to American citizens.

That will change when I take office on January 20, 2017.

So, to everyone listening, I will promise you real hope and change and not the hope and change that candidate Barrington Martin promised, because his hope and change brought about a bad economy, burdensome regulations, and radical laws that are unconstitutional.

The most basic role of government is to protect the people and without law and order there will be chaos.

It is time for an assessment of our great nation to be stated and not the lies from the media or the people who are part of the establishment.

We need something better to work with.

At this convention though, you won't hear any lies.

You will only hear the truth, even if the left-wing media says it is dark and grim.

No matter what I say, they will try to spin it negatively because they do not like us.

They and the United Labourists have a deep hatred for freedom, liberty, and the pursuit of happiness, unless it fits their criteria.

But at this convention, we shall honor the American people, as you guys are the most important part of becoming president.

Not only we will honor you but we will get straight to the facts about the issues plaguing the nation now.

So here are the facts.

We have made decades of progress in combatting crime but all of that has been potentially rolled back due to the Martin administration.

In Martin's adopted city of Chicago, crime increased nearly five times the rate of every other city.

In our largest cities, there was a 33% increase in crime, and that has been the largest increase in the past 30 years.

In DC alone, crime and homicides increased over 60%, and there is nothing stopping it.

Everything has risen by an average crime rate of 55% during the past year and it is only getting worse.

We have 225,000 illegal immigrants here with criminal records that were ordered to be deported by a judge but they are currently roaming free and that could potentially risk American lives.

The amounts of new illegal immigrant families have increased by double and triple the rate since 2014.

And the United Labourists say there is nothing wrong with this being an issue.

They don't care that these illegal immigrants are coming here to our country and harming us.

They rather give them aid and comfort under the false pretense of asylum because they support illegal immigration and open borders.

Every day, every week, tens of thousands of these illegal immigrants are being released to our communities, and we have no way of tracking them, since they don't wear ankle monitors.

Instead, they are expected to wait for their asylum claim to be heard in a court of law, but they never show up, so they could be anywhere.

We need to end this but the United Labourists will say that I and you are heartless.

But they are the ones that are heartless, because they do not want to enforce border security.

The United Labourists believe we should admit anyone into our country because that is immigration, but the truth is that is not legal immigration.

That is chaos and anarchy, because they are mixing illegal immigration with legal immigration.

They say it is immoral to support a secure border because they don't want to protect our borders.

And, just last year, we had more instances of illegal immigrants killing innocent Americans.

We have illegal immigrants that were arrested for killing innocent Americans before and they were caught and arrested, but then they were released on bond, and then they killed again. And then they were deported to their home country.

But then they crossed into our border illegally again and they killed innocent Americans another time.

I met countless families that you have heard from who have spoken up against illegal immigration, but it seems the United Labourists and the Martin administration does not care about this issue.

And what about our economy that the media says is the best it has ever been, thanks to the Martin administration?

Well, our economy has not been the best as it should be since this current administration has taken office.

We have seen record-low GDP rates around 1.2% and the economists and the left-wing media that supports the United Labourists and the Martin administration believes that is the new normal.

Well, that is not normal, because we need growth, and lots of it, so Americans can prosper.

And what is even worse is a record 6 out of 10 African-Americans live in poverty, while nearly 80% of African-American youth are unemployed and can't find any work.

And the saddest case is that three million more Hispanics and Latinos are living in poverty today because of unemployment compared to 8 years ago.

It is a staggering statistic but the United Labourists seem not to care anything about it.

Since the year 2000, 17 million people have completely left the workforce, and people have been making $7,000 less.

Our trade deficit for goods this year is a whopping $950 billion.

So think about that for a minute?

You know what we can do with that money if we don't have a deficit?

We can fix our infrastructure, such as our roads and bridges, because they are such in bad shape.

And, President Martin has doubled our national debt to $19 trillion and it will increase by another trillion before a new president takes office on January 20, 2017.

We will fix that once I get into office.

And let's address our military and what is happening abroad.

You know remember when Iran held our navy sailors hostage?

Well that was such a disgrace that when I'm president we won't let that ever happen again.

And it was such a disgrace two months ago when we gave Iran $150 billion in cash.

You know where that money will go?

It will go straight to funding terrorism and terroristic activities to support radical Islamic terrorism and you can thank the United Labourists and the Martin administration for that.

Iran is the threat and they seem to want it both ways.

Well, when I am in power, that won't happen anymore.

We will restore peace in the Middle East and we will make sure we restore order back to our military.

But it doesn't end there.

Do you remember when the Martin administration made his remark about a red line in Syria?

Well, Martin never kept it.

And his administration saw the rise of the Victory World Front and the Islamic State.

But he has crippled our great military by not letting us engage the enemy by capturing or killing them.

Instead, he wants us to hold peace talks and to release prisoners from Guantanamo Bay in Cuba.

Ladies and gentlemen, this is the micromanaging of the military because President Martin won't let our great military defeat our enemies abroad, and it is the legacy of Cynthia Norwell Anderson.

That is the very definition of not putting America and Americans as the number one priority.

We must hold our elected officials responsible.

You know, the political elite and the big campaign donors are lining up to support my opponent, Cynthia Norwell Anderson, because they know she will give anything to them if they donate to her or her corrupt foundation that doesn't do anything.

I have no patience for injustice, because it seems there are two types of justice here in America.

One is for common folks like you or me and then there is the other justice system.

In that other justice system, it seems people like Cynthia Norwell Anderson are protected from being prosecuted for actual crimes.

Now, that isn't fair.

And what's even more surprising is that Anderson was cleared by Carl Ronald, the director of the Central Bureau of Domestic Investigations, even though actual crimes were committed.

She had an illegal email server somewhere in a bathroom and she was protected from being prosecuted.

That isn't right.

And if you or I did any of that we would already be in jail.

That isn't equal justice.

That is a travesty and we won't have it anymore.

Trust me, if Cynthia Norwell Anderson is elected, there will be no change, because she will be at the behest of her special interests and all of the lobbying groups, because they want some special deal in return for giving her large amounts of money.

When you have the CBDI director saying Anderson was extremely careless and negligent, you know she isn't right for the job.

Millions upon millions of United Labourists will join our new movement because they will see America is better off without someone like Cynthia Norwell Anderson's failed policies.

She supports countries in the Middle East that discriminate against the LGBTQ community but she and her fellow United Labourists say that they are good for the LGBTQ community.

It seems there is a double standard here, because you can't support one while you are saying you are for the other.

Well, as president, I will protect the LGBTQ community from any hateful actions committed by people.

Anderson won't change anything.

And she will even not force pressure on NATO.

I will make sure all NATO countries pay their fair share of defense spending towards that alliance, because the United States can't be held responsible for making the fair share payments of other countries.

We must put our foot down.

And I will also renegotiate NAFTA, because the current condition of that trade deal has a bad impact on our economy.

It was written by the special interests in support of the special interests.

And when it was written it was such a bad trade deal that we as a country got taken advantage of.

We were told it would be good for our workers, but it has taken away jobs from many of our proud American workers.

And many of our workers know that it is a bad deal, so when I'm elected I will renegotiate NAFTA, so that it never hurts our workers or our economy ever again.

But the same can't be said about my opponent, because she will keep the current agreement in place.

And then there is the issue about energy.

My opponent does not support the coal industry because she believes wind and solar energy are much better for the environment.

She knows wind and solar energy costs too much and will be a burden for the American people.

But she thinks we should no longer use gasoline in our engines.

She does not like fossil fuels and wants to harm the oil industry.

Well, let me tell you something.

Solar and wind energy cost too much money to build and maintain because the equipment is expensive to begin with and then you need many of those solar panels or wind mills to power a city.

It costs more to install the equipment and to maintain it than to use it.

But they say it will be more energy efficient and it will reduce the cost of your utility bill.

Sure, it might lower your utility bill dramatically, but it is not a good idea or policy, because the average American can't afford tens of thousands of dollars to install equipment.

But the United Labourists don't care about that, since they believe it will combat climate change.

The real story here is that we know that carbon does not contribute to the cause of climate change, as climate change is a natural cycle of the environment.

Climate change has always been happening since the beginning of our solar system.

The United Labourists don't want you to know that because they want to falsify their data.

Well, we are going to put American energy first when I become the next president of the United States of America.

We won't ship manufacturing or steel jobs to overseas countries, as we need to support our American workers.

If they want to eliminate fossil fuels, then what will we use to power our vehicles?

Do they believe everyone will buy electric cars?

Yes, that is exactly what they believe people will buy?

But the thing is electric vehicles can cost up to double or triple the amount as a regular gasoline-powered car, and then there is the special plug you need to have in order to charge it.

Not every business or gas station might want to install those special plugs for the electric cars.

And then you will have to keep charging the vehicle because the initial charge won't last that long.

So, eliminating fossil fuels is a bad idea and it will cost us as Americans too much money.

And we will fix our economy and stop this restrictive tax system.

We will bring back the jobs and we can do this by lowering our corporate income tax to a flat rate of 13%.

You will hear the United Labourists saying that we support Wall Street, but what they don't realize is that many Americans own and operate a small business in which they are the only employees, and they pay their salary from the money they make to survive.

We need the corporate tax rate equal across the board so that it can be fair to all businesses, so that we can build the economy and create more opportunities for jobs.

But that is not all, because we will also lower the individual tax rates to much lower rates, because you know people work hard for their money and the government doesn't need all of that.

And besides, they waste your money anyways, because the United Labourists like to spend it on their welfare programs.

Well, my plan is to reform the economy, and you need to lower the tax rates to do that. Only then will you see job growth.

"But I'm not done there, because we will get rid of these many burdensome regulations that restrict the function of business, and then the economy can prosper again."

Throughout my campaign, I have seen the tragedy of our public school systems, and I will make sure that the local school boards and the state get back their control, because we don't need the radical unions and the federal government telling our students what to do.

Schooling is a local and state issue only and it should stay that way, so we say no to this crazy concept of the Natural Foundation plan that makes no sense at all. And we shall succeed.

But we are not done just yet.

We will protect our second amendment because we need to defend ourselves from the criminals."

We will only appoint Supreme Court justices who support the constitution and interpret it as it was originally written.

We will support our veterans because they need help after coming home from the battlefield.

Our Veteran Administration is such in of dire restructuring that our veterans are dying because of long wait times and negligence.

And that brings us to MartinCare.

As your president, I will make sure that MartinCare is repealed and replaced, or just repealed.

It is such a bad law because of how it forces you to buy insurance or you will have to pay a fine.

Ladies and gentlemen the individual mandate is unconstitutional.

But we will make sure it is repealed and never replaced, because people shouldn't be forced to pay a fine for not buying a product that they don't want.

The bad thing about MartinCare is that it increased healthcare premiums across the board by upwards of hundreds of percentage points, and people can't afford that.

So, we will make sure people can buy health insurance over state lines, because currently there is no competition in the state markets.

If you have Medicare or are funded through the Veterans Administration, then those are the two programs that only work across state lines, but using out-of-state coverage from regular health insurance plans won't work in other states.

So, we are going to fix that.

At this time I would like to thank the entire evangelical community for believing in my campaign.

I would like to thank my family.

I would like to thank all of my supporters and all of you who are here tonight.

Together, we can do great things, but my opponent will just continue on the same failed policies.

Together, we can achieve this, and we will make America into a prosperous economy again.

We will help businesses and we will make sure all of those burdensome regulations are eliminated.

We will fix our infrastructure and our failing schools.

We will make America stronger.

We will make America safer again.

We will make sure we can achieve anything because we need to be on the world stage again.

And we will make America prosperous again.

Thank you and God Bless."

People began cheering with excitement, as that was the end of the National Centralist Convention of 2016.

With history in the books, it remains to be seen what happens next.

And that could be anything from a surprise and even something expected.

It all remains critical in deciding what happens next.

And with that, Katrina wraps up the convention and makes sure everything is cleaned up before leaving for the national campaign of Carlton Winters and continuing her job as a spy to target the campaign of Cynthia Norwell Anderson.

It is just a part of the history books now.

VI

"This just in, we are getting reports of a cache of 25,000 emails being leaked by Forum Page just days before the start of the United Labourist

National Convention; so this seems to be a huge embarrassment to not only Cynthia Norwell Anderson but also for Stephanie Donavan-Candy, the chairwoman of the National United Peoples' Traditionalist Labor Workers Party Committee, and we could expect a resignation in the near future," said Ryan Fisch of Wolfe News Channel, the top rated channel for conservatives that don't want to listen to propaganda.

"Breaking News, we are just learning that Forum Page has leaked hacked emails from the server of Cynthia Norwell Anderson," said Roman Anthony Andrews.

It would be inevitable until Donavan-Candy resigns, because the emails also implicate her about fixing the election for Cynthia Norwell Anderson over candidate Elias Dominic.

That is just as bad as the old days of Tammany Hall.

"This just in, Elias Dominic is asking for Donavan-Candy to resign, just 1 day before the 2016 United Labourist National Convention," said Ryan Fisch.

It is too early to tell, but it isn't looking good for Donavan-Candy, but she might survive, yet there could be chaos and a bunch of distractions out of the ordinary.

Of that time, there is just the time to decide what is right for the future of the party.

That will be the day when there is unity and that will be the day when people don't behave themselves.

For all other purposes everything else is redundant because it doesn't need to make sense.

And that includes how the United Labourists will react to this email leak in the future.

It will surely start our as an attack against the political establishment but then it will transform into a political attack against the opposing political party.

That is just normal in politics and still is popular today.

VII

Today is July 25, 2016, the first day of the 2016 United Labourist National Convention, and everything seems fine, but people should think otherwise.

There is just the opportunity for everyone to be conceited in an effort that doesn't make sense.

"Let's get this convention started," said Stephanie Donavan Candy to the audience.

"Good Afternoon everyone, the next four days are going to go by so fast, but we have the greatest supporters in the world, so let's show them our class and unity," said Donavan-Candy.

Meanwhile, as the convention is going on inside, Katrina is paying some people to protest outside in order to demand change, and they are exactly the same people that protested at the Centralist convention, so it should be no surprise that these people are social justice warriors with nothing better to do.

"Hello, I am with a local union, and I want to know if you are tired with the same old agenda by the political establishment and how no one cares about the little guy, so I'm asking you to join the fight of demanding change and social justice, because we need it, and if you join in we will pay for your meals, housing, and transportation, if you need such amenities," said Katrina to a group of people in order to start protests in the streets outside of the nominating convention for the United Labourists.

With that, they bought Katrina's lie and started to protest.

"No justice, no peace, no justice, no peace, no justice, no peace, no justice, no peace," said repeatedly the group of protestors outside the convention.

"Stop the steal, stop the slaughter, stop the attacks, stop the steal, stop the slaughter, stop the attacks, stop the steal, stop the slaughter, stop the attacks," said the group of protestors outside of the convention.

"We won't rest until all cops are arrested; we won't rest until all cops are arrested; we won't rest until all cops are arrested," said the group of protestors outside of the convention.

"We want justice, we want action, we want justice, we want action, we want justice, we want action," said the group of protestors outside of the convention.

"No war, no sanctions, Israel must go, No war, no sanctions, Israel must go, no war, no sanctions, Israel must go," said the group of protestors outside of the convention.

"Self-defense is not a human right, self-defense is not a human right, self-defense is not a human right," said the group of protesters outside the convention.

The protestors kept on chanting until their voices were heard and then they didn't care what people said to them.

"I say healthcare, you say human right; healthcare, human right, healthcare, human right, healthcare, human right, healthcare, human right," said the group of protestors outside the convention.

"If we don't get what we want, we shut it down, if we don't get what we want, we shut it down, if we don't get what we want, we shut it down," said the group of protestors outside the convention.

"This is what democracy looks like, this is what we want, this is what freedom is, this is what we need, this is power, this is what democracy looks like, this is what we want, this is what freedom is, this is what we need, this is power, this is what democracy looks like, this is what we want, this is what freedom is, this is what we need, this is power," said the group of protestors outside the convention.

"We want these racist cops out, we want these racist cops out of our neighborhood, we want these racist cops out of our homes, we want these racist cops out of our lives, we want these racist cops out forever, we want these racist cops out, we want these racist cops out of our neighborhood, we want these racist cops out of our homes, we want these racist cops out of our lives, we want these racist cops out forever, we want these racist cops out, we want these racist cops out of our neighborhood, we want these racist cops out of our homes, we want these racist cops out of our lives, we want these racist cops out forever," said the group of protestors outside the convention.

It is a never-ending protest of anger and deceit and there is nothing that can be done to end it.

There could be something better to do but no one wants to do that.

It could be that these protestors want their voices to be heard by the people inside the convention.

It could be that these protestors are dissatisfied with political action.

It is believed that these protestors want and demand change now.

And that is exactly what they want because they won't stop until actions are taken.

It is a case that must be determined to what takes place in the future but they want reparations when they don't even deserve them.

There is a time and way for everything to be solved.

And then there was the rest of the world thinking about something more important.

Today was the second day of the convention, and it would be crucial to see what happens next.

"Good evening everyone, let the roll call of the states begin now, and we will show everybody how we elect with democracy and unity," said Stephanie Donavan-Candy.

"Ladies and gentlemen, please welcome to the stage, Lisa Bennett-Hawthorne, the secretary of the National United Peoples' Traditionalist Labor Workers Party Committee," said the announcer.

"I call this session to order, but before we begin it's customary for delegates to speak on behalf on any candidates and to nominate candidates, so let's give a warm welcome," said Bennett-Hawthorne.

"Madam Secretary, for years we had no diversity in any of our elections, and finally, this is the year when women can speak up about the horrible things men do to us; women are finally fed up with men and other people taking advantage of us, and it has grown into a movement that even the most powerful are afraid of; so it is my privilege to nominate the first women presidential candidate to a major political party, Cynthia Norwell Anderson, and the next president of the United States of America," said an Anderson supporter.

"Madam Secretary, I will second the nomination of Cynthia Norwell Anderson, because it is time we have a female in charge of the highest office in the land, and it is time we bowing down to the misogyny and racism that is rampant in male culture," said another Anderson supporter.

"Madam Secretary, for years we had income inequality and class warfare present in our everyday lives, and that is still present today, but I can see that changing, because this is the time that we as a party need to give people access to free healthcare, help the future generation with college, get rid of student loans, and offer the chance for corporations to pay everyone a living wage, so I now have the privilege of nominating the best person for the job that can lead us to a better future, in which Wall Street and the political elite will take responsibility, Vermont Senator Elias Dominic, the only one who has the guts to tell the people the problem that America faces in the future if nothing is done to fix it," said a Dominic supporter.

"Madam Secretary, I have the privilege to second the nomination of Elias Dominic, because it is time we hold the corporations and Wall Street accountable for their illegal actions, and it is time to move forward with this political revolution so that people can be treated fairly once and for all, so I am seconding the nomination of the great Senator from the great state of Vermont," said a Dominic supporter.

"Okay, it is my pleasure, to certify the official candidates of the National United Peoples' Traditionalist Labor Workers Party, and now it is time for roll call," said Bennett-Hawthorne.

"Alabama, you have a total of 60 votes, how do you wish to cast them," asked Bennett-Hawthorne.

"Madam Secretary, thank you, the state of Alabama has champions all over our state and not only in football but in people who support our civil rights, and we proudly cast 50 votes for former Secretary of State Cynthia Norwell Anderson and 9 votes for the great Senator from Vermont, Elias Dominic," said the delegate from Alabama.

"Okay, Alabama, you cast 50 votes for Anderson and 9 votes for Dominic, and I will count the other vote as an abstention," said Bennett-Hawthorne.

"Alaska, you have a total of 20 votes, so how do you wish to cast them," asked Bennett-Hawthorne?

"Madam Secretary, Alaska, the state that is threatened most by climate change, Alaska, the state with our receding glaciers, Alaska, the state that makes the United States of America as an Antarctic nation, and Alaska, the state with rising water levels, casts 6 votes for the next president of the United States of America, Cynthia Norwell Anderson, and 14 votes for the progressive candidate firebrand Elias Dominic," said the delegate from the state of Alaska.

"Alaska, 6 votes are cast for Anderson and 14 votes for Elias Dominic," said Bennett-Hawthorne.

"American Samoa, you have 11 votes, so how do you choose to cast them," asked Bennett-Hawthorne?

"Madam Secretary, American Samoa, home of the cleanest air in all of America, the home to many members of the military, and American Samoa, the last place for the sun to set in America, American Samoa proudly casts 3 votes for Elias Dominic and 8 for the next president of the United States of America Cynthia Norwell Anderson," said the delegate from the island territory of American Samoa.

"American Samoa, you have cast 3 votes for Dominic and 8 votes for Anderson," said Bennett-Hawthorne.

"Arizona, you have a total of 85 delegates, so how do you wish to cast them," asked Bennett-Hawthorne?

"Madam Secretary, Arizona is the home of many women-elected leaders, the state that is a place for diversity, and Arizona proudly casts 34 votes for Senator Dominic and 51 votes for Cynthia Norwell Anderson the next president of the United States of America," said the delegate from the state of Arizona.

"Arizona, you have cast 34 votes for Dominic and 51 votes for Anderson," said Bennett-Hawthorne.

"Arkansas, you have a total of 37 delegates, so how do you wish to cast them," asked Bennett-Hawthorne?

"Madam Secretary, Arkansas, the first state to recognize that hope does exist, the state home to Secretary Anderson where she led the first initiative for pre-k education be funded sufficiently, and Arkansas, the state filled with hope and change for our children and future generations proudly cast 10 votes for Elias Dominic and 27 votes for the next president of the United States of America Cynthia Norwell Anderson," said the delegate from the state of Arkansas.

"Arkansas, you have cast 10 votes for Dominic and 27 votes for Anderson," said Bennett-Hawthorne.

"California, you have 551 votes, so how do you choose to cast them," asked Bennett-Hawthorne?

"Madam Secretary, California, the state that is the most progressive in the nation, California, the state that is leading the battle against the threat of climate change, the state that is moving away from fossil fuels and towards renewable energy, the state that is focused on reducing CO2 emissions to get rid of pollution, California, the state that is focused on clean air and clean water, and California, the state that stands for everything against the views of

Carlton Winters and for a $15 minimum wage proudly cast 221 votes for Senator Elias Dominic and 330 votes for the next president of the United States of America Cynthia Norwell Anderson," said the delegate from the state of California.

"California, you have cast 221 votes for Dominic and 330 votes for Anderson," said Bennett-Hawthorne.

"Colorado, you have 78 votes, so how do you choose to cast them," asked Bennett-Hawthorne?

"Madam Secretary, Colorado is home to sand dunes and the Rocky Mountains as well as many national parks, and as United Labourists we are proud to fight every day to protect these sacred lands because they belong to America, and we proudly cast 41 votes for Senator Elias Dominic, 36 votes for the next president of the United States of America Cynthia Norwell Anderson, and 1 abstention," said the delegate from Colorado.

"Colorado, you have cast 41 votes for Dominic, 36 votes for Anderson, and 1 abstention," said Bennett-Hawthorne.

"Connecticut, you have 71 votes, so how do you choose to cast them," asked Bennett-Hawthorne?

"Madam Secretary, Connecticut, the state with the most progressive delegation in Congress, the state with a progressive governor and one of the most progressive legislatures in America, and we cast 27 votes for Senator Elias Dominic and 44 votes for the next president of the United States of America Cynthia Norwell Anderson," said the delegate from the state of Connecticut.

"Connecticut, you have cast 27 votes for Dominic and 44 votes for Anderson," said Bennett-Hawthorne.

"Delaware, you have 32 votes, so how do you choose to cast them," asked Bennett-Hawthorne?

"Madam Secretary, Delaware, the home of vice president Walter Ross, the home of a unanimous United Labourist congressional delegation, a unanimous state legislature with control by United Labourists, and one of the first states to sign the constitution, proudly cast 9 votes for Elias Dominic and 23 votes for Cynthia Norwell Anderson the next president of the United States of America," said the delegate from Delaware.

"Delaware, you have cast 9 votes for Dominic and 23 votes for Anderson," said Bennett-Hawthorne.

"United Labourists Abroad, you have 17 votes, so how do you choose to cast them," asked Bennett-Hawthorne?

"United Labourists Abroad represents the more than 9 million U.S. citizens who live outside the United States of America, and the home of Elias Dominic's older brother, Terry Dominic, so we cast 10 votes for Elias Dominic and 7 votes for the next president of the United States of America, Cynthia Norwell Anderson," said the delegate from United Labourists Abroad.

"United Labourists Abroad, you have cast 10 votes for Dominic and 7 votes for Anderson," said Bennett-Hawthorne.

"District of Columbia, you have 44 votes, so how do you choose to cast them," asked Bennett-Hawthorne?

"Madam Secretary, I am the mayor of the District of Columbia, the capital city of the greatest country in the world, the United States of America, so we cast 5 votes for Elias Dominic and 39 votes for the next president of the United States of America, Cynthia Norwell Anderson," said the delegate from the District of Columbia.

"District of Columbia, you have cast 5 votes for Dominic and 39 votes for Anderson," said Bennett-Hawthorne.

"Florida, you have 246 votes, so how do you choose to cast them," asked Bennett-Hawthorne?

"Madam Secretary, Florida, on behalf of Florida, the sunshine state, and Florida, the home to our great United Labourist Senator Frank Reginald, and the state that will go blue for Cynthia Norwell Anderson, Florida cast 72 votes for Senator Elias Dominic and 163 votes for the first women president of the United States of America, Cynthia Norwell Anderson," said the delegate from the state of Florida.

"Florida, you have cast 72 votes for Dominic and 163 votes for Anderson," said Bennett-Hawthorne.

"Georgia, you have 117 votes, so how do you choose to cast them," asked Bennett-Hawthorne?

"Madam Secretary, it is a great honor to be here, where Georgia is the epicenter of civil and human rights, where the march for social justice has begun, and Georgia, the peach state, the home to our 39th president, Joseph Nathan, a United Labourist, proudly cast 29 votes for Senator Elias Dominic and 87 votes for the next president of the United States of America, Cynthia

Norwell Anderson," said the delegate from the state of Georgia.

"Georgia, you have cast 29 votes for Dominic and 87 votes for Anderson," said Bennett-Hawthorne.

"Guam, you have 12 votes, so how do you choose to cast them," asked Bennett-Hawthorne?

"Madam Secretary, Hello from Guam, the home of a very diverse group of people, and Madam Secretary, we have traveled through 9 time zones to make sure we have a president who is sensitive to our needs and to make sure we have a president who supports our rights as defined in the United Labourist platform, so Madam Secretary, we proudly cast 2 votes for Senator Elias Dominic, 1 abstention, and 9 votes for the next president of the United States of America, Cynthia Norwell Anderson," said the delegate from the island territory of Guam.

"Guam, you have cast 2 votes for Dominic, 9 votes for Anderson, and 1 abstention," said Bennett-Hawthorne.

"Hawaii, you have 34 votes, so how do you choose to cast them," asked Bennett-Hawthorne?

"Madam Secretary, Aloha from Hawaii, the Aloha state, the most beautiful place in the world, the birth place of our great president Barrington Martin, and Hawaii the state where you can convert to 100% clean energy and stop using fossil fuels that pollute our sacred environment, so Hawaii cast 19 votes for Senator Elias Dominic and 15 votes for the next president of the United States of America, Cynthia Norwell Anderson," said the delegate from the state of Hawaii.

"Hawaii, you have cast 19 votes for Dominic and 15 votes for Anderson," said Bennett-Hawthorne.

"Idaho, you have 27 votes, so how do you choose to cast them," asked Bennett-Hawthorne?

"Madam Secretary, Idaho, the gem state, the state with the most mountain peaks in the lower 48 of America, and the longest undammed river in America, we proudly cast 20 votes for Senator Elias Dominic and 7 votes for Cynthia Norwell Anderson," said the delegate from Idaho.

"Idaho, you have cast 20 votes for Dominic and 7 votes for Anderson," said Bennett-Hawthorne.

"Illinois, Illinois, you have a total of 183 votes to cast, so how do you choose to cast them," asked Bennett-Hawthorne?

"Madam Secretary, the great state of Illinois, home to our great president, Barrington Martin, the great Senator Phil Arnoldson, and our soon to be Senator, Trisha Freeman, so for Elias Dominic we proudly cast 74 votes for the Senator that started our new progressive political revolution and for the next president of the United States of America we cast 98 votes for Cynthia Norwell Anderson," said the delegate from Illinois.

"Illinois, you have cast 74 votes for Dominic and 98 votes for Anderson," said Bennett-Hawthorne.

"Indiana, you have 92 votes, so how do you choose to cast them," asked Bennett-Hawthorne?

"Madam Secretary, in 2008 Indiana for the first time turned blue since 1964 to help elect the first African-American president in the history of the United States of America, and 4 years later we again sent a member of the United Labourists to the Senate, and this November we are going to send Cynthia Norwell Anderson to the White House to become the next president of the United States of America, so it is my honor and privilege to cast 43 votes for Senator Elias Dominic, 1 abstention, and 48 votes for the next president of the United States of America, Cynthia Norwell Anderson," said the delegate from the state of Indiana.

"Indiana, you have cast 43 votes for Dominic, 48 votes for Anderson, and 1 abstention," said Bennett-Hawthorne.

"Iowa, you have 51 votes, so how do you choose to cast them," asked Bennett-Hawthorne?

"Madam Secretary, we believe in equal pay and dignity for everyone, and we proudly cast 21 votes for Elias Dominic and 30 votes for the first woman to be nominated to a major political party in the United States of America," said the delegate from Iowa.

"Iowa, you have cast 21 votes for Dominic and 30 votes for Anderson," said Bennett-Hawthorne.

"Kansas, you have 37 votes, so how do you choose to cast them," asked Bennett-Hawthorne?

"Madam Secretary, Kansas is home to a rich history of activism from us United Labourists, and is the home and birthplace of Catherine Nolan, the mother of our great president, Barrington Martin, and Kansas proudly cast 23 votes for Senator Elias Dominic and 14 votes for the next president of the United States of America, Cynthia Norwell Anderson," said the delegate from the state of Kansas.

"Kansas, you have cast 23 votes for Dominic and 14 votes for Anderson," said Bennett-Hawthorne.

"Kentucky, you have 50 votes, so how do you choose to cast them," asked Bennett-Hawthorne?

"Madam Secretary, the commonwealth of Kentucky knows the beauty of Kentucky Bourbon, the world's finest Whiskey, as well as bluegrass music and our great grass, so Kentucky proudly knows what a winner looks like, and we cast 27 votes for Senator Elias Dominic and 33 votes for Cynthia Norwell Anderson, the next president of the United States of America," said the delegate from the state of Kentucky.

"Kentucky, you have cast 27 votes for Dominic and 33 votes for Anderson," said Bennett-Hawthorne.

"Louisiana, you have 59 votes, so how do you choose to cast them," asked Bennett-Hawthorne?

"Madam Secretary, Louisiana, the home to New Orleans, and the state that is threatened by the threat of rising water and hurricanes as well as the disappearance from the rest of the continental United States because of climate change, we have two great candidates who will acknowledge that we need to change, so we the delegation of the great state of Louisiana proudly cast 14 votes for Senator Elias Dominic and 45 votes for the first woman in the history to become president of the United States of America next January, Cynthia Norwell Anderson," said the delegate from Louisiana.

"Louisiana, you have cast 14 votes for Dominic and 45 votes for Anderson," said Bennett-Hawthorne.

"Maine, you have 30 votes, so how do you choose to cast them," asked Bennett-Hawthorne?

"Madam Secretary, Maine is a rugged and independent state known for their loggers and forests, and we take great pride knowing that we can achieve the future in reducing our threat to the climate, so we know we can provide a better future to our children and future generations by sustaining our forests and to help guide the future of our state towards a better future, so Maine proudly cast 18 votes for Senator Elias Dominic and 12 votes for Cynthia Norwell Anderson," said the delegate from Maine.

"Maine, you have cast 18 votes for Dominic and 12 votes for Anderson," said Bennett-Hawthorne.

"Maryland, you have 120 votes, so how do you choose to cast them," asked Bennett-Hawthorne?

"Madam Secretary, the great state of Maryland, the home of the and the birthplace of late Supreme Court justice Thurgood Marshall, the home of Francis Scott Key, and the United States Naval Academy, so we proudly cast 36 votes for a great man Elias Dominic and 84 votes for the next president of the United States of America, Cynthia Norwell Anderson," said the delegate from the state of Maryland.

"Maryland, you have cast 36 votes for Dominic and 84 votes for Anderson," said Bennett-Hawthorne.

"Massachusetts, you have 115 votes, so how do you choose to cast them," asked Bennett-Hawthorne?

"Madam Secretary, Massachusetts, we have worked for the common good, we are first in public education, the state that started with it all by dumping tea in the harbor, and we are ready to fight for our nation, so we cast 46 votes for Elias Dominic and 68 votes for Cynthia Norwell Anderson, the next president of the United States of America," said the delegate from the state of Massachusetts.

"Massachusetts, you have cast 46 votes for Dominic and 68 votes for Anderson," said Bennett-Hawthorne.

"Michigan, you have 147 votes, so how do you choose to cast them," asked Bennett-Hawthorne?

"Madam Secretary, Michigan, the home of the Great Lakes and to the people who build stuff for Americans, we cast 66 votes for a great Senator named Elias Dominic and 81 votes for the next president of the United States of America, Cynthia Norwell Anderson," said the delegate from the state of Michigan.

"Michigan, you have cast 66 votes for Dominic and 81 votes for Anderson," said Bennett-Hawthorne.

"Minnesota, you have 93 votes, so how do you choose to cast them," asked Bennett-Hawthorne?

"Madam Secretary, Minnesota, the home to many great people and the home to Hubert Horatio Humphrey, who told everyone to get out from under the rug of states' rights and to move towards human rights, so we the delegation of Minnesota cast 47 votes for Senator Elias Dominic and 42 votes for the next president of the United States of America, Cynthia Norwell

Anderson," said the delegate from Minnesota.

"Minnesota, you have cast 47 votes for Dominic and 42 votes for Anderson," said Bennett-Hawthorne.

"Mississippi, you have 41 votes, so how do you choose to cast them," asked Bennett-Hawthorne?

"Madam Secretary, Mississippi, the home of the blues and to many great singers and songwriters, Mississippi, the home of the greatest river in the world, and to some great species of American fish, we cast 33 votes for Cynthia Norwell Anderson and 7 votes for Elias Dominic," said the delegate from Mississippi.

"Mississippi, you have cast 7 votes for Dominic and 33 votes for Anderson," said Bennett-Hawthorne.

"Missouri, you have 84 votes, so how do you choose to cast them," asked Bennett-Hawthorne?

"Madam Secretary, the great Show Me state, the home of Harry Truman, a state united to change this country in a better direction, proudly cast 35 votes for Elias Dominic and 49 votes for the next president of the United States of America, Cynthia Norwell Anderson," said the delegate from Missouri.

"Missouri, you have cast 35 votes for Dominic and 49 votes for Anderson," said Bennett-Hawthorne.

"Montana, you have 27 votes, so how do you choose to cast them," asked Bennett-Hawthorne?

"Hello, Madam Secretary, from the great state of Montana, known as Big Sky Country and the treasure state, the home of our great governor who is protecting our public lands, environment, and our rivers from harmful use by the big polluters, and this year the state of Montana will send the first woman to the White House, so we proudly cast 12 votes for Senator Elias Dominic and 14 votes for Cynthia Norwell Anderson the next president of the United States of America," said the delegate from Montana.

"Montana, you have cast 12 votes for Dominic and 14 votes for Anderson," said Bennett-Hawthorne.

"Nebraska, you have 30 votes, so how do you choose to cast them," asked Bennett-Hawthorne?

"Madam Secretary, Nebraska is such an amazing state with very hardworking people, and because our splitting of votes on November 8 for the Electoral College will turn blue and drown out the red, so one of the most diverse delegations in the history of Nebraska proudly cast 13 votes for Cynthia Norwell Anderson and 16 votes for Elias Dominic who electrified the movement of the United Labourists," said the delegate from the state of Nebraska.

"Nebraska, you have cast 16 votes for Dominic and 13 votes for Anderson," said Bennett-Hawthorne.

"Nevada, you have 43 votes, so how do you choose to cast them," asked Bennett-Hawthorne?

"Madam Secretary, Nevada, the fabulous Silver State from Lake Tahoe to Las Vegas, with a diverse population, we proudly cast 16 votes for Senator Elias Dominic and 27 votes for Cynthia Norwell Anderson, the next president of the United States of America," said the delegate from the state of Nevada.

"Nevada, you have cast 16 votes for Dominic and 20 votes for Anderson," said Bennett-Hawthorne.

"New Hampshire, you have 32 votes, so how do you choose to cast them," asked Bennett-Hawthorne?

"Madam Secretary, the state of New Hampshire, and to a town called Unity, where Cynthia Norwell Anderson endorsed Barrington Martin in 2008, and home to the city of Portsmouth, where Elias Dominic endorsed Cynthia Norwell Anderson in 2016, so New Hampshire proudly cast 16 votes for the great Senator from Vermont, Elias Dominic, and 16 votes for the next president of the United States of America, Cynthia Norwell Anderson," said the delegate from New Hampshire.

"New Hampshire, you have cast 16 votes for Dominic and 16 votes for Anderson," said Bennett-Hawthorne.

"New Jersey, you have 142 votes, so how do you choose to cast them," asked Bennett-Hawthorne?

"Madam Secretary, New Jersey, the home of the Garden State, with two great United States Senator and a diverse state, and the state that will send the first woman to the White House in American history to empower feminism and breaking the glass ceiling, so we proudly cast 45 votes for the great Senator from Vermont, Elias Dominic, and 90 votes for the next president of the United States of America, Cynthia Norwell Anderson," said the delegate from the state of New Jersey.

"New Jersey, you have cast 45 votes for Dominic and 90 votes for Anderson," said Bennett-Hawthorne.

"New Mexico, you have 43 votes, so how do you choose to cast them," asked Bennett-Hawthorne?

"Madam Secretary, we are from the state of New Mexico, and are proud of our great veterans, the home of the Navajo Code Talkers, and now our state proudly cast 16 votes for Senator Elias Dominic and 27 votes for the next president of the United States of America, Cynthia Norwell Anderson," said the delegate from New Mexico.

"New Mexico, you have cast 16 votes for Dominic and 27 votes for Anderson," said Bennett-Hawthorne.

"New York, you have 291 votes, so how do you choose to cast them," asked Bennett-Hawthorne?

"Madam Secretary, New York, the Empire State, the birthplace of women's rights in Seneca Falls, the place with great leadership as well as dignity that enacted a $15 minimum wage, marriage equality, and paid family leave, the state proud of our partnerships with organized labor, a very proud supporter of Puerto Rico, the home of the dean of our great congressional delegation that is set to retire, the proud home of our great former president George 'Percy' Anderson and the home of our great former senator and the next president of the United States of America, so we proudly cast 108 delegates to Senator Elias Dominic and 181 delegates to the next president of the United States of America, Cynthia Norwell Anderson," said the delegate from the state of New York.

"New York, you have cast 108 votes for Dominic and 181 votes for Anderson," said Bennett-Hawthorne.

"North Carolina, you have 120 votes, so how do you choose to cast them," asked Bennett-Hawthorne?

"Madam Secretary, the great state of North Carolina, the Tar Heel State, the state with great basketball teams and very delicious barbeque, home of Fort Bragg the largest military base in the world, the only battleground state that will give us the first woman that will become the next president in the history of the United States of America, Cynthia Norwell Anderson, the state that proudly supports our military, and the state that will repeal HB 2 once we take back control of the governorship and the state legislature, so we proudly cast 48 votes for Senator Elias Dominic and 70 votes for the next president of the United States of America, Cynthia Norwell Anderson," said the delegate from North Carolina.

"North Carolina, you have cast 48 votes for Dominic and 70 votes for Anderson," said Bennett-Hawthorne.

"North Dakota, you have 18 delegates, so how do you choose to cast them," asked Bennett-Hawthorne?

"Madam Secretary, the great state of North Dakota, home of five great tribal nations, and the nonpartisan organization to combat corporate money from entering into political contributions over 100 years ago, we proudly cast 14 votes for Senator Elias Dominic and 7 votes for Cynthia Norwell Anderson," said the delegate from North Dakota.

"North Dakota, you have cast 14 votes for Dominic and 7 votes for Anderson," said Bennett-Hawthorne.

"Northern Mariana Islands, you have 11 votes, so how do you choose to cast them," asked Bennett-Hawthorne?

"Madam Secretary, welcome from the Northern Mariana Islands, and today we stand here for the first time to proudly cast our votes, so we proudly cast 2 votes for Senator Elias Dominic and 9 votes for the next president of the United States of America, Cynthia Norwell Anderson," said the delegate from the Northern Mariana Islands.

"Northern Mariana Islands, you have cast 2 votes for Dominic and 9 votes for Anderson," said Bennett-Hawthorne.

"Ohio, you have 160 votes, so how do you choose to cast them," asked Bennett-Hawthorne?

"Madam Secretary, we are the great state of Ohio, the state that finally made it possible for anyone who loves each other to marry, the state that made marriage equality possible, so we proudly cast 62 votes for Senator Elias Dominic and 98 votes for the next president of the United States of America, Cynthia Norwell Anderson," said the delegate from the state of Ohio.

"Ohio, Ohio you have cast 62 votes for Dominic and 98 votes for Anderson," said Bennett-Hawthorne.

"Oklahoma, you have 42 votes, so how do you choose to cast them," asked Bennett-Hawthorne?

"Madam Secretary, Oklahoma, the home of the 38th tribal nation, and we are happy to be here today, and 8 years ago today we made history by nominating the first African-American to the presidency of the United States of America to a major political party, and today we make history again by nominating the first woman candidate to a major political party to that same very office, the presidency of the United States of America, so we proudly cast 22 votes for Senator Elias Dominic and 20 votes for the next president of the United States of America, Cynthia Norwell Anderson," said the delegate from the state of Oklahoma.

"Oklahoma, you have cast 22 votes for Dominic and 20 votes for Anderson," said Bennett-Hawthorne.

"Oregon, you have 74 votes, so how do you choose to cast them," asked Bennett-Hawthorne?

"Madam Secretary, the great state of Oregon, home to 9 tribal nations, home to the Pacific Ocean, and home to over four million of some of the most wonderful people in America, we proudly cast 34 votes for Cynthia Norwell Anderson and 38 votes for Senator Elias Dominic," said the delegate from the state of Oregon.

"Oregon, you have cast 38 votes for Dominic and 34 votes for Anderson," said Bennett-Hawthorne.

"Pennsylvania, you have 208 votes, so how do you choose to cast them," asked Bennett-Hawthorne?

"Madam Secretary, we are from the commonwealth of Pennsylvania, and we are honored to award 82 votes to Senator Elias Dominic and 126 votes to the next president of the United States of America and the first woman in history that will be elected to the White House, Cynthia Norwell Anderson," said the delegate from Pennsylvania.

"Pennsylvania, you have cast 82 votes for Dominic and 126 votes for Anderson," said Bennett-Hawthorne.

"Puerto Rico, you have 67 votes, so how do you choose to cast them," asked Bennett-Hawthorne?

"Madam Secretary, the island territory of Puerto Rico, being the only all Latino delegation at this convention, the home to a tropical paradise the future 51st state, and we proudly cast 23 votes for the great Senator from the state of Vermont Elias Dominic and we also are proud to cast 44 votes for Cynthia Norwell Anderson, the next president of the United States of America and the first woman president who will be elected to the White House, and the person who will sign our referendum to admit us as the 51st state of the United States of America," said the delegate from the island territory of Puerto Rico.

"Puerto Rico, you have cast 23 votes for Dominic and 44 votes for Anderson," said Bennett-Hawthorne.

"Rhode Island, you have 32 votes, so how do you choose to cast them," asked Bennett-Hawthorne?

"Madam Secretary, we are from the great United Labourist state of Rhode Island, home of some of the greatest coastlines and beaches in the world, as well as our great New England Shellfish, and Rhode Island the smallest state in the union, so we proudly cast 13 votes for Senator Elias Dominic and 19 votes for Cynthia Norwell Anderson, the next president of the United States of America," said the delegate from the New England state of Rhode Island.

"Rhode Island, you have cast 13 votes for Dominic and 19 votes for Anderson," said Bennett-Hawthorne.

"South Carolina, you have 59 votes, so how do you choose to cast them," asked Bennett-Hawthorne?

"Madam Secretary, the Palmetto State, the home of the first in the south primary, South Carolina, with a rich history of progressive politics and change, South Carolina is proud to cast 13 votes for Elias Dominic and 46 votes for the next president of the United States of America, Cynthia Norwell Anderson," said the delegate from South Carolina.

"South Carolina, you have cast 13 votes for Dominic and 46 votes for Anderson," said Bennett-Hawthorne.

"South Dakota, you have 25 votes, so how do you choose to cast them," asked Bennett-Hawthorne?

"Madam Secretary, from the great state of South Dakota, the land of Mount Rushmore, the home of the Black Hills, the home of the Lakota people, the home of great grasslands, the home of our great farmers who serve the people of America each day with farmed fresh food and Ethanol, the home of Ellsworth Airforce Base, and South Dakota, with one of the best economies in America, the home of many great national parks, so we proudly cast our 25 votes in the following manner: 10 votes for Senator Elias Dominic and 15 votes for the next president of the United States of America Cynthia Norwell Anderson and the person who will lead us into the future," said the delegate from the state of South Dakota.

"South Dakota, you have cast 10 votes for Dominic and 15 votes for Anderson," said Bennett-Hawthorne.

"Tennessee, you have 75 votes, so how do you choose to cast them," asked Bennett-Hawthorne?

"Madam Secretary, the great state of Tennessee, the state that ratified the 19th amendment to give the women the right to vote, proudly cast 23 votes for Senator Elias Dominic and 50 votes for the first woman president of the United States of America, Cynthia Norwell Anderson," said the delegate from the state of Tennessee.

"Tennessee, you have cast 23 votes for Dominic and 50 votes for Anderson," said Bennett-Hawthorne.

"Texas, you have 251 votes, so how do you choose to cast them," asked Bennett-Hawthorne?

"Madam Secretary, Texas, the great Lone Star State, the home of the 36th president of the United States of America Lyndon Baines Johnson, and the state that will finally turn blue in November, proudly cast 72 votes for the progressive Senator from Vermont, Elias Dominic, and 179 votes for Cynthia Norwell Anderson, the next president of the United States of America," said the delegate from the state of Texas.

"Texas, you have cast 72 votes for Dominic and 179 votes for Anderson," said Bennett-Hawthorne.

"Utah, you have 37 votes, so how do you choose to cast them," asked Bennett-Hawthorne?

"Madam Secretary, the great state of Utah, home to 5 national parks, the Beehive State, and the number one state of volunteerism, proudly cast 29 votes for Senator Elias Dominic and 8 votes for the next president of the United States of America Cynthia Norwell Anderson," said the delegate from the state of Utah.

"Utah, Utah, you have cast 29 votes for Dominic and 8 votes for Anderson," said Bennett-Hawthorne.

"Vermont, you have 26 votes, so how do you choose to cast them," asked Bennett-Hawthorne?

"Madam Secretary, Vermont passes," said the delegate from the state of Vermont.

"United States Virgin Islands, you have 12 votes, so how do you choose to cast them," asked Bennett-Hawthorne?

"Madam Secretary, the people of the Caribbean, the United States Virgin Island, the island of tropical paradise with excellent tourism, the home of Alexander Hamilton, and we understand the importance of deserving the right to vote under the American flag, so we proudly cast 12 votes for the next president of the United States of America, Cynthia Norwell Anderson," said the delegate from the United States Virgin Islands.

"United States Virgin Islands, you have cast 12 votes for Anderson," said Bennett-Hawthorne.

"Virginia, you have 108 votes, so how do you choose to cast them," asked Bennett-Hawthorne?

"Madam Secretary, the beautiful home of the commonwealth of Virginia, the place where it all began in Jamestown, home to 8 presidents of the United States of America, home to many of our founding fathers, home to one of the largest naval bases in the world, home to many members of our great military, and home to our next vice president of the United States of America, Senator Tony Dennis, so we proudly cast 33 votes for Senator Elias Dominic and 75 votes for Cynthia Norwell Anderson, the next president of the United States of America," said the delegate from the commonwealth of Virginia.

"Virginia, you have cast 33 votes for Dominic and 75 votes for Anderson," said Bennett-Hawthorne.

"Washington, you have 118 votes, so how do you choose to cast them," asked Bennett-Hawthorne?

"Madam Secretary, we are the state of Washington, and we are a proud state that believes in building bridges and not walls, and we gladly believe in fighting the threat against climate change, and standing up for the working families of America, so we proudly cast 74 votes for the progressive voice, Senator Elias Dominic, 42 votes for the next president of the United States of America, Cynthia Norwell Anderson, and 2 abstentions," said the delegate from Washington.

"Washington, you have cast 74 votes for Dominic and 42 votes for Anderson," said Bennett-Hawthorne.

"West Virginia, you have 37 votes, so how do you choose to cast them," asked Bennett-Hawthorne?

"Madam Secretary, home of some of the most compassion people when any disaster strikes, the home of putting people first, proudly cast 19 votes for the next president of the United States of America, Cynthia Norwell Anderson, and 18 votes for Senator Elias Dominic," said the delegate from the state of West Virginia.

"West Virginia, you have cast 18 votes for Dominic and 19 votes for Anderson," said Bennett-Hawthorne.

"Wisconsin, you have 96 votes, so how do you choose to cast them," asked Bennett-Hawthorne?

"Madam Secretary, Wisconsin, the Badger State, the state where Americans still create and manufacture products, the state where cheese is made, the home of shipbuilding, tools, beer, and the paper industry, the state of Wisconsin cast 49 votes for Senator Elias Dominic and 47 votes for the next president of the United States of America, Cynthia Norwell Anderson," said the delegate from Wisconsin.

"Wisconsin, you have cast 49 votes for Dominic and 47 votes for Anderson," said Bennett-Hawthorne.

"Wyoming, you have 18 votes, so how do you choose to cast them," asked Bennett-Hawthorne?

"Madam Secretary, the state of equality, the state with many firsts, the state with the first national park, the first national monument, the first state to give women the right to vote, so we are proud to cast 7 votes for Senator Elias Dominic and 11 votes for Cynthia Norwell Anderson, the next president of the United States of America," said the delegate from the state of Wyoming.

"Wyoming, you have cast 7 votes for Dominic and 11 votes for Anderson," said Bennett-Hawthorne.

"Vermont, how do you choose to cast your 26 votes," asked Bennett-Hawthorne?

"Madam Secretary, I am the chair of the Vermont United Labourist Party, the state where the political revolution began, the state that will lead us into the future, and the state with great leadership that will combat a modern-day McCarthy, Carlton Winters, so we proudly cast 22 votes for Senator Elias Dominic and 4 votes for the next president of the United States of America, Cynthia Norwell Anderson, and now it is my privilege and honor to introduce Senator Elias Dominic," said the delegate from Vermont.

"Thank you, and hello Madam Chair, I move to suspend the rules and procedures of this convention and I move that all votes cast by the delegates of this convention be mirrored in the official record, and I also move that Cynthia Norwell Anderson be selected as the official nominee for the National United Peoples' Traditionalist Labor Workers Party for president of the United States of America," said Senator Elias Dominic.

"Thank you, thank you Senator Dominic; the Senator from the state of Vermont, Elias Dominic, has requested to suspend the rules and to nominate Cynthia Norwell Anderson by acclamation as the presidential candidate of the National United Peoples' Traditionalist Labor Workers Party," said Bennett-Hawthorne.

"Is there a second," asked Bennett-Hawthorne?

"All in favor of the motion say I and all opposed say No," said Bennett-Hawthorne.

"No one opposed, okay, the AYEs have it," said Bennett-Hawthorne.

"Have a great rest of the night and the rest of the week," said Bennett-Hawthorne.

With that, Cynthia Norwell Anderson became the official nominee for president of the National United Peoples' Traditionalist Labor Workers Party and the first female candidate in American history of a major political party, so it was proclaimed.

Everyone was happy and cheering because it was one of the most historic nights in the history of a major political party.

No one ever thought this day would arrive but it is here now and everything will just be part of the past now.

There are no words for what the people who support Cynthia Norwell Anderson can say right now because they are excited about winning in November.

Tonight is the third night of the convention and there is only one speaker left of the night to give a speech, with Tony Dennis already giving his acceptance speech for vice president, excluding the closing prayer of the night's events.

"Ladies and gentlemen, please welcome to the stage, the current president of the United States of America, Barrington Hashim Martin," said the announcer to the audience.

"*Thank you.*

It is a pleasure to be here tonight.

You know, it is exactly twelve years ago that I first attended and spoke at my first United Labourist convention, and it was such an extremely rewarding experience.

My two daughters attended as well along with my life, and what time has passed.

My daughters always tell me how my hair has changed and all of the things that has happened since I been there.

That was a long time ago, around the summer of 2004, and a lot has changed since then and now.

So, I would just like to reflect back on the progress that we have made as a country together and what we need to move forward, because it is a time of opportunity for everyone, and it is a time for everyone to unite in order to make history again.

Tonight marks the eve of Cynthia Norwell Anderson's acceptance speech of the presidential nomination for the United Labourists, and at the moment, we are at a historic feat in America when a woman can become the presidential nominee of a major political party.

This is the best thing that could happen to America, as she is the leader of the free world.

Tonight, let's reflect of what we did to get here, and how we as a party fixed the problems faced by America in the past.

When I took office, we were in the midst of one of the worst possible economic crises in the world.

The economy was tanking and the big banks did not want to accept responsibility.

We had banks and financial institutions taking advantage of the poor.

There was simply no accountability or action taken by the banks to fix the crisis. Instead, they foreclosed on homeowners.

Instead, a new problem created.

Automakers were on the brink of survival and people soon had to decide if they wanted to buy coupes and small sedan or SUVs, and that was a serious issue.

Our economy was on the brink of collapse.

But now, we are back on top, with our 401(k)s soaring and a booming economy, with 15 million jobs and counting since I took over as your president.

Our auto industry set new records with production facilities all around the world. It was one of the worst recessions in nearly 80 years and it was at a time when no one thought we could recover because we were in such a financial mess.

But today, unemployment has reached ten year lows and we are at the height of our game.

We finally declared healthcare is a human right in America after nearly a century of trying to help Americans live better lives, and not just a privilege for the very few.

After the rise of Middle Eastern Oil, we finally stopped relying on foreign energy needs, and we are moving towards with becoming the number one oil producer in the world.

And we have tripled our effort and gains on clean energy.

Together, we have done great on energy, but that is not all we have achieved.

We finally declared justice against the most dangerous terrorists in the world, Osama bin Laden, and we have already brought home many of our troops home from abroad that were stationed in Iraq and Afghanistan.

But we can do more and we did.

By using diplomacy, Iran can no longer get their hands on very dangerous nuclear weapons.

And we opened a brand new chapter with Cuba by opening up a new relationship

We helped students out with their college debt by instituting strict policies. We helped institute policies that protect everyday American from fraud.

We helped cut in half the number of veterans living on the streets because of homelessness.

We proved with kindness and love that anyone can marry making marriage equality possible.

America and Americans have learned countlessly that nothing is impossible and no matter what obstacle we might face we will get things done.

And we brought almost 200 countries to the table to help sign into a new climate treaty, because we saw what was happening to our planet, and they could see the threat of climate change as well.

By many standards and measures, America is stronger than ever, and it continues to grow every day since the day of our founding.

But make it clear, we still have things to improve on.

And tonight, I am here to tell you with every victory there will be some setbacks, but we do have some more work to do, and I am here to explain that.

Today, we still fall short of helping the needy.

There are still many families living from paycheck to paycheck.

This results in children suffering because they don't know if they are going to survive or live under a roof for another day.

Today, we still have many people struggling, even though the economy is the greatest it has ever been in our history.

There is still poverty in our neighborhoods and we need to fix that.

We are currently working on criminal justice reform and we are seeing how many unjust crimes that have been committed against innocent people.

My office is personally working with local communities to help make sure violence and gun violence comes to an end, because we have too much casualties based on people owning weapons that they shouldn't.

We will make sure that ends.

And, as we continue, it will only get better, so there is more to look forward to.

But, this November, there is a big choice.

We could either move forward with our proven agenda or all of our progress will be set back over the past few hundred years, and we can't afford that to happen.

We still have time to give people the raise they deserve and we will be working towards a living wage of at least $15 per hour, because people and families have bills to pay, and they need to provide food and shelter in order to provide.

We need to help our children in school by fixing our failing public school systems.

There is a need to provide better education and that will ultimately help society to better educate the future generations.

It is a fact that our children must learn the right way by engaging in universal programs that promote unity.

We are not the best country in the world like we used to when it comes to education and that is just a disappointment because we have some of the brightest people and best universities in the world but there is still a knowledge gap.

We can fix this and we will but we need to make sure our streets are kept safe first."

If our streets aren't kept safe then there will be crime and the children can't learn because their education would be disrupted, so it is a thing of trying to end this senseless violence.

We still have time and we can do it.

But November is only a short time away, and if we don't get out the vote, you will have someone you will regret in office, and you don't want the failed policies from a certain political party that brought you the recession that nearly killed our great economy.

No, you want a person who will able to institute reform.

Look, this is a fundamental choice, so you can decide to vote for a person who makes up all kinds of nonsense or you could vote for someone such as Cynthia Norwell Anderson who has the most experience in decades to lead this country to a brighter tomorrow.

There is a case of proven leadership in one of those people but the other one just feels it is fine to discriminate against Mexicans and people from the rest of the world.

The other candidate just keeps on repeating some racist and hatred against innocent people and he has no regard for human rights.

So, you could either vote for that mess or you could vote for the best record, Cynthia Norwell Anderson.

America is a beacon of hope with some of the best people in the world.

We allow people to live here and they can accomplish anything if they set their hearts on it.

We have the American dream. People are able to break down barriers here because other countries make it impossible.

We are a country of hope and change and we embrace everyone regardless of what they believe.

And that is the America that I know.

That is the America I was born in.

That is the America I want to live in and not some dystopian future that blocks out people looking for better jobs just because of their skin color, because we are better than that.

Look, 8 years ago, Cynthia and I were rivals, and she gladly endorsed me at the convention, and she was a very tough opponent to beat because she had one hell of a team.

And for that, I rewarded her by offering a job in my administration after I won when I took office in January, so it is a time we must unite, even if we are opponents trying to win one of the most powerful offices in the free world.

But this isn't about me.

This is about her and why she is the best for the office of the presidency.

I still remember that day on 9/11 when she demonstrated her strong tenacity on the problem of terrorism.

She has fought for everyday Americans when she was the Senator from New York.

She made sure her constituents were protected from harm. And then in 2008 I asked her to become the next Secretary of State, and she did a tremendous job at it.

She made sure that there was justice for the innocents killed by Osama bin Laden almost 15 years ago.

And she was in favor of the mission in targeting him.

It does not matter if you had the most experience or least experience, because nothing can really prepare you for the job of the presidency.

You will have to just wait and see every day.

But Cynthia has been in that role by sitting in the Situation Room and she has observed the demands of the job, so she knows what it takes to lead a country.

She has been part of those important decisions and truly understands the threat of a global crisis.

She knows something is important at stake when taking care of our children, our elders, the working family, the soldier, the veteran, and the small business owner.

She always listens to the people, even if America is in the midst of a crisis.

And she never quits because she always wants to get things done.

And that is the Cynthia that I know and that is what she will do for America.

She will fight for you and everyone who deserves a chance to succeed.

Just look at her running mate, a person with proven experience and a track record.

He always gets things done and he knows when there is a problem that needs to be fixed.

He was the governor of Virginia during one of the most tragic shootings in the history of America.

His record is just spotless with amazing leadership.

And then you have Carlton Winters, and he doesn't really have a plan, because he says he wants to keep out Mexicans.

He doesn't really seem like a facts guy.

He really has no plan to solve anything.

Everything he says is just nonsense.

Sure, he might be a businessman, but he does not know what it takes to take operate a government.

Look, he is facing lawsuits from many people and is being sued for fraud. Does that sound like the person you want to run a country?

No, it doesn't, because he will wreck our economy and he will bring down everything, resulting in chaos.

Let me tell you something, a business is not the same thing as a government, so if you run a business that doesn't really qualify you to run a country.

He doesn't even pay his workers or contractors.

Everyone who has ever worked for him feels cheated, and that is not the person that should lead America into the future.

Do you really believe that some 70 year old person disregarding rights to people will be good for America?

Well, if you do, then you will probably end up voting for him.

But if you are actually concerned about your everyday life, then you will vote for Cynthia, because she will make sure the economy grows, that your bills will be paid, that healthcare is a human right and not just a privilege for just the few.

She will do that and more because she cares. Carlton Winters favors a tax cut in favor of the wealthy class but Cynthia believes in a fair tax code that makes sure everyone pays their fair share of taxes to the government.

Cynthia is for higher wages and wants to see every day Americans prosper.

She will grant you better benefits.

Wall Street will no longer be able to get away with what they do because they will be better regulated with much stricter enforcement.

And if you want any of that you should vote for Cynthia Norwell Anderson.

Let me tell you more about what Cynthia will do.

If you care about our national security, then rest assured, because she will keep you safe in a dangerous world.

It is clear that Cynthia is well-respected around the world.

She works well with our intelligence teams and everyone around the world to make sure Americans and American interests are kept safe from the dangers of today.

Our troops trust and believe in her.

Our troops has pounded ISIL into a pulp but there is still much time left to go until they are fully defeated, and Cynthia won't rest until they are obliterated.

But the other person does not see it that way.

Carlton Winters and his base believe in some sort of conspiracy that there is a more dangerous terrorist organization that is out there called the Victory World Front.

He cites evidence but I never heard of the Victory World Front and neither have my members of my administration.

I don't even believe if any of our loyal supporters have even heard of it.

So, really, you have a tough guy saying a terrorist organization exists without any evidence, and then you have a proven leader with an excellent track record.

Who would you rather vote for?

And now Carlton Winters called our military a disaster by saying we don't get things done.

He says America is at its weakest points in decades.

And he also says NATO is not holding up to their commitment.

Well, he is either clueless or making things up.

He fails to see our troops working with our allies in order to combat our enemies.

Instead, he cozies up to Russia and the allies of Leninov.

He does not know about the billions of people who go to America just to experience a new life that will be a beacon of hope, freedom, dignity, and human rights.

He rather calls America a turbulent place that lost its greatness.

He says he wants to see America prosper, to see America stronger, and to see America great.

Well, America is already great.

It is already strong and it remains the most prosperous country in the world to this day.

And I will say that is one reason why Carlton Winters will lose.

Our democracy depends on helping everyone helping each other and not leaving our allies behind.

Carlton Winters is just selling the American people short and that is another reason why he will lose in November.

He has no real solutions, and everything he says will set us back over 200 years.

America doesn't depend on any single person or entity because what makes it great is everyone who live and work here.

It relies upon all of us to live in harmony.

Our power does not originate from a king or a prince but from some immortal declarations that was declared right here over 200 years ago.

We hold these truths to be self-evident, that all men are created equal; that together, we, the people, can form a more perfect union.

That is who we are and no one can ever take it away from us because we believe we can shape our own destiny in order to combat tyranny committed by an abusive government.

We have done it before and we know we can stop it in the future.

America has always relied on us working together. And Cynthia knows that is necessary to get things done.

She knows nothing is black and white.

Cynthia knows it takes compromise to get things done in order to succeed and she knows democracy never really works if we keep demonizing each other.

She knows we can and must fight for progress in order to move things forward with time.

Cynthia knows we can have a fair, just, and lawful immigration system with open arms for anyone that wants to escape the threat of gang violence and economic poverty.

She knows about the constant economic inequality plaguing the inner cities and how it must be difficult to help people with the American dream.

And I know it can be frustrating with democracy because people are divided on the issues.

But I promise you that we can work together and that Cynthia will be there for everyone.

We can work together on the issues to make this country more united than it was ever before.

If you want to fight for the future of this country, then it is important we combat climate change to stop the harmful effects that we did to our atmosphere, and you can support Cynthia.

If you want to stop our children from getting killed by gun violence, then you will vote for Cynthia because she will make sure commonsense gun laws are passed so she can sign them into law and to finally stand up to the gun lobby.

If you support economic equality you can vote for Cynthia because she will fight for a better wage.

If you support the right for all to have universal healthcare, then you can support Cynthia, because she will make sure no insurance company denies anyone health coverage that they need to stay alive.

And I know, Cynthia and I do have our critics, but they are purely meant to be divisive and hurtful.

That isn't the America I know with all of that divisive rhetoric because the America I know accepts people for who they are and never discriminates against anyone.

Sure, America has gone through several different times, but we always come together to help each other when in need.

And sure, my time in office hasn't caused everything to be fixed, but with Cynthia at the helms of our party, we can move forward with our agenda of finally making America into a better place.

But you, the American people, have brought me up by giving other people help when they couldn't fight for change anymore.

It gave me hope because you helped to elect the first African-American president in the history of the United States of America.

And that is surely a change for the hope of bettering our society, because it says anyone can break a barrier to seek what you want.

You've vindicated me before and this hasn't been the last but it was not the first time.

You showed the world that we can work together by engaging in diplomacy without killing innocent people overseas.

You helped everyone to realize that times are changing and that certain things are no longer acceptable today.

And many of you have never been involved in politics until now, because you saw no interest, but today you see this is probably one of the most important elections in your lives.

You are the organizers of this new movement and nothing will be possible without you.

So tonight, I am asking all of you to continue to support my friend, Cynthia Norwell Anderson, and to vote for her in November, because she has proven time and time again that she can lead us into a bright future.

She is the best hope for progress not to die.

Tonight, I ask you support Cynthia the same way as you did with me, because of her integrity of leadership.

Twelve years ago when I addressed this convention, I offered my expression and message of hope, and we have gotten a long way since then.

Every day we are making progress and we can help make America a better society to be more inclusive.

And for these past almost 8 years in office, you have vindicated me, because you have seen me worked with Cynthia and our allies around the world, hoping to make sure nothing goes haywire.

So, if you're ready, then I'm ready to pass the baton to Cynthia Norwell Anderson, to be the next president of the United States of America and the first woman president in the history of our country.

Thank you all for this incredible journey during this past 8 years and we can achieve more progress with Cynthia Norwell Anderson as the next president of the United States of America so that we can move forward with our goal of progress."

Barrington Martin's speech fired up the crowd and it was surely the best thing all week, but it shows America what people might want, and that is just the beginning of it all.

And today was probably seen as the best night of the convention.

But like that, the third night of the convention concluded after the closing prayer.

Tonight is the last night of the convention, and it is already underway, as there is excitement to hear from Cynthia Norwell Anderson give her much anticipated acceptance speech.

And then it was time.

"Ladies and gentlemen, delegates and alternates, please give a very warm welcome to the stage, Cynthia Norwell Anderson, the official 2016 presidential nominee of the National United Peoples' Traditionalist Labor Workers Party," said the announcer.

"*Thank you!*

Thank you for being such an amazing audience and thank you for your support.

You know, this weak has been inspiring not only for me and you but for all those young woman out there who never thought that we could break the glass ceiling by becoming a presidential nominee of a major political party.

And to them, well, you persevered, and now we made history by breaking that glass ceiling.

To all of my family, I would just like to thank all of you for being here and supporting my campaign.

And to all of my supporters, your campaigning for me has worked to break the barriers of change.

Without you, we wouldn't be here on this very historic night.

Tonight is a time of change because of what we have accomplished in a very short time.

This week we heard hope from George Anderson.

This week we also heard hope from Barrington Martin.

And America continues to change for the better of society because of progress.

It is accurate and a fact to say Barrington Martin made America a stronger and more prosperous country.

And I would like to thank Elias Dominic and his campaign along with his supporters.

You have started a cause that has opened up to our young voters.

Your campaign has started the change for economic injustice, social injustice, and climate injustice.

Your causes are our causes because we need to fight to make sure progress continues on a path that does not turn back over 200 years of history.

We need your ideas and passion because they are important for progress to continue.

And that is the only way we are going to win, with progress, so we need to move forward.

Everyone, welcome to Philadelphia, the city that was the birthplace of our nation, where everything begin over 200 years ago.

We know how it all began and we are here to make history.

We are here to make sure that we continue the path of radical change brought by 13 unruly colonies in order to defeat a tyrannical King and his parliament.

We are here today to reflect about what they did.

Because that took courage and we are at a time when certain people want to turn back progress.

We are a moment of reckoning and it seems powerful interests want to break us apart.

They want to make sure we won't be able to accomplish what we need to accomplish.

We are losing our bonds of trust and respect from around the world.

And we must acknowledge that we must not anyone or anything to divide us no matter what.

Our founding fathers embraced change because they grew tired of what the British were doing to them.

And we can achieve that same change today.

Listen, we heard Carlton Winters last week, and his message for America was darkness and division.

He will guide us to midnight rather than to a morning in America.

You don't want that because America will fail under his leadership, and he wants to separate us from the rest of the world.

The rest of the world are already down at us and think we are an embarrassment to all of society.

He has made his plan clear of turning back progress, and we can't let that happen.

Now, we know what America is up against.

But he wants us to fear everything and that America is currently facing an inexistent threat from around the world.

He wants to divide us.

He wants us to be afraid.

He wants to make sure we listen to his propaganda.

Well, we will not be afraid.

We will not let him divide us.

Instead, we will rise up to the challenge and will make sure love always win.

We will make sure to continue towards progress and no one will tell us what we can and can't do, because this is America, the best country in the world that allows freedom of expression and speech.

We won't allow any religions to be banned because that goes against our constitution.

And we won't build a wall, because we should welcome anyone fleeing poverty and violence with open arms.

America is a welcoming country and it should remain that way and it shall.

No, instead, we will build an economy that supports the American people of the Middle Class, and not the Wall Street special interests.

We will make sure the billionaires and millionaires pay their fair share of taxes so that everyone is treated equally.

We will move toward a more progressive tax system that doesn't favor the rich.

Too many people have not received a raise in years and we will make sure they do receive a raise.

We will make sure that people are paid a living wage.

And we need to make sure the millions of immigrants are not afraid to contribute to our economy because they are the backbone of our nation, so they will not be afraid because of the threat of deportation.

We won't allow them to be deported because we love our truly patriotic immigrants who support our economy and way of life.

We have a chance to finally fix our immigration system and it will work.

We will build a path towards citizenship for all those immigrants who are already contributing to the economy, because they deserve it, and we will grant amnesty to anyone that fears for their live in their home country because of gang violence and economic hardships because of the difficulty it is to find a good paying job.

We will open up our arms toward freedom, liberty, and the pursuit of happiness.

America is a country of hope and change.

We have the best and most powerful military in the world.

We know the threat of terrorism and we are defeating it head on by engaging the enemy properly.

We know the problem of income inequality, and we know we must make sure the working-class can survive because they are the backbone of our economy.

We must fight for a better tax system that is fair to everyone and we shall make it a goal to help anyone in need.

We must fight the threat of climate change.

We must fight the threat of the on-going crisis that students face when paying off student loans.

We must fight for renewable energy.

We must fight for everything that the American people stand for because progress is good.

So, don't let anyone tell you otherwise, because they won't get far in office.

Last week, Carlton Winters indicated that he can fix everything and he repeated said that throughout his campaign.

Well, he must be forgetting that we have troops fighting on the front lines, that the police are fighting crimes across the country, and the doctors and nurses who are helping to take care of people who need help.

He is forgetting about all those people like teachers that educate students, the entrepreneurs that help move us towards the future with their inventions, and the mothers that must grieve when their child dies from gun violence.

Carlton Winters is just a person that wants to take credit for everything when other people are in fact responsible for it.

He thinks he can take advantage of the weak and poor.

We know he has no plan and he isn't about to develop one that will guide us towards the future.

He says he has experience in business and that is why you should vote for him.

But all he did was stiffed his employees and vendors, so don't count on him doing anything good for the better of society.

You have seen me first hand working as your first lady for eight years.

And then I was the Senator from the state of New York for another 8 years.

After that, I ran for president and lost to Barrington Martin but he rewarded me with an experience that not everyone can accomplish.

He asked me to be his Secretary of State and I accepted the job.

So, I was the Secretary of State for four years in addition to my other political experience.

But let's not forget that I was also a great first lady when my husband was the governor of the state of Arkansas.

I don't know how you could top that but Carlton Winters says he is more experienced than me.

We'll see about that in November to let the people decide.

And I bet you that I will win, because people with experience in public service know what they are doing.

So, you all know about Carlton Winters already, but my campaign actually wants to solve problems.

It's not just about the rhetoric like with Carlton Winters but it is about the issues.

You can say something but then you must act on it.

And we put a team together and gathered facts and found out we have what it takes to win.

You know, we have seen some courageous people here this week, and we know what we have to do.

Because of changes in our laws, we have people who now can get an education.

We have challenged the rhetoric from the Centralists in power in the Senate and the House of Representatives.

We have gotten so far since this country was founded over 200 years ago.

For the first time in history in the United States of America, a major political party, with the help of the people, has nominated a woman for president, and that is a major goal towards progress.

We have seen what the people want and need in order to survive in this great country.

We finally recognized that healthcare was a fundamental human right and not just a privilege for the few.

We took control of our environment by agreeing to the Paris Climate Deal in 2015.

We gave immigrants a path towards a better future and we can still do more for them.

We took on the gun lobby in many progressive states and now no one can purchase military-style weapons.

We took on the economy and the big banks and now it is better than it ever was.

We helped increased education in inner cities so our students will be able to learn better.

We are taking on the threat of climate change by moving towards renewable energy.

We are going to take on campaign finance reform so that the rich and the Wall Street financiers can no longer influence us.

We will make sure our military is able to defeat the enemy so that no more innocent people die.

We will take on immigration and welcome anyone that wants to be here.

We will provide for a better tax code that is fair and progressive for all of America.

And we will do more.

We will accomplish so many things when I'm president, and you will see the difference between rhetoric and getting things done.

So, let's empower everyone.

Let's empower those little girls and boys across America who wants to make it in America like me.

Let's empower the people who work hard for their money to make an honest living.

And let's empower anyone who enjoys America and wants to achieve the American dream in order to be successful.

You know, the United Labourists are the party of working-class Americans but we need to do more so you can be successful.

So, I want to empower everyone to live better lives, and that will be my promise from my first day in office until my last.

I know we can do more.

I know our economy can do better because it isn't working as it should.

I know that America thrives when the middle-class thrives and is successful.

And that's why we need a progressive justice on the Supreme Court, in order to get money out of politics, so that nothing is corrupt.

We need to overturn Citizens United because it empowers the threat of Wall Street financiers corrupting our politicians by lobbyists and the special interests. And we will accomplish that.

For too long our economy has suffered because corporations got rich off of us and they simply don't care.

They are taking advantage of our workers and immigrants who just want to make an honest living.

They are taking advantage to tax loopholes so they can pay less money in taxes.

They are moving overseas because they don't want to pay their fair share in taxes, so they believe they need to pay less.

They have wrecked our economy and that shouldn't stand.

We don't need the 1% to dictate to us what needs to be accomplished because we have the freedom of speech to decide what we want to achieve.

And on day one, I will make sure Wall Street and the corporate interests won't be able to get what they want.

I am fighting for all of you because all of you represent America in her finest moment of success.

We need to keep American jobs here and not ship them overseas because America deserves better.

We need a person with strong leadership to take on the issue of everything.

You need to ask yourself if Carlton Winters has the capacity to become the next Commander-in-Chief of our great country and military and to lead us towards a better future.

He says he is a businessman and always gets things done but he can't even handle a little bit of criticism.

Face it, he will ruin our future and set progress back nearly over 200 years.

He is not the one you want as your president.

I couldn't imagine how he will fix a crisis in the oval office.

He would fail and everyone will be calling on him to resign.

Let's put aside this mean rhetoric and put on the shoes of other people, the people who constantly are attacked by people who want to target the innocent, the weak, and the poor.

We will protect the minorities, the LGBTQ community, the Hispanics, the Latinos, and any other group of people who are part of the American minority.

We have let them all down and all that Carlton Winters will do is to set back progress by not allowing them to participate in the American way of life.

Right now you have to stand up to all of the bullies and the hate that is heard around the world.

You have to realize that we need to protect the people that are the weakest and poorest because they cannot simply defend themselves.

And the founding fathers knew that.

They knew that we had to change in order to succeed.

And that is why we succeeded, because we knew what we had to do to survive.

That is the story of America and we are still here today after 240 years because we knew we must move towards progress to provide for a better future for everyone.

So let's build our own destiny and we can grow stronger together in a much better way because America will be better off and greater once we moves towards greater progress.

Thank you and God bless all of you here tonight and during the week of this convention."

With that, everyone began to celebrate, after the first woman to be nominated as a presidential nominee for a major political party in the United States of America gave her acceptance speech to an excited crowd.

And it was just a spectacular event with much fanfare.

All that was left was the closing prayer of the convention, and that too soon shall come, and it will just go down in the history books of America.

America, as we know it, is in a center of new attention, and that is the best for all, so says the people.

FOUR

I

Excitement and anxiety from critics and supporters of Cynthia Norwell Anderson from around the world became aghast in either tears of joy or nervousness when they learned CBDI director Carl Ronald was reopening the investigation into her missing emails.

It was a surprise no one could understand that supported Anderson.

But Katrina and the campaign of Carlton Winters were glad it was reopened because it meant that there was actually something there to look into.

Today was a marvelous day for all with the exception of Cynthia Norwell Anderson, her campaign, and the people that supported her.

It is a bright day for transparency, at least according to the critics of Cynthia Norwell Anderson.

Anderson's critics are saying that this reopening of the investigation means that CBDI director is taking the crimes committed of Anderson seriously.

It also means that the CBDI director is trying to be as transparent as possible but that is something to be discussed in the future.

"Breaking news, CBDI director Carl Ronald has confirmed that he is reopening an investigation into the emails of Cynthia Norwell Anderson, which is prompting backlash from several leading United Labourists and the supporters of the Anderson campaign but is prompting praise amongst the supporters of Carlton Winters," said Roman Anthony Andrews.

It was just as described, and that wasn't anything new.

The supporters of Cynthia Norwell Anderson are starting to claim that this will have a negative impact on her progressive campaign and it will lead to her loss.

Several pundits in support of Anderson have already decried of the effort of reopening the investigation by saying there is nothing there while the critics of Anderson are saying that she knowingly engaged in unlawful behavior that put our national security at risk for having a private server in order to escape from supplying her records to the parties that demand them under the Freedom of Information Act.

It was just a case of people saying stuff again.

There is already chaos coming from within of the National United Peoples' Traditionalist Labor Workers Party in an attempt to try to figure out what is happening.

And the Centralists are just eating it up.

The goal is for an October surprise and that is what is happening to the Anderson campaign, but by an unexpected friend.

It couldn't get any worse and the supporters of Anderson are just livid about what is happening to their candidate because they view director Ronald as the new enemy of the people for reopening an investigation that seems nonsensical to them as they feel there is nothing there.

That is just how they feel and they believe it to be that way because they want double standards, according to the Centralists and people critical of the United Labourists.

It is for that reason why many of Anderson's supporters believe the reopening of this investigation will lead her to losing the presidential election.

They consider it an all-out war bent on destroying the life of an innocent person who really didn't do anything wrong but they failed to explore all of the facts thinking that Anderson is just above the war, at least according to how the Centralists view it.

But there is a much larger problem of trying to stop an election.

It goes against the very word and meaning of the constitution.

Then something happened again, and it seemed to infuriate both sides to say the least.

"Breaking news, we are just learning that CBDI director Carl Ronald is closing the investigation into Cynthia Norwell Anderson's emails and has concluded no new information was discovered, and we are also just now learning that all of the emails recently discovered were just duplicates of previous emails," said Roman Anthony Andrews.

But it seems that the United Labourists and supporters of Anderson feel betrayed again because the election is only two days away, making it look like a victory for Carlton Winters, yet Anderson still leads in the polls and has a 99.99% chance of becoming the next president of the United States of America, so if they believe that then they should have nothing to worry about.

It is just the small price to pay but soon it will be all for the best and this will just be a note in the history books.

And that seems to be what is taking place right now.

Already, the supporters of Cynthia Norwell Anderson are blasting director Ronald for closing the investigation two days before the presidential election.

They view it a threat to democracy and they believe it is wrong to influence the political arena with such nonsense.

It will be all over before they know it but it is just following protocol so they must be patient and wait for the outcome on Tuesday night.

It could be a long night and the election might not be decided until the early morning of the next day, so people will be glued to their television sets.

It all seems to just be a little too crazy to watch the pundits analyzing what they see as a threat and what they view as necessary to happen.

That is just the beginning of something that will just create more chaos and division.

II

Election Day has arrived and everybody is anxiously waiting to see who will win.

No one knows who will become the next president of the United States of America but the pundits all believe there is an extremely clear consensus that it will be Cynthia Norwell Anderson because of the polls and her popularity amongst everyone.

Well, that is jumping to a conclusion before the people decide and it won't be known until the votes are counted by the precincts and the election staff.

So, it seems unwise to make a claim that doesn't exist yet until the votes are tallied and reported.

That just seems to be the most responsible thing to do.

But no one actually believes that, so the time will come when people rethink their solutions.

So it remains to be seen at what will happen next.

"Breaking news, we are waiting for the first polls to close, so stay tuned to us for the latest election coverage for the 2016 presidential election and who will win," said Roman Anthony Andrews.

And there it was, the most important night in the history of the country, because it would decide the next president of the United States of America.

"The first polls have officially closed and we are waiting for live results from Indiana, Kentucky, Florida, Georgia, South Carolina, Virginia, and Vermont in the next hour or so," said Roman Anthony Andrews.

"We have an all-star lineup so please stay tuned for the latest updates in the election coverage, but right now it is still too close to call in Georgia, South Carolina, and Virginia, while Florida still has some polling places open in the northern part of the panhandle," said Roman Anthony Andrews.

But as of now, we can project that Carlton Winters will win the states of Indiana and Kentucky and Cynthia Norwell Anderson will win the state of Vermont," said Roman Anthony Andrews.

"Let's now turn to Aaron Campbellson who is at the magic panel," said Roman Anthony Andrews.

"So far tonight Carlton Winters is in the lead with 19 electoral votes while Cynthia Norwell Anderson is trailing him with 3, but expect that to change as we get in more states later on, and that can happen very soon and probably in an hour or so, which could put Anderson in the lead, so we expect many outstanding states to be called soon, and back to you Roman," said Aaron Campbellson.

"Okay, thank you for that insight Aaron, and now stay tuned for a very important projection; we can now project that the state of West Virginia is called for Carlton Winters while it is still too close to call for the states of North Carolina, so let's go to our all-star lineup to get their opinions on the night's events," said Roman Anthony Andrews.

"I generally believe all is lost for Carlton Winters if he fails to win Ohio, North Carolina, Texas, Florida, and Pennsylvania, but I don't think he will be able to win because Cynthia Norwell Anderson is expected to beat him in a landslide, but let's just wait to see what's going to happen tonight," said Gina Tucker.

"Okay, we can now project that South Carolina has been called for Carlton Winters, but in 10 minutes from now we expect live results from 20 states plus Washington DC, so stay tuned," said Roman Anthony Andrews. "

Right now it is still too early to tell if Carlton Winters has the momentum to win, but we might know in the near future, yet this could last well into the morning and that could mean bad news for the Anderson campaign because it might show Carlton Winters with a fighting chance, which would result in an upset victory and possibly bad news," said Leslie Cohen the national political correspondent of National Media News Network.

"Okay, it is the top of the hour, and we can now make several major projections so stand by; we can now project Carlton Winters has won the states of Alabama, Mississippi, Oklahoma, and Tennessee while Cynthia Norwell Anderson is projected to win the states of Connecticut, Delaware, Illinois, Maryland, Massachusetts, New Jersey, Rhode Island, and in the non-state of the District of Columbia; we are still waiting for Florida as the polls are now officially closed there and also for some other states that are too close to call and some other states that are in more than one time zone so we won't know any information on those results until all polling places have officially closed, but let's go to the magic panel to see who is ahead and who is behind," said Roman Anthony Andrews.

"Right now Cynthia Norwell Anderson is in the lead with 75 electoral college votes while Carlton Winters is trailing her with 66 votes with 129 votes still undecided," said Aaron Campbellson.

Okay, we can now make a projection that Carlton Winters has won the state of Arkansas, giving him a much needed win, but he is still trailing with 72 electoral college votes to Anderson's 75, but expect more live results in the next hour," said Roman Anthony Andrews.

"It is now the top of the hour, 9:00 pm Eastern Time, and several states have either closed their polling places and or are now reporting their live results while others are too close to call, and get ready for a major projection; okay, we can now project that Carlton Winters has won the states of Kansas, Louisiana, Nebraska, North Dakota, South Dakota, Texas, and Wyoming while Cynthia Norwell Anderson has won the state of New York; the states of Arizona, Colorado, Michigan, Minnesota, New Mexico, and Wisconsin are still too close to call, so let's go to the magic panel with Aaron Campbellson," said Roman Anthony Andrews.

"Roman, Carlton Winters is currently in the lead again with 137 Electoral College votes while Cynthia Norwell Anderson is trailing with 104 Electoral College votes while 190 votes are still undecided because those states have yet to be called; as we look at the map here on the magic panel it seems Carlton Winters is winning where he is supposed to but the question is can he actually keep it up to firmly close the gap on Anderson and preventing her from winning," said Aaron Campbellson.

"Thank you Aaron, and now we can report on the next states that will close in the next hour, so please stay tuned to us for the latest coverage," said

Roman Anthony Andrews.

"Okay, it is the top of the hour again, and more states have closed, so let's go to Aaron Campbellson at the magic panel," said Roman Anthony Andrews.

"Roman, the states of Idaho and Oregon haven't officially closed yet because they are located in more than one time zone, while it is still too close to call in the states of Iowa, Nevada, and Utah, but we are expected to project a winner soon in the state of Montana, so we will just wait and see to what will happen," said Aaron Campbellson.

"We can now make a projection for 3 states; okay, we can now project that Carlton Winters will win the states of Montana and Missouri while Cynthia Norwell Anderson is projected to win the state of New Mexico, and back to Aaron Campbellson," said Roman Anthony Andrews.

"Roman, we are seeing the voters deciding democracy tonight, and so far the exit polls do not match what we are seeing, so expect Carlton Winters and Anderson going back and forth with the lead in the Electoral College," said Aaron Campbellson.

"Okay, get ready for a major projection; we can now project Carlton Winters will win the state of Ohio while Cynthia Norwell Anderson will win the state of Virginia and Colorado, so it seems Anderson has put the brakes on Carlton Winters for at least one needed state that could make a difference in the outcome of this election, and back to the magic panel," said Roman Anthony Andrews.

"Yes, Roman, we are seeing that both campaigns seem to be performing very well, but we still have some time to go until we find and determine a clear consensus, so the bottom line here is tonight will be a very long night," said Aaron Campbellson.

"It seems like a night that is up to the people," said Roman Anthony Andrews.

Everything about the election was just kind of interesting, as the media and the establishment were expecting Anderson to be ahead by many Electoral College votes because they expect her to win the same way as Barrington Martin did, but that did not seem likely, so the media just had to see what would happen next, or else there would be a consensus that Carlton Winters didn't win fairly.

And then something happened, but it was just as predictable to happen this way.

"If you are currently tuning in, please standby for a major projection, because it is the top of the hour of 11:00 pm Eastern Time, so don't change that channel; we can now project that Cynthia Norwell Anderson has won the states of California, Hawaii, Oregon, and Washington, putting her over the edge of the Carlton Winters campaign while Carlton Winters is projected to win Idaho and the much needed state of North Carolina," said Roman Anthony Andrews.

And it was just keep coming, as the night grew older and the dawn of a new day was almost here.

It would be something big for everyone to see what will happen next.

"We are just moments away from a major projection; okay, we can now project Carlton Winters will win the states of Florida, Utah, and Iowa, putting him on the path toward potential victory, but he still needs to win other states to seal the victory," said Roman Anthony Andrews.

And then it was chaos, because the inevitable happened that no one saw coming.

"Breaking news, we can now project Carlton Winters will win the state of Georgia, so let's go to Aaron Campbellson at the magic panel to see the potential paths for victory," said Roman Anthony Andrews.

"Roman, if you look at the math, there isn't much of a path for Cynthia Norwell Anderson, as Carlton Winters is just winning everywhere across America," said Aaron Campbellson.

"Okay, we now turn to our all-star lineup of panelists," said Roman Anthony Andrews.

"Congratulations to both of you because your side has clearly won and I can see it in the writing when there is no path to victory anymore, but I would just like to say what we saw here tonight is a backlash against the minorities because tonight we saw oppression will win once again and more people will find it difficult to live in America so they might see the results differently," said Terrell Dominique.

"We can now go to the victory center of Cynthia Norwell Anderson where she and her supporters will celebrate if they somehow win the election tonight or early in the morning," said Roman Anthony Andrews.

"Right now we are seeing a loss of excitement from the people and supporters here as they continuously wait for more results, but they don't know what to think of the current situation because they seem to feel lost, and there is a sense here that their dream of the first woman president of the United States of America won't come true, so they are starting to realize that by crying or getting a bit nervous of the news that Carlton Winters will become the next president of the United States of America," said Ryan Margherita.

"Okay, thanks for that updated information Ryan, and now we go to Aaron Campbellson who is currently at the magic panel to give us the live update of the current Electoral College vote at the magic panel," said Roman Anthony Andrews.

"Roman, Carlton Winters is currently in the lead with 244 Electoral College votes while Cynthia Norwell Anderson is trailing with her 209 Electoral College votes, with 82 undecided, so if we look at the map it will be impossible to say how the Cynthia Norwell Anderson campaign will win this election at this point in time," said Aaron Campbellson.

"Thank you Aaron, and now we must wait for the live results from a few outstanding states, so please stay tuned for the latest updates and we will be right back after these announcements," said Roman Anthony Andrews to the people who are watching the news.

All was a loss of words for what was happening tonight and it seemed there is no path for victory for Cynthia Norwell Anderson.

This won't end well for some people because they will be in tears about what to do next and maybe they will try to target the Electoral College in order to sway some of the voters to become faithless electors.

That is certainly something that might happen on December 19, but it remains to be seen. But that seems to be a bit of a stretch to say the least.

"We are about to make a major projection so stay tuned; okay, we can now project that Carlton Winters will win the state of Pennsylvania, putting him on the path to victory and nearly giving him the required number of 270 Electoral College votes, and we can also call Alaska for Carlton Winters along with the 2nd Congressional District of Maine," said Roman Anthony Andrews.

A short time later there was something happening at the victory center where the Anderson campaign would celebrate with her supporters should she win.

"Ryan, are we learning anything new about the Anderson campaign and the future of it," asked Roman Anthony Andrews?

"Roman, we are just learning her campaign manager is going to speak soon, but wait, I think he is coming to the podium now," said Ryan Margherita.

"Folks, it's been a very long night and there are still votes to count, but don't get discourage yet. We can still win this but now I would ask for everyone to go home to get some much needed rest and we will announce something tomorrow."

"Okay, you heard it here from Nathaniel Coruschi, the campaign manager for Cynthia Norwell Anderson, who has told everyone to go home and has yet to concede defeat, but we are hearing reports that Cynthia Norwell Anderson will not show up and instead will stay in her home waiting for more results," said Ryan Margherita.

"We are still waiting for several outstanding states so please stay tuned to our coverage if you want to learn what happens," said Roman Anthony Andrews.

And then something drastic happened that was not expected to in the history of the two-party system.

"Breaking news, we can now project that Carlton Winters will win the state of Wisconsin, breaking the blue wall that once belonged to the United Labourists, and we are now learning that Cynthia Norwell Anderson has called Carlton Winters in order to concede during a hotly contested battle of the campaign season," said Roman Anthony Andrews.

And it happened again for another unexpected surprising turn of events that left the supporters of Anderson stunned and in disbelief because they thought she had a chance.

"Okay, we can now make a major projection; we can now project that Carlton Winters will become the next president of the United States of America, marking a bitter battle over the past 18 months after accusing all of his opponents of something sinister, but we still have a few outstanding states to declare, but let's go to Aaron Campbellson for an update again," said Roman Anthony Andrews.

"Roman, if you looked at what happened tonight, it seemed impossible to the establishment, but Carlton Winters is expected to win in Arizona and Michigan, which should declare him the winner in a matter of days or weeks, so we won't find out today, so I think tonight or last night because it is the next day, that the unconventional candidate won due to his policies and how he approaches everything and the American people seem to like that," said Aaron Campbellson.

"Okay, we are learning now that Carlton Winters is about to give his victory speech, so let's listen in to see what he has to say," said Roman Anthony Andrews.

"*Thank you, thank you, you have all been all wonderful throughout the entire campaign.*

A few moments ago I received a phone call from my opponent, Cynthia Norwell Anderson, and I would just like to thank her for a hard fought battle, but clearly my message is better.

Anyway, there are still a few outstanding states but we are expected to win there.

And in the coming days and weeks, I will start the process of getting people together so that I can take the oath of office on January 20, 2017.

I would just like to thank my campaign manager, Katelynn George, the first woman to lead a conservative Centralist presidential nominee to victory, and my campaign chairman Mr. George Charles, a great man who understands that we must listen to the people and understand that socialism, communism, and Marxism must be rejected.

But most of all I would like to thank all of my supporters, because without you we couldn't have won this election.

Again, I would like to say thanks to all of you and I hope you have a great rest of the night or whatever is left of it and God Bless."

"Okay, you heard it there, Carlton Winters gave his victory speech and is forming a transition team to take over the presidency when he assumes office in January of next year," said Roman Anthony Andrews.

And just like that, Carlton Winters officially became the president-elect of the United States of America.

"Today is November 10, 2016, and we can now confirm that Carlton Winters has won the state of Arizona, but we are still waiting for Michigan," said Roman Anthony Andrews.

And then it happened again, which was unsurprising at this point in time, so it remains unhinged.

"Breaking news today is November 28, 2016, and the state of Michigan has certified the election results, and Carlton Winters has won that state as well, so this brings his tally up to 306 Electoral College votes, making it one of the largest upsets since Barrington Martin won reelection 4 years ago," said Roman Anthony Andrews.

It was now clear that the only way to deny Carlton Winters his win was through the Electoral College but that too would not lead to a victory for some white knight or the election of Cynthia Norwell Anderson, and it was just like that.

III

The Electoral College has met already and Carlton Winters is unanimously selected as the next president of the United States of America to begin his term on January 20, 2017, but there were 7 faithless electors who didn't vote for their chosen nominee.

"Breaking news, there were 2 faithless electors who didn't vote for Carlton Winters and 5 faithless electors that refused to vote for Cynthia Norwell Anderson, and this brings the tally to a total of 304 Electoral College votes for Carlton Winters and 227 Electoral College votes for Cynthia Norwell Anderson, so Carlton Winters is a lot closer to victory," said Roman Anthony Andrews.

All that was left was a joint session of Congress on January 6, 2017 to officially certify the results.

And then it happened, the Vice President of the United States of America, Walter Bryant Ross, and now officially certified Carlton Winters as the 45th president of the United States of America and Timothy Simon as the 48th vice president of the United States of America, with some people booing the results.

Meanwhile, Katrina is nowhere to be found in the vicinity of the Washington DC area.

Who knows?

It could all be just an elaborate ruse to set up and frame a duly elected president.

But there are just more important issues to deal with.

She could be back in the year 2005 or it could be that she is currently hiding.

No one actually cares until they find something that they don't like and that is probably what is going to happen, so it will be an issue to deal with for the next several months as everything else is determined in a way that makes no sense at all.

But the details lie in the message of what is being portrayed because everything could be good and then something bad happens because someone might have an agenda.

It is all the reason why nothing makes sense at all and it will be the reason why chaos penetrates all layers of government for the reason of forming discord from within in order to alienate and divide the people.

That is just the crazy thing that always happens because it is gospel to certain people, which makes it all too crazy and certain for doom.

And it will solve nothing because that has always been that way in the way of the people.

Before long, everything will come to an end, but in the meantime no one cares a bit, and that will probably be something to tell the future of the world about the historic election of a nonpolitician to the White House in some sort of unprecedented action.

But there is just the epitome of what will come next, and that will be the agenda being set by the administration of Carlton Winters.

So it remains to be seen until there is time and when it will be necessary to declare nothing.

The most important day arrived and it was filled with fanfare and excitement from supporters of Carlton Winters and for people who wanted to watch the inauguration of a newly-elected president being sworn in by the chief justice of the Supreme Court.

But there was another event happening at the same time.

Thousands of people who support and are part of the female empowerment agenda started marching against the idea of Carlton Winters being sworn in as the next president of the United States of America because they don't like his agenda or politics.

It was just amazing that these people want to say that Carlton Winters is anti-women, all because he doesn't support abortion.

And it was just like that, because they didn't care, as they were just the extreme elements of the United Labourist movement.

It was all too familiar.

But before long, Carlton Winters was on stage ready to take the oath of office with the people and his supporters watching.

"Do you, Howard Carlton Winters I, solemnly swear that you will faithfully execute the Office of the President of the United States, and will do the best of the ability, preserve, protect, and defend the Constitution of the United States," asked Chief Justice Franklin Howards?

"I, Howard Carlton Winters I, do solemnly swear that I will faithfully execute the Office of the President of the United States, and will do the best of my Ability, preserve, protect, and defend the Constitution of the United States," said Carlton Winters.

It was official, Carlton Winters was now the 45th president of the United States of America, and Timothy Simon officially took the oath of office as the 48th vice president of the United States of America after that in a much anticipated event of the century.

Meanwhile, Katrina was watching the events from a distance in order to avoid anyone spotting her.

But on the other side of town, things were already in despair, as angry rioters decided they had enough of what America stood for.

Sirens blazing, as people started to panic, as rioters started to light businesses and vehicles on fire.

One by one, they flipped over a limo and any object that were in their way.

Angered at what they saw as the new president, they threw Molotov Cocktails into the streets and roads, lighting them up with sparks of fire.

Windows were broken with shards of glass everywhere in the vicinity of the area.

People were panicking as the masked rioters were just causing chaos everywhere.

It was just a sight to see and that would be at the center of attention.

And then all hell broke loose, with businesses burning to the ground and the police called.

It was a tragic event and no one knew what was happening, but just pure chaos.

And then out of nowhere, Katrina disappeared again, but this time into a glimmering flash of a bright white light that just seemed all too very familiar.

IV

Suddenly, there was a loud noise that sounded like the crashing of a jet engine, but it was probably anything.

Out of nowhere, Katrina was buck naked in a hotel room in the present day, and a news report came up looking for a mystery person clearly resembling that of her, but it was all just pure luck.

"Breaking news, we have learned someone by the name of Katrina Maribelle is at the center of investigation for being a Russian agent, but we don't have any information to confirm this yet, because we are just learning this information now, but meanwhile there is a new controversy surrounding the size of the crowd that attended the inauguration today saying it was the largest in the history of America, but we have information saying it is not the largest crowd in history," said Roman Anthony Andrews.

Katrina smirked and quietly turned off the television, and then went on to take a shower and then get dressed, so that she can go travel where she needs to go next.

There is everything but certainty, yet there continues to be chaos in the streets with no end in sight, as there is just no ending to the violence by these rioters.

It seems they have nothing better to do but de dressed in black all over to disguise their identities so they don't get caught by the police.

This is just another attempt to stop the free flow of democracy.

Such a sad attempt is taking place to undermine everything that America stands.

And no one wants to intervene because it is just very violent of what is currently going to happen if nothing stops them from wrecking society.

That will be the day when everything dies in a fire because the world will change after seeing a global event of mass proportions.

It is just the exact thing that must take place, and there will be chaos everywhere.

People will not know what to do because all will be clueless, and it will be the end of the world as they know it just to survive a catastrophe.

A short time later, Katrina got out of a steaming hot shower with her sexy but slim naked body glimmering from the steam of the water and put on some clothes so she could leave to go somewhere.

It is not that known but it is expected to be classified.

And then, just like that, Katrina disappeared again, not to be heard or seen by anyone.

It was either a coincidence or was planned from the very beginning in order to get something done.

V

And then, there was a beacon of hope, or some people thought, as a bright flash of white light suddenly appeared out of nowhere, bringing it a crowd of spectators that then suddenly went back inside to seek shelter due to a loud crashing sound that was all too familiar that sounded like gun fire and thunder and lightning shaking a tree that ended in disaster.

All were afraid and it just frightened everyone because they didn't know what to think, as it caused something bad to rekindle in a long ago memory.

Suddenly, something drastic started to happen.

Bright flashes of white light started appearing out of nowhere, like it was predicted from a message of God.

It was like something from an apocalypse that seemed all too familiar in a way that there is constant chaos and destruction of everything in search of the enemy.

No one wanted to go outside as they were all just too afraid of what might happen to them.

It could be a trap or it could be a part of their past in order to plague them for the rest of their lives.

But it is just the thing of the past, so says history, and that is the place to stand in the case of nothing like before.

Something could be going wrong or it could be the center of attention but no one actually knows what will happen to them due to the threat of fire

Then, there was a sudden change in light, as something ominous seemed to have occurred.

The bright flashes of white light turned to bright orange, signaling a threat to the community and possibly the rest of the world for some unknown reason.

And it happened, like something from a movie, as the bright flashes of light turned to flames.

No one knew what was happening and it seemed all too sudden.

Suddenly, the roads and streets were up in bright red and blue flames as white smoke started to appear turning to gray and finally to pitch black all in a sense of something unknown.

It could be something dangerous or it could be completely harmless, but there is just no sign in sight that signals anything like that because nothing seems like it is supposed to.

But that is not all too easy to describe because no one has ever saw this before.

This is just the beginning of something new.

Hastily, someone or something appeared out of a bright flash of white light, but no one saw who or what it was because of the heavy flames and the thick smoke.

But just like that the flash of white disappeared after a few short seconds, and then someone finally appeared at the end of the light.

It was like a reassurance of the future but something just wasn't right. The person finally revealed their identity and it was Katrina Maribelle.

She was just as excited as always and then she picked up a newspaper lying on the ground that read 'WAR IS IMMINENT AFTER HITLER INVADES POLAND,' which was the headline of the lead story on the front page of the Daily London Gazette, the oldest newspaper in all of the United Kingdom.

It was just all too familiar and Katrina developed a smile of happiness.

The people probably knew war would be imminent but they never saw Katrina, as she was already hidden in a safe house that no one else even knows about.

There was just the threat of war and it would happen in a matter of days.

It would be a surprise to no one as the entire continent of Europe will take part in the potential war.

Things could get worst by the minute and it will just drag on for years.

VI

The day was September 1, 1939, and all of humanity was lost, as no one knew what to do.

Katrina could care less about what was going on and she thought everything was normal as it should be. But there was something to be worried about.

It would concern the future of the European people and how they should respond to the threat of war on their borders, but to the greater extent it would be European countries against many other European countries, because they enemy is located throughout Europe.

It is just the way the world operates.

So it would be tempting to see what would happen in the case of no war.

Everything was just happening so fast that no one knew what would happen.

And as it stands, the threat of declaring war is imminent and will be in a matter of days.

The threat of war would put everything in chaos.

People would have to start rationing their food.

The water supply would be limited.

The financial markets will collapse.

The economy will lead to an economic meltdown.

The people will be displaced causing widespread homelessness and no one would be able to escape the possibility of losing their family fortunes and wealth.

Soldiers will be everywhere and they will be placed throughout the neighborhoods waiting for something to happen.

There will be destruction of property and valuables causing chaos and havoc amongst the town and city folk.

The people will suffer from PTSD and other mental illnesses due to the prolonged threat of war.

The quality of life will decrease for everyone except those lucky few who know.

And everything will be in a terrible position.

But the worst thing that will happen is the government will all of a sudden take advantage of the people and society.

And the people will be afraid to rise up because they might get arrested.

The threat of a dictatorship is an imminent possibility and it might lead to other governments being overthrown, leading to worldwide panic and disaster due to fascism, national socialism, communism, Marxism, and the people at the top deciding what is legal and what is not.

No one will be able to escape the wrath of the new government but the people at the top shall be immune from almost anything.

Committees will be formed to control the people.

Criminals will get to decide if you live or die.

The threat of worldwide surveillance will be imminent and very possible in every home, place of business, and building, in order to keep an eye on the people.

Speech will be heavily regulated and everything that goes against the government and the dictatorship will lead to an arrest, where death shall be the sole sentence.

The youth will get involved starting in high school but it will then gradually move down to junior high and eventually to elementary school students so everyone can be indoctrinated.

And the older people who were born before any of this will either not say anything by keeping quiet or they will join the ranks of the dictatorship, as the other third option will be immediate arrest.

Violence will be an everyday occurrence as people will fight for their lives.

People will steel and cheat because they won't have anything better to do.

And crime will be rampant in the inner cities or ghettos with no chance of decreasing.

It will just be a very depressing environment, so everything in and around the capital cities shall be heavily fortified while the Midwest and other places in middle America will try to live on as normal but with the threat of an out of control government.

And this will just be the start because nothing can predict the start or ending of anything.

As the threat of catastrophe rises there will just be more chaos in the midst of a crisis. It all stems from something that could be caused by a small minor change or detail in the fabric of history and time, but it is impossible to predict anything.

Before long, the people will just get used to everything, but then there will still be those who plot in secret to escape this tyrannical dictatorship in a plan of trying to overthrow it.

And they could get caught, with a new threat arising, by it being the creation of new laws being passed by the dictatorship or the government.

The legislation would try to target and punish terrorism and terrorist acts by them being defined as trying to overthrow a legitimate and duly elected government.

The threat would be to silence the people but eventually some will get caught by planning more attacks while others will meet and plan in secret and will only strike when the people realize what is going on is wrong and when the government and dictatorship are at their weakest.

That will be the day and it just might work, so it seems.

VII

And then it happened.

On September 3, 1939, two days after Hitler and his group of radicals invaded Poland, France and Great Britain declared war against Germany, beginning another world war.

Tanks will soon by rolling out into the streets and soldiers will be deployed overseas in order to defeat a common enemy they see as a threat to the future of civilization.

People will be drafted into the armed forces of their home country.

Conscription notices will go out for the sole purpose of trying to recruit and train the best people.

The armada will show up on the coasts and will build up to lay claim to the enemy and their allies.

The Air Force will do flyovers to get a better glimpse of how to proceed with the mission.

The Marines will try to scout out places of territory in order to sneak attack the enemy whenever necessary.

The coast guard will patrol the seas and will close off everything to anyone that poses a threat to the national security of the country.

It won’t be long before people get annoyed at seeing warships, planes, and tanks storm neighborhoods in order to protect the country or to invade it.

Chances are people won’t care or they will hide and cower in fear because they won't know what will happen next.

No one will know who is an enemy and who is an ally.

It will just be so awful that the people will get used to it but they must in order to get on with their lives.

Everything will just seem normal as usual and no one will be able to stop that.

And then, all hell broke loose.

It was a campaign to impose economic warfare against the German Nazi forces in an attempt to try to stop their actions.

The people wouldn't know what to do because they fear prices might go up due to a decrease in trade and commerce from the German state.

It is a thing to be reckoned with and time will tell.

Pressure was building for the British government to act because there was nothing stopping Hitler from committing his atrocities against the people of other countries.

Eight months has passed and Hitler decided to invade the country of Denmark and then to occupy it because he felt threatened that it would all collapse if he didn't protect interests.

Then sometime later, Hitler did the same thing to Norway, as a way to protect his interests for the new German state.

It was a way to get around the British naval blockade put in place to stop Hitler and Germany from additional damage.

But Hitler knew he had to do more in order to stop the threat of being defeated.

It would be a risk he would just have to accept but at a cost of deploying more of his men in order to get things done.

There was a war going on and it seems people did not know what to do.

So it seems there is an attempt to get to the bottom of what is currently at the forefront to determine how to fix the threat but it is still unknown about how to strategize in an attempt to wage war against a common enemy who tries to sabotage democracy under a false pretense.

Sooner or later there will be something more serious to consider and it will not be the same as it always has.

For that purpose there will nothing short of surrender because it will be the generals who will decide.

And then something more serious did occur to the point of dire and utter importance.

News reporters started to report Hitler was preparing to invade Holland and Belgium.

It would be an all-out war because they had something Hitler wanted, which was land to build up his all-important Reich.

Boom!

Something just happened that will change the face of the world as people know it.

"What's happening," said one person

"Didn't you hear, we are being invaded," said another person.

There was something afoot and it seemed there would be a case to own it.

That wasn't the case for everyone because they saw it differently in the eyes of hopelessness.

Suddenly, bombs were dropping everywhere from the air by enemy airmen on the houses and buildings in Holland and Belgium.

It was a time of being afraid and a time of trying to see if the people will live to see the next day.

The populace was scared and they had the right to be.

It was a case to hide and seek shelter before anything else bad happens.

And then one after another, more bombs dropped, in order to annihilate the current people in power in a way to gain control.

The allies were facing tremendous pressure from their citizens, as there was no immediate action.

It was time to test what will happen and who will be held responsible.

Something needed to be done and if not then there will be hell to pay.

Troops were everywhere.

The people were scared and didn't know what to do.

It was a case that anyone could be an enemy agent because something bad had occurred.

Tanks were everywhere and bombs were still dropping from the sky to kill the innocent civilians.

People were scrambling in order to avoid being killed.

Something just didn't seem right and it was just the height of the new age so people thought.

And then it was announced on the news and radio that the great city of Rotterdam was destroyed in a matter of hours.

The people were angry and no one expected people to survive.
It was such a sad day and nothing and no one could see that.

The day was now May 13, 1940, three days after Hitler and his Nazi Party invaded and took over Belgium and Holland, and now three days later the prime minister of Britain, Neville Chamberlain, has resigned due to the political pressure from the Labour Party.

All was lost but hopefully Winston Churchill could do something about it that will turn everything around.

FIVE

I

Warplanes buzzed from the sky above of the United States Naval Base at Pearl Harbor in Hawaii. Shots were fired and bombs were dropping in all locations below. The people of Hawaii were afraid. And soon, they knew they were under attack.

The day was December 7, 1941, and it was in the early morning hours when people were starting to go to leave for work in order to pay their bills.

It was something of a surprise and soon people would feel the pain of not knowing what will happen in a case like this.

It was just surreal because no one saw this coming.

Clearly, something has caused this to occur in a situation like this.

Everyone was just so surprised but it wasn't even over.

Soon, another round of fire and bombs started, and it was the same thing happening all over again, as the people thought the warplanes turned around.

But they just flew back to attack the Pacific Fleet of the United States Navy more.

The enemy forces just wanted to completely obliterate everything they saw.

And they did because it was just good weather.

Everything was clear with partly cloudy skies.

There was nothing wrong with visibility and all seemed to work it as a surprise attack against the United States government.

And then the warplanes finally turned around after bombing what they saw as a threat to their national security and interests.

The enemy planes left the airspace and landed at their aircraft carrier to head back off to Japan in an attempt to attack more.

The people felt betrayed and they didn't know what to think. The aftermath left 2,403 innocent people dead with 188 United States Air Force planes damaged while 8 warships of the United States Pacific Fleet were either damaged or destroyed.

It was such an intense but short battle that no one saw this coming, but the Japanese believed there was a threat to their national security and interests so they attacked.

It was just too hard to comprehend.

It was one day later, and America still was in turmoil.

Quickly, the President of the United States of America, Franklin Delano Roosevelt, took action and demanded Congress to declare war against the enemy state of Japan for attacking America.

Before long, something happened and it was at the behest of the United States Congress.

And it too was declared.

On December 8, 1941, the House of Representatives voted 388-1 while the United States Senate voted 82-0 to declare war against Japan, and then it was approved by the president in a matter of minutes.

Three days later there was another two declarations of war, one against Germany and the other against Italy.

It was unanimous, as the House of Representatives voted 393-0 and the United States Senate voted 88-0 to declare war against the Nazi-state of Germany.

And then, war was soon declared against the fascist state of Italy in a unanimous decision.

The House of Representatives voted 399-0 while the United States Senate voted 90-0 to declare war on Italy.

It was just to defeat the terror of Hitler and his allies.

And soon, all three declarations of war were signed into war by the president of the United States of America, Franklin Delano Roosevelt.

No one knows what will happen next but there will be conscription after more conscription notices going out everywhere.

The threat of war has become imminent and it will change the lives of everyone forever.

Soon, there will be chaos, but it is just too soon to tell. But it won't be long from now until the people start feeling the effects of war.

The country and the nation will face a test.

Can the leader of the free world lead America to victory?

Could his replacement end the war if something drastic happens to him?

There is not a clue in sight of what will happen but there is no way out of the tunnel.

But for now, there is still hope.

There is still time for change and the belief nothing bad will happen.

It is a time of need for everyone to realize because there might not be much time left.

People will learn their fates something soon but it won't be long until a travesty occurs.

People will start to realize that war isn't that so great and then there are those who have experienced the first war against the common enemy before.

It won't be long until now before something bad happens and that is just how it is.

But the effects of war will be dire when they go into effect.

The government shall ration everything from food to fuel in an attempt to support the mission.

Food shall become scarce because of the war.

Soldiers need to eat too.

Fuel for vehicles shall be scarce and be rationed because of the need for military vehicles needing to fight in a war.

There will be a lack of clothing because no one will be able to produce enough due to the war.

Factories will be converted to war planning facilities in order to build military machines.

The army will set up temporary bases everywhere in order to target the enemy.

Safe houses shall be established in order to hide from enemy agents in a time of need.

Houses and buildings will be demolished by bombs.

The largest cities will be destroyed and devastated and people will need to come together in a time of need.

Everyone would have to conserve everything because there won't be enough to go around.

Rationing would just have to stay around until it is no longer needed and the people will need to get used to it.

But the time for rationing is not today, because Congress approved three declarations of war.

And as time goes on, there will be a greater chance or possibility rationing happens because the goal is to support the mission of defeating the common enemy in a time when there is a national security issue and threat to the interests of the United States of America.

And then it happened.

It was now the spring of 1942 and there was a problem.

There was a lack of food because of the war.

There was a lack of fuel because of the war.

There was a lack of clothing because of the war.

The Japanese cut off production to the United States and her allies because of the declaration of war.

And there was a lack of tires being produced, so there was just the case to conserve.

People were devastated about what will happen but they have been warned months before about the effects of war by people.

And it would result in doom and chaos as people try to survive in the midst of a national emergency that no one can figure out.

It would be the case about trying to solve a problem about trying to defeat the common enemy.

It is the case to determine what will happen.

There will be no indication of whether people will have a job.

There will be no indication of how many people will survive.

There will be no indication of when America will win or defeat the common enemy.

There is just no indication of anything.

It all remains a mystery due to the complex nature of negotiations and diplomacy.

And in the midst of this, a country needs to survive, so the people are funding the war effort by purchasing several hundreds and thousands of war bonds in an effort to help out the troops.

There was no time to waste because time was money and if no one was working then there will be no one fighting against the terror of Hitler and his radical agenda.

So, there is a crisis to be solved, and the government needed to act quickly, because they believe they can save the people from facing the full effects of war but it hardly ever works but propaganda might.

There is just a time of chaos for everything and soon there is the case to distinguish the case of nothing to save humanity.

Quickly thinking, the United States government thought, America should be saved from every aspect of the war, and that is what they want to do.

Just like that, the United States government launched their new goal in mind, the food rationing program in order to limit the intake of food people can buy for a day, a week, or a month.

It was just the effort to stay afloat.

People will now request to receive a ration book so the stores and government can track their daily, weekly, or monthly purchases.

The government was ready with their boards to commence and begin rationing around the country in order to support and help the war effort, and that included helping the allies.

And a short time later, there were additional rationing boards installed in order to start rationing fuel.

It would be a nightmare scenario but it is happening in the case of what to do in a time of need.

The people were asked by the government to first donate any scrap rubber because the Japanese seized the factories that produced the majority of the rubber for America.

It was a request to help make sure there were enough tires for the vehicles because there would be a short supply.

But with all of this, there were rules put into place in order to make sure everyone followed the rationing program as a way to institute the fair share requirement of promoting equality amongst all that are receiving and participating in food rationing.

It was part of the goal of the newly-created government agency known as the Office of Price Administration in order to control the prices of everything.

Only the person described in the ration book could use the stamps to purchase any eligible food at an eligible retail store and they set forth each ration week last from midnight to midnight on Saturday.

Set forth, the rules put forward by the Office of Price Administration strongly imply for the ration book and stamps to be stored in a safe and secure location and that the parents be responsible for the ration books and stamps belonging to any and all of their children.

Put forth by the Office of Price Administration and the local rationing boards, the stamp must be detached and witnessed by any and or employees responsible for being the cashier of record for the hour or day at the time and any mutilated stamp is void and is ineligible to be used to purchase items.

Put forth, any lost, destroyed, mutilated, or stolen ration book must be reported to the local rationing board.

Put forth, any person who sets foot and is admitted to the hospital for more than 10 days must surrender it to the hospital administrator and upon leaving it shall be returned to them.

And put forth, whenever someone dies, that ration book must be turned in to the local rationing board.

Questions regarding rationing should be directed to the local rationing board.

It ceased to amaze no one that these were the conditions set forth by a government seeking to control everything.

But the truth is that everyone has to follow it because any violations might result in going to prison for not listening to the rules and regulation set forth.

And that wasn't going to be accepted by all.

The people won't stand for intrusion and interference in their lives because they will stand up for what they believe in.

There will be riots and protests.

People will burn down buildings.

And the government will start cracking down.

And then there will be automatic confiscation of everything.

The result will be a dystopian society in a time when there is no hope for the future.

There won't be anything to worry about because there is just nothing.

The economy will spiral out of control into extinction to a place that no one wants to visit.

People will be out of jobs and there will be a lack of them being made available.

The soldiers will have to react quickly in a time of need and there will be a need to decide who the enemy is and who the friend is. It will just all be out of control.

The world will be in chaos and therefore people must and will find a way to exist.

Chaos will just be a thing of everyday living and it is the hope of all humanity that something will change for the better.

That is just how it works and it might never succeed.

But too many people will die before the carnage of war ends.

And in a time of peace there is none because hope does not exist when there is war due to a lack of war.

It is just an attempt to disguise as propaganda in order to try and promote a unified message that doesn't seem to be true.

That is what it will all be, propaganda, because that is the goal of the government in this time of need.

It is a warning to all not to wear everything when there is a case to be decided against war.

And for the better of the nation, there will be new people rising.

There will be the resistance that rises up in order to combat these atrocities of this government.

The resistance shall rise up in accordance with their proven and excited commitment of getting things done in order to spread a message of love and hope to target and combat all of the lies and falsehoods set forth by the government propaganda.

Some things will never change but it is hope that is all needed.

Out of this though, there will be a time of need and hope, but it is a time that the resistance shall be targeted in a case of retribution to target the innocent.

And the propaganda will never disappear until there is a lack of discipline in the higher ranks of government.

There will just be obedience until the end of the war and the people as well as the resistance will try to find a way around it.

The black market is born and it is at the behest at the resistance in order to bring back control.

II

Meanwhile, the media kept spreading the lie of Russian collusion, by indicating that Russia helped Carlton Winters win the 2016 presidential election because their candidate, Cynthia Norwell Anderson, failed to win that election in November.

But now, it is 2017, and there is a new president in power, that of

Carlton Winters, and he is here to stay.

However, the threat remains that the United Labourists will try to stop his agenda by saying he wasn't fairly elected. And then it was finally done, as many Centralists and United Labourists wanted, that CBDI director Carl Ronald has been fired from his position.

So news was expected concerning the firing and it was just not a surprise.

"Breaking news, we are now getting word of the termination letter of Carl Ronald, and it offers contradicting statements about why he is being fired from his position, so we will keep you updated on this news that is just coming out," said Roman Anthony Andrews.

Interview after interview, the United Labourists just started to rally against president Carlton Winters, because they just didn't like him since he fired the most hated person in their political circle.

That isn't a surprise but now they accuse Russian collusion.

Yet both attorney general Albert Hearlk and deputy general Miles Reymond gave the recommendation to terminate Carl Ronald in addition to the reason given by Carlton Winters, but the haters and critics were just not having it.

They just gave their full support behind the now fired CBDI director and the critics were not done just yet because they believed in the opposite of what they want.

With a little over a week later, something dire happened, and it was not for the better of the country.

Deputy Attorney general Miles Reymond is now believed to appoint a special counsel in the case against Carlton Winters and the possibility of Russian collusion.

"Breaking news, we are now learning that Deputy Attorney general Miles Reymond has appointed a special counsel in the matter concerning Russian collusion and the Carlton Winters campaign," said Roman Anthony Andrews.

The critics of the president will now say something exists even if there is nothing there.

It is all just a game to them because they think they got the president now on a crime of collusion but it isn't a crime to collude, since that isn't defined in the law regarding elections.

But they will say that by receiving information from a foreign power to gain an upper hand is a crime, but there is no evidence that such information was given to the campaign.

It is just a tantrum they are throwing because they believe the wrong person won the office of the presidency.

They believed Cynthia Norwell Anderson was the most experienced thing since the invention of sliced bread because she is a woman.

That just tells the critics that she and her supporters only voted for her based on her biological sex or gender since they believe she will be a better president than Carlton Winters and also because she will promise so much free stuff to everyone who doesn't want to work because they just want to rely on government welfare.

This isn't the first time it happened and it won't be the last, as there are enemies out there that want to ruin the life of an innocent bystander just to gain traction by spreading lies and falsehoods against people.

Of course, the critics are praising this move against the president, as they believe it will lead to his impeachment, so say the members of the United Labourists.

But they are missing the whole point, because there is a much larger picture.

The only reason why Deputy Attorney general Miles Reymond appointed a special counsel is because he felt pressured by what Carl Ronald did, by releasing his unauthorized notes to the public knowing it is property of the Department of Justice and giving it to sources outside the jurisdiction of the CBDI is a violation of the law due to it being regarded as special and privileged information.

And there is also the fact is that Miles Reymond pressured Albert Hearlk to step down from the Russian collusion and interference investigation.

Something does not seem right but it is just the epidemic of corruption.

So, the critics and people against the president are going to pounce at this notion that Russia helped Carlton Winters win the 2016 presidential election, because they claim there is just no other way that their candidate lost.

Well, the critics of Cynthia Norwell Anderson will say that she was a very flawed and weak candidate, because of her numerous scandals during her time as Secretary of State, the scandal in Arkansas, and the attempt to give away the natural resources of America to a foreign power that could be a threat to the national security and interests of America.

And besides that, the Centralists will also claim that she will continue Martin's apology tour of America.

And the United Labourists and the supporters of Cynthia Norwell

Anderson have been panicking ever since November when Carlton Winters was declared the president-elect of the United States of America.

It was just a surreal experience for them because they thought they had it in the bag.

They thought they were ahead by a lot and that Carlton Winters had no chance of even winning the election.

And they believed the flawed opinion polls that didn't really measure the supporters of Carlton Winters because most of his supporters rarely told the opinion polls who they were voting for because it could lead to harassment and public shaming.

But, supporters of Cynthia Norwell Anderson nevertheless seemed outraged that a white man won back the presidency after the African-American won the presidency over eight years ago.

The critics of Carlton Winters thought it brought back America back to the dark ages during a time when most people didn't have rights and slavery was rampant throughout the world.

Throughout the 2016 presidential campaign, the United Labourists had a theory that because Barrington Martin was in office then they would have an upper hand in winning the next presidential election for Cynthia Norwell Anderson.

And then they were surprised that Carlton Winters said he would have to wait to see if he will accept the results of the election, yet there seems to be hypocrisy, because many United Labourists immediately started to reject the results of the presidential election.

It was set to become something divisive in the aftermath of what they thought would be another historic election.

So far, it seems the staunchest critics of president Carlton Winters are now having panic attacks or feel afraid for the people of America.

They fear for the illegal immigrants.

They fear that the corporations will take advantage of everyday Americans.

They fear that another financial collapse is going to happen.

And they fear that people are going to pay less in taxes because they know that will invigorate the economy.

It won't be long now until there are calls for impeachment but there already are because they just don't want the president to be Carlton Winters.

There are already reports of deep state resistance from within the Department of Justice from remaining Martin supporters.

It was just the cause of attention for some inferior tactic.

And the media is just eating this up because they have nothing better to do.

Nearly two weeks have passed since the appointment of the special counsel and there seems to be activity at a storage locker owned by former campaign manager for Carlton Winters, Gary Bouchfer, and it seems the media will have a field day with this information when it is reported to them in the near future.

III

It is the early afternoon of August 9, 2017, and there seems to be something big that might be reported soon.

It seems one of the most liberal newspapers in the country is going to report on the news that the home of Gary Bouchfer has been raided in the predawn hours of July 26, so it seems the newswire will pick it up soon.

The critics of the president will go wild with the report and they will say this is evidence of corruption but they will still forget that it might not even be related to anything.

The critics can say all they want but it will lead to nothing but government waste that they support in order to impeach Carlton Winters.

They might claim that this shows that the current president doesn't care about corruption because he hired some person with connections to Russia.

And they simply won't care if they are proven wrong, because they already declared everyone guilty without any hard evidence.

That will be a sad day for America but it is just shenanigans as usual for the resistance.

No one will care but that is the case of the thing that is accepted now, until the past comes back to haunt them.

So, no one will even care.

"Breaking news, we are just learning that the special counsel has launched a predawn raid on the home of former campaign manager for Carlton Winters, Gary Bouchfer, but we are still reading through the details of this report, so stay tuned, and we will have reporters give us the latest facts in the case," said Roman Anthony Andrews.

"Roman, we are just learning that this predawn raid relates to Gary Bouchfer's tax documents and foreign bank accounts, as it relates to his ties to foreign governments and members of political parties that support the Russian president, but we are also finding out that Bouchfer has given those same documents to Congress already, yet we are just learning that a source close to Bouchfer says he expects to be targeted by the special counsel," said Jeremy Dustin Scott.

"Thank you for that updated information," said Roman Anthony

Andrews.

The news kept spreading like wildfire and it seemed the critics of the president won't stop until they caught someone they didn't like.

But the first question to ask would have to be is the association concerning collusion, because so far no evidence exists yet.

Instead, this might just be an attempt to remove a duly-elected president from office.

But there is just more to the story than before.

More news will be rolling out and it seems there is no end in sight to stop this madness.

And then, there is just more news rolling out from the newswires, so no one can actually understand what is happening.

But a new story is just about going to be released and it concerns Gary Bouchfer and him being a target of the special counsel, so this is the next revelation the United Labourists must by hoping for, or else they will have nothing to go on.

"Breaking news, today is September 18, 2017, and we have new facts and details about the special counsel investigation regarding Gary Bouchfer, the former campaign manager for Carlton Winters, and we can report that Gary Bouchfer is a target of this special counsel investigation and that he was told to expect to be indicted, but we will keep you updated on the latest news concerning about this story and more," said Roman Anthony Andrews to the people watching from home and at work.

The critics pounced again and they thought this was just a fantastic revelation that they would finally get the president of the United States of America.

They thought this was the best thing since the ham sandwich but they rarely realized what is going on because of their hatred for Carlton Winters. But that is nothing new.

And again, there is now another news story set to be released that Gary Bouchfer has been the subject of a secret court order since 2014 so CBDI investigators and Department of Justice officials could secretly surveil his everyday actions without him knowing anything, and that remains to be somewhat consequential because Bouchfer is not even a foreign citizen of the United States of America.

The critics of Carlton Winters will try to pounce on this new information again by saying that the president only hires corrupt individuals.

It is more of the same from those United Labourists, but there is really no reason why Bouchfer should have been the subject of a secret surveillance order.

They just can't handle the fact that their candidate failed to win the presidential election, so they constantly make up excuses in an attempt to destroy a person's life, even if there is no actual evidence there.

And that should warn the rest of society, so the whole theory is just to determine why they want to target innocent people without first checking the facts.

Of course, the United Labourists will never do that, as they will lead a witch hunt until they get what they want, which will never actually happen, so they will actually be wasting their time and they will realize everything after America decides to reconfirm the presidency of Carlton Winters in a second term as president and when they lose the House of Representatives again after potentially taking control in January of 2019, they will lose again in November 2020 and the Centralists will control the House of Representatives again in January 2021.

But then the members of the United Labourists will claim they lost because of racism in an attempt to try and divide the country more.

All they want is for a do over in order to redo the 2016 general election so that they can take the House of Representatives, the Senate, as well as the office of the presidency.

But that won't get far due to possible challenges, and if they think about traveling back in time, well they don't really have a chance, unless of course, propaganda.

It is their fault for losing because the people had enough of the establishment, and instead they wanted change.

A day later, on September 19, 2017, a news story concerning Gary Bouchfer is about to be published again.

This time it will indicate that the special counsel is set to investigate the past 11 years of Gary Bouchfer, and that is an indication that the special counsel is looking for something because they actually haven't found anything linked to Russian collusion.

It is just another sign of a witch hunt.

Of course, the critics will be quick to say that the special counsel has found something and it is in fact related to the case of Russian collusion, but the question is about actually proving it.

And then they might say they don't need any evidence because they don't like anyone or anything connected to Carlton Winters.

It will only be a matter of time until there is a crisis of politicians trying to one up each other and that will be the day of reckoning and chaos throughout society.

And just as people thought there was an end in sight there was more stuff to come.

The resistance just tries to find a way to try to produce smoke where there is no fire.

For some reason the resistance is going to try to say that everything is proof of Russian collusion.

But then they will try to say that it is Russian interference when their claims are proven to be false.

It is just something to be in the crosshairs of a successful republic for the reason that remains to be unknown.

People are so preoccupied with hating the president because they do not like that he won over their favorite chosen candidate who they would just crown to continue the polices of Barrington Martin.

It is a reasoning that is of no surprise to the supporters of the president.

It is all the same and it shall never change for the better of the country without first having some sort of new political revolution.

That is the day when the people could rise up in order to support the goals and ideology of socialism, communism, and Marxism all under one roof.

It would be a tragic day in America because the radical leftists would control and dictate everything and the people will only become pawns of the government.

And there will be a group of people who will try to escape in order to save humanity.

But then there are others who will become fierce supporters of this new radical leftist government because they say it is all about law and order, as they see anyone opposed to socialism, communism, and Marxism as the enemy of the state.

That is nothing new and it will always be that way and for the foreseeable future unless somebody rises up and challenges them that will result in an unknown future.

Thus, it remains to be seen, because there will be a third group of people that won't know what to do because they will either stay put and try to stay out of trouble or they will do something that might get them into trouble.

No one knows what will happen in this type of future but if people are not careful then this will happen, causing chaos and destruction everywhere, to the point of nothing more than crazy things that will be no more.

But, the United Labourists and the people against Carlton Winters have something new to discuss as of today, September 22, 2017, because of some new news story that has just surfaced on the newswires.

Already, there are reports that the United Labourists are seizing on the recent revelations that Russian agents have tried to target or hack the election systems of about 21 states or jurisdictions within the continental United States of America.

That is a report from the Department of Homeland Security, but it also stated that the only successful attempt was in the state of Illinois, a place filled with United Labourists.

So, the underlying theme that people should take away here is that the majority of states or jurisdictions within the United States of America are safe.

Yet, the United Labourists and the fringe that oppose the current president of the United States of America will say he is unfit for office and because of the attempted election targeting by Russian agents that proves Russia is the reason Carlton Winters won because they cheated for him and hacked every electoral system in the United States of America.

And of course, that is just ludicrous, because they are just making things up, but when you have well-known Senators and members of Congress who oppose everything you do, then there is an opinion that people might develop in a way that is corrupt and unreasonable.

There might be more revelations after this mostly unsuccessful hack of the electoral systems from the September 22 report, so it remains to be seen what will happen next.

This will result in something graphic and it might turn to the people to make a grave and wrong decision.

It will be the point of no return and at the most crucial time in history there will be trying to make up something new as a way to get to the bottom of the agenda.

But, there is nothing hopeful, as it remains a mystery of what the special counsel will actually do next because they are not after the truth.

Everything is more of the same so there might be nothing short of a catastrophe.

The goal of the resistance and the United Labourists is to make everything politically motivated in a time when no one wants to be defeated.

And the hope of humanity stands still for the purpose of making the truth seekers look foolish.

The story of Russian collusion is of interest to the people who only oppose the presidency of Carlton Winters because they never wanted him to win, as there is a theory that Cynthia Norwell Anderson was the best person and most experienced to lead the country in decades, which is probably some sort of exaggerated claim.

But they won't care because they will say they are trying to protect the country from what they believe is a madman.

Yet, their goal is to change America into a progressive country that does not like the idea of how America was founded in the first place.

But if they fail, then they will try to create a crime, something that won't stand up in a court of law but will stand up in the court of public opinion, so now it would relate to trying to see if the president actually did commit any high crimes or misdemeanors such as bribery or extortion.

It is just another political move and that has always been the case about why they hate the president and will believe anything.

It is the rise of the surveillance state and the surrendering of the freedom, liberties, and the foundations that America was founded on.

For that reason, that is nothing more than a pipe dream from those people. And it too shall be the reason why there is a case to target innocent people without any evidence.

IV

News broke just now on September 26, 2017 that the special counsel is now partnering with the Internal Revenue Service to investigate Bouchfer on possible federal tax violations.

The story is breaking just now and already the United Labourists and opponents of Carlton Winters are having a field day with what is happening because they all believe this shows evidence that Gary Bouchfer is a tax cheat who knew what he was doing, but there is still something missing.

This has already caused an avalanche of support to go after the campaign staff of Carlton Winters in a way to demonstrate that the political establishment is in control and that change will be against the law as it relates to revealing corruption by the people in power.

That is just the case that needs to be stated.

But that must still wait in an attempt to determine what will happen next.

And then, a United States Senator belonging to the United Labourists is saying that he expects criminal charges to be filed against Gary Bouchfer and Vincent McLoughlin soon in an enthusiastic manner.

There is still the question about how the Senator knows this, so it remains to be seen if there is any certainty to this question.

But news and more revelations could soon be released shortly.

The timing is just strange but it is how it is due to the fact that the people who oppose the president want to get rid of him and spread false rumors in order to distract everyone.

They claim it is for the better of our country.

But little do they know that it isn't helping their cause and many of them already know that.

The only problem with their theory is that there is a lack of evidence supporting it, so they just make stuff up in order to please their far-leftist base of people who oppose freedom, liberty, free speech, the freedom of religion, and the pursuit of happiness to form a surveillance state that supports big government.

That is nothing more than a pipe dream of hopelessness and a threat to democracy.

And then it hit again, a news report just released revealed that Russian agents bought advertisements to appear on Social Media Enterprises flagship social media website to target specific areas in the United States of America but it fails to mention any collusion or election interference.

Already the critics that oppose Carlton Winters are making a false claim that this report proves that Russia helped him become president.

It is just the same old hoax that they keep on promoting while not providing any evidence and trying to create a narrative that has yet to be proven.

That is just a case of people trying to find something or invent it if it doesn't exist because their choice did not win the presidency.

It is always the same and it never shall change unless there is an actual revelation.

No one can tell those people that there is anything wrong with the current president because there is nothing wrong with him and his administration but they already he is a threat to democracy in America just because they hate him.

And then they try to panic when he isn't even harming the country.

Everything is always a game to them and it just keeps on repeating until the time runs out.

Time will eventually run out but then again on September 28, 2017 there was another news report, and the critics and the United Labourists just seized on it again, claiming it proves their claims, but they fail to cite or to provide any evidence whatsoever.

This time a report cites that they have the evidence that fake news contributed to the election of Carlton Winters for the purpose to make sure Cynthia Norwell Anderson does not win.

It is a theory that does not seem to make sense and the Centralists are already ripping it apart, because it fails to say how many Americans it influenced when they can't report the actual number of people who fall prey to it.

And many people who voted for Carlton Winters already made up their minds months in advance, so the undecided voters in the general election were persuaded by policies, and not some fake news.

It is a cry for help in a time when no one can understand the situation that is going on.

The resistance is trying to start a coup against a duly-elected and legitimate President of the United States of America.

Everything remains a mystery and it shall always be that way when trying to tell a member of the resistance that there is nothing wrong with the current presidential administration in power because they cannot just get it into their heads.

They are all stubborn and believe a police state is for the best of the country, since they believe it is good to target anyone that has been or is associated with Carlton Winters.

That is a damn shame but it is now or never.

Nothing can convince them but that will never change until they have seen the light of day once they realize high taxes for just making money is government theft.

Until then, the society will be on the brink of collapse, because of all the crazy laws that have been passed by a socialist, communist, or Marxist regime.

And that is a dangerous trend of supporting people who just wants to take control in order to control how and what people think and do.

It won't work for all except for those in power.

Everyone else will feel the pain of a bad decision of helping corrupt individuals take away hard-earned money and placing it into the pockets of cheats and liars in order to make sure that only the people in power have the money.

The resistance and the United Labourists know this but they still refuse to accept it, as they think it is their duty to control the lives of the people, as they believe they know what's best for society.

But they are just forgetting something.

They are forgetting about the constitution.

They are forgetting about the declaration of independence.

They are forgetting about the true intentions of the founders of America. They are forgetting about the Bill of Rights.

They are forgetting that America was founded on the Judea-Christian values of society.

They are forgetting about the freedom of speech and the freedom of religion.

They are forgetting the pursuit of happiness and the right to freedom and liberty everywhere.

But most importantly, they are forgetting about the role of government, because the rights of the citizens don't come from government as they come from a divine God, yet they still reject that idea for some reason or another because they believe government grants the rights of everyone and that is how they see everything in the role of government, that the rights are derived from government.

It is just a case of not wanting to obey the constitution.

The very basis and ideology of big government and a surveillance state is a threat to the democracy of the people and society but the United Labourists along with the members of the resistance are willing to remove democracy if it means getting rid of Carlton Winters and anyone who supports him and his policy agenda.

It is something that is reminiscent of the days of corruption for which socialists, communists, and Marxists were in control of everything.

Before long, the resistance and United Labourists will say there is nothing wrong with being fascist, because already it seems they are engaging in fascism by trying to silence people with differing opinions, views, and beliefs, yet they say Carlton Winters and any of his supporters are fascists all because they oppose him and the constitution.

They rather see the death of America like Iran does so they can remake America into a land that eliminates freedom of speech, freedom of religion, freedom of the press, the pursuit of happiness, liberty, and everything else that is supported by and established by the founding fathers of America.

That is such a shame but it is nothing new.

They will just keep claiming Russia did it without any evidence, so they believe.

And then, Social Media Enterprises announced it would send the United States Congress thousands of advertisements bought by agents of the Russian government, on October 1, 2017, again sounding the alarm for the resistance and the United Labourists that collusion did indeed cause the wrong person to win the presidency, but that is an excuse and they know it, yet they won't stop it because they need something to talk about.

It will all disappear in a short while, as another story will replace it.

So just like that, on October 2, 2017 another news story came out saying that Russia is using the same tactics and methods as corporate America does in order to influence the American voter.

But then a short while later, Social Media Enterprises stated only 10 million people saw the advertisements bought by the Russians, yet there is no indication how many of those people voted and how many of those people were eligible to vote.

Yet, already, the United Labourists and the resistance are trying to spin it by saying Russia helped Carlton Winters by stealing the election for him.

It is just more of the same and it will continue to happen until they invent something new.

And then, one day later, on October 3, 2017, the Senate Intelligence Committee, headed by a weak Centralist and also be a United Labourist who opposes Carlton Winters is said to release a report that Russia has indeed interfered in the 2016 election and that there is a need to fix everything now so that it doesn't happen again.

But there is just no evidence that Russia did interfere in the election to help Carlton Winters win, but it is only stated due to the fact Cynthia Norwell Anderson lost the election.

Something will soon replace the most recent news reports so that the people who oppose Carlton Winters and his administration will be united and enthusiastic that something bad will happen for him, but it will only lead to something that isn't even related to the craziness of everything.

That is just how strange people have been acting, which is actually deranged when other people start to think about it.

However, nothing will change their minds until they feel the pain of socialism, communism, and Marxism in a different country than America, as America is seen as the best country in the world with hope, liberty, and the pursuit of happiness.

They will only realize it when they are jailed in a rogue country such as Cuba, Venezuela, or Iran.

Only then will they realize that they were wrong and they will make an attempt to change their ways and beliefs, if they actually see socialism, communism, and Marxism as a stain on society and immoral to civilization.

That will be the day but there is always the chance they refuse to accept facts.

They seem to think they will get what they want when they know they are on thin ice.

Inventing conspiracy theories is nothing new to them but they will say that the Centralists are making up the conspiracy theories, but they will not recognize what they say as being classified as a conspiracy theory because they believe everything they say and do is the gospel and actual fact.

Many people can see through that but then the supporters of the resistance and the United Labourists will say that the Centralists are to blame for everything.

So, it isn't so crazy to say that there is a threat on the horizon, but everything will be replaced with some other news story.

But something happened.

It will just create a distraction and further divide the country.

Some people will say it is warranted while others will say it is unconstitutional.

That is just about to be replaced with another news story about to be published or reported on and it will surely get the attention of the resistance and the United Labourists.

"Breaking news, we are just learning that Alexander Christopoulos, a former foreign adviser for energy for the Carlton Winters campaign, will plead guilty in a court of law after reaching a negotiated plea deal with the special counsel about giving false testimony to CBDI investigators that were investigating Russian collusion and the campaign of Carlton Winters, so we expect to know more about this in the coming days, but we know now that this is the first time that the special counsel investigation has evidence that demonstrated members of his campaign had ties to Russian officials," said Roman Anthony Andrews.

Already, the members of the resistance and the United Labourists were seizing on the fact that a former campaign official for Carlton Winters has pleaded guilty for some sort of process crime. Several Senators that are United Labourists are already saying that this demonstrates that President Carlton Winters is a bad actor and has several bad actors in his campaign and in his administration.

They believe that this plea deal demonstrates that the Russians stole the election away from their chosen candidate and anointed majesty, Cynthia Norwell Anderson, because it says something about links between the campaign of Carlton Winters and Russia.

That shows they will just lie about anything, because they just have hatred for the president that they won't overlook.

It is just a sad day in America when they want to skew everything in their favor by not waiting for the full story.

That is just the point of everything they are saying in regards to this breaking news story on October 5, 2017 and they are doing it to every other news story that hits the newswires so they can spread their propaganda.

It is always about something that has to do with nothing.

Suddenly, something happened that the members of the resistance and the United Labourists might enjoy.

Today, on October 27, 2017, a grand jury for the special counsel has just delivered their first indictments for the special counsel investigation.

It surely will lead to proof that there certainly was Russian interference that helped Carlton Winters to win the presidency, but that won't be the whole story, as it won't be reported entirely.

Instead, they will certainly be happy that the president might be impeached soon, even if there is no evidence linking Russia helping anyone.

But it won't even make any difference whatsoever because they think they can just get away with a bunch of lies and propaganda.

And the news is just breaking on the wires now so reactions might be immediate.

"This just in, we have the first indictments from the special counsel investigation, but we do not know at this time the people or entities that were indicted because that is still under seal, so we will have to wait and see what happened today in a few days or so," said Roman Anthony Andrews.

Critics of the president began to speculate about who it was but they were united in saying it was evidence that Russia helped him steal the 2016 presidential election.

Whether it shows evidence or not, there seems to be a rationale amongst the liberal media crowd that Carlton Winters is guilty until proven innocent.

Something dangerous like that should never be tolerated because it will just lead to a police state in the near future if all of those people keep it up, and eventually they will believe it is necessary to pass bad legislation that is unconstitutional in nature that infringes on the rights of the people.

There is some certainty to that but it can be prevented.

But there is no reason why they would want to investigate the truth.

Instead, if they can't find anything then they will try to manipulate the facts in order to get an indictment that is closely affiliated with the president, only because the person indicted did not tell the special counsel what they wanted to hear.

That just shows you that the special counsel is not seeking the truth.

The actual truth is that in at least one case the special counsel will try to invent some charges because no crime was committed, and in that same situation, the people being targeted actually lie, but instead forgot something due to a lapse in memory, but that is common to forget something.

So then, the people or person being targeted will try to revise or update the special counsel with the things they might have just forgotten by looking at specific evidence suggested to them.

And that could refresh their memory.

So, there is no intention to ever to lie to the special counsel, because forgetting something is not actually a crime, but it will lead to a crime if the special counsel is upset that they couldn't get any of the information that they wanted.

Because, the special counsel has already made up their mind, as they developed that if people being targeted are telling them the truth then that truth being told by them isn't actually the truth because they did not include information that was already gathered.

And what this tells everyone is that the special counsel is inventing a crime saying if you forget stuff because of a memory lapse we will send you to jail.

That is just a violation of the constitution and should be condemned by everyone, but the resistance and United Labourists support the idea of forgetfulness as a new crime, because they think it will lead to the impeachment of the president that is currently presiding in the White House.

The crime of forgetting is only a crime in those countries that do not support the very idea of a small government and restricting the role of what a government can do.

It is a crime for which there is no standard to ever be even tolerated in a civilized world.

It is a crime in countries that seek to only destroy civil liberties, freedom, along with the pursuit of happiness, freedom of speech, freedom of religion, and freedom of press.

It is a crime only in those certain countries that seek to suppress speech that goes against what the government wants.

The very basis is to limit what people can do so that only the government can be in control of everything.

The ultimate goal is fascism by restricting and silencing other views, beliefs, and opinion.

The ultimate goal is to turn toward socialism, then to communism, and to finally adopt a Marxist state that takes money away from people and redistribute it to the people who don't deserve it because they either don't want the money or they believe people must work hard to earn it.

And by refusing the money, then the people will be subject to criminal action because they disagreed with the intentions of the government.

And the resistance and the United Labourists are all fine with all of that, because they believe it is necessary to fund all of these welfare programs so that people won't have to work.

It is just a way to get more voters and to rely on the government for everything.

Stuff like that is just wasteful spending but the media just enjoys it for the fact that it might lead to something new.

The people must realize that something is going to hunt them down if they don't keep on checking with the world.

Surely, there will be a time when a lapse in memory will become some sort of crime because someone or some entity did not remember some particular message or event.

It will lead to chaos and destruction while the resistance and the United Labourists will rise to power in an attempt to seize control from the people who support the idea of a limited and small government because the resistance and the United Labourists believe government needs to be involved in everything.

That is just how bad everything seems to be.

Such a tactic described is a fishing expedition but can also be called a witch hunt.

And people are just letting it happen blindly because there is just no accountability.

News reports on October 28, 2017 indicate the first indictments had to deal with Russian meddling.

Once reported, the resistance along with the United Labourists felt excited with jubilation that there was finally some evidence of Russian collusion, but little did they know it had nothing to do with collusion.

This is just the tip of the iceberg but the resistance and the United Labourists are so full of hatred and moronic behavior that they fail to see the bigger picture.

They are just trying too hard but they always try to make something up if they become distressed.

But something happens that is about to shake up everything.

The day after, on October 29, 2017, it is revealed that the special counsel has seized 3 of Bouchfer's bank accounts.

Immediately, the liberal news media and the pundits seize on that news and are convinced that Gary Bouchfer is a bad man because the special counsel has found he helped the campaign of Carlton Winters to collude with Russia.

There is no mention of Russian collusion and what even seems interesting is that this case does not have anything to deal with Russia.

The resistance and the United Labourists have never been more excited in their lives, as they now believe the special counsel is going after people close to the president, and they believe this is just the beginning that will lead to the indictment and impeachment of the President of the United States of America, even if the constitution says that the president can be impeached by the House of Representatives and put on trial in the Senate.

The president is immune from being indicted by an outside entity, as that is deemed unconstitutional, which would ultimately cause a constitutional crisis.

And the resistance and United Labourists are already saying the president is causing a constitutional crisis but that is just simply not true, because it is they that want to cause a constitutional crisis by trying to eliminate the president from power because they don't like him or his policy agenda.

Then the next day arrives.

On October 30, 2017, the news media reports that Gary Bouchfer has surrendered himself to the CBDI after being indicted just days ago, and the resistance and United Labourists are just in awe and excitement because they believe it will lead to the downfall of the President of the United States of America.

They are overly joyed that they will be able to see the light at the end of the tunnel and that Bouchfer will now turn against Carlton Winters.

It is still early in the day but there is just more news to come.

Surely they think it is the happiest day in the world but they are already doing their rounds on liberal media networks saying that this news about Bouchfer means there is proof and evidence that Carlton Winters colluded with Russia to steal the election away from their anointed choice Cynthia Norwell Anderson.

But the resistance and the United Labourists are too quick to pounce that they are making up stuff again that doesn't even make sense.

They are saying this is evidence of Russian collusion but it has nothing to do with that.

The case against Bouchfer actually has to deal with money laundering, conspiracy against the United States of America, along with racketeering.

Still, the resistance and the United Labourists believe it has everything to do with Russia, while just saying a bunch of nonsense in the name of their ideology.

It couldn't be further from the truth but they don't care because they are the resistance.

That seems to be intentional, so they don't even hold members of their own movement or ideology accountable the same way as the Centralists.

Surely the resistance cares about what they are actually doing but they rather harm America because they never believed in the founding values and beliefs of America to begin with.

All they care about are alleged injustices, most of which are not really injustices, as it is only in their minds that there is a problem to begin with.

So, it is just something that is fictitious in nature.

But something might just appear on the news later on in the day or sooner because of Russia.

On that same day, the second to the last day of October, news just broke again that Alexander Christopoulos has pleaded guilty to one count of lying, according to the special counsel.

The news media picked it up and all of the leftist pundits, the members of the resistance, and the members of the United Labourists all pounced on the theory that Carlton Winters only hires liars and people do not know what they are dying.

Eventually, they will call any campaign official sketchy because of ties to Russia.

But as the news is coming out, more information is revealed.

National Media News Network is reporting that Alexander Christopoulos has engaged with someone known as Andres Zerafa that is linked with the Kremlin in Russia.

Zerafa allegedly told Christopoulos that he had extremely damaging information on the campaign of Cynthia Norwell Anderson from Russian officials in the form of several thousands of emails, but there is no evidence that any information was ever traded between both parties.

That seems to be an indication that people will be willing to accept information about another political campaign if they had any help that would help other political campaigns.

But then, the resistance and the United Labourists have made it a crime to get dirt on other people, as they see it as Russian meddling and a threat to democracy.

Well, it is neither of those options, and opposition research is done all the time, but it is only illegal when foreign government officials are paid to gather opposition information due to bribery, and yet Zerafa is not even a foreign government official.

It is just another tactic of hypocrisy that is employed by members of the resistance and the United Labourists.

They want to bring the country down to a crisis in order to get their way.

And it just remains to be seen when it will all be over, as people believe anything more will damage the country to the end of time in chaos and destruction.

Chaos and destruction will rue the day when people need to care for their lives in a time of need.

It isn't all that special but life is more important than the constant complaints from the resistance and the United Labourists.

It is just a lame excuse from them in order to seek attention.

That has always been the case and it will be that way forever and eternity unless there is such a nuisance that prevents that.

For that purpose, there is a time to say nothing is off the limits.

It isn't as crazy as it seems but it is normal throughout the time of existence.

So there must be speculation about what is going to happen in the near future with an abundance of caution.

VI

On November 10, 2017, the notorious Washington Bulletin released another nonsense publication saying that there is ample evidence indicating that Russia helped influenced Carlton Winters to win the 2016 presidential election, all based upon flawed and biased analysis.

It remains to be seen if a liberal newspaper headquartered in the nation's capital can be unbiased in their reporting.

That is something that must be known or there is just a curse that will continue to haunt the world.

But still, when this analysis report was released, the same people that opposed Carlton Winters seized on it by saying he stole the election away from Anderson with the help of Russia.

They just do not comprehend that it is a flawed and biased analysis intended to say that Carlton Winters shouldn't be the president because we didn't vote for him.

It is all of the same repeated nonsense as always and it continues to stay that way until something else happens.

All the same people will just appear in the news as they have always appeared and it will be the time to go against the sands of time.

There is a case to be made about the time in need in order to get to the bottom of anything.

They hypocrisy never ends and it will continue unless someone finally decides to stop it.

Notorious liberal newspapers are hoping that doesn't happen due to the fact that they want chaos and destruction to continue.

And it will be at the center of attention for reckless decisions.

They are trying to create some sort of smear campaign by using anonymous sources that shall not be named due to the possibility that they don't exist.

If they do exist then they are not even telling the truth, because anyone can be a source, but that means they got the information from some place unrelated.

They are trying to ruin the country and create a national crisis because they just hate the person in the White House.

It is all a sham and it should be stopped, but just when people thought it could be over, another story is published by the Washington Bulletin in a case that seems familiar again saying absolute nonsense.

And then there seems to be something huge.

News is breaking today on December 1, 2017, as there is a lot of speculation that someone is about to plead guilty in the special counsel investigation.

It could be about Russia or something else.

There is just the case the resistance will go with the Russian narrative.

It is the exact reason why people don't know or learn anything from the liberal media, because they have too many people on that say something that has yet to be proven or the people being interviewed are just making something up.

So, maybe, that is why the people that watch certain channels create hoaxes and conspiracy theories that have no standing.

Still, there is just speculation about what is going on in the minds of people that question what is being said on the news because there have been countless times that journalists have gotten the story wrong.

Speculation is just growing on who will be indicted next by the special counsel.

Some people believe it is Carlton Winters that will be the next one to be indicted but there is a problem with that as he is immune from being prosecuted since he is subject to the whims of Congress.

Others think it could be Carlton Winters Jr. because they say that taking a meeting with a foreign lawyer is an act of collusion.

Then there are the people that speculate it could be anyone associated with Carlton Winters.

The members of this so-called resistance movement against the president and his policy agenda are just wasting their time because they won't get to see the light of day when something bad happens to their movement.

It is all speculation and it is just the same as always without regard to the truth.

And then, a breaking news story just appeared on the newswires indicating the person to be indicted won't be indicted because a plea deal was reached between the special counsel and the defendant.

So, it seems there is no story to tell, but then more information is released. It is reported that former National Security Adviser Lt. Gen. Vincent McLoughlin is about to plead guilty to one count of giving false testimony to federal investigators in exchange for the special counsel not to go after his son.

The news is breaking constantly about the case and the crazy pundits are having a field day and they still believe it is the best day in the world.

Already, the resistance and the United Labourists are saying that this proves the claim of Russian collusion in the election because they say that he lied about talking to a Russian ambassador.

But they failed to realize that it was his job to lead the transition of important national security interests so that Carlton Winters will be prepared before taking the oath of office.

It is part of the requirement for the job to adopt a foreign policy before taking over as the next president of the United States of America.

But they refuse to accept that because they say the wrong person won the election.

That is just their opinion but they will never stop their claims because they just can't face the truth and accept the outcome.

It is always about something that they think is proper.

And with the recent revelations of the events, many members of the media are happy with joy and excited as hell, because the majority of them are part of the resistance or are staunch United Labourists.

It is just that bad in the terms of a country.

The members of the resistance are still at it because they refuse to accept the outcome of the election but when Carlton Winters said he might not accept the outcome of the election so that he can wait and see if he ever needed to file a lawsuit in regards to the results they had a field day saying he wouldn't accept the outcome of an election.

So, the resistance believes it is just fine and dandy to criticize a presidential candidate about what he says but not fine when they are doing the exact same thing.

It is just hypocrisy and the resistance and United Labourists do not want to admit that a double standard applies to them and them only.

That is not justice but they want to have their cake and eat it too.

There is just more breaking news about the former national security adviser, as the liberal media is reporting that Vincent McLoughlin was a rogue and renegade agent.

It is something that is being done from within the White House because they are trying to distance themselves from someone that is considered a disgrace now.

The media is just giddy as ever because they are trying to say that the administration is embarrassed at the actions of the former decorated army general.

Something is just part of ordinary life and that will never change for the better of society.

People do not care about what is happening and everything will eventually fall apart.

Slowly but surely a new order will start.

The Broadcasting Corporation of America News Agency or BCA News is reporting that they have just learned through anonymous sources that Vincent McLoughlin will testify against the president in a court of law in the near future.

Soon, all the members of the resistance started to go along with the report of becoming a state's witness against a sitting president because they all believed some biased reporting from a renegade news correspondent in the name of democracy.

The resistance was happy and they even started to celebrate in the streets.

It seemed like everything was going their way until it didn't.

There is just something wrong with the news being reported that has to concern Carlton Winters.

A sitting president can never be indicted because it is written in the constitution that is left up to Congress to decide.

But they do not even care about that, as they forgot about it or they have never read the constitution.

And if they did read it then they have a different perspective of it because they say it should be a living document that changes with the times because of Progressivism.

They fail to understand the very basic concepts of what the founders wanted but they simply do not care that they are wrong because they believe they are always right.

It is just a sham and a sad day in America.

It will all come crashing down sooner or later and then it did for the better of the country.

The BCA News correspondent that reported the news regarding Vincent McLoughlin turning state witness against a sitting president has been suspended for 4 weeks, and the claim they said was only because he said candidate Carlton Winters and not president-elect Carlton Winters.

So it was only due to something that described Carlton Winters in the wrong context in terms of an appropriate noun.

But that is not the end of the news regarding this shameful reporting.

It was alledged that Vincent McLoughlin would become state witness against Carlton Winters because of the comments and views his former boss made concerning the defeat of the Islamic State.

So now if someone says they will grind the Islamic State into a pulp so that they don't terrify and kill people around the world, then it is viewed somehow as a threat to democracy.

And democracy is never better because threatening to kill the enemy abroad is not a threat to democracy, as the enemy is a bunch of terrorists.

It's a good thing that the BCA News correspondent was suspended but then the members of the resistance stated that the suspension was an attack against the freedom of the press and democracy.

As always, they were quick to attack the decision.

The crazy attacks from those resistance members just want to have it both ways because they do not know what they want to see in America.

It is just part of life but they don't care about hypocrisy.

They believed the news report to be truthful because they wanted it to, as it targeted Carlton Winters and his policy agenda.

They are just full of themselves because something is just crazy in them.

So, they believe the BCA News correspondent that wrote and presented the story was wronged when they suspended him.

That is such a double standard but it is just crazy to say that.

But since the news story was retracted the resistance is just screaming now and getting nervous that maybe they just won't get Carlton Winters.

Something needs to happen now and soon before the resistance seizes on more false reporting.

It isn't the end of the world but to the resistance if they don't get the president on anything then they might give up hope and that will result in chaos and confusion because they thought the president did indeed did something illegal that would warrant indictment or impeachment proceedings.

It will surprise them when nothing happens to him in regards to the special counsel investigation but then they will say it was fixed from the beginning.

They will attempt to cry wolf again because they didn't get what they wanted in the beginning.

They will get very frustrated and angry that they couldn't get Carlton Winter's head on a silver platter as they would like because there is just no evidence.

It is a fry car for help in a need of a much bitter crisis.

There is just the case that needs to stand but they are acting like a bunch of hysterical babies.

Everything has always been this way and it seems it isn't going to end.

And just like that, the resistance seized again against the president for the comments he recently made.

They criticized him for saying that he felt very bad for McLoughlin.

The media just ate that up and said he was wrong to feel bad for his national security adviser because they claim it was wrong for him to work with Russia to develop a better relationship with them for the United States of America.

They want to keep it as the status quo because they blame Russia as the enemy that stole the election away from their anointed candidate.

It certainly won't be crazy but they are just crazy as hell due to all the procedures that must take place.

That is likely to never happen because they will argue that the president is always wrong, even if they support it, due to it coming from the person that they didn't vote for because they believe he should not be the president of the greatest country in the world.

It is surely the best thing in the world to impeach him.

But they just don't stop at anything because a breaking news report has just been released accusing Bouchfer of writing an op-ed with someone in Ukraine.

The prosecutors for the special counsel alledged that Bouchfer secretly co-wrote an op-ed piece with a Ukrainian journalist with ties to the intelligence agencies of Russia while out on bail.

The resistance as well as the United Labourists seized on this information and said it is proof that Russia stole the election for Carlton Winters and that the president only hires bad people that are against the democracy in America.

And they said it is time to lock everyone up that is associated with Carlton Winters. It is just the same old thing again but then they become overjoyed again for the purpose that the prosecutors are seeking to revoke the bail for Gary Bouchfer because they believe he has violated the terms of the bail as well as being a threat to the rest of the world.

Just now, people were dancing in the streets for something that was just crazy.

It would seem that they just want to be happy about something that other people don't really care about, but they don't care, as they are not a part of Middle America, as they don't like what Middle America stands for.

It is just a case of elitism.

The case has never been clearer and it seems there is only one way of moving forward.

The people must never look back at what is happening to the country or else there will just be confusion about what is happening in the world today.

It will just be a case to figure out the reasoning behind this type of organization.

And there is just something that isn't about what is going to happen.

The resistance and United Labourists are nervous and afraid that the president will fire the special counsel but they have no evidence of that, as Carlton Winters has repeatedly said that he has no intentions of firing the special counsel because that would be politically devastating.

It is just the case of everything wrong with society.

And before something is set to begin it will be over, just like everything else.

They claimed that America pulling out of the Paris Climate Deal was bad for democracy because they say it will be bad for the environment.

But they do not like it when the president criticizes the CBDI.

It is just strange about what is happening, but tomorrow is a new year in America and there are just better things to deal with.

VII

The New Year has approached and now it is January 3, 2018, but there is word that Gary Bouchfer is about to sue the special counsel because he believes the special counsel has too much power as no one even elected the special counsel so it seems the special counsel reports to no one and the resistance and United Labourists are just fine with that.

It just shows you that they support a police state.

But there is just something going on that needs to happen.

The resistance and the liberal media might just laugh off this lawsuit by Bouchfer's lawyers or they could take it seriously.

But then it just hit the newswires and people are just now reacting to it.

Already, the pundits are laughing their asses off, because they seem to think Bouchfer has no case.

What's even better is that they say they feel sorry for Bouchfer because of his nonsense lawsuit that they claim is nonsense due to the fact they believe it has no chances at succeeding in a court of law.

It is just something that is intriguing to them.

But soon enough the pundits and the resistance make their way onto television news programs claiming this latest lawsuit by a former associate affiliated with Carlton Winters proves that he is hiding something because he knows that Russia stole the election.

Members of the resistance are going on every news network to make their claims even if they know it is false, but they simply don't care because they just want to target anyone associated with the president.

It makes it clearer that there is just a campaign to get anyone that is affiliated with the current administration.

They liked that Bouchfer's lawyers filed the lawsuit against the special counsel because they say it demonstrates that Bouchfer himself is an agent of Russia and is willing to make up stuff in order to get out of going to prison for a very long time.

It is just something that they want but they are just part of the problem due to the fact that they are only doing this because it is Carlton Winters that they hate.

For that very reason, they have no claims of credibility.

It is just the thing that they say is the real reason because they want the president to be impeached just because they hate who he is and that is just plain moronic and idiotic at the same time because they don't understand anything.

But it never gets old, yet it never ends, so it will continue forever and forever.

That is the only thing that is the life of their movement until it dies in a slow death.

And then the Washington Bulletin published something more.

Several leading House United Labourists are urgently calling on Shrieker and Social Media Enterprises to investigate and then combat Russian bots and trolls on their social media platforms.

It seems the reasoning behind this is because the United Labourists know that there is no Russian collusion that ever stole the election away from Cynthia Norwell Anderson, but they are just going with the narrative in order to please their base and to also say that Carlton Winters does not deserve to be president because we never liked him.

They are just using this as a charade because they know Carlton Winters won fair and square in the 2016 election, but they need to make up an excuse as to why they didn't win.

It all makes sense, but to them the idea of Russian collusion is the better option forward, because they say it explains everything, even if they know it isn't true.

The United Labourists are just digging a hole deeper and deeper without getting anywhere after getting rebuked from their critics about the Russian collusion narrative.

Everything is about Russia because they need to find evidence of something related to their theory or else they will have to make something up again.

It is just the pit of the iceberg and it continues to grow.

The majority of the people, mainly every single voter who was eligible to vote in the election, said that no one influenced them to vote for Carlton Winters.

And then the media picked up on the narrative saying that Russia influenced their vote for Carlton Winters, even though only a handful of people saw the advertisements, probably near 0.01% of the population, yet still the resistance, United Labourists, and the media ran with the narrative that Russia influenced the 2016 presidential election.

It is a clear sign that they cannot comprehend anything.

Many supporters of Carlton Winters have already debunked this narrative that Russia influenced their vote but they seem not to comprehend that Cynthia Norwell Anderson failed to campaign in several northern blue states that were supposedly safe for many other United Labourists in the past.

And they also can't comprehend that she failed to win the election because her message was largely unsupported in Middle America.

Nevertheless, everything is a repeat of the election, claiming it was stolen from her, but no real evidence is ever cited because it lacks the support and credibility of the facts.

In every instance, there seems to be something wrong, but it just keeps coming back to this same scenario that the United Labourist could not believe that they lost an election after 8 years of Barrington Martin being in office.

Of course the same political party will lose the presidency after 8 full years of being in office, because of change, as the people get tired of the same old policies over and over again.

So, the people vote for a different person for president that is affiliated with some other political party.

And that has always been the case most times but with a few exceptions.

They cry out against the Electoral College because they say it isn't representative of a true democracy.

Well then, the reason there is an Electoral College is to make sure that the smaller states are never ever disenfranchised by the much larger states.

In a sense, it makes sure that California, Florida, Texas, New York, and other larges states don't decide the outcome alone.

And by establishing it this way it allows all voices of America to be heard and not just the people that live on the coasts.

It is a question of equal representation but it seems none of the members of the resistance and United Labourists gets that so they rather eliminate the Electoral College.

But now the Washington Bulletin has published another piece saying that the special counsel is interested in seeking answers as to why Carlton Winters fired McLoughlin and Ronald.

It is a mystery why this is being asked in the first place because the special counsel already knows the reason why.

It is just a diversion tactic and possibly a trap.

Now though, the many members of the resistance are applauding this move, because they believe it shows malice and intent to obstruct justice.

There is a problem with this accusation concerning obstruction of justice because Carlton Winters, and two top officials in the Department of Justice released the reasoning behind why Carl Ronald was fired, and ultimately Carlton Winters himself said he fired McLoughlin because he lied to the Vice President.

So it seems that the United Labourists and the resistance are relaying a sham, a hoax in fact, in order to lie to the American people.

The goal is to mislead the public by spreading propaganda into the sphere of influence.

It is a sign from someplace that the resistance and United Labourists are losing the upper hand, so they must start accusing people of committing obstruction of justice.

But just then, on the same afternoon of January 23, 2018, they are now making the claim of an abuse of power for the firing of Carl Ronald.

Yet, they seem to forget that they viewed Ronald as the enemy of the state and of democracy because of what they viewed of giving the election to Carlton Winters.

They blame Carl Ronald for Cynthia Norwell Anderson losing.

So now it is perplexing to see them defend him because they didn't like that Carlton Winters was the one to fire him.

It is all a case of extreme jealousy.

And it will continue until someone dies in a deadly fire for which there is no escape, which will become the crime of the century, so there is no hope or change for anything.

The resistance and United Labourists are hopeful that Carlton Winters did commit malfeasance in office because of what he did to disgraced former CBDI director Carl Ronald, as they view that as the end of the world, as well as obstruction of justice because they say the intent was to make sure that the Russia investigation be interfered with.

It is something ridiculous because there is no truth to that, as the investigation could continue on without him, as the replacement will take over, and career agents do the work.

So, they do not have any actual standing in their arguments about the president.

It is just so weak that they can't think of anything else. Something just needs to occur in a nick of time that will stop everything.

But before long, the Washington Bulletin decides to publish another one of its attack pieces, this time two days later on January 25, 2018.

The journalists or reporters that wrote the piece are accusing of Carlton Winters of trying to fire the special counsel in June 2017, but then they claim that he backed off when the White House Counsel said he would resign.

Yet there is more to the story they claimed.

The piece also reported Carlton Winters would consider firing deputy attorney general Miles Reymond because it was him that appointed the special counsel to begin with.

Soon, it was all over the airwaves, and the United Labourists and the members of the resistance were up in arms.

They were so furious because of the possibility Carlton Winters considered firing their hero, which was the special counsel.

They viewed the special counsel as some sort of divine God while also criticizing God at the same time because they refuse to accept him as a divine being.

Instead, they rather attack religion and say that it is not good for society.

And soon they will claim Jesus was a socialist, with no real evidence to back it up.

But as soon as it was on the airwaves, the people that hated the president wanted to see him impeached.

It was like they saw him as a threat to democracy and freedom.

One prominent United Labourist Senator exclaimed that this was the worst day in the history of our democracy, as it is a threat to the future of our existence.

Another prominent United Labourist Senator said the attempted firing was an embarrassment to the rest of the world because it presents obstruction of justice in the highest form.

And then a prominent United Labourist House member said this demonstrates flagrant disregard for the rule of law and a violation of the constitution of the United States of America.

Another prominent United Labourist House member said that the action represents an abuse of power and obstruction of justice, as the president does not care about the rule of law.

And then, there were prominent members of the House and Senate that called for impeachment because the president thought about firing the special counsel, yet all of them were part of the resistance and the United Labourists.

They are all claiming it is a threat to the democracy when really it's not, since America is a federal republic, so that derails their argument.

Their shenanigans are all the same as they are seeking a cry for help due to revealing their true selves to the public at large by claiming that they are the true supporters of freedom, liberty, democracy, and the pursuit of happiness.

But they refuse to accept that the special counsel is indeed a witch hunt, because they actually support police state tactics by saying it should never end.

And that is just plain wrong, because the special counsel was based on a lie to begin with.

There was no reason to appoint it and there was no reason why it was needed.

Moreover, the memo appointing the special counsel points out no crime to investigate except for crimes found during the normal process of the investigation.

And with that, collusion is not even a crime, so everything is illegitimate to begin with, but it seems that none of the members of the resistance and the United Labourists get that, as they are just too preoccupied with getting the president for crimes they made up due to not liking him.

There is nothing unusual about what is happening according to the resistance and the United Labourists, but that is because they fail to align with Middle America, as they don't really care about the Middle Class due to the resistance and United Labourists being arrogant, since they care more about identity politics.

But sooner or later they will try to attack and cause another issue.

Then everything will begin again with the same issues being debated over and over again.

VIII

An abundance of caution was something to be careful about, as there was a new talk of the town today.

And it was only the last day of January, so there is still time to go.

But today the issue was the Ruelas Memo and why some House United Labourists are taking issue with it.

Prominent critic of Carlton Winters and noted member of the United Labourists, David Lorman of the House Permanent Select Committee on Intelligence, decided to attack the Ruelas Memo for being too transparent.

It's all about a plan to target the president and the United Labourists think it might work. They don't want the truth to be told.

They want to create a fictional narrative that does not fit the current evidence.

Ranking member David Lorman believes it's his thing to do in order to put out a narrative that targets the president because he says it is imperative to convince everyone in America that Russia stole the election from Cynthia Norwell Anderson.

Lorman constantly believes Russia is to blame for why Carlton Winters won the presidential election but he fails to cite any real evidence whatsoever.

Lorman keeps saying the evidence proves that Carlton Winters was in talks with Russian officials to collude in the 2016 general election, but the transcript do not actually say anything like that due to the matter that he wants that to be the case.

He's just so desperate to prove that he is right that he is willing to spread lies, falsehoods, and propaganda to the American people.

That is just his way of telling America that he does not care what the people think because he believes he is always right even when he knows he is wrong.

And then Lorman is trying to criticize the Ruelas Memo again, saying that new information was added that was never even approved by the committee in order to create a false narrative.

But there is no false narrative coming from Congressman Ruelas, as he has seen the very same evidence firsthand, the same evidence that Congressman Lorman saw, but David Lorman believes there is evidence to support his claim of Russians colluding because he knows nothing exist.

The media does not like what Ruelas is doing because they developed the same narrative that believes in the hoax concerning Russia engineered the election for Carlton Winters in an attempt to attack America.

That is just jealousy coming from the people that do not like that their choice didn't win.

For all other purposes, David Lorman is now saying that it is not the same memo as before, so then he believes it must not be released or else it is a threat to the national security of the United States of America.

That could be true or he could be covering up for some people that he knows committed some form of wrongdoing.

It is a case that screams corruption. But the will never learn their lesson, since they are so determined to believe something that doesn't exist.

Lorman's goal is to cause confusion amongst the masses in order to persuade everyone that his theory about Russia collusion is the only reason why Carlton Winters won, but he continually fails to identify and of the evidence that exists, because none exists supporting his theory, as the real reason Carlton Winters was due to people not liking his opponent, Cynthia Norwell Anderson.

Nothing will ever change until it leads to something that is new to the world.

And then it was the day of February 2, 2018, so it was certain that the president will declassify the Ruelas Memo.

The day is still young so it might take a while to be released, with all of the bureaucratic structures within the confines of the CBDI and many national security agencies.

It wouldn't be a surprise if some officials within the national security agencies and the CBDI try to redact certain names, sentences, or paragraphs, because they might say keeping those in would amount to revealing sources and methods.

That might be claimed by the resistance, the United Labourists, and other people that are opposed to it being released because it most likely embarrasses people that did something wrong.

The people opposed to the release of the memo just don't want to be called out after they were caught red-handed with doing some inappropriate things, such as misleading federal judges, just because they didn't like certain people so that those people could be investigated in a biased and unnatural way.

Time will tell when they are finally caught but the American people that support transparency won't understand why anyone would be against the releasing of the memo.

The American people will then understand that the people opposing the release support a police state that surveils anyone whoever they want to and whenever, as it allows many or all of these national security agencies to unlawfully track people. It is a sign that demonstrates big government because they don't care for the constitution as it was written.

They want to replace it with something more sinister, something more evil, and something that leads to totalitarianism.

They do not want America to succeed any more than a tyrannical despot that seeks to destroy every part of civilization.

There is a threat to their rule and they know it but they will try to stop anyone before they succeed.

The people will rise up.

They will see the threat of totalitarianism and they will take to the streets. They will make sure the totalitarianists will never succeed.

The people will march in uniform.

They will form a blockade along the roads to stop the threat of military force.

And there will be fire, chaos, and destruction if no one decapitates the person in charge.

Everything will then result in a revolution to take back the country and it soon will be new leadership in charge.

And the people will rise again in order to make sure this never happens again.

The threat of a true democracy is a threat to their rule and they know it for better or worse.

And that is why they don't want the Ruelas Memo to be released, because they know it will lead to freedom, life, liberty, and the pursuit of happiness.

They do not want that to happen so they will try to divide most of the country with propaganda.

It is a plan but it will work only if the people allow it to.

That is the point of everything, and it will lead to a global case of a diplomatic row.

But it was now later in the day, and there is now word that President Carlton Winters will declassify the Ruelas Memo in a matter of moments.

It will be determined for the accuracy but there is no word on how the members of the resistance and United Labourists will respond to any of it.

They could be mad and angry as hell or they could be happy and not panic.

But they will most likely be mad and angry as hell and will later become nervous and then start to panic, because they fear that the president will be re-elected to a second term in office, and that would be their worst fear.

It just shows the people that they can't handle the truth.

That is something to really fear about and it won't be long until it might happen.

The strong intent of blocking anything because of many government cover-ups is not good for the country and it certainly demonstrate what is wrong with people in power.

Because these people want to harm America by not supporting freedom and liberty as well as anything that has to do with the promotion of a written constitution, because they regard everything as living and changing with the times.

It needs to be kept and viewed the way it was intended.

And if it's not, then the resistance and United Labourists will try to restrict not only the constitution, but the Bill of Rights, because they want to promote a police state that surveils everyone without regard except for their friends at the very tippy top of the food chain.

So there will almost certainly be high crimes and misdemeanors and corruption to the extent that no one will ever abolish or remove them from power because it will be impossible to do so.

That will surely be the death of democracy as we know it and no one will be able to stop any of it.

At last, the Ruelas Memo was declassified and released in the early to mid-afternoon, and it was just as expected.

There was outrage coming from the resistance and United Labourists as originally expected.

They were just angry as hell because they believed releasing the memo would amount some sort of threat to national security.

That was not the case, as found by the few independent journalists and reporters who saw through the deception from the resistance and United Labourists.

There was no threat to anyone and it was just as expected.

The memo revealed that the dossier was the basis for everything, but the far-left believed otherwise.

The memo did not reveal any sources or methods.

Instead it revealed a plan of trying to take down a person that sought to become the next president, all because of hatred.

It was a case of deception because every bit of that dossier was already proven to be false and based on lies from Russian sources.

And it was the case that the United Labourists and resistance believed Russia was responsible for their person losing, yet the dossier came from Russian sources, so they can't have it both ways.

They can either blame Russia or support Russia.

But by accepting the dossier that means they support the Russian government, while also saying they opposed Russia because of collusion.

It is just hypocrisy and that is just crazy and a double standard.

IX

Outrage after outrage filled the airwaves, as the resistance and United Labourists spoke out against the releasing of the Ruelas Memo, and it was only February 3, 2018.

The resistance and the United Labourists can't handle whatever they are going through. It could be that they are having some sort of mental breakdown and do not want to seek help because they are just acting so crazy.

It's possible they believe what they are saying because of their still crazy belief that Cynthia Norwell Anderson won the election.

Then they say Anderson won the popular vote because the popular vote is the true and actual form of democracy.

They claim the Electoral College is outdated but they fail to see that it helps prevent the larger states from making decisions in the end.

Still, they claim Anderson won 3 million more voters than Carlton Winters, but they fail to reveal that most or all of those 3 million votes are from the blue United Labourists state of California.

Their claim of Anderson winning the popular is just saying that the people that voted for someone else such as Carlton Winters does not even matter.

Their views present the real threat to actual democracy because of what they are demanding but the media will probably shrug it off, at least according to the Centralists, because many of Anderson's supporters will say an attack against their candidate is just one of many right-wing conspiracies.

So it seems that there are still too many people that support a form of socialism, communism, or Marxism, because they believe the government should be in charge of everything.

That just shows a break in traditional values, as there is a price to pay if you do not join their bandwagon.

And they call themselves the resistance because they think they will rise up and take back control.

They might think that but they will ultimately lose.

No one can tell them anything and it seems they will not even concede if they lose.

Before it's all over, they will throw another tantrum, because of what they see as a threat to society in their minds.

And it indeed happened again when the president proclaimed on Shrieker that the Ruelas Memo vindicates him in the Russian collusion investigation.

But the resistance as well as the United Labourists was not having it, because they decided to make up their own claim of saying that it is nothing more than Russian propaganda.

They just can't handle the truth as it seems.

Then the pundits started appearing on their favorite shows as always and saying that the president is living on his own little fantasy world.

They do not like what he is saying because of their own prejudiced views.

It seems they will stop at nothing and continue their hatred by saying a bunch of nonsense.

Some are saying that the president is having his own mental breakdown and that he needs to seek help now or the country will go into chaos.

Others are calling for the president to be removed from office and are asserting the 25th amendment, and are saying that he is a threat of the country because they say he is unstable.

But they fail to realize that Timothy Simon would be a nightmare for them, as they will just use the same tactics and methodology against him, because they will hate his views on abortion and other issues.

The issue remains to be seen and it will be the time and place for something to see.

And then, David Lorman will say he and his group of many United Labourists colleagues will vote to release a counter memo attacking the Ruelas Memo and saying that it is nothing more than propaganda because it doesn't tell the truth.

So, the United Labourists believe they will be the savior in protecting the special counsel, but it has nothing to do with the so-called special counsel, because they are really out to get the president, as they have revealed that in their commentary and on the airwaves by saying he is not to be trusted because we don't like him.

That is usual coming from them due to their base being the resistance that wants a do over for failing to win the 2016 election in November.

It is just a case that they can't handle but they are now saying that their memo will tell the truth and actually prove that the special counsel is correct in its nature for pursuing baseless charges against the people they despise.

It is just something sort of a cover up that makes no sense at all but no one will win against them.

They still have to debate the issue of when to release it but there could be a delay due to the nature of the wording.

But they are certain that they are right and everyone else is wrong because that is what they believe in.

It just amazes the people that didn't vote for them because of the resistance against the president, but they are not even surprised at what is happening.

Two days have passed, and it is now February 5, 2018, but there is a debate in the House Permanent Select Committee on Intelligence to decide if the new memo put forth by the United Labourists should be released, as the United Labourists believe it will prove their point that the Russians helped the campaign of Carlton Winters and made it possible that his opponent will never win because they claim Russia hates her.

That is all a ruse and will not bring up any new information.

Instead, it could very well prove that Ruelas was right in the beginning.

But the United Labourists and resistance will try to say that is not the case, because they very well believe it will reveal new and troubling information that the people will start to demand answers from their members of Congress.

It could also backfire but then they will claim it won't because they say they are always right.

That just shows the people that they are unaware of Middle America

.

At last, the committee is about to vote on whether to release the memo put forth by the United Labourists.

If it is not released then they will cry obstruction and abuse of power and if it is release they will say exactly the same thing.

That isn't anything new from them but they are just obsessed with this Russian collusion narrative since their choice did not win back in the month of November in the 2016 election, so that could be the cause for feeling petty about the current White House.

But they won't just stop this kind of nonsense.

That seems likely and it will be the time of the century in order to make up new evidence and crimes.

Then it was decided.

It was a unanimous vote from all members of the House Permanent Select Committee on Intelligence.

The news hit the airwaves as soon as the vote was over.

The supporters of the rebuttal Memo are saying that it is a great day for transparency but the Centralists on the committee never said they were opposed to releasing it, so this claim by the United Labourists seems to be just another propaganda attempt.

It was their chance to celebrate in the streets once again and they thought nothing was going to get in their way.

They are rejoicing on the news networks with many of their favorite pundits and news anchors.

It just couldn't get better than that for them, as they thought this was their chance to take charge of everything in the mindset of their truth.

It would finally be the time to take charge on what they believe is the true corruption but that won't get them anywhere in the confines of the truth. It is just something is going to happen that will turn against everything.

And then it was revealed to be at the center of what will happen next.

The David Lorman Memo as people called it will go the president's desk to see whether it shall be classified, but it might take some time if there is any sensitive information in there.

It is just impossible to say if and when the Lorman Memo will be released, because there could be and are more important issues at hand that the American people care about. Middle America does not really care about this because they know there are better and more important things that matter in their lives, as many don't care about the obsessions that United Labourists have with Russian collusion.

The people have money to make and they need to survive in order to live and work because they care about achieving the best possible outcome that exists to better promote their career and possibly be assigned to a higher position in the future if they have the potential.

But the resistance and United Labourists seem to not care about that as they call it reckless and endangerment.

So no one will know when the president will make a decision, because he says he has better things to do that matter more than releasing a bunch of propaganda.

At long last, the president made an announcement in regards to the David Lorman Memo.

He indicated that he would not release the memo to the public because it still contained numerous details and information that are said to be classified because of sources and methods.

Without any hesitation, the resistance and United Labourists balked at the decision, saying that it was just another attempt of blocking the truth and transparency.

It was just one more excuse from them again because they didn't get what they want, so now they have to revise it if they want it released to the public. Time will tell if the United Labourists want to do that.

But they did not relent.

They just kept on attacking the president saying it was an attack on democracy.

They claimed it was an infringement on the first amendment.

They went on the airwaves one after another and continued to sprout their propaganda by saying this was the worst thing in the world to happen in over 200 years since the founding of this country.

It was the same thing over and over again with just repeated nonsense and the same old rhetoric.

People were not surprised at what they were watching due to the same spin being said over and over again.

It can be such tiring of listening to the same old stuff again that has been debunked, but it seems they will just complain about everything, from helping the people in poverty to protecting national security.

The resistance and United Labourists just don't care for the common man and it shows it deeply.

It just shows that everything is a game to them and that has always been the case.

That is something that will try to be distorted but it's true for some reason or another.

That is just as crazy as the rest of the world and it continues to be that way for the eternal right of mind.

And that is why it will take a while to determine if the Lorman Memo is to be ever released.

Soon, the American people forgot about the Lorman Memo, but then today, February 23, 2018, the resistance and United Labourists received a new shiny object, and they will probably spin the same narrative as they have always did.

It was again breaking on the airwaves and this time it was about the Russian collusion investigation again.

The most adamant critics of the president started saying this was evidence of Russian collusion.

It had to do with a new superseding indictment against Gary Bouchfer, this time about being an unregistered foreign agent to a foreign principal, giving false information to investigators, and conspiracy against the United States of America.

The resistance and United Labourists seized on this new indictment about the crimes allegedly committed by Bouchfer.

They say that by being an unregistered foreign agent that proves

Russia stole the election for Carlton Winters.

But that proves nothing.

It means Bouchfer worked for someone else, which is not even closely related to Russian collusion.

The same thing was repeated all day long and it was just the beginning of what will be a long battle.

Pure nonsense is the name of their strategy and they even made an attempt to call the Ruelas Memo the worst thing that happened since the Saturday Night Massacre, in which the independent counsel was fired from his job.

They cried about that then and they are crying about something not like that today.

It is just crazy how they think but it will always remain some sort of mystery.

But there is a chance of hope that everything will change for the better of the country.

Then, it finally happened, as the resistance and United Labourists were just overjoyed.

Congress fixed the problems with the Lorman Memo and it was released on February 24, 2018, a day after a new indictment was filed against Bouchfer.

They were saying how it vindicated their theory of Russian collusion but then there was no evidence of that, so they still spun the lie of Russian collusion.

It was just another sad attempt and the delay was due to including classified information.

Before the day was over they thought they succeeded, but only to their base.

But they believed their spin was such a success that they don’t care whatever happens.

So it was just another day in the fantasy world of crazy people to the extent that people actually believe their theory is good and to always be trusted.

But that is not how it is as it is not true.

Another big day arrived, and it was February 28, 2018, the day that Gary Bouchfer pled not guilty to the new charges in the United States District Court for the District of Columbia.

News was just breaking on the case and the pundits believed Bouchfer made the wrong decision.

They already have decided to convict him in the court of public opinion because he worked with some unsavory figures that are said to be friends of the Russian government and Leninov.

Pundits felt sorry for his not-guilty, as they believed that there was overwhelming evidence against him.

That could be the case but no case should ever be decided in the court of public opinion.

It would be fine if they just stated their opinion why but they don't really do that in this case, as he worked for Carlton Winters.

It is indeed possible that Gary Bouchfer will be convicted of the charges against him because of the damning evidence of not paying taxes, but there is something wrong with a case if they say a person lied when there is no evidence that they intentionally lied.

So, if that was the case, then it would be an uphill battle for conviction on that particular charge during deliberations because the defendant might not always remember every single detail.

It's basically the crime of forgetting that is charged if the special counsel does not get what they want, and then they will try to say that it is also obstruction.

Well, if someone has a faulty memory or they just do not remember some particular detail, then that is not intentional.

The person or defendant fully believes that they couldn't remember, and that can be due to a lapse in memory, as people often forget certain things, since they have more important issues to deal with.

It would be hard for a jury to convict on a lapse in memory if the defendant truly believes that they didn't lie, but it will be appealed if there is a conviction.

Some people might not like that but facts are facts.

People are people.

And people always make honest mistakes, but it is always possible that anything can be taken out of context because of some rogue prosecutor that wants to get a person because there is a particular person that they are targeting.

It is always the same old thing but this is what the special counsel has come to.

That is exactly what is happening to Eugene Frozn, or at least that is what he has been saying for the past year or so, as he believes he will be indicted because he won't tell the special counsel what they want to know, as he isn't that type of person to flip, but no one actually cares about what is going to happen.

It would be a travesty if Frozn was convicted if he ever faced trial, because the prosecution would have to mislead everyone, saying that he intentionally lied to obstruct justice.

Well, if it wasn't intentional and he did indeed truly forgot about information, then the jury would have to acquit, as there would be no case for obstruction of justice because that is connected to perjury, and since he did not recall certain information due to memory issues, as is common with most people, then there will be no other choice than to acquit the perjury charges as well.

But there is no case yet and no indictment filed, yet Frozn believes it could be soon because he is always addressing the issue.

So it remains to be seen in a time of disarray when there is chaos and destruction because that will result from the special counsel to make up flimsy charges against innocent people because of a lack of some or any cooperation.

That is just something that the members of the resistance as well as the United Labourists will never understand, because they have a very deep hatred for the president.

The time has come that a decision needs to be made if Bouchfer will stay true to his word of not flipping, but the resistance believes he will, and that could result in a problem because he might lie.

But now a new problem has arisen involving the president's former personal attorney, Harrison Nicholas, who has come to the attention of the special counsel involving something sinister.

The Washington Bulletin is now reporting that on March 6, 2018 the special counsel is seeking a bunch of information regarding the Winfell Tower Project in Moscow, Russia for some reason or another, but the project was aborted to focus on the election of Carlton Winters.

Since that revelation, they have accused Carlton Winters and his company, the Winfell Organization, of being guilty because he wanted to build a hotel in Russia.

Members of the resistance and prominent United Labourists have already seized on the information regarding the proposal of Carlton Winters and his business to build a hotel in Russia immediately after the Washington Bulletin reported that the special counsel wanted to interview witnesses from within the Winfell Organization and Harrison Nicholas regarding the issue of documents.

It was just a firestorm and so it seemed the special counsel had no case of Russian collusion, but the supporters of the special counsel did not see it that way, as they believe this somehow confirms that Russia stole the election for Carlton Winters.

That isn't a valid argument but people will still believe anything, so it remains to be clear what is real and what can be now deemed as fake news.

Such an immediate response to something that are biased about just shows they can't handle anything because they are disillusioned by their new found glory of hatred and contempt for the president in office.

There is just more information needed before a decision can be made and it is just about as clear as day that nothing is about to demonstrate that.

And then it happened.

There was just something interesting going on outside.

Boom!

A crashing sound was heard from everywhere.

Cars started piling up.

Lightning struck the clock tower.

People soon started to hide because they did not know where to go and it seemed futile.

They thought about the worst thing that could happen to them, which was death.

But it was just confusion.

Everything was a distraction.

And it was just another vehicular accident because someone didn't pay attention.

Or it could be a distraction on purpose to blame a political party in order to make a statement.

That is surely something not unprecedented, as it has happened before.

But the people just want to know what is going on so they can just get on with their lives and move forwards a time that offers ease and the same old environment of life.

It never gets old and it will always remain the same.

X

Anger and frustration started rebelling against the Centralists from critics of the president, members of the resistance, and from many outspoken United Labourists about a decision they thought was wrong and too quick to decide upon.

It was just reported today on March 12, 2018 that the Centralists of the House Permanent Select Committee on Intelligence have officially closed their investigation into the Russia matter.

But there is a problem, as the United Labourists objected saying evidence exists while Centralists are saying it is based on a fictitious narrative from a dossier gathered by someone that hated the president to begin with.

Just as the story hit the airwaves, the reactions started to pour in, and they were all negative, saying Centralists are trying to hide the truth.

It wasn't even surprising that the United Labourists objected to the conclusion of the investigation and its results before it was even released, as they have been saying that they won't support it because they believe Russia stole the election in order to help Carlton Winters ascend to the White House.

But the report from the Centralists in the House Permanent Select Committee on Intelligence does conclude that Russia did have a role in the 2016 election cycle by trying to interfere in order to create some sort of discord, yet it also stated that there was no details or evidence of collusion between the Russian government and the campaign of Carlton Winters, as Russia did not favor any candidate during the presidential election.

The United Labourists balked at this theory put forth by the Centralists, but they knew they couldn't disprove it, as no evidence indicated Carlton Winters worked with foreign officials in any attempt to stop Cynthia Norwell Anderson.

Immediately, the resistance and the United Labourists took to the airwaves, after the conclusion was made public, and they just kept saying the same old things over and over again like how they lost because of a Russian influence campaign organized in order to steal away the presidential election away from their anointed choice.

They keep making the same old rejections that never make a lick of sense.

But they will never stop until they get what they want, which is to manufacture a crime or to mischaracterize testimony in order to send innocent people to jail.

Yet, the final report has not been issued, because it still needs to be checked for sources and methods.

The United Labourists and resistance again object to this idea, as they see it as a transparency problem, even if they have a problem with transparency by keep on denying the truth.

It is just the same as always but it will remain that way.

So here will be a public report and a non-redacted report, so that people can know what actually happened, but the resistance and United Labourists will still have a problem with this, since they just want everyone to believe Russia is to blame even if they acknowledge they do not have any evidence supporting it.

The conclusion from the memo is only from the draft, so everyone that criticized it should just wait and see, but they won't because they think Russia is to blame for everything due to the fact they didn't win back both houses of Congress or the presidency.

It is just a lost cause for them so no one should even care about their situation.

It takes time to complete to make sure it is safe for national security reasons.

That is just another reason why the opponents will be against transparency.

The next day arrived, and it was March 13, 2018, but then something that was expected occurred, and it would be surprising if it didn't.

David Lorman decided to attack the draft report saying it is just incompetence and a bunch of Russian propaganda.

Lorman then says he and his United Labourist colleagues will draft a report on their own, indicating he opposed and does not like the initial conclusion of what could be released.

The news started breaking the story about Lorman's proposed report on the Russian investigation, and everyone in the media praised it, saying it demonstrates guts, courage, and strength to stand up to a falsely and wrongly elected president of the United States of America and to Russia.

The resistance and the United Labourists just went with the message, saying it is a product of transparency in order to demonstrate the wisdom of the truth and of the first amendment.

All were happy this was happening but they were just in their own little fantasy world dreaming of what it would be like if the president was impeached.

Some people will never learn in the case of the evidence but that is just life.

Sooner or later there will be a heavy grasp of coordination in order to determine what is real and what is false regarding Russia, because there is just no evidence of wrongdoing.

Lorman is just the tip of the iceberg and he believes everything he is doing is for the good of the country, but that can be further from the truth since his colleagues are the resistance and are United Labourists, so they don't really want to reach the truth according to most of Middle America.

The reckoning has arrived, and it was March 22, 2018, the day that the House Permanent Select Committee on Intelligence will decide to release the classified report concerning the Russia investigation.

It will probably be along party lines, and that is rich for a party that says they always support the idea of transparency, but the United Labourists are just opposed to many of their ideology when it comes to Carlton Winters.

In the early afternoon the vote was over and it was decided along party lines to be released with all Centralists supporting the release while all United Labourists opposing it.

Then the news broke about the vote, and all of the pundits started to scream by shouting that the release of the classified report to intelligence agencies was part of the Russian disinformation campaign to hide the real truth about what happened in 2016.

There is nothing new about that but that is just hypocrisy about saying they support transparency.

They still think it is a travesty.

But the redacted report has yet to be released, so it will be very interesting to see what the resistance and United Labourists make up that time in order to spin their narrative.

The release of the redacted report finally arrived, and it was just as expected.

On April 27, 2018, the Centralists released their report clearing Carlton Winters and his campaign associates while the United Labourists released their rebuttal report saying that everything in the report put out by the Centralists is wrong and inaccurate.

There was a firestorm of outrage from the left because they just did not like what was in the report because it didn't contain any evidence of wrongdoing.

The members of the resistance and United Labourists started appearing on their favorite shows saying how the release of the majority report was a threat to national security and a bunch of Russian, but that was all they could provide. And it is another day with the dawn of a new arrival.

Today was May 8, 2018 and there was something that was going to be released, and it might surprise the resistance and United Labourists, so there might be hell to pay.

The Senate Intelligence Committee has just now convened and is ready to vote on an upcoming issue that could divide the country further into chaos and destruction.

It was the vote to release a very short report about what happened during the 2016 election.

No matter what happens the resistance and United Labourists will say this is proof of Russian collusion.

That just shows everyone else they don't really care about anything.

There is just a comprehension problem or they just don't want to look for the facts.

It is about time they learn their lesson in order to get out of their own little fantasy world.

And it is now time to learn the facts and not cherry pick the data.

The debate in the committee has ended and now the vote is about to take place.

By a majority of the members, the committee votes to release the short report about what happened in the 2016 election and that will soon be on the airwaves.

The report concludes that no vote was ever changed by Russia trying to hack the voting system but it does say there was intent to undermine any and all confidence in the voting process.

Then, it hit the airwaves.

The resistance and United Labourists seized on the claim that the goal was to undermine the presidential election, but they fail to assert the first part of the conclusion saying no vote was ever changed by Russia.

They never say this on air because they know it destroys their claim of Russian collusion but they are still going with the debunked claim of Russian collusion.

Prominent Senators and members of the House of Representatives from the United Labourists appear in mass on their favorite television news program in order to lie to the country and to the world.

They start to spin the same narrative over and over again about how the report represents proof of Russian collusion.

It all represents something further from the truth in order to send a message that the truth doesn't matter.

That is just how it seems now in a sense of craziness that no one agrees about because there is a sense that no one understands.

The critics of the president start to pounce on the report saying that he knew all along this was happening.

They claimed again that he stole the 2016 presidential election away from Cynthia Norwell Anderson and how he being president is bad for democracy because of the Electoral College.

And then it is about abolishing the Electoral College next and trying to replace it with a national popular vote via a compact with many states.

So the supporters of this plan will say when they reach the magic number of 270 from a certain number of states that agreed to the compact, they will award the popular vote.

Well, there is one thing wrong with that, as it is not even legal, since a constitutional amendment is required.

It will also eventually be struck down in the United States Supreme

Court immediately.

There is just no sense going that route, and there are at least two large states that will never to this, which are Texas and Florida

But it is still an argument about Russia.

It will always be about Russia because there is just something that is so attractive about a place that people say is controlled by a mad man that wants to ruin America by undermining everything.

That probably makes it to be the opposite, because there is nothing available.

It is just the case that there is nothing more than hypocrisy.

Everything else will be determined by misery.

And then it was July 13, 2018, already past the date when members of the special counsel started to investigate Eugene Frozn's finances along with his tax returns for some particular reason, but hey they are just looking for new evidence to invent.

But now the day is new, and the news media has reported that the Department of Justice is set to begin some sort of unknown press conference in a sense that seems all too familiar.

That is just how it seems and it is the sense of entitlement.

No one knows what the July 13, 2018 press conference is going to be about but it could be about the arrest of another drug kingpin.

There can only be speculation what will be addressed.

It could be a surprise to many or it could be just very interesting.

Nothing will be off the tables and it will be decided what to do next if something doesn't go the way of either political party.

There is just the time and place for everything.

And then there will be the ranting and raving by the resistance and United Labourists no matter what happens because they will just complain about everything for no particular reason.

It is concurrent with everything that if this is about indictments, that the resistance and United Labourists will pounce again and say that there is evidence of collusion.

They will make a claim that has no standing even if they know it because they just believe it to be true since they want it to be true but they know it will never be true because there is just a lack of any evidence supporting their claims.

People will just think of anything to get to the bottom of nothing.

And then people started to appear at the podium.

It was the deputy attorney general Miles Reymond as attorney general

Albert Hearlk hasn't been seen in months because Reymond forced Hearlk to recuse himself from the matter over one year ago.

No one knows why but the reasoning could be due to being power hungry and that he isn't really a supporter of president Carlton Winters to begin with.

That could be the case or it could be that it wasn't conclusive.

But, the press conference is just about to start, so no one should say anything.

The deputy attorney general has just announced that the special counsel has indicted 12 Russian military intelligence officials for crimes of hacking the security and computer networks of the National United Peoples' Traditionalist Labor Workers Party Committee as well as for stealing emails belonging to Cynthia Norwell Anderson and trying to influence the outcome of the 2016 presidential election.

The deputy attorney general also accused the Russian military intelligence officials of stealing the personal information of voters for inferior purposes.

He continued to lay out the conspiracy that they tried to accomplish, and just like that the press conference was over after a matter of less than twenty minutes time.

And then the liberal media seized on that information saying to their audience through their pundits that this demonstrates Russian collusion, but they still refuse to see the much bigger picture.

Lorman and his cronies seized on this new indictment saying that there is now proof that Carlton Winters was never legitimately elected, but he doesn't have any evidence to support that claim.

It is still all based on the unverified claims made by the hoax dossier from some former British spy who has an axe to grind against the sitting president.

It is just the case that is purely nonsense based on a bunch of lies, which is the primary basis for the investigation to begin with along with Carl Ronald intentionally releasing documents to cause the appointment of a special counsel.

It is all the same and this isn't the first rodeo.

Everything will be over when the fat lady sings, which is never, as the resistance and United Labourists want a special counsel investigation until they will take control.

But there is a new battle to brew so that is just the thing to begin with in the end.

Meanwhile, Carlton Winters was in Helsinki to hold a summit with the Russian president, Dmitri Leninov, and the press conference between the two men has just concluded on July 16, 2018.

Already, the media has said he has committed treason without any evidence to cite it.

And now many in the resistance and the United Labourists want to see the notes of the translator that recorded everything.

They claim that it's in the important of national security, but that is just an excuse, because they also said that no one should talk to Russia.

That is their reason because they believe Russia should not be able to exist because they want to control everything.

The media is just outraged at what happened and it seems that many that support Carlton Winters are disappointed in him for saying that he does not believe Russia tried to interfere with the 2016 election.

But the resistance and United Labourists take it to a whole new level by saying the president is a stooge for Russia and is a current foreign asset of the KGB because they said he believed Russia was not involved.

While there were many people disappointed in the president's poor remarks because he possibly dismissed his intelligence agencies, that doesn't mean they were actually accurate.

It could be some sort of mistake due to a certain issue such as fatigue.

Sometimes people are tired and don't know what they are doing after a long flight and never-ending negotiations.

Then the resistance and United Labourists also say that there was very damaging evidence of Russian collusion because President Leninov said he wanted Carlton Winters to win because he said America wants to develop a stronger relationship with Russia in order to have better deals.

And that really ticked off the resistance as well as the United Labourists, but the president of Russia and the president of the United States of America saying they want to work together to develop a better international relationship.

Even more, the resistance and United Labourists cry wolf saying there is very clear evidence of Russian collusion because they cite Leninov as saying that he wanted Carlton Winters to win and become the next President of the United States of America, so that has to be evidence that Russia stole the election from their anointed choice.

Well, that is just plain wrong, as it is surely a case in not even paying attention.

Eventually, a few days later, Carlton Winters makes a clarification that he indeed believes his intelligence agencies and says he unintentionally misspoke due to fatigue.

The majority of his supporters and base forgave what he said but not the members of the resistance or the United Labourists, as they still don't like that he won.

But it was just a new day yet again.

Today is the dawn of Gary Bouchfer's trial for tax and bank fraud in the Eastern District of Virginia.

It's already off to a fast start, as the judge in the case wants to select a jury as soon as possible.

July 31, 2018 is ready for what's to come as there is an abundance of hope that the prosecutors will get what they want in the trial.

And then the jury is quickly selected in a surprise to everyone that thought it would last longer.

The trial is off to the start of the opening oral arguments and is set to take the stage in a few short hours.

It is almost very certain to be a show trial and a spectacle for people to watch in order to get into the process of convicting innocent people before they are even put on trial to begin with.

The trial enters its first day with very few hiccups but the judge demands to know what the prosecution is doing in order to prove their case to the jurors.

People are watching and waiting every day for the end of the day each day to see what has occurred.

They want to know what the prosecution did, what the defense did, and what the judge said.

Everyone was excited and it couldn't be more chilling.

The time will tell when everything arrives at a tipping point because that will be the time when the judge would have enough of the prosecution and ask them questions about their case.

Thankfully, that day has arrived, and it has almost been every single day that the judge asked questions concerning the prosecution's case against Gary Bouchfer.

It seems the judge is getting very annoyed at the prosecution because he wants the prosecution to show actual evidence that can prove Bouchfer knowingly committed tax and bank fraud and tried to hide it.

The resistance and the United Labourists are now and have been getting fed up with this judge because they don't like that he is questioning the prosecution.

It's a constant game of shenanigans and nothing will ever be the same, but something is about to happen.

Just like that, the trial of Gary Bouchfer is over, on August 21, 2018, without his lawyers calling on any witnesses because they believe he will win the case, but time will tell if that was a mistake, because there is word a verdict has been reached.

But there is now word that the former personal attorney for Carlton Winters is set to plead guilty in the Southern District of New York to 5 counts of tax evasion, 1 count of bank fraud, and 2 counts of campaign finance violations.

And the resistance as well as the United Labourists is happy for joy and celebrating in the streets as they believe this guilty plea means corruption.

Still, there is no evidence that any campaign finance violation was committed, as that is just a fictitious crime engineered by the people that are against Carlton Winters.

The verdict for Gary Bouchfer was announced and the jury found him guilty on 8 counts of filing false tax returns, defrauding banks, and failing to declare foreign bank accounts.

However, there was a hung jury on the other 10 charges, so the jury was dismissed and was excused.

It was a happy day for the people that support the police and security state because they were saying the guilty verdict represented evidence of Russian collusion without providing any evidence to back it up.

And it was just something they were proud of.

Nearly a month later, on September 14, 2018, Gary Bouchfer decided to plead guilty to the remaining 10 charges as well as the other outstanding charges that have yet to be decided because there was no trial yet.

With that, it seems Bouchfer will avoid a retrial and a second trial in a different location and that will save the government money.

And the guilty plea is celebrated by the same people as always that believes Carlton Winters is guilty of colluding with Russia.

There is just craziness everywhere with no one understanding the basics of life.

XI

Hell broke loose, as attorney general Albert Hearlk resigned at the request of the president, on November 7, 2018, just one day after the United Labourists won the midterm elections by taking back the House while the Senate was still in control of the Centralists.

It would be a rude awakening in the near future but there is just hell to pay in January as the resistance will be back in control of the House of Representatives and will conduct a bunch of reckless investigations.

At the same time, Carlton Winters has already appointed a person to replace Albert Hearlk, and the resistance and United Labourists are already outraged about the appointment of Edwin Grovel as the acting attorney general that will replace Hearlk, because they did not like that the president bypassed Miles Reymond for the job.

So, they are angry for no reason at all, and they are just crazy.

Chaos and destruction erupts in the streets on November 8, 2018, as people start protesting for the resignation of Albert Hearlk.

Thousands join in the streets.

They all form in lines and united in conviction

People start chanting.

People start marching.

They start going down the streets and neighborhoods.

People are watching them.

The media are out trying to interview some people.

Cameras from above catch a live shot of the protesters.

Everything is broadcasted back to television viewers.

As the protesters march on, other people in front start to chant again and again, in order to demonstrate conviction.

Nothing ever stops.

They shout against the resignation of Albert Hearlk.

They shout against the current president.

They shout against the appointment of Edwin Grovel.

“What do we want? We want the special counsel,” chanted the angry protesters repeatedly.

“Is anybody above the law? Nobody is Above the Law,” chanted the protesters.

The people were watching from home.

It was a spectacle for everyone to watch.

The hashtag #ProtectSchmidt was trending on Shrieker.

Supporters alike were waiting to see what will happen, but they all agreed on one thing, that special counsel Joseph Charles Schmidt had to be protected from Edwin Grovel, because they feared Grovel would end the investigation led by the office of the special counsel, and that would be one of their worst nightmares to say the least.

But the protesters just kept on marching until they were tired and they kept on chanting and shouting, thinking people will listen to them. It was just all a distraction, because it didn't matter, as the president kept on saying that he has no intentions to ever fire Schmidt, even if he wants to.

Members of the resistance and the United Labourists will never listen to that because they will say that statement is just false.

The far left will stop at nothing, as they continue to be hysterical about something that is none of their business.

They fear for their safety but they have nothing to worry about.

They fear for their future but life hasn't been this great since the 1920s.

They fear for the future of their children but the world is not a safe space.

They create propaganda for fear of climate change.

They fear everything because of radical talking points that have no basis.

They fear for the safety of others by saying guns should not be in the hands of anyone.

But there is a second amendment and criminals will never follow the rule of law.

They constantly complain about the way of life but they have yet to move to Canada as they said before the 2016 election if Carlton Winters became the president.

Life has never been better.

But they are disillusions due to the way they believe everything should be.

Every street corner in every major city and metropolitan area was just filled with the masses of people.

They had professional demonstrators.

They had prominent members of the House of Representatives that opposed the presidency of Carlton Winters.

They had actors and actresses speaking on stage nearby on massive grass lawns with portable stages.

Every prominent demonstrator spoke on the stages set up on the grass lawns while protestors marched in the streets.

They were just mad as hell and wouldn't take it anymore.

It was surely a peaceful protest but everyone was angry.

There were socialists.

There were communists.

There were Marxists.

There were people that just wanted to watch.

Everybody marching in the streets just hated the president and wanted to demonstrate that they don't like him.

They decried the tax cuts law.

They decried the repeal of the individual mandate.

They decried the progress on the question of peace in the Middle East.

They decried everything he did even though they would have supported it if Cynthia Norwell Anderson instituted the same policies as Carlton Winters did.

It all demonstrates hypocrisy and that is the root of why they don't like Carlton Winters whatever he does.

It all amounts to jealousy.

But the protestors claim they are feminists, even the men, so they support the rights of women all while wearing vagina hats that they say is about protecting abortion and providing equal access to women in need of services.

Sure, that sounds great, but it is all about saving abortions in killing innocent babies.

They just all complain about nonsense.

They support illegal immigration.

They support higher taxes.

They support a government-controlled state and economy.

The protestors just want to say they are against the president but that is not true.

They want to see him indicted but since that is unconstitutional they want to see him impeached because they just don't like his policies.

It will just be anarchy everywhere.

That will bring chaos and destruction to the point of everything going down in flames.

The event kept going well into the late afternoon and eventually there were benefit concerts at night to support abortion and access to welfare in a few major metropolitan areas that were organized by local supporters.

That is the thing about community involvement.

That is nothing sort of crazy but it is what it is.

The protesters continued until they all left.

They chanted.

They organized in a circle of supporters to pray that the president will be impeached.

It was a major protest picked up by all national news media and they continued to air it all day, at least the liberal networks did.

The liberal news media networks even sent their reporters there to watch as it all went down and it just continued to go out of control.

And the protestors had their say.

They talked to the media.

They told reporters what they wanted to happen.

There was no mention of them being afraid of the president, as some of them said they will attack him because of his policies.

It was almost the beginning of the next morning and they had all left after the concert.

The protestors left a complete mess behind with garbage piling up everywhere on the streets.

Everything looked like a disaster but that is just how it went down.

Cups were everywhere filled with beer or possibly some sort of wasted food.

The media didn't care and it was just a new day.

They just went on their way and started to focus on something that would be about the president again.

And then it was December 12, 2018, the day of reckoning for the former personal attorney of Carlton Winters to see what he has to say about his old boss.

The judge sentences Harrison Nicholas to 3 years in federal prison for what he did.

At that moment in time, everyone that opposed the presidency of Carlton Winters said there was proof the president violated the law and thus he must be impeached.

All the same talking heads and pundits from the resistance and the United Labourists are just at it again without realizing they are wrong due to their hatred of the president and his policies.

It wouldn't be complete without Harrison Nicholas attacking his now former boss because the now disgraced attorney is now trying to get a better deal, or at least he was until he was sentenced.

Then on December 18, 2018, a federal judge in the nation's capital accused Vincent McLoughlin of possible treason before taking it back due to some confusion.

The judge apologized but not before the resistance and the United Labourists took advantage of the ill-informed comment.

And on a sign of good luck, the judge again delayed the sentencing for another 90 days to allow McLoughlin to continue his cooperation with the special counsel to see about his future.

But that soon passed because there was another event that was just about to happen.

On December 22, 2018 at midnight, a partial federal government shutdown began all because the United Labourists refused to protect the border from illegal immigrants.

The resistance and United Labourists became furious due to the fact that the federal government shut down.

They blamed Carlton Winters and the Centralists because they believe the construction of a border wall is a waste of taxpayers' money, as they believe a technological wall will be better for the public.

Well, the border patrol agents say a physical structure is needed to protect the southern border, yet the United Labourists and resistance still do not want to support that idea.

The resistance and United Labourists somehow believe that technology will prevent illegal border crossings, but they fail to realize that a technological wall will only allow border agents to actually watch immigrants illegally crossing into the border, as it won't actually cause a decrease in illegal border crossings.

Thus, that is why the border control agents demand an actual physical barrier.

That is just something that isn't worth it for the United Labourists and the resistance, as they believe it is just immoral.

With the government shutdown still taking place, Carlton Winters is not traveling to Palm Beach anytime soon because he wants to get a deal if the United Labourists are willing to accept funding for a border wall or some type of steel slats barrier.

And on December 28, 2018, the Centralists in the House Judiciary Committee releases their final report into the Russia probe early just a few days before the United Labourists take over, and they condemn officials at the CBDI and demand a second special counsel be appointed in order to get to the bottom of why there is just a double standard.

Another year has arrived and it is almost the same as before.

The government shutdown is still alive and well, and people are now starting to get angry, as they blame the United Labourists for not actually doing anything.

On January 2, 2019, a foreign company is fighting a subpoena to hand over their records, and the resistance and United Labourists are crying wolf yet again because they say this is proof of Russian collusion.

On January 3, 2019, one day later, the 116th Congress is convened under the control of United Labourists for the House of Representatives and under the control of Centralists for the Senate.

On January 4, 2019, a federal judge extends the term of the grand jury for the special counsel by another 6 months, and the resistance as well as the United Labourists says this is evidence of Russian collusion, which still falls short of the claim.

It was just constant craziness again and again and they just keep making stuff up.

On January 10, 2019, the House-led United Labourists hold their first hearings, and it is an affront to transparency since it was a closed door hearing, but they just complained after it was over because they didn't get what they want.

On January 15, 2019, Arthur Laird appeared before the Senate Judiciary for a committee hearing to replace former attorney general Albert Hearlk.

And the United Labourists are all upset that he wouldn't commit to recuse himself from the special counsel investigation.

That made them all furious as hell.

On January 18, 2019, a spokesman for the special counsel issues a rare public statement by saying the claim being made by some sort of online publication is inaccurate and false.

And then all hell broke loose for some reason or another.

It could be a coincidence or it could be the end of the world.

There is just a lack of public data to conclude what will even happen.

That will surely cause some sort of interaction again between the United Labourists and the resistance in order to decide what they will do next.

The people deserve to know.

But hell is just waiting for the next victim, as hell is the office of the special counsel, because it just wants to invent evidence to go after anyone who advised Carlton Winters.

That is just something that will have to change and soon it could be all over in a matter of weeks or by July of this year, at least for the grand jury investigating the Russian probe, since there is a maximum of 2 years in which it can investigate crimes.

And that will be bad news for the resistance and the United Labourists, because they just want it to last forever until they can get the president.

It is just a bunch of anarchy from chaos and destruction.

XII

Loud bangs were everywhere causing people to check the commotion on the outside of their homes.

It wasn't clear what was happening but there were just a lot of people outside waiting for something to happen.

Then there was a banging on the front door of a house.

"CBDI, open up, we have a warrant to search your house," said the person in a shouting voice.

Soon, a bunch of CBDI agents and members of the local SWAT team in Broward County entered the house and collected vast amounts of evidence because they wanted to.

And then, the CBDI agents handcuffed a person and took him to a CBDI car. The car sped away into the early morning heading to Miami to get to a processing station and a federal court.

Everything happened so quickly but it was also caught on camera by National Media News Network on January 25, 2019, in what seems to be a much publicized raid in order to humiliate a person.

Then it was announced that a grand jury empaneled by the special counsel has indicted Eugene Frozn a day before on 5 counts of lying to the House of Representatives, 1 count of obstructing justice, and 1 count of trying to tamper with a witness.

The indictment was released to the public and the same talking heads started saying how this case was a slam dunk but it didn't add up that way, as the special counsel was hiding exculpatory evidence and they know they are hiding it because it would ruin their case.

Eugene Frozn was released hours later on a surety bond of no more than $250,000.00 on his own signature and recognizance, so he didn't have to pay a cent.

The United Labourists and resistance still continued to say that the case against Eugene Frozn is airtight but they fail to realize that texts and emails have been taken out of context because it was just cherry picking by a prosecutor from the special counsel with ties to Cynthia Norwell Anderson, so that is just a conflict of interest.

But half of the obstruction charge is linked with lying to Congress, while the other half is linked to the charge of witness tampering.

Something doesn't smell right, as this case against Eugene Frozn seems fishy.

Already, Eugene Frozn and his team of attorneys know that the texts and emails were taken out of context and that the special counsel is trying to withhold exculpatory evidence.

His attorneys know that there is exculpatory evidence because the full texts of messages and emails have been publicly available, at least some have.

Yet, Eugene Frozn is charged with 5 counts of perjury, but it is certain that Frozn himself and his attorneys believe that Frozn just had a lapse in memory.

The conclusion from Frozn and his team of attorneys is that the special counsel is trying to make forgetfulness into a crime of perjury, and that is just bad for democracy.

It is a bad day for the country and everyone.

The special counsel is trying to take every message and email out of context and making it possible for failing to remember an event or a key detail as a crime.

It is night and the federal government is now reopened after 35 long days.

And then, the day is now February 1, 2019, so Eugene Frozn is about to appear in federal court in a DC Federal court.

Already, the resistance and United Labourists kept on saying the same talking points of saying how the case against Eugene Frozn is a slam dunk and airtight, and they say he should consider asking for a pardon from his friend Carlton Winters.

But they fail to include any exculpatory evidence in their analysis, as that would be beneficial to the defendant.

Yet somehow National Media News Network knew about some type of unusual grand jury activity on a Thursday morning, and they were just waiting with their vans and vehicle outside of Frozn's house with no other news media in sight.

And they attacked anyone that said the special counsel leaked the indictment and raid in advanced notice to their network, because they said it was some unusual grand jury activity.

That is somehow very interesting and intriguing of how just one news network speculated about another indictment being issued and they also had a hunch that the same person might be arrested the same day.

And then they say it was unusual grand jury activity.

Their explanation just doesn't make any sense, because they were the only news organization at the scene of the arrest of Eugene Frozn.

Not everyone is buying what they are saying about how they found out about it, but then they cite speculation.

So it is not that surprising when National Media News Networks all of a sudden becomes angry about questioning their information and saying that the office of the special counsel tipped them off in advance.

They were so outraged that they sent their media reporter stooges on air to keep on saying the same line of unusual grand jury activity.

And again, the American people questioned the raid on the home of Eugene Frozn, except for the resistance and the United Labourists, since they support a police state that surveils everybody all while supporting socialism in a collapsing state of Venezuela.

The prosecution is trying to withhold evidence and they know it but it remains to be seen if and when a federal judge finds this information, and once she does she will be extremely angry and possibly impose sanctions on the prosecution.

And the prosecution will be dumbfounded because they had a belief that the judge would always support them, but they will be sorry when punishment arrives.

And the resistance and United Labourists will then become angry at the judge and say she is a stooge for the president, but that has no merit at all.

The resistance and United Labourists will just be angry that they couldn't get what they want and they will become angry for losing while also supporting the idea of withholding exculpatory evidence is a very good idea, even if it is unlawful.

But then something happened that changed history forever and there was just the start of panic and chaos everywhere leading to the possibility of destruction in a matter of minutes.

It was just the beginning of the end.

SIX

I

Darkness approached everywhere with a bright orange haze taking over the entire United States of America. Dark Ash lay on top of skyscrapers and buildings everywhere. It looked like a volcano has just woke up from a long nap but it was more than that. Sirens were blazing with people screaming everywhere in all directions. It was just chaos and destruction as people were panicking and didn't know what to do. It felt like a surreal experience and déjà vu all over again.

The people were reacting strangely and didn't know what to do, as they are just so very surprised and befuddled.

And there were just more problems to the point it could cause severe respiratory problems.

In a matter of minutes, smoke started to rise from everywhere. Bright red and orange flames started to appear and it just made everything worse.

People were screaming from the presence of danger raging right in front of them.

There was just no light.

Everything started to change right before the peoples' eyes. It wasn't anything that anyone has ever seen before.

Clouds of pitch just took over the once blue sky of hope and it soon made everything dreary and equal.

People were trying to find out what was going on but they felt scared and panic.

There was a cause for concern that the world would soon end, because of the dark ash, the orange haze, and the rising smoke from the flames.

It just all seemed like an apocalypse was here so they had to protect everything they had.

It was such a sad day in America because no one knew what to do in this time of need.

It was certain that some people believed it was only a dream but it is not.

This was surely a surprise to everyone because there was no warning whatsoever.

There must have been something that caused this to happen.

As the panic ensued, trees began to burn up from out of nowhere, and soon more panicked as time passed by.

Buildings started to change shape and height.

Cities turned to ruin.

Everything was just like a disaster from a very long time ago.

Roads crumbled to stone in some places.

Businesses were broken into.

Windows were smashed in by bombs and grenades.

There was broken glass everywhere.

Entire cities were falling apart and there was nothing people could do about it, because it seemed fruitless.

Monuments started to collapse under their own weight.

The whole world seemed like it was dying.

But that was not the case.

Europe and Asia were fine.

Nothing was happening in Africa.

And no one cared for Australia.

It was only happening in the United States of America.

Things continued to happen that no one could explain.

It seemed like a natural disaster because everything was broken or was breaking.

An earthquake could be possible, but that wouldn't explain why all of the buildings changed.

To the people this is just the sign of an apocalypse because that is the only way to explain what is happening.

That is the only way that could really be the right thing to say because something just doesn't feel right during this craziness.

Everything was just falling apart and there was nothing that could be done about it.

All hope was lost and it remained in the hands of the people that tried to escape as soon as they could.

And then something more extreme happened.

The ground started to shake and the people started to panic again.

It was a never-ending crisis filled with constant bickering and people praying to survive from whatever was going on so they wouldn't die.

Everywhere was a disaster area and it soon became very obvious that something was very wrong with society, as the world might soon end.

Quickly thinking, a group of people in Los Angeles started to try and rescue as many people as possible before the ground ate the city and people alive, but it was not certain, as there was just too little time, since no one knew what will happen next.

It was nerve wracking because nothing was even known at the same and it seemed that people were trying to hide as the best that they could just to survive.

But there was just too much damage to the buildings, streets, roads, and other infrastructure everywhere.

It was just so dismal that nobody could escape the wrath of whatever was in the works by Mother Nature.

Suddenly, there was a change in events.

Everything stopped but it still remained the same.

The sky was still engulfed in dark pitch clouds with the bright orange haze still covering up everything.

Cars and other vehicles were still damaged from the ground cracking and rumbling.

There were still fires everywhere with smoke rising from the bright flames.

Then, all of a sudden, the clouds of pitch disappeared with no signs of ash left over, but bright flashes of white light were now appearing all over the place, possibly causing people to think that it was lightning, but it just wasn't the same, yet it kept bouncing everywhere thinking where to go in order to find a good landing place.

There was just uncertainty, as now everything was replaced with a never-ending overcast of thick orange haze resembling some sort of mixture between smog and fog with a combination of smoke and dust, so it is just so puzzling what's happening.

People are having hard time breathing.

Everywhere they go they start to nearly collapse.

The air is causing respiratory problems and people are now starting to die everywhere.

It is just so perplexing that no one knows what is happening.

Out of nowhere, a group of shadowy figures dressed all in black and covered from head to toe in protective clothing appear, and then the flashes of light disappear behind them.

It was the Victory World Front.

Meanwhile, Katrina was waiting for something to happen in a strange sort of way in her safe house wearing nothing but her panties while lying in a nice and comfortable bed.

It was just so tempting to think what would go on in the midst of a crisis but there was just the case of trying to see what to do in the war effort.

Everything was fruitless and it too soon will become a thing of the past. There is just an effort to avoid anything at all costs but that might just be a pipe dream.

People will develop a sense of need and then there will be a case of abandonment.

Nothing will be able to escape the wrath of the new disaster.

The day is just nonexistent and it will always be that way until the rest of society has something to say about it.

But the people are just poor pawns in a government-controlled society.

It is September 1, 1939, and Hitler has just invaded Poland.

Everyone is on alert as the armed forces of each country determine what they will do next.

It could be war or it could be no action.

The populace is alert as there might be imminent war.

Men might be conscripted to join the war if there is one or they might just dodge it by running away, making excuses, or hiding from the authorities.

Nothing is certain.

Everything is just in disarray and war could be inevitable, as France and Great Britain could strike soon.

Leadership will be tested and if it fails there will be pressure from their constituents.

There will be resignations and then there will be negotiations.

There will be distractions and then there will be peace deals.

There will be nothing but chaos as people will just try to survive in the midst of destruction.

All hope will be lost and it is just about time to understand what could happen in a time of war.

It will be total annihilation against the enemy and each alliance will face combat and casualties.

Something is just not right and everything is just going so quick.

The world is waiting for something to happen and that will be the day when something strikes back

II

It was September 3, 1939, and war is imminent against Germany for invading Poland.

It is certain it will happen today before anything else does in a time of need.

And just like that, France and Great Britain declared war on Germany for attacking the sovereign nation of Poland.

Now it is more than ever that many Europeans will see combat while their families wait at home to see if they ever come home.

Tanks are rolling down the streets on tank trailers after mere moments of the joint announcement of a declaration of war against Germany in order to get to their assigned units to protect the country and the capital of London of Great Britain.

Military squadrons are being sent to go to Poland in order to fight the common enemy.

The local draft boards are notifying potential soldiers that they might need to fight in a war.

France and Great Britain will try to send their best people in a time of need. There is just something that needs to happen soon or it will be the last of the European nation.

More countries will soon join in as there could be more action by the Nazi Empire of Germany.

Alliances will be formed on all sides in order to defeat each other.

It will be that point in time when there is common unity and a declaration of peace that people will end the war.

It will only be then when the enemies realize they are losing that they will give up.

That day will be decided upon learning that they can no longer win the war.

And that too shall be a lesson.

But it is a lesson that is decided by the fate of each nation taking part in the action.

And so it began, military planes started their engines and flew off with soldiers on board to combat the enemy.

One by one they left the airfields of Great Britain and France to fly over Germany and drop bombs, or so the people thought.

It was just too early to know what will happen next.

Germany has refused to listen and now there is war against them from France and Britain.

It is just a matter of time until someone gets hurt form an explosion or something else.

And just like that, Great Britain already had her first loss, with the sinking of the passenger liner the SS Athenia.

It was a huge loss for a major military power.

About 98 passengers and 19 members of the crew died after a German U-boat fired torpedoes at it left the port of Liverpool.

About 1,100 lives were on board and just fewer than 300 were Americans.

The event was such a travesty that something had to be done but it could already be too late to get to the bottom of the situation.

A decision was made, and on September 4, 1939, the Royal Air Force decided to raid all German warships in the vicinity of the area of Heligoland Bight.

Some people said it worked while others said it was a waste of time, but the truth of the matter was that the Nazis were waiting for that attack from the British Air Force.

The Nazis knew this was going to happen so they thought ahead and abandoned the ship while leaving behind bombs all in a matter to trick the allied forces.

And the British thought they would have won but it was all a trap.

Hundreds of men died on the German warships because they tripped over a wire that ignited an explosion.

It was more tragic than the day before.

Just two days later, on September 6, 1939, the newly-elected South African government declared war against Germany after parliament decided to stop remaining neutral.

Life was just getting worse for everyone.

It will soon reach the height of the nation and no one could save anyone, for there will be fear and chaos everywhere.

But it just got worse for Germany, as Egypt broke off all relations due to the invasion.

It was just the price of war and the rest of society.

Three days later, on September 9, 1939, Poland was under assault again, in the city of Warsaw by the 4th Panzer Division of Hitler's newly-formed Armed Forces.

There was nothing that could be done, as Warsaw was now completely under siege from all sides.

It was a devastating defeat but at no time is there an imminent threat to Great Britain and France.

It is just the beginning of the end for a weak European nation all because something was at the center of attention.

More attacks will soon arrive but it could be now or in stages so that everything can be a surprise attack.

That is just the situation at hand and no one will be able to stop that.

The country will continue to fall behind and it is just now or never to decide what will happen next.

And it was just the time again for everything to continue all over again, as nothing seemed like it would go away.

It was like something from an old movie but something wasn't right.

Just 16 days later, on September 17, 1939, it was an all-out war and attack against Poland, led by the Russian Red Army of Soviets arriving on the Eastern coast, and now outnumbered Polish troops were advised to travel to the neutral nation of Romania, a country that seems to be safe for now, but time will tell how long it stays that way.

Nothing could save Poland now because it was clear Hitler wanted it for his own selfish reasons in order to maintain his German Reich so that he can maintain order and help protect the ethnic Germans.

It was a plan that no one could deny but it wouldn't last forever, as that would mean he would have to admit defeat if he didn't get his way.

It would be a miracle for something to bad happen to the Germans and their allies, but such an action might be too early in the hopes that it could change the path towards a more favorable solution, and hopefully a new action will take place to ensure the safety of all people.

It will be for that very reason why no action will be taken and that soldiers will fall behind the line of a lack of leadership.

Things would soon change or so people thought, as it was just the same thing every day.

The Nazis kept on attacking for the sole purpose of trying to pursue world domination in a time that is suspicious to the rest of the world and of society.

France and Great Britain were nowhere to be found as they kept on facing setbacks from Hitler's attacks, and the people did not know what to do except to exert pressure on their government officials by telling them to stand up to the tyrant Adolf Hitler.

Pressure was mounting on the prime minister of Great Britain to take action but he did not do anything to help the allied forces.

It was a shame of what was happening to the world, as this could be solved, if anyone took action to stop the events from continuing into downfall and oblivion.

There was no time left to defend against the enemy as they were just too strong to defeat.

It wouldn't be long now and it wouldn't help them to stop the influx of bombs and grenades into their territory.

That is the last of the straws that could bring chaos and destruction.

People were just experiencing the carnage of war and it wouldn't help them now.

It would be an act of war to be against the war but the propaganda was just so obvious in a time of need and poverty to determine if there would be peace and action.

It was just the case that nothing would happen, as 1,200 Nazi aircraft just bombed the city and capital of Poland, Warsaw, on the 24th of September of the year 1939.

Time was indeed running out and it seemed all too obvious that something needed to change.

It happened again, just two days later, on September 26, 1939, more Nazi aircraft attacked, and this time it was against the Royal Naval base at Scapa Flow, but it was the first failure of the new German empire, and it will be their last, as Hitler ordered propaganda to say that they sunk the HMS Ark Royal, yet it was just a sham.

British forces tried to shoot down the first Nazi aircraft they saw but it missed with spectacular failure.

It was something that had no words for the military officers.

Everyone was just flabbergasted at the timing of events, and then it has fallen.

III

News breaks that Poland has fallen to the Nazis and Hitler's new German empire on September 27, 1939, and no one could describe the type of action that would have reversed it.

There was just sadness everywhere with 200,000 civilians dying in battle.

Poland will now be subjected to a war of redistribution of land amongst Germany and the Soviet Union with each country getting their share of 660,000 Polish prisoners of war to be divided in an unequal number.

That was just the beginning of the end for Poland to cease to exist as it once did independently from all burdens because on the 6th of October 1939, the last Polish troops stop fighting in the war against the Nazis.

It was certainly sad but Prime Minister Neville Chamberlain fell right into Hitler's trap by rejecting the last peace offensive.

That was just a bad sign that something wouldn't go as plan as the allies hope. It was a war until the end.

Hitler will soon launch his next strategy against the Western power of Great Britain and Chamberlain would regret the peace offensive that he never even thought about.

It was just that as the days rolled by with nothing happening until that fateful day of October 14, 1939, when the Nazis launched a surprise attack against the British ship HMS Royal Oak at Scapa Flow in Orkney, Scotland, after a German U-Boat torpedoed it.

Altogether, 800 died as a result, and it was just a sad day for all to watch.

Something had to be done but no one knew what to do. It was just that time wasn't on their side.

But as the days passed, there was just peace, and the people thought it was the end of war, until they heard the Russian Red Army of the Soviets invaded Helsinki that allowed over one million troops into Finland on the 30th of November.

Helsinki was bombed by the Soviet aircraft in order to get a handle on the situation.

It was just pure carnage and no one expected the same thing to happen twice.

There was just overwhelming force from the enemy at times that the allies thought about giving up while they still had a chance to surrender.

It was at a time when everything counted, but nothing stopped the Soviet Union from invading Finland without a declaration of war.

It was just that easy in order to make sure no one could escape.

But there was some hope for a winning future.

It was certain to collide with the enemy and the allied forces.

There was a chance to defeat or even weaken the German armed forces under control by a mad man.

It would be time to launch an all-out attack. But it failed on December 13, 1939, when the German battleship, the Admiral Graf Spee, launched a quite powerful and dangerous sneak attack against British forces off the coast of a river plate estuary in Montevideo, Uruguay.

It couldn't get any better for the Germans but someone informed them that the British would attack them there and win if they weren't prepared to take on the enemy.

It wasn't pure luck but it was strategy that surprised many of the British naval officers off guard because they thought they had some sort of advantage with their intelligence people and their superior radar, but it was just a coincidence they lost to people that want to kill them.

That was such a waste of time to target the Germans.

Time was of the essence but it wasn't kind to the Soviet Union for what they did to Finland.

On December 14, 1939, the Soviets were expelled from the League of Nations, but the government vowed to fight back.

It was certain that something would happen, but Katrina was surely in the midst of something more interesting.

It was about the future of the world and to save humanity or so other people thought.

Intrigued with the presence of war, Katrina decided to join the British Army, as a way to give back to her community, but in a way that will haunt the rest of society forever.

But it wasn't as expected, because it was just an advisory role to the generals and other commanding officers.

There was just the timing of everything but no one cares about that, since it just seems too irrelevant.

And so, it was settled, for the time that it took it will be the time of a life for people to enjoy whatever they could.

It would be the attention of the state and towards something special not knowing what to do and how to do it everything.

It would be the crime of the century to wait and see what happens next and for the immediate future of humanity because war is war and there is no way around it.

There is no excuse to support it and there is no support for the war to not take place.

The war will have to take a life of its own due to the factions that determine everything from the beginning in a way that undermines everything.

That is life and that is when there is a time to go to the front lines by not doing anything.

It will just be a time for everyone to understand why war matters and why it must take place or else there will be no peace at all.

But it was just the right time to say and do nothing and possibly to stay unengaged in everything, for opposition to the war is a crime against the state and is punishable by death.

The people won't stand for that and that is why people must take a stand by supporting it or else.

And it was time to go to combat.

Stripping down to nothing but her sexy yet gorgeous slim naked body, Katrina puts on regulation panties and a regulation bra, followed by a regulation jacket blouse, then military regulation army trousers, along with military regulation socks and boots.

Everything so perfect now but it was just the way it had to be, so Katrina placed a nametag found in her pocket of the tunic.

It was an officer uniform with the insignia and rank of colonel. It was just the right of passage, but to escape notice from anyone, Katrina puts her long silky hair in a bun so that no one notices that she is a woman and it is also standard operating procedure.

Upon her head, she places a military regulation visor cap with the rank and insignia of colonel, in the hopes that it will provide her time to think of something next.

The dawn of military and war theatre has already begun and it is just about time to think what will happen next.

Katrina is ready to take the next step but it is a good thing that she has a closet full of these uniforms in her safe house.

It is just the time that will be seen as an obstacle.

And so, she departs the safe house to report to the British military intelligence corps, where she will serve as an advisor to the British chiefs of staff and several other units in order to report on the latest intelligence so that Britain can better develop their strategies to defeat the enemy.

It is just a way to defeat a rogue nation.

Life as people knew it would change significantly.

IV

Nearly almost a month since joining the British army as a senior military officer, Katrina has got her hands full with gathering intelligence for the British military so that the generals can revise their strategies in order to try and defeat the enemy.

But she isn't complaining as she is used to working like a man.

It is just that she has got her hands full because there isn't that much she can do because she believes the work is just too easy due to the fact that she wants to do more work.

Surely, there is more work that can be done in the line of duty, but her role is as an adviser, so she has to gather intelligence and then report back to the generals in charge of military intelligence.

But the swing is in the opposite direction, as there might be some sort of choreography that determines the side that will win in the end.

It is purely for show and that is how people know what they need to do.

People in the war will just take action and it will be in the best interest to take back the role of the government and give it back to society.

Alas, that will never happen, due to the matter that it is purely speculation.

There is nothing that can be done now until someone takes responsibility.

Only then will effective leaders will take the mantle and win.

Chaos and confusion ensues in the ranks of the military in Britain as the Minister of War is terminated from his position on January 5, 1940 due to a lack of getting things done and also being very unpopular with the British ministers of parliament in the House of Commons.

The sadness is short lived as Prime Minister Chamberlain replaced the Minister of War with someone favored by high-ranking commanders that opposed him to begin with.

It is just a war of words from the people in control and the people who follow the orders, because the established military commanders don't care for the ranks of the other military due to them being political appointments.

It is just a fact of life.

Then all hell broke loose on January 8, 1940, as the government of Great Britain had to institute the implementation of ration books, causing the people who live there to purchase limited amounts of butter, bacon, and sugar, due to an extreme shortage.

It is only the beginning and things will soon become bleaker.

People will have to live on a limited amount of food thanks to the war.

Nothing will save the people now unless the war comes to an immediate halt but that will never happen until one side wins and decides to declare victory.

The campaign is against time and it is uncertain when everything will be over.

And it will be a vigorous campaign against hatred and discrimination to the point of a heated debate that people will argue for and against the war by making unpopular laws.

It will be a very long battle with mortar fire and bombs galore as well as deciding how to approach the situation at hand in a time of need and chaos.

That is just the fact of life and it will be at the end of time to declare no victory.

But everything just got worse, as the Soviets continued their war on Finland by sending thousands of troops and equipment in order to take over the country, and the resistance vows to fight against this rise in power by an unelected government.

On February 1, 1940, there was just a change in power and nothing could save the Finnish people now.

They would have to fight as hard as they could and it would be until the end. It is just something to think about, yet something must present itself in order to find a way by taking control of the situation.

That time is not now because it will be known at the time before of imminent defeat. Everything is present.

Finally, there was some good news, as the government of Great Britain announced all merchant ships in the North Sea will be armed, but just one day later, on February 15, 1940, the Nazis announced that all British merchant ships will be classified as warships.

And it was just chaos, because Germany knew what was going on, yet Britain fell into the trap set forth by the Nazis.

It was a genius idea and the British government sought to play that game against a power-hungry executive who used the emergency powers to declare himself of everything over the government.

It's an all-out offensive led by different governments in order to get better control of the situation in a place of nothingness.

Sooner or later, there will be a time when the British government will need to make a tough decision, and it will be one of the hardest choices to decide.

On February 17, 1940, British officials had to make that order, by now ordering and helping 400,000 children to evacuate from the cities to more rural areas, in order to escape the wrath of war.

Time will tell if this is the correct decision but it must stand to protect the young and innocent from dying in something tragic.

On March 13, 1940, the war is over between Finland and the Soviets, as a truce is agreed upon, but it is just short-lived, as there are worse matters at hand.

War just made a turn on March 20, 1940, as the French government under the leadership of Daladier has been overthrown in Paris, and the new premier of France was Paul Reynaud.

The timing couldn't be worse.

It was going all downhill from here, but with the rise of a new government, then things might get better.

It is just a waiting game and people will have to get to the bottom of everything.

Nothing is going as planned and there is a deep mistrust of the government due to inaction by the British cabinet.

Someone needs to solve this situation now before it gets out of hand and more people die from a government that is showing no signs of leadership.

People will take the time to appreciate something better other than war or else there will be chaos and destruction for the future of society.

It just gets worse and worse every time there is inaction on the battlefield.

That is such a shame but there is now a new goal in mind to fight against the common enemy.

It is surely a part of the plan but it could fail.

Then, on April 8, 1940, the Royal Navy started to get smarter, by laying mines all throughout the waters of Norway.

It was a sure thing to work but that didn't stop the Germans from anything.

They knew about this tactic and invested in equipment that could detect the mines and other explosive devices.

It was just a waiting game to see how the British will respond.

Everything could all be a distraction, but the Nazis also developed some sort of device that could destroy any underwater explosive.

It was just a thing that the British and other allied forces had to deal with, because that was just the beginning of everything.

One day later, on April 9, 1940, Germany takes a full step forward and immediately invades Denmark and Norway for lacking protection from the allies.

It is just the beginning of something else and that will have to stand the test of time.

V

Bombs drop from below, as Germany begins its invasion on Holland, Belgium, and Luxemburg on May 10, 1940.

War is now picking up speed and chaos is ensuing all across Europe, as they are starting to panic that more innocent people will die as well as their future being bleak from a shortage of everything.

It is the worst thing that could happen to anyone and it is just a sign of cowardice and weakness.

Time will be of the essence to see who will stand up against the Nazis, because it sure wouldn't be Britain, and France is still nowhere to be found.

But there is a change in guard, as Prime Minister Neville Chamberlain sudden resigns due to a lack of leadership and from deep mounting pressure within the walls of parliament.

This could be the start of something immediate and wonderful but it is a sign that just might work.

A new prime minister is appointed to lead the attack against the enemy of Germany.

His majesty, King George VI, appointed the honorable Winston Churchill to take the lead against a powerful Germany in order to win the war that no one has won yet. It was a bold move and it couldn't be at a better time.

Immediately, there is a change in strategy, but there is no knowing if it will work.

On May 11, 1940, Churchill gave the order to bomb Berlin, the capital of Germany.

The plan is met with applause from the people but there was something wrong.

The members of the cabinet thought something would go wrong.

There is just a sense of frustration and uneasiness that something isn't just right.

It sounds strange but it has happened before, and no one ever wants to repeat that again.

This could be a sign that something is indeed very wrong and that it is only the beginning for Britain and France to have several thousands in mass casualties.

That is the most dreaded thing that anyone will want to know because it is a sign that something isn't working.

It means that there isn't really a plan to help anyone.

But there is something or someone that is embedded from within in order to make sure Germany wins and that the allies have no chance at all.

Surely, that sounds like a familiar story due to it being a familiar story, as it has happened before, and this wouldn't be the first time it would have happened.

But there is no indication if they will even happen, as the Royal Air Force sent 3 warplanes to Germany in order to fight them in the war.

This could be a sign of victory but it isn't the end. It is only a sign that the government is taking a stance against hatred and discrimination in a matter that doesn't support appeasing the enemy that is known to the world as being complicit in mass murder.

Something must change and this is hope, so it will be in the interests of how to proceed, as Britain could actually win in a time of need that is the time of the century.

It is just about protecting the freedom and liberty that everyone loves in order to stop any government takeover and it is for that reason why nothing can be seen as it is planned because it might actually in the opposite happening.

The plan to send 3 warplanes to Germany could be a good one but it might backfire if they are not careful.

Everything could go down in flames and people will be angry.

The people will demand answers about what went wrong.

There will be investigations.

And it will only be a matter of time again until German appeasement is the official strategy in order to defeat the enemy again.

But there will be fierce opponents of these new investigations, and they will say that new generals are needed to come up with something new.

It could just be a waste of time but it is just the same as usual.

The time is now and Germany needs to be defeated.

There is just devastation across France, as on May 12, 1940, they are ambushed by German soldiers in the Northeastern town of Sedan in a careful but thought out plan.

French soldiers are just flummoxed at what happened to them, as they thought they were winning, but this wasn't so, and now it is seen as a major setback to victory.

If something doesn't happen soon then there will be nothing left but utter chaos and destruction because there will be no rules or anything that can support civilization.

It will all be anarchy, a thing that no one wants to ever experience in their lives, because people can make their own rules in which they decide what is right and what is wrong.

The most immoral thing could now be legal while the most moral thing could be considered illegal.

It is all a matter of time until something like this happens, and when it does there will be mass protests.

People will start rioting and they will rise up to show some much needed support to the leaders of the new movement.

There will be the revolution that no one thought could ever happen and it will be like living in a train wreck.

Nothing will be present but devastation and it will be all the fault of the people who supported the revolution.

They rose up in order to say that had it with rules, laws, regulations, and civilization in general, because they believe a rule of law and order is bad.

The whole world will soon collapse, and that will be the end of most of society for the rest of time, until someone decides to rise up again in order to hold someone accountable.

But the British decide to fight back by launching a new campaign in order to defeat the dreaded Nazis.

On May 14, 1940, Great Britain launches the Local Defence Volunteers, in the hopes of getting as many people as they can in order to defeat the enemy, but there is a setback that could ruin it all before it all began, as the German Air Force suddenly attacks Rotterdam in order to send a message to the allies, and it causes an immediate impact of mass casualties.

Over 30,000 innocent people have been seriously injured or killed, whether it was in the line of combat or civilians alone, and it is the time to deploy a more effective strategy.

Just one day later, on May 15, 1940, General Erwin Rommel of the Nazi German Army sent his tanks to attack France in Philippeville, and it went as planned since France was weak because of a failed government due to failed leadership, so they knew it would be only a matter of time until the country loses its government.

France faces a fierce battle between Germany but it is just a loss of words, as they are highly outnumbered in a duel that could decide the fate of the war.

Meanwhile, at the same time, General Georg-Hans Reinhardt of the Nazi German Army advances his tanks and troops 37 miles west of the Meuse, indicating that Hitler means business.

It is just the same old thing that will happen again and again without repercussions, so there must be another way to defeat the enemy.

But there is a major setback.

Holland has fallen and is now under the threat that Hitler will control it for the rest of time.

The surrender of Holland is a sad day for the allies as they think how to strategize next.

Day after day, the allied forces keeps on losing traction in the war against Germany, and nothing can be done even though France and Britain try to focus on the common problem.

It isn't working and the people are still suffering from the lack of food and beverages as the war continues.

It feels as though life will never go back to normal.

Something needs to happen soon but even though a new general was appointed to head the allied forces, it was still the same.

For some reason the Germans keep on blocking the allies due to some strange reason.

They must know something that no one else does or it could be pure intelligence.

That is just life because there might be a person deep within the allied forces who is giving away intelligence to the enemy that is Germany.

A mole or double agent could be at work in order to get a much preferred outcome.

It has been done before but no one has questioned the legitimacy of it.

Life as usual is the same and reinforcements come to save any and all British and French troops at Dunkirk in an evacuation attempt on May 26, 1940, but just two days later, on May 28, 1940, there is devastation yet again, because Belgium has fallen to the Nazis.

The populace is not surprised of the defeat, as National Socialism is sweeping across Europe, so parents and grandparents are mindful to protect their children and grandchildren to avoid any type of propaganda that might lead to brainwashing.

Young children and teenagers are especially prone to this and might develop a new identity towards fascism.

Therefore, it is just that the populace does not give up due to this recent setback because it might lead to the enemy winning.

But there is news of happiness, as the allied forces were able to save more than 330,000 troops in the line of fire at Dunkirk, after the evacuation has ended on June 5, 1940.

There is nothing but jubilation and excitement, as new hope arises that the now saved troops will be able to save them from the war and defeat the Nazis.

Time will only tell and it will depend on the goal in mind.

The strategy will determine if the allies will be the victor in the end but it could just be a trap.

Yet hope has dwindled again for the allies, as for three days straight, the Nazis have either ambushed France or have increased their attacks significantly in order to stage a fight to take down the government in a fit of rage.

The news breaks.

There is nothing more that can be done, as now there could only be chaos.

Somme and the Aisne are now on the brink of being taken over by foreign powers or the enemy because troops have surrendered in a fierce battle that was against France from the beginning.

It was just sad to hear this.

Chaos and destruction continue to ensue as there is another war on the brink of the horizon.

It could make matters worse.

And people will soon fall to the interests of propaganda.

More news breaks. It is just as expected.

Prime Minister Benito Mussolini of Italy announced on July 10, 1940, that he has decided to declare war on France and Britain in order to expand Italian colonies in North Africa by expanding into or taking over British and French territories.

The announcement infuriates the people as well as the governments of France and Britain and they vow to take action against the new enemy of Fascism as well as the continued threat of National Socialism.

Things just got more complex but there is a threat that new ideologies will replace values and belief with something that supports immorality, government surveillance, and the rise of a police state.

It is just that reason why France and Britain are now fighting against time in order to protect their people.

But the news is just the same as always.

Nothing can be done and it has been the same as always.

But with the rise of a new threat there is unity.

But it wasn't meant to be, as there is a threat of a strong foe to the east of them.

There could be another collapse and it could be within days of an advance.

So nothing is certain.

There is just a warning but the people are starting to panic, as the people of France could be next to face the wrath of Hitler.

It is just a sign of a failed strategy.

Something needs to happen and it must happen now or there will be no future left.

There is a meeting amongst important diplomats to discuss the threat of a German advance against France but nothing is known of it except that Paris is considered and declared an open city for warfare on June 11, 1940, so it looked like it was about over.

Two days later, on June 13, 1940, French troops abandoned Paris in what seems to be an ambush from Germany.

The Nazis take control of the city and declare victory over France, as they believe they have defeated one of the allied governments.

Just three days later, the cabinet of Paul Reynaud is ousted from power by the French general Henri Petain of the last war with Germany.

There is new leadership and the general wants the French people to know that, so he announces to all of France on June 17, 1940 that they need to stop fighting and to also try to seek an armistice from Germany if they are willing to accept.

But it is short-lived, as the announcement is interrupted by the news the Royal Air Force started to bomb Bremen and Hamburg in a new attempt to take back the country.

However, the German Air Force strikes the British back by ambushing them in the clouds.

It is sabotage and then several hundred warplanes belong to the Royal Air Force go down in flames.

And the British thought they were winning.

A day later, on June 18, 1940, the French resistance rises up against the Nazis occupation of France, and it is just a show of force with unity to tell the Germans to go back where they came from.

The Germans refuse to listen and start to occupy and take control the city of Paris in an alarming rate only because they believe they can.

On June 20, 1940, Italy invades France from the Alpines, making sure no one can escape.

The goal is to make the remaining French troops to give up.

Italy wants to make sure there is no threat to their future and it just works out to be a strategic victory if they can take control of an allied nation in order to seek their overseas territories.

Something is just in the midst of the new threat of civilization. Something is dire for the need of the craziness in society.

It is just pure speculation but nothing can be understood like what the French and British are going through.

There is war everywhere and it is just starting, so people should just get ready for the long haul and wait it out until it ends.

VI

Sirens ablaze throughout France with utter chaos and panic as no one knows what to do.

The townspeople of Paris gather everywhere in all known and possible directions outside in order to see what is going on.

It is a sign that something big is going on and the people of France don't know what is going to happen to them.

It is a sure sign of the beginning of the end of the old society.

There is just so much uncertainty in a case that doesn't feel like anything is happening.

Suddenly, people run from their homes and start screaming that France has surrendered to Germany.

The people of Paris are now at a loss of words again.

They can't describe the situation but they must hide or they could end up as collateral damage.

The dawn of a new day will go up in high flames as society collapses.

It is all ending now and there is just something that needs to be dealt with in order to stop it from happening but the war is taking over all parts of Europe.

Nothing is sacred anymore.

Planes are buzzing above and people are looking up everywhere in order to see the noise but it is all covered in clouds.

Then there is light, as the clouds clear up.

People are pointing up and are worried at what they see.

It could be all for show until the people paying close attention spot swastikas on the body of the planes.

They run and scream in order to hide as now they know Germany has won and they had loss.

It is surely sad but that is just the beginning.

An announcement is made on June 22, 1940 to all of France, saying Paris and all northern regions will be under control of the Nazis while the south shall be under control of French general Petain.

The people of Paris are horrified, as they do not know what to do.

They don't want to be occupied by a foreign power.

It is just something horrific.

The people of France start to panic.

They take to the streets in order to start a riot.

They proclaim that this is just bad and is not worthy of a true Republic.

They demand answers but there is nothing that can be done to stop it because the damage has already been done.

Hundreds and even thousands carry to the streets with torches in hand to take down the headquarters of the Nazis but they find nothing.

It is just a case of nothing.

They are too quick to judge because they are just too quick to realize that the Nazis will take control of government buildings.

And it is just a rush to judgement.

France has fallen and Britain could be next if they don't change their strategy.

Time will tell but it is about time that something happens to the end of time.

Hitler announces to his commanders to begin the Battle of Britain in which Germany shall take control of all of the United Kingdom.

It is a sure thing he can win, so on July 16, 1940 he initiates his plan of how to take away Britain from their current government.

It just might work but it will take some time and planning.

Hitler's generals and admiral agree to a total of 250,000 air and sea troops because they believe it is necessary to use both the Air Force and the Navy in order to take control of Britain.

It might be more than necessary but it could increase the chances of winning. The goal is to take London by force in order to take South-East England by storm.

But there could be a problem if they are not careful.

The British could ambush the Nazis with a special show of force from allies and the people.

There is no indication of winning but it is still in the works of what might happen.

Planning will ultimately determine the success of anything.

And if there was any chance of escaping, it would have to be quick, as the king and the rest of the royal family would have to move to a safe house or somewhere they can feel as though no one would find them. It is just the way it goes to the brink of extinction of a once great country with a lot of pride and glory.

People must be unified in opposing fascism and National Socialism or else civilization is doomed for eternity.

The day is August 1, 1940, and the Battle to take control of Great Britain begins, with a fleet of 5,000 warplanes positioned in France, Belgium, Holland, and Norway.

Hitler orders all Royal Air Force squadron planes to be shot down with no survivors left as well as to destroy the entire fleet of Royal Air Force planes.

The royal family is put on alert to gather and pack their belongings in case of a possible abduction by the Nazis, and that is just the beginning of the immediate warning of impending doom, because there is word that they will be placed on a list to be executed so that Hitler can officially take control of the British government and execute the members of parliament as well.

It is just something that isn't surprising anymore.

The British are outnumbered by 5 to 1 and there is a likelihood of strong surrender or occupation if the Royal Armed Forces do not have a perfect strategy in order to defeat the Nazis in battle.

The warning was ultimately heightened and the royal family alerted because the government feared the abduction would cause surrender to the Nazi Reich.

It would be the worst possible fear that Hitler could win yet another country by outmaneuvering it by occupation or making it so that surrender will be imminent.

Should that happen then the people will take to the streets and demand answers from their representatives in parliament.

It would sure be hell but that might not even happen because there could be a lack of global action against the royal family.

It could be the 1600s all over again but there is just nothing stopping Hitler from completing his plan.

That is just the type of situation that exists.

German planes continuously attack Great Britain in order to better secure the monarchy.

It is a never-ending campaign and something that most people are used to by now.

An all-out aerial attack is being waged by the German Air Force and it is going as expected.

Something more could happen but it could be a surprise.

And there could be a breaking of a trusted alliance in the hoping it will lead to seizing more land.

That is just a betrayal of trust from an important ally during the war effort to remove the allied forces from power.

Something needs to happen by taking action now or else it could lead to more chaos.

The constant attacks continue, even if the German Air Force has lost a few planes already, but that is expected since the British Air Force is fighting back against their enemy.

Then something dramatic happens where no one expected it to happen.

A Greek cruiser is destroyed on August 15, 1940, and it is rumored the Italians are to blame for sinking it.

The allies are angered and promise to fight back but it is just more rhetoric.

The rumor must be correct because 5 days later, on August 20, 1940, Italy announces an all-out blockade against the Mediterranean and African territories of Britain.

This was probably planned from the beginning and the Italians knew the cruiser was in the way, so they destroyed it for the purpose of making sure nothing prevents them from taking British territories hostage in the name of fascism.

Suddenly, German bombers were seen from above by the people of London, so they started to realize something is wrong because they might be next.

Bombs start dropping down from above and people start screaming and shouting fleeing in panic because they don't want to die at such a young age in the middle of their lives.

It is only a matter of moments until many bombs ruin St. Giles and Cripplegate.

Something must have happened because no part of London was supposed to be attacked, unless it was a strategic plan by Hitler to think of something new.

The attacks are just getting closer to home but with the people now panicking in London, something must be done to silence Hitler.

A show of force or something that might send a message to Hitler might mean that this war shall not be tolerated anymore.

Churchill responds with a swift but just message of revenge saying he will obliterate the Nazis into the past by bombing their planes and airfields in the aftermath of the devastation.

The people of London are overjoyed and they cheer for the future, but there is just something to it that might not even pan out.

Everything could be a diversion and that might just cause the whole plan to get out of hand so there must be a backup strategy to determine the precise plan of action.

A night attack against Germany begins on August 25, 1940 to take revenge against the Nazi Reich for what is deemed an accidental bombing but the British government says it was intentional because Hitler wants to take control of the government and parliament so he can have more land in order to kill more innocent people.

Berlin lights up with mortar fire from above but the Germans were expecting this to happen, so the German Air Force started forming when no British warplane was looking.

The Nazi planes came from behind and then launched an assault against the British just when they were deploying their last round of bombs on the German capital.

It was another sneak attack by the Nazis and it was just as usual.

Germany was able to sink all but two planes and it was time to plan more engagements to show Britain that they were going to fight back against this night attack.

There was damage but it could be fixed within a reasonable amount of time.

But there were no survivors from the Royal Air Force bombers that attacked Berlin in the night, except those in the two planes that escaped due to sheer luck.

The German people stood strong and it was just as they thought in the aftermath.

But London needed to act first in order to make a deal with a new or possibly old ally.

It just needed to be done and struck so that if anything bad this happen to their fleet of ships and planes, then they could find some more time by leasing ships from allies.

It would be a desperate attempt for safety and to secure a possible win against Germany and Italy but there is just no sign that it could benefit anyone but war.

So it could be a sign of weakness that the allies are running out of options.

Nevertheless, an agreement was reached between the governments of the United States of America and the United Kingdom after the President of the United States of America, Franklin Delano Roosevelt, signed the Anglo-American Lend-Lease Agreement on September 3, 1940, but in return for receiving 50 war destroyers from the previous world war Britain agreed to a 99-year lease for the United States Armed Forces to use several of their naval and air force bases.

It is a done deal and both parties get something in return in hopes of that they can potentially defeat Hitler and Mussolini.

For that one reason, there is hope for the people, as they celebrated in the streets once they heard of the favorable news of additional equipment to support the war effort in a time of need.

The equipment might be dated but if it is the best that they can come by then it will have to do it.

And so far, not many people are having doubts about the equipment, but then there are some that say that the equipment is just too old that it won't efficiently detect enemy ships.

That could soon turn into a conspiracy theory and might lead to propaganda being deployed in order to stop people from hearing them.

It is precisely why people might not want to say anything that criticizes their government, because that could lead to their prosecution in a wrongful manner.

The day was now September 7, 1940.

But the celebration was just short lived yet again, as Hitler began his blitz against London in order to secure the capital to take it.

The royal family was put on alert again in order to gather and pack their belongings for one more time just in case they need to evacuate to another location in the hopes of not being kidnapped.

About 500 German bombers are escorted by roughly 1000 fighter jets in order to surprise and scare the people of London, but it was different from their usual attacks.

People were frightened.

They didn't know what to do and they were afraid of what might happen if they were inattentive to the situation at hand.

Babies started to cry.

Children started to panic.

Everyone wanted to huddle together in order to find some sort of safe place because the skies were just so loud.

People looked out their windows and spotted German planes with a swastika on them.

They were surprised.

They didn't know what to do.

They didn't know if they were going to die.

They were afraid for their lives and didn't know if this was their last night to live.

Parents and grandparents urged their children to back away from the windows because of what might happen.

It was soon aware that this was a retaliatory act for what Britain did to Berlin just days ago.

The people had to protect their homes and their families so they will survive. It is a time that is all too familiar of daily raids.

The allies have done it but so far not much has been done about it. The case is just about to get no better.

It is all for a common cause.

Everything will fall and it too will be at the end of times in which there is nothing more but the development of a dystopian society so that the whole world could become a socialist utopia.

German warplanes have started dropping their bombs on everything they see with a light on.

Quickly thinking, the parents and grandparents pull away their children and grandchildren away from the windows and then they close all of the curtains to hide any light to avoid being detected.

But it doesn't last long, as the Germans can spot targets from above with visible light, so they start bombing, thinking it contain allied forces that seek to destroy them.

Explosion after explosion, there is nothing stopping the Germans, as it just keeps on going for no particular reason.

Then there is no noise but then it comes back.

One after another, German warplanes start to attack the airfields of the Royal Air Force, in order to deter the British. Runways and taxiways were ruined beyond repair.

It seemed like destruction from the end of the world.

The Germans kept on attacking and further destroyed the airfields of the British Air Force.

They didn't want them to regroup.

For nights on end, this is what the people of London had to endure and they didn't want to die.

People were afraid and they had the right to be, as they didn't want to depart their bodies for something that frightened them.

It was just as though they needed to take quick actions.

It was too late, as there was nothing that can be done.

The airfields were just beyond repair and it is just the same as before in the mind of society.

Quickly thinking, the British Secret Service had to think about the royal family, before they were kidnapped.

Hitler already had his eyes set on Buckingham Palace so there was a reason to be afraid.

On September 15, 1940, British Secret Service agents along with paratroopers, launched a secret mission by evacuating the royal family from above and placed them on an unidentified plane.

It took nearly five minutes and any longer would be a problem for all of Britain.

Within less than an hour, the members of the British royal family were whisked away to a private mansion in Worcestershire, England, a place that no one thought about.

About ten minutes later, Nazi kidnapping squads repelled from above in order to break into the palace but they were just too late, as the royal family has already escaped.

It took less than an hour to get the royal family to safety and the Germans were flummoxed about what to do because they thought the British government would surrender to Hitler in a time of war.

Immediately, Churchill and the British Parliament were briefed on the matter about the successful escape of the royal family as well as the Germans breaking into the palace in order to kidnap them.

Churchill is glad that the royal family is safe but he now has to think about something in order to try and defeat the Nazis.

Just three days later, on the morning of September 18, 1940, the Nazis seize control of the British skies.

It was surely a very sad day for the people of London because they wouldn't know what will happen next.

Prime Minister Churchill will have to think of something fast and it needs to be soon or else Britain would be the next to fall.

Devastation hits the British public on September 28, 1940, and word is Germany has outnumbered Britain by 5 to 1 in an aggressive war against the British Armed Forces.

Still undeterred, Winston Churchill refuses to give up, as he believes there is still time to win the war and defeat the Nazis as well as Hitler. It is just a tough day to experience when the Royal Air Force has lost so much, but Hitler still has more stuff up his sleeve before he plans to formally occupy Great Britain.

While the British were facing a war of their own, no one bothered to notice that Egypt on September 13, 1940, was invaded by Italy, and it was just a case of trying to help the allies trying to defeat Germany in a time of need.

But Operation Sea Lion was a success so far and soon Hitler might finally take the United Kingdom and have his way of occupying it if there isn't any hindrance to his future or current plans.

There is still no threat that the allies will win but that will always be a possibility.

And now it is one month later, October 28, 1940, so there is a time and place for everything, and Mussolini intends to prove himself to Hitler that he can get things done as well as providing support and loyalty to the Nazis in a time of need.

Mussolini must not fray from the path and so he decides to prove himself to the Axis Powers of what the allies call the common enemy of hatred and discrimination taking over Europe in a vile campaign to spread chaos, destruction, anarchy, and lawlessness in order to help spread the weakness of the Western powers.

With the war continuing as planned, Prime Minister Mussolini approves a plan to invade Greece, and it is without a doubt a risky yet very actionable plan because the fascist leader believes he can take down their soldiers before anything happens.

There is just a problem if Hitler and the other leaders of the Axis Powers will accept the invasion as proof of loyalty to them.

It could fail greatly causing innocent people to die but the goal is to occupy the land in an attempt to force the Greek government out of power without something to think about.

Mussolini wants the land in order to grow his new fascist empire to spread his message of propaganda against the entire Western world in an attempt to silence the speech of everyone else by saying freedom and civil liberties are bad for the environment.

That is just the type of craziness that will lead to violence and more chaos in an attempt to grow out socialism, communism, and Marxism.

People will revolt and they will demand answers.

Later that day, Mussolini launches his campaign to seize the Balkans, in an attempt to say he has the guts to be a loyal member of the Axis Powers so Italy can be an official member.

So far after a week, the campaign has been a success, but the allies are getting nervous there will be a new threat against freedom and civil liberties.

On November 11, 1940, the Royal Air Force finds out that it has some undamaged planes so they immediately decide to attack the Italian Navy in Taranto of all places.

But there is doubt whether the Royal Air Force would be able to win at sea because they are using obsolete bi-planes that no one even uses anymore.

The immediate thought is these planes would be able to destroy Italian Naval Battleships.

It will be interesting to watch but it is not put on hold.

In the afternoon, the campaign begins, and there are already several problems.

A few of the bi-planes seem to be having trouble keeping flight due to the weight of the torpedoes and bombs attached.

The Italians see the planes and think it is quite funny that Britain is resorting to obsolete planes in an attempt to win.

The British are now outnumbered by 7 to 1 after a surprise attack by the Germans and Italians due to intelligence given to them from a trusted and important source.

As it turns out, bi-planes were not able to damage the battleships, due to a united campaign led by Germany and Italy in an attempt to squash the British.

Immediately after the British led attack started it failed significantly by not realizing the payloads were too heavy and that Germany and Italy shot down the planes with their own planes within minutes of seeing them.

That is just intriguing.

It is just another sad day for the allies as they face defeat yet again in a humiliating way for which they thought they would win.

Something isn't right, as the allies thought they knew everything about the Axis Powers, but it turned out to be wrong.

The whole situation is leading to an investigative report on why there are continuous losses but it could fail to acknowledge the reasons why they might be losing the war.

There could be a trap.

Or there could be a mole or a secret agent giving away privilege information away to the enemy.

No one can cite a reason for why Germany and Italy has somehow overcome the force and power of the Royal Air Force and Royal Navy.

It must be that an anonymous source is embedded within the British Military for some reason or another.

The investigation could reveal a culprit but that is highly unlikely due to no one knowing who it is, leading to believe that someone high up in the Nazi ranks is trying to sabotage them by tracking their every movement in a sly manner.

It is probably a massive troll bent on trying to fool the allies in a convincing way and then making it look like they are using a failed strategy in order to win the war.

There is just something about this that doesn't make any sense at all because it would be considered treason if there was a British soldier giving classified information to enemy agents in a time of war, since that would mean that that person is indeed a mole or a double agent in order to prevent the allies from winning the war.

And the punishment is death for the purpose of treason.

But there was another reason to fight harder in order to win the battle.

There has been another air raid by the German Air Force, and on the day of November 14, 1940, the city of Coventry was bombed and is all but destroyed in a spectacular yet sad manner.

A fourteenth century cathedral was ruined and the lead roof flowed like a river down onto the ground in which everyone started to flee and panic that no one has ever seen in a few months.

This will just keep on happening until someone wins the war in a fit of rage.

But it will take some time in a need of war because no one knows who the enemy is, as they could be anyone, even in disguise, so no one is ever to be trusted.

It was just attack after attack and win after win, as the Italians and the Germans have just not lost much ground since the war has begun.

Time is now indeed running out, but the situation just got worse, as the ninth Italian Army just defeated Greece at Koritsa on November 22, 1940.

This is just a blow to the allied forces as they were counting on the Greeks for superior fire power and strength just because of their historical heritage of winning several countless wars.

The allies try to counter with their attacks on the Axis Powers by implementing Operation Compass on December 9, 1940, but there is just no chance that Britain can survive by trying to disrupt Italian forces in Egypt.

It is just a waste of time but the British can do whatever they want in order to win the war.

It will take luck and strength for the British to win in a desert campaign in the middle of nowhere but there might be a surprise waiting for them before they even know it.

And they will be sorry they ever messed with the Germans and Italians. It is just too early to tell but nothing can predict the outcome of the future.

It will all be for nothing and will lead to further new embarrassment in all forms.

That is just the case that it needs to be in the form of a new nightmare.

As Operation Compass proceeds, there is just silence, and no one knows what will happen.

No one knows how long it will last and if it will even succeed.

That is just the epitome of life because if parts of Egypt are captured by the allies then it will continue into the New Year. But if they lose the battle against Italy, then Egypt will be part of Italy forever.

That is just a threat of extinction and no one wants that.

The battle continues but there is another setback.

Allies have failed to capture Sidi Barrani, as they thought they have would capture at least one town or region controlled by Italy.

It was just another devastation to take the control back from an enemy power.

The Germans and Italians got word of a possible invasion in Egypt from a trusted intelligence source, so Hitler sent some of best troops to the town of Sidi Barrani and other places within the surrounding areas.

It was pure genius and on December 11, 1940, Britain and her allies were once again ambushed by surprise in what would be trench warfare to the death of civilization.

Nearly all allied soldiers died or were injured as they fell into holes and trenches while the Germans and Italians snuck up behind them in a sort of game.

Casualties were high and are just the beginning of a new fatal war to go against civilization.

The desert leaves no traces behind and it is everything wrong with the way the war is being fought.

Soon there will be nothing left but a place of doom and catastrophe.

It is just the fact of life but no one wants to ever admit defeat.

The wounded and unharmed retreat after a resounding defeat in which they thought they could have won.

Some wars are just not meant to be won and that might be the case here. It could all be a lesson of what not to do but the Germans and Italians just knew that the allied forces would arrive, so it means they know something, and it shall reveal itself long enough.

That is just the case of the situation at hand.

A new year is just about to begin and that will just lead to further devastation to anyone involved in war whether fighting or supplying all of the weapons.

The time is just now to fight back and it is the same time of when people will suffer and then they will decide if they want to face death or just live a normal life.

Time is up and it won't last long.

It is February 10, 1941, and there is a new sign of the threat of war is on the rise. South African military forces try to seize power away from Italy and Germany but they just fail to get enough support from the allies due to unexplained reasons that don't make sense, so South Africa has to commit to an invasion alone.

But there is still a problem with everything, as Germany has now turned to taking Africa with the help of Italy.

So that might not pan out for South Africa, even if Britain has some forces in the near vicinity of where South African forces are going.

It is just about timing.

The South African forces already crossed into the border from Kenya into Somaliland on January 29, 1941, but they must wait to plan their attack because no one is helping them.

But the Germans and Italians receive some intelligence that the South Africans are planning to invade parts of Eastern Africa to stop the Nazis and Italians.

Britain then tries to encircle German and Italian forces to Benghazi, but it is a trap set by the Axis Powers, because Benghazi was all part of the plan to begin with.

The plan immediately backfires for Britain and Australia, as the Germans and Italians backup forces were waiting for them in what seems to be an apparent sabotage.

It was a deadly day for the allies and it all goes downhill from there on February 6, 1941.

Four days later, on February 10, 1941, Mussolini and Hitler come to an agreement for Mussolini to support Italian forces in North Africa with German Armed Forces.

It is just the new dawn of the century.

On March 2, 1941, Bulgaria joins the ranks of Germany and Italy by officially joining the Axis Powers, which now gives Germany the necessary access to invade Yugoslavia and Greece, and that is what Germany does to grow their empire on April 6, 1941, the same day that British forces attempt to occupy Ethiopia to prevent an Axis uprising.

But one month earlier, on March 6, 1941, Britain officially invaded Ethiopia, yet it wasn't a threat to the Nazis or Italians because the Axis Powers viewed Ethiopia is a non-issue in the sense that it was about desperation.

On April 4, 1941, the combined German and Italian forces have now officially captured Benghazi, and just six days later, on April 10, 1941, German forces have officially captured Tobruk.

Seven days later, on April 17, 1941, the Royal Yugoslavian Army is forced to surrender, making it possible for the Axis Powers to seize and occupy the land and the region surrounding it.

Great Britain, however, was facing a shortage of planes and troops due to the constant attacks from Germany and Italy, so they must consider drafting additional people, making it possible there will be more casualties in the name of war.

It is just the beginning but that won't stop the enemy from launching an all-out attack against their natural foes.

The state of the union for the allied forces is just dismal at best.

And there is nothing that can help it, with the exception of a new ally entering the war, but no one knows when that will happen.

Meanwhile, Germany continues its battle against Britain in the capital city of London on May 10, 1941, and there is no plan to stop it, as Italy is now joining the relentless campaign against the British capital.

The goal is just to overwhelm the British public into giving up and surrendering so that no one is in the way.

Things officially heat up on June 22, 1941, as the Soviet Union, under the leadership of Josef Stalin, officially agrees to join the ranks of the Axis Powers, in order to make sure that the Eastern Front is protected from allied forces.

Everything will be far from over now but things take a drastic turn when the South African forces officially surrender at Gondar in Ethiopia on November 28, 1941, in a way that turns the odds against Britain.

The war is only heating up and nothing will get better.

It is all a lost cause from now until the end.

SEVEN

I

Buzzing from above with clear but partly cloudy skies with a deep but too familiar tone, the same that happened in Berlin and London was at it again in a mysterious sounding of one, as people are barely awake and some are about to go to work.

It is an early morning day on December 7, 1941, as a familiar sound of warplanes fly above in a flyover in order to do who knows what to a naval station.

It was just an annoying sound of repeated noise and the people wanted to know what was happening but then something happened.

Everything disappeared as though it was just some sort of practice run.

But something didn't feel right.

It was like they were still here but no one knew where.

People didn't feel safe.

It just felt like another one of these surprise attacks but from where.

And then, it hit the people, as they now knew the war was coming for them.

Immediately, the planes turned around and started dropping bombs galore on everything in sight.

The Japanese has officially declared war on the United States of America by dropping bombs and torpedoes from above.

It was a clear sign that they wanted to destroy every bit of the United States Pacific Fleet stationed at Pearl Harbor Naval Air Station in Hawaii as their planes flew over the island territory.

People from left and right were starting to panic as they did not know what to do.

It was just a surprise and no one knew what was happening.

The Japanese just wanted to destroy everything to prevent the United States from entering the war.

There was just chaos and destruction everywhere as now the people thought about what it will be like until the war ends.

They might be next and it could be a matter of days or even hours until there is a new threat on the horizon.

That will be bad but it won't be the first time it would have happened.

Bombing was just continuous and no one could stand it.

The United States Naval sailors were surprised by a sneak attack and they were rendered powerless so they couldn't act.

For 11 minutes straight beginning at 0753 hours there was a torpedo attack and then it was followed by Japanese bombers.

By 0800 hours all of the US fighter planes were destroyed.

Soon, an explosion was seen from above and by the people who lived on the island, as they saw smoke nearby that was coming from the naval air station.

Then it was confirmed, the USS Arizona was hit and it started an explosion that continuously to cause more imminent danger to the rest of the island and soldiers.

Then, at 0837 hours, the Japanese bombers turned back, and people thought they were safe.

The United States Government has issued an alert to all people to seek shelter as soon as possible because of a continued threat from the attack.

The military wanted to act fast but it was not fast enough because there was nothing that can be done.

There can be more attacks so the people must take cover for the duration of the attack.

It is not clear but there seem to already be casualties.

But no one could catch any luck, as Japanese bombers appeared over the island of Hawaii again at 0840 hours to resume their action against the United States of America.

It was another round of bombing and Japan had one goal in mind.

About 167 Japanese bombers flew over Ford Island and then bombed it while also bombing Kaneohe Naval Air Station and Hickam Field.

It was just a message to be sent to prevent a nation from entering the war.

All of a sudden, it was finally over, and the first wave of bombers returned to their aircraft carriers around 0950 hours while the second wave was just departing for Oahu to leave.

People were astonished and panicking because they didn't know what has happened.

They just knew that there was an attack against their country and action needed to be taken.

Then an assessment will be made about what to do next.

An announcement was made hours later and it was learned estimates were up to over 2,000 people that died in the bombing of Pearl Harbor.

It was such a tragic event that no one wanted to remember what happened.

No one wanted to live with the burden about having to protect their family members now due to deranged actions caused by an unproven theory.

It was just so sad that people didn't want to be here anymore.

No one wanted this experience to be the norm because it will just frighten away tourists which will take away some much needed revenue for local and state governments.

There was such an outpouring of sympathies and emotions to the deceased and members of the families.

The United States military didn't know what to do but they knew they must move on in order to think of the future strategies in a time of war.

There will be hell to pay and that was a promise made by politicians on both sides of the political spectrum.

The damage was done and it was time to decide what to do next.

It is just incomprehensible at what the Japanese did to this great country.

But it was too late and the United States would have to decide if they would declare was against a foreign power.

It would be the hardest decision to be made but it might be necessary in order to stop tyranny from taking over civilization.

No one wanted to face death again like this ever before and it will be a reminder for all that survived.

Already, rescue crews are trying to save the people from Pearl Harbor that survived the bombings and attack.

They would need to announce the true victim counts that died, survived, or wounded.

The people of America would have to deal with the wrath of Japan and the Axis Powers if there is war declared.

President Franklin Delano Roosevelt was briefed on the disaster at Pearl Harbor and he was immediately inflamed at what happened to the soldiers stationed there at the naval air station.

He wanted to act quickly to show strength, force, and courage against the Japanese.

The president was just angry and frustrated at the situation that took place and he vowed he would seek immediate action in order to punish the Japanese.

It was a sign he was taking everything seriously because he believed the Japanese decided unanimously to declare war against the United States of America.

The idea was clear to him.

The president would ask Congress to declare was against the enemy state of Japan.

It was just dire that everything was clear to the people.

They have been attacked and a foreign power declared war on them.

That wouldn't go likely and it looked like everything will change for the better.

Time would tell about who is right and who is wrong.

Then it happened, President Franklin Delano Roosevelt asked both houses of Congress to declare war against Japan.

And they responded to him with immediate action. Almost every politician was angered and dismayed by the actions taken by Japan and they knew they had to do something.

It is about justice and courage and to preserve freedom, liberty, and the pursuit of happiness to keep everyone prosperous and safe.

The United States Congress took immediate action by saying they will vote on declarations of war as soon as they are written.

The people of the United States of America cheered this on, as they believed it was the best and only decision necessary in order to take on the enemy.

It is now time to take the appropriate action against the enemy and that is the only purpose to move on with prosperity.

On December 8, 1941, both houses of Congress overwhelming voted to pass declarations of war against Japan.

It was meant as a sign to say to the rest of the world that no one attacks the United States of America and gets away with it.

The United States of America had to act or else they would just be exercising weakness and Hitler and Japan would laugh in the face of all of the American people.

It would be a mockery if no one took action against a real threat of imminent war.

And so it went to the office of the president for final signature and he signed it as soon as it was received by him.

It is unanimous.

The United States of America has officially declared war on a new enemy state, the island nation of Japan.

Newspapers soon published their lead headline for the next day and it was just all unanimous.

All of them printed the declaration of war on the front page as their lead story.

The government of Great Britain has a new partner in the United States of America joining them as an ally in favor of defeating the enemy in the war.

It was clear to Great Britain.

They had to act or face the wrath of the British people.

Knowing they had a chance of winning the war now against Hitler and Mussolini, the British government decided to take a bold plan of action that would ultimately test the waters of sanity.

It would take confidence to face a true enemy

That would demonstrate courage and strength throughout the world to tell society that bombings on foreign soil will amount to a declaration of war and will never be tolerated.

Britain took action for the first time since entering the war with a very clear path.

The British government declared war against Japan just moments after the United States of America did on the same day.

It was a bold move to take this step and the people overwhelmingly supported it. There was just the case of celebration again.

Three days later, the United States Congress passed more declarations of war, this time against Italy and Germany, in an attempt to fully support the allies in a never-ending situation.

The declarations of war were unanimous and had the support of the

American people.

Everyone applauded it and there was just nothing wrong about it.

The United States of America was willing to go all-in to stop a few menaces by destroying society as they knew it because it would lead to mass chaos and destruction with full anarchy throughout the world if it wasn't stopped.

This was the most reasonable as well as one of the most appropriate choices that has been decided in order to make a stance that the governments of the United States of America and Great Britain will take retaliatory action against those that attack innocent people and the soldiers of their great armed forces.

It was a sign that people would have to think about and it will be known to the end of times.

Everything is about to change and that might be for the better to demonstrate a show of force and the stance of going to war will eventually weed out weakness in order to be united against the common enemy of the Axis Powers.

The time is now and it is the force of the people that shall decide the end of times.

II

Hitler responded with immediate action as soon as he learned of the declarations of war against Germany and Italy on the same day.

It was a day he decided to demonstrate he was more powerful than anyone else.

That is just what needed to happen.

The prospect was just grim for the future and no one wanted to live in such a world and then news broke about what Hitler has done in order to secure his base and support.

Germany has now declared war against the United States of America on December 11, 1941 for declaring war against them.

It was soon a threat of back and forth remarks trying to deepen the divide of an already fragile society.

There would be chaos and destruction but nothing before the case of something more sinister to the extent that nothing is as it seems because of the threat of a divided country.

That is just something that must be dealt with in order to plan for the future of the war but not before to decide if there will be any more threats.

And then it happens again.

There was another surprise attack from the enemy at hand and it now threatens to further destabilize everything.

The Soviet Union has launched an assault against the United States of America in a way to capture the surprise of the American public and from politicians.

December 31, 1941 was a day that would live in infamy until the end of civilization, because just after midnight Soviet bombers led an air assault against the territory of Alaska.

People were awakened to loud but mysterious noises that they never heard before and it was just the beginning.

Just a few minutes later, several hundred enemy planes from above dropped bombs on known military bases operated and owned by the United States of America in an attempt to prevent an attack on the Soviet Union before it can happen but it was just about the same as always.

The people were afraid and didn't know what to do while some slept throughout the entire campaign.

But the air assault on the territory of Alaska proved to be an easy one for the Soviets, as no one was able to spot them, due to advanced stealth technology obtained from an unknown source.

Bombs galore dropped one minute after the other and it was the surprise of a lifetime.

It would be known as the attack on midnight of New Year's Eve for the rest of eternity and it was justly named.

The sky lit up with flashes of light, as the several Soviet bombers dropped bombs from above.

Elmendorf Field in Anchorage was the first to be attacked as it was located in a major civilian area, followed by Mark's Air Field in Nome, Ladd Field in Fairbanks, and Fort Wainwright, all simultaneously without losing any momentum.

The Soviets were just invincible and the United States of America could not spot anything.

There were just repeated flash bangs and unfamiliar sounds.

It sounded as though that the world was ending but it was more than that.

As people tried to sleep, they wondered what has happening to their once quiet towns.

They were now full of noise that sounded like some form of severe thunder and lightning.

Buildings started to shake and then the earth started to crack.

The roads seemed fine but nothing was immune from attack.

Air fields were being pulverized and obliterated.

Industrial facilities were flaming up.

Airplane hangars were no longer to be found.

There were just explosions everywhere as they light up the sky with beautiful colors.

It looked like a sign from God that the world was never meant to be.

Buildings everywhere were up in flames as smoke started to rise from above.

Grass was burning and so were the trees.

Sidewalks started to turn to ash and dust and then the streets were blasted into craters.

Everything was just being destroyed and it seemed to be the end of the world and the beginning of an apocalypse as people knew it.

Some people wanted to go outside while always tried to see what was going on because they didn't know what was going on.

They wanted to see why there was a bunch of noise going on outside.

It would be a mistake they would soon regret as they quickly went back inside and tried to hide their children and other family members.

They saw enemy planes from above that resembled the Soviet insignia.

And it was a warning to them all as they wondered why someone would do this to some isolated territory.

There was just a weary conclusion of hope and it was just a sign of a new threat.

There is just nothing but humanity in the way and the Axis Powers want to destroy that.

Something isn't right and it must be the solution of the problem.

It was known as the Blitz against Alaska and the world stood in fear as everyone was defenseless.

No one knew why Alaska was under attack from the Soviets but some speculated that they wanted Alaska back because it was just a massive piece of land that could support the facilities of the Axis Powers, and particularly the Soviet Union.

Before long, the air assault was over in less than three hours, while the Soviet bombers were headed back to their aircraft carriers off the coast of Alaska.

And then it was morning. Immediately, the United States military learned about the air assault by the Soviets and they thought about having to alert the Congress and the President of the United States of America.

It was just something that needed to be addressed before senior government staff finds out.

Someone would be fired if no one was alerted and it would soon lead to new actions being taken against the enemy but that would be when a new threat is foreseen.

And that threat is now.

President Franklin Delano Roosevelt is alerted and Congress is then alerted about the situation.

It is a sad day and people are demanding answers about why no one did anything.

The President informs Congress about the new threat and quickly informs them that he urges that a declaration of war be issued against the Soviet Union.

Congress takes up the decision and it is to decide what it will do.

News starts to break that that were several witnesses who saw the Soviet bombers and they describe it as an assault after midnight.

Many of the witnesses said they did not know what was going on until they went outside to see what was happened and they described the Soviet insignia to reporters and investigators alike.

Air traffic controllers repeatedly said they saw blimps on their radar but then disappeared for no apparent reason, but they did then report that they thought they heard bombs dropping from above.

And the question would be why they didn't report it.

Well, the air traffic controllers said there was no signal or tone at the other end to alert anyone.

It was just a sign of sabotage.

Quickly, Congress is told of the information from the investigators and the reporters, while the president is privately briefed about the same information.

And soon, within the last hour, the Soviet Union has taken the responsibility for bombing Alaska on national television and radio, and they say it was an act of pride to target the innocents.

The president was infuriated and so were the members of Congress in both chambers.

They wanted answers and they wanted names.

They claim the American people have the right to know who and what did to our great and thriving country.

It was soon learned that Congress would write up another new declaration of war and it would immediately go into effect after it was signed into law by the president.

It took action and sometime but on January 1, 1942, the United States of America declared war against the Soviet Union.

The day was glorious and it marked an extraordinary time of existence.

Nothing will stop the allied forces now but there is always the very looming threat of the rise of the Axis Powers with their advanced weaponry from some unknown sources.

The day is now January 9, 1942, and Japanese forces are now leading an attack against the Philippines, in an attempt to gain more territory for the Axis Powers.

It was a sign of not giving up but it was also a sign of trying to gain the upper hand like the Axis Powers have did repeatedly did once before in the name of war.

It was as usual as the rest of the claims by the people but it is now normal and that is just a problem.

On the following day of January 10, 1942, the allies tried to set up a post in the southwestern Pacific in order to strategize their next plan of trying to stop anymore invasions by the Axis Powers.

The campaign is short-lived as Japanese and Soviet forces lead a combine air assault just a few hours later against them.

Allied forces are trying as hard as they can to try and maintain a stable ground.

But Singapore surrendered to the Japanese after the presence of an overwhelming defeat and being outnumbered by 3 to 1.

The President of the United States has had it and he wanted to stop the Japanese before they attack more.

There was condemnation by the United Labourists against the Japanese Americans.

And it was just brutal racism and discrimination as some people has said.

Anti-Japanese sentiment was just growing like wildfire and it was not going to change in a moment's notice.

Members of Congress started to state the support for the war if the only goal was to defeat the Japanese menaces of the world.

People started growing tired of the inaction of the allies and they wanted change.

That all changed on February 19, 1942, when the President of the United States of America, Franklin Delano Roosevelt, signed into law Executive Order 9066 that ordered all people of Japanese Ancestry that lived in the country to be sent to internment camps as a retribution for what Japan did to Pearl Harbor.

Americans celebrated in the streets because they believed this was the best decision ever made while prominent Centralists denounced the executive order as a ruse to take away civil liberties from innocent people that did not even do anything wrong.

United States Marshals and CBDI agents started to knock on the doors of known Japanese-Americans in California and Hawaii while many business owners in the territory of Hawaii opposed the order because it would ruin the economy.

Several prominent and well known white business owners everywhere across the territory of Hawaii staged protests because they thought it wasn't right and they believed the Japanese were so ingrained into society that the economy will collapse because nearly all businesses were Japanese owned and operated.

The minority in Hawaii had a belief that many businesses will shut down because of internment causing chaos and panic everywhere.

It was just a bad idea and the local politicians stood up to President Roosevelt in the name of morality.

The White House backed down from the internment of Japanese Americans in Hawaii but then there was just more bad news.

On April 9, 1942, allied forces in Bataan surrender while the Philippines surrender to Japan.

Americans are taken hostage and are then interned at labor camps.

Roosevelt and Congress are outraged as hell as with the American people demanding answers.

Some things never change but it is just a cry for help.

No one even knows what they are doing and people of all creeds are fed up with the American military, as they have faced defeat after defeat.

Americans and Britons alike are demanding change and to fight more and more vigorously in a time of need.

Underway is the battle of Coral Sea but already it is proving to be another disaster as the Soviets, Italians, and Germans have joined Japan in a united front against the combined forces of Britain, Australia, and the United States of America.

The allies thought they could win this one but they took on heavy damage from early on after they were completely assaulted by an abundance of warships and bombers.

It was an immediate assault against the allied forces led by the Axis Powers, but it was all over within a day after May 4, 1942.

The aftermath was just devastating as the allies had nothing left they could do.

Much of the Pacific Fleet was all but destroyed and it would only be a matter of time until this would be reported back to Washington DC for an update what to do next.

A few ships of the Pacific Fleet still remained but they are nowhere near the Coral Sea as they are on the other side of the Pacific Ocean close to the Midway Atoll.

News of the defeat breaks to the American people and Congress as well as President Roosevelt as mad as hell for what happened.

They want to know how the Axis Powers defeated their forces in the South Pacific and soon Congress holds hearings by demanding answers.

People are starting to panic that the war will be lost in a matter of months and that is making the members of Congress to demand answers in order to avoid any new types of embarrassments.

But Congress is told by the admirals that allied forces were just outnumbered by the combined forces of the Axis Powers of Germany, Italy, the Soviet Union, and Japan in a surprise sabotage attack from all sides of the ocean.

Members of Congress in the joint hearing gasped and are deeply surprised from the new information, but they soon learn that the Axis Powers have obtained advanced stealth technology and has implemented it on all of their planes, helicopters, vessels, and military equipment in order to avoid detection.

Senators stood still and members of the House of Representatives did not know what to say about any of this information.

Everyone was shocked including the guests observing everything.

Soon there was speculation from many in the room that there could be a mole or double agent embedded within the allied forces but they had no proof of anything.

Questions resumed and the admirals didn't know how to respond to any of it but speculate.

Then a hypothetical came up and asked if it was even possible if any of the Axis Powers had any advanced information as well as knowledge of the planned battles or campaigns planned by members of the allied forces.

And the admirals replied saying it was very possible, which shocked the whole room.

After a full day, the federal government had to think about what to do but they just had to continue with their main strategy of hoping that the Axis Powers will mess up.

Military officials remained optimistic that they could still win at one last stand, the Battle of Midway Atoll, in which they have learned that the Japanese will try to capture the group of islands in another attempt to gain traction and additional land.

Should that happen then there will be a collapse of all hope.

Sadly, on June 4, 1942, the Japanese led another surprise assault against the United States of America by destroying or severely damaging the remaining Pacific Fleet with help from Germany, Italy, and the Soviet Union on all sides.

Tragedy struck again and there was nothing that could have been done to prevent it.

The Japanese has successfully captured the Midway Atoll in the North Pacific.

Bombs went flying everywhere with shrapnel killing the allied forces immediately, including most of the members of the Pacific Fleet that took part in trying to prevent the capture.

Nearly two thousand United States Navy sailors perished that day, with only a few hundred surviving from minor or major injuries inflicted upon their bodies.

It was just a bad day for the allies.

But it just got worse, as the combined Australian and British forces lost nearly five thousand sailors while only seven hundred remained alive from major injuries to their bodies.

The executives officers on board already know that Congress would be demanding answers yet again and it would be in the immediate interest of what to do next.

It seemed everything was foiled again by some secret source from within the allied forces.

Nothing can stop the Axis Powers from winning now and it will only be a matter of time until the white flag is flown in the name of defeat.

That is just the consensus of the people that see it as is because there is nothing that can save the world now.

It will surely be a case of what politicians try to think to do next.

Something is just in need of a new victory but it won’t be the allies anytime soon.

Things do change and that might be for the better of society in a time of need.

News broke quickly to the American public that they have been yet again defeated by the Japanese of the Axis Powers.

Congress is soon briefed and the President is made aware of the current situation.

They are shocked beyond belief that the Japanese has won again but they don't give up yet as they try to decide what to do next.

They realize time could be running out and soon a decision must be made.

No one has seen this before but the United States of America has won a war on all fronts like this before, so they still have hope.

But strategy is the most significant issue and so far the Axis Powers gained the upper hand in everything.

There is just one thing that must be remembered.

War is war.

Over four months later, on October 23, 1942, recoup British forces attempt to attack the German Army at El Alamein in North Africa, but it is soon realized that they have been sabotaged again, as the combine Italian and German Air Forces immediately launch an air assault against anyone that ever entered the decoy camp at El Alamein.

It was a trap from the beginning and the allied forces fell for it once again.

Something just doesn't feel right and it could be the sense that the allies should be winning but someone knows something that is changing the course of history in order to create a new society bent on supporting the ideology of a coup to challenge the establishment.

Nothing can be at the time of need more than time because something needs to change before there is anything more drastic.

People just want to know what will happen to them in the near future and that is especially important right now because they don't know if the allies are going to win the war.

But there is just the case about winning the war now.

The world is changing and soon there will be a new civilization that shall decide the future of society.

III

An unidentified blip appears on U.S. radar but soon everything is just engulfed in stormy weather, and it is a sign of caution.

United States of America Air Force traffic controllers start to look puzzled as there are no clouds in sight.

They contact General Command in hopes of getting some sort of accurate response about why this is happening.

Someone somewhere there is a person watching laughing at everything going on.

But there is just more of this happening everywhere, as the Gulf Coast and the Western Pacific of the United States are experiencing the same problems as the Eastern Coast is facing.

Blips are appearing everywhere on radar and then disappear again with the sign of stormy weather, according to the radar equipment.

It is just a sign that something is up but everyone is puzzled as to what is happening in the midst of an international war.

General Command is contacted several times and they seem to be puzzled as well because there are no indications of any clouds being present anywhere.

And now, the same thing is happening off the Alaskan coast, so it seems all of this is a coordinated attack against the United States of America in order to send a message.

It will be just too late about what might happen next but the United States might be prepared to fight for their lives.

The situation is just too tense to understand and it seems to all be coming to an end, so that might just be the end of society as we know it. But there is just the craziness of society.

It is just past midnight of the New Year of 1943 on the Eastern Coast, past 1900 hours on the Pacific Coast, past 2300 hours on the Gulf Coast, and past 2000 hours on the Alaskan Coast.

Something big is going to happen and it will be soon.

General Command is perplexed at the high amount of calls coming in from all of the air and naval traffic controllers.

They just don't know what to do because this is the first time this is happening.

This could attract negative attention from the people if no one figures out soon enough what is going to happen.

It could attract the attention of Congress as well as the president but the military must decide before anything else happens.

A coordinated attack by the Axis Powers is the last thing the United States of America wants as it could lead to their eventual defeat.

Suddenly, air and naval traffic controllers can hear mortar fire coming from all directions but they don't know who and for what reason so they contact General Command to see if they can find anything that might explain the situations they are facing.

It fails to stop, as the noise is just getting closer and closer, and there is just no sign of anything, but then explosions are heard.

Within a matter of seconds, controllers are able to see smoke and flames are rising up from the runways.

Then all of a sudden, it happens again, but with more than ever in a way that sounds terrible.

Second after second, minute after minute, mortar fire kept on being heard, and the controllers did not know what to expect, but then it hit them.

Everything around them was burning up in flames, as they soon realized the United States was under attack from the Axis Powers in an attempt to fully take control of the United States of America.

They try to notify General Command but no one responds.

There is just dead silence in the control towers, as they fear the worst.

Then minutes later, they can see and hear torpedoes and bombs everything.

Torpedoes launching from off the coast of warships continue to strike everything in sight while bombs drop below from warplanes to devastate everything.

It is just full fire as there is no stopping a fleet of warships from damaging everything.

It seems like this is just a lost cause but there must be more to do.

There is just something that has to be known.

But everything is in disaster.

Quickly thinking, the controllers try to engage the warships, but it just gets worse.

More torpedoes are fired and more bombs are dropped from below.

No one responds as the ships get closer and closer to shore, but there is nothing that can be done.

There is nothing that can save anyone now and it remains to be seen.

It is half past midnight on the Eastern Coast, and the Germans have just landed off the coast of Virginia Beach, Italy on the Gulf Coast, Japan on the coast of San Francisco, and the Soviets on the coast of Alaska.

No one knows what's happening, and soon there is just dead silence, as there is a lack of awareness.

And then, loud blasts can be heard, as the control towers go up in flames and smoke.

Cities and towns start to burn and neighborhoods start to panic as the people do not know what to do after they are awakened by strange noises.

They look out their windows but can see nothing but fire in the near vicinity.

Everything around them is being destroyed as they ponder how to escape this eternal hopelessness.

General Command puts out an alert to all control towers warning of an imminent invasion by the Axis Powers but no one responds.

There is just utter silence, as the officials back at Langley and Quantico ponder what to do next.

The people try to escape but it is too late as their houses start to burn in flames with thick white smoke.

They all try to make a desperate attempt of trying to pray that this all ends now.

But it is just hopeless.

No one saves them from the burning flames of hell led by Germany, Japan, Italy, or the Soviet Union.

It is just too late to do anything and soon General Command might have to notify the President of the United States of America as well as the members of Congress.

There will be hell to pay as prominent Senators and members of the House of Representatives will be demanding answers from commanders in charge of military operations.

No one wants to see that but it is just a colossal waste of time.

The enemy is already on shore but they are waiting for the right time to attack.

It is still unknown when the Axis Powers will set foot on dry land.

That will be the time when all hell breaks loose as there will just be an ambush of everything.

Before long, there will be a collapse of everything in the midst of a national crisis.

There is just nothing that can be done and that will be the final defeat.

An attack grows greater and greater after no response but it is not too soon to notify President Roosevelt and the members of Congress.

That will be the day when people will be ousted from their posts because there will be nothing to stop anything.

It will all be for a lost cause and soon there will be an imminent attack against all that support the freedom, liberty, and pursuit of happiness granted under the constitution of the United States of America because it will be no more.

IV

President Franklin Delano Roosevelt is notified of the imminent air, sea, and land attack by the Axis Powers from all fronts by General Command just after 0100 hours.

He's told that the Axis Powers have successfully and skillfully penetrated the radar systems and they will be here soon to start an invasion.

Alarmed, the president notifies his cabinet, but he soon realizes that Congress must be alerted, because there is just precious time left to defend the country and defeat the enemy.

General Command is told to use anything in their inventory and artillery to defeat the Axis Powers in the hopes that it will provide more time.

But the Axis Powers are just waiting for the perfect time in order to strike with their new secret weapon, an atomic bomb, which will be the death of a once prosperous country.

It will only be a short matter of time until it strikes from all coasts and then a land, sea, and air invasion shall commence in order to take control of the American government.

And it will be a surprise to everyone how they did it.

That will be the day when a new civilization shall emerge from the ashes while people will learn to cope by just embracing hate and discrimination.

Congress is alerted and they are surprised and mad as hell that they are going to lose.

All hope seems lost and they know it is only a matter of time until they set foot on dry land.

They quickly must think of something that will extend the war such as appropriating more funds to the war effort in a way that sends a message that the United States does not give up.

But it has little chance of working because the enemy is already here and they are ready to fight when it's time, so the new appropriated money would be just a waste of new funding.

It will be eager to watch but there is no end in sight as it will just be the beginning of the new world. There is just nothing that can be done as everything is going downhill.

The world is on the brink collapse and Great Britain is all but defeated.

France is nowhere to be found. Germany is on the rise.

The Axis Powers are just defeating everyone for the greater good of the country.

That greater good is leaving the people reckless without knowing what will happen to them.

There is a great chance of an uncertain future as soon as the Axis Powers complete their attack against the United States of America and the rest of the allies.

No one ever saw it coming but it will surely be a lesson for everybody to learn that there are some people that will provide some inside information to the enemy nations.

It is just all a sham for a thing of irrelevance that doesn't seem to matter anymore but this is just the start of the new age.

The war has just begun and there is just a sign that the allies will be defeated in a matter of moments before anything can be decided in the near future.

Time is of the essence but it will test the sands of time by declaring the extinction of a once great nation.

There is just a lack of time to get things done before the attack.

Planes can be heard buzzing over the National Mall and there is a high possibility the enemy is ready to attack or they are just pouncing at the chance to scout the exact location of where they might drop the bombs in order to win.

People start to be awakened from all the noise they are hearing outside and they want to know what is happening and if they will survive for their remaining part of their lives.

This might be the end for some but not all because of collateral damage.

That always happens and it won't be the last time.

Otherwise it is just a normal night everywhere as people just want to get some sleep hoping they will wake up without anything bad happening.

It is just the hope that something doesn't happen but there is no certainty if that is the goal of anything.

It is just still quiet with nothing happening except for the planes buzzing in the sky trying to scout out a location.

That is just normal and it will continue until there is peace or something else.

Soon there won't be anything left and that is just sad.

And it won't be the first time that happens in the chance of a lifetime.

All of a sudden, missiles can be overheard above the skies, and the members of Congress start to panic in a special session in the middle of the night.

It is just chaos with one member speaking on top of another, knowing they need to immediately think of something before it is too late.

There is just something strange going on that they feel will happen soon.

And then there are more missile launches, one after another and by the dozens, heading in a manner to destroy Washington DC.

Members are panicking because they think there is nothing left to do and they don't know if there is enough time left to write a bill.

Members freeze and turn to catatonic state as they realize that time has run out to act but one member quickly writes a bill on a piece of paper and introduces it to the floor.

It provides for additional funding in an immediate manner.

Quickly read, it is just one sentence long, and it is put to an immediate vote, but there is no knowing if it will pass in time in order to evade surrender or to be signed into law by the president.

The electronic vote begins and within one second everyone voted yes, and the House passes it off to the Senate.

Within seconds of receiving the bill, a Senator introduces the bill from the House and puts it up for a vote, not knowing if it will pass or not, in an attempt to provide safety and security for the American people and for the country in a last ditch effort to see if there is any chance of survival.

It is the only chance the leaders of the free world will have to try to save the country from an imminent invasion.

But it is still uncertain what will happen next, as most people might not even find out until they wake up.

There is just little time to spare before the world finds out and that is just a sad state of affairs to deal with in an unwinnable war.

Debate is quick to end and Senators are panicking about what to do next in the event of a failure to act in time.

They claim that no matter what is done to try to stop the Axis Powers there might not be enough time to really stop them from annihilating the country and blowing it up into billions of small pieces.

Surely, the Senators are trying to do what's best for the country, but they do not want it to be too late, as anything could happen.

It is about the heart of the matter, but they just go with it.

A vote is scheduled after just five minutes of debate, and in a stunning manner, all Senators voted to approve the additional funding for the war in an immediate effect to try and defeat the Axis Powers.

It is just one last shot and it will be very well the final one at that since the Axis Powers are waiting to set foot on dry land.

So it won't be long now.

President Roosevelt is notified that Congress has approved immediate funding to try and defeat the Axis Powers.

But there might not be enough time because it has to travel all the way to the White House.

It could be just too late and Germany would have already taken over the Eastern Coast of the United States of America.

Soon enough, the legislation arrives at the White House before any more damage is done.

It is immediately signed and becomes the law of the land.

But not a single person knows about it because they are more concerned about their livelihoods.

And just like that, the people are alerted via radio and a national television announcement from President Roosevelt saying that he has approved more and immediate funding to try to defeat the enemy but says time might be limited because the enemy has arrived and is waiting just off of our shores ready to pounce.

It is a startling announcement to all of those who are awake and are tuning in to the broadcast from the President of the United States of America, as this might be the last time they might hear from them due to an imminent threat off the shores of the country.

But they fail to know that they are nearly on dry land and are waiting for the perfect time to launch their attack against the homeland.

There is just no certainty now and it could be soon until many millions of innocent people die from a rogue attack by the Axis Powers.

It is just too soon to understand the basic fundamental aspects of life before the end of times.

Something isn't just right and it will continue into oblivion until there is a new beginning.

Soon, everything will be gone, and the people will have to move on, just like they were told to do by the president if America does not win this war.

It is just the price to pay and it will continue until there is no more.

That is the extent of the future for America if Washington falls to Germany, because the coordinated has already begun.

Surely, that should shock everyone, but it won't happen until it finally happens.

That is just a part of life and it is just about time.

Nothing is ever left behind but today is the dawn of a new world.

V

Fire and fury emerged from the sky as bright balls of orange flames deep with passion start to launch everywhere from above in a scene that only takes place in a movie but this is real and they are hitting and damaging all in sight to inflict the greatest damage possible.

People are awakened by loud blasts of sound that seem awfully scary and unfamiliar and they try to look out the window only to see large flames of balls of fire that are hurtling their way towards their homes.

Panic ensues everywhere but it just keeps on coming with full force.

All of a sudden, sparks of fury light up the sky, like a lightshow or something, but soon everything changes, as they start hurtling down towards neighborhoods in a way that seems all too familiar.

People are feeling like the world is only going to end but there is just more and more in the vicinity.

Just a few moments later, torpedoes and missiles make way towards buildings, and are just destroying everything in sight and lighting buildings on fire resulting in rising smoke.

In a matter of minutes, it seems the entire city center is on fire, but there is no end in sight, as fire keeps on spreading everywhere.

Congress is panicking right now as they know time might be finally running up and the war is lost.

There is something that can stop any more damage and destruction everywhere.

Panic and chaos ensues as the people realize they are going to die tonight or are going to die under the threat of trying to flee.

It won't be soon enough until someone arrives in order to save any innocent people from dying.

Still, there is just nothing to do in the near vicinity.

It is all hopelessness as the military fighter jets are soon deployed in order to stop the threat from continuing but it is just too late again as German warplanes shoot out missiles forcing the American fighter pilot to eject from their seats and their planes crashing down into trees or other buildings and even in a grassy field or street.

Nothing will be in the vicinity of anything until there is chaos and that has begun to commence the future of the new world.

Something is just happening all over again, as the people move to the streets and finding abandoned cars with no one to be found. It looks like an abandoned town.

This looked like it has happened before but there is just chaos and panicking everywhere in the midst of destruction and the people are starting to demand answers but they realize they are going to die if they don't move within the next few seconds.

It will only be a matter of time until all hell breaks loose because this is only the beginning and it soon will be in the midst of an unwinnable war.

Time is of the essence and that will be the time of total annihilation.

And then, a crowd of German warplanes can be seen buzzing from above, with bombs dropping everywhere and no end in sight, and it is only the start.

A few seconds later, more bombs drop, followed by torpedoes that strike nearby government buildings, then missiles from above that light the grass on fire.

It is all leading to something that might lead to the destruction of the end of the world.

But then there is silence with no one in sight from above.

The people cheer but they hear something falling from above that they do not want to know.

Suddenly, there is an immediate boom and the ground lights up on fire while creating a deep crater near the vicinity of the White House.

There is nothing but damage everywhere.

The U.S. Capitol is nearly spared but there is damage to the White House.

Congress is alerted and then all hell starts to break loose. Then, the power goes out, and members are nearly scared.

The White House is safe but it has sustained heavy damage from the nearby explosion.

President Roosevelt is found safe by his cabinet but then all of a sudden shots are heard and there is no one left to remain in sight but an unknown shadowy figure.

It is just something tragic and backup arrives, just after the disappearance of the shadowy figure.

It was like no one saw the person who shot the president and his cabinet because of all the commotion from the German invasion.

But it is all part of the plan in order to overthrow the government of the United States of America.

And nothing will ever get in the way of the Axis Powers.

Commotion is heard outside by people screaming and there is just no indication of survival until the sunrise.

There could be more bombs like this but no one will take a chance.

Everyone is just panicking and showing signs of chaos and then there is the bad news of who will lead the country.

Congress has been notified and they are completely mortified.

The president has been shot and it is believed to be fatal.

There is a huge gaping hole of what was once the roof of the White House.

Vice President Henry Wallace is the next in line to succeed Roosevelt and he is quickly sworn in before any other damage can be done.

There is not much time left and it is very likely the country will fall immediately to the Axis Powers.

But all of a sudden something happens, and it is just the thing that doesn't sound that great.

Footsteps can be heard near and it all sounds to be quite fishy, as there is just complete darkness everywhere with no good signs in sight.

The footsteps are getting closer and closer and there is no place to hide.

Adrenaline is rushing and there is just an amplified sense something is going to happen soon.

The people are panicking outside but they do not know what has happened at the White House.

They do not know he has been succeeded by the Vice President.

All hope is lost, as the footsteps are getting closer and closer once more.

And then it stops for a few short moments before the new president can concentrate about what to do next.

Suddenly, people dressed all in black and covered from head to toe, blocking every noticeable part of their body as possible, approach the new president while heavily armed with weapons, and there is just silence, as the president throws his hands up in the air and says "I Surrender, America Surrenders, to the Axis Powers," but the people dressed all in disguise shoot him anyways.

A helicopter can be heard from above and the masked and disguised men grab on to the rope and climb up as it just moves away.

Without a trace they all disappear into the night but the end is not in sight yet, as Congress has yet to found out that the new president has been shot.

This could be the end if there is more to come when the government is at its weakest in a time of need from the effects of war.

Quietness ensues after there are no signs of survivors and it is just suspicious.

Then warplanes can be heard from above and suddenly the sound of a bomb can be heard.

It strikes, causing a deadly impact, killing everyone in sight.

The U.S. Capitol has been hit.

Everyone is dead inside.

There are no signs of survival.

Germany has defeated the United States of America.

It is a sad day for the world to endure but then there is just the case of everything else.

VI

German warships start their assault on the eastern coast, and soon the Soviets, the Italians, and the Japanese all join in and attack from where they are stationed.

It is just about to get started and no one will realize what is even happening because everyone is fast asleep, well most of them are, but when the sun rises it will be the beginning of a new world, a world that in which America has fallen, a world that will not be the same as yesterday because it was long gone after the Axis Powers found out how to defeat the freest country in the world.

There is just nothingness as people are unaware about what is going to happen in the middle of the night in the nation's capital of Washington DC and all across through America simultaneously in several different time zones.

When they all wake up it might as well be over for the survivors of the night.

National Socialism has arrived on the coasts of the United States of America and it has brought it perks with it in order to spread fascism, racism, eugenics, antisemitism, and negative forms of nationalism, making it seem all fine and good for all to experience, but it is just a way to spread propaganda so support can increase overall.

It is about making sure the people fall in line with the new government so that there can be no surprises in a time of need and disarray because soon it will all be crashing down in a matter of hours and days.

The campaign to take America has commenced and there is simply nothing that can be done to prevent it as it is just too late to convince the Axis Powers to turn back.

Missiles are in launching positions as the combined forces of the Axis Powers count down until they finally attack America all at the same time and it is just quiet with nothing but the wind in the hair of people who shouldn't even be out in these conditions.

But it is just quiet as night as there is just the sign of not being aware about anything to the extent that it will be a surprise to all when the sun finally rises.

The combined forces are ready to fire to destroy everything in their way in order to take out historical buildings and anything else that stands for American freedom and liberty.

They are ready and it is now or never before anything else happens.

Warships have commenced the countdown and the missiles fire from all sides starting with Germany, followed by Japan, Italy, and finally the Soviet Union, all in sync with each other in order to perfectly align the goal of inflicting as much damage as possible.

Bombs then drop from above in a manner that tries to inflict great pain and suffering on the people.

And then, German U-Boats fire torpedoes from offshore to just annihilate everything in sight because nothing must remain from the old Empire. It seems crazy but it gets the job done.

The sky is lit up with bright orange sparks that soon ignite to form red and orange flames and soon the ground below starts to shake with severe and an extreme catastrophic nature causing people to wake up in the middle of the night.

Flames start to appear and smoke rises up from several homes and buildings across all communities and neighborhoods across America, as now there is a sign of catastrophe.

Trees start to crack and the sidewalks break away from the streets and roads.

The earth has now opened up to reveal the dirt of the planet and soon one by one the streets and roads start to collapse from the immense pressure from the blast impacts.

Within minutes of impacting buildings, homes, neighborhoods, and communities across America, the second round of missiles, torpedoes, and bombs launch from their stations and then strike their targets in a matter of seconds.

Not all have collapsed as bridges still remain standing connecting the cities to the other parts of the state and that is still hopeful for the people that want to escape before they die.

The survivors might have a chance to seek shelter elsewhere but nothing is certain because the impacts are just getting stronger by the second each time it hits a target.

There is nothing that can be done to stop anything.

But no one might even make it to sunrise since death might arrive soon for most people.

This is just the certainty of war on the horizon between the people who oppose and support it but that will only create what the Axis Powers want: chaos and destruction in the form of an uprising due to political turmoil and an uncertain future.

That is just the fact of life but they want anarchy.

It will be an uprising like no other and that is certainly not unheard of but this could be different in the sense that there is a new goal in mind by killing each other unmercilessly in an attempt to get back at each other due to a failure to act by the government of the United States of America, and that will surely be a spectacle to watch, because people will kill each other over a false pretense to begin with based on assumptions that everyone could be saved from going to war.

And that is when the complete takeover of America shall commence because no one will be able to get in the way of the Axis Powers taking control since they are all fighting each other in protests and riots by demanding accountability.

The perfect time to strike is when no one is paying attention to anything as the world is being destroyed around them as they argue for no reason at all.

Nothing is apparent as ever as this precarious situation with all of the people up in arms over something that doesn't make sense to most people but it has to do with the possibility of dying imminently and wanting to live much longer.

The people do not want to die but they must in order to make room for the future, as they are going to die anyway, at least most of them are, because they will be killed by the combined forces of the Axis Powers in an attempt to lead to what seems is a better tomorrow.

But the truth of the matter is death will be the result of occupying America and that has already begun in a ruthless but successful coup.

There is just sympathy for everyone all around facing the wrath of the Axis Powers, as there seems no way out and all hope seems hopeless due to the fact that there is no one to lead the country anymore.

It is just something sad and intriguing at the same time because no one ever saw this coming, so it was especially surprising that the allied forces failed to win at all costs by trying to win the advantage.

It was like the allied forces knew what they were doing but somehow somewhere the Axis Powers just had the upper hand by having someone provide information to them concerning the campaigns that will take place during the war.

No one ever had a chance and that is surely a despicable act of retribution towards the good people of the world in a way that undermines society to provide for the generation of people that were born into a dismal life of the Great Depression.

The time of everyone is the time that the people will rise up to demand change but that is probably too late to happen now.

It is just the kind of chaotic manner of not knowing what to do next that will stigmatize everything.

Surely something can be done to stop this but it will take an incredibly amount of courage and conviction in order to take on the Axis Powers from further destroying society senselessly in a way that does not promote the foundational values and beliefs set forth by the founding fathers those many years ago in Independence Hall.

And then there will be victory for all.

VII

Explosion after explosion kept on going all through the middle of the night with a deafening pulse sent to all that could hear the wretched noise of multiple rounds of torpedoes, missiles, and bombs exploding into buildings or the ground and streets of neighborhoods, communities, cities, and towns of America.

The smell of the thick heavy smoked filled the air vents everywhere that was near and it made a choice of harming the people by invading all homes and businesses with an odorless gas that no one could see or taste, but all they could smell was the smoke rising from the flames of fires from the many explosions throughout America.

Everything was spreading like wildfire and there was no stopping it before it could spread more.

It was going to be a long time before sun rise but not many might be alive in the morning when many people wake up.

And then it was morning.

The smell of gun fire and smoke woke up the survivors who failed to hear what happened during the middle of the night and it was just a disaster zone with nothing that can be done.

The rotting corpses of the dead bodies from the victims of the night spread throughout America and the air and it was just a rotten smell that smelled like a mix of rotten eggs and onions in the sense that sulfur was taking over the entire landscape of humanity.

The scenes outside were just devastating and it all resembled a battlefield from the Battle of Antietam fought back in 1862 but this time millions of innocent people died of the result from a coordinated response from the Axis Powers in a time of glory and pride.

It was just a war zone outside and no one knew what they would find if they ever ventured out to see what happened during the wee hours of the night and for all they know it could be something very normal such as a fight or an act of violence that just takes place always in the heated places of politics or disagreement.

There was nothing but silence as the soldiers of the Axis Powers have finally set foot on dry land as the sun was rising.

German soldiers secured the remains of the White House and the U.S. Capitol as a way to determine if anyone was alive and survived the attacks by the missiles, torpedoes, the bombs, or even the most dreaded atomic bomb that sent soundwaves everywhere.

It was an immediate impact to all within the center of the explosion and anyone outside of the center felt an impact that was so severe that it rattled the houses and buildings all across the DC area.

It reminded everyone the horrible aspects of war during a time that could wreak havoc on society because of political disagreements that had a determination of the outcome.

Society today remains hopeful but only the justices of the Supreme Court remain alive in an underground bunker beneath the building after they realized something would happen soon but they have no idea of what went down in the middle of the night.

No one ever saw this coming but it was now more than a reality now that the United States of America surrendered in her overnight hours with Henry Wallace giving away the white flag and then being shot dead for his treason, and then with the attack against Congress all perished inside leaving nothing inside but dead bodies and ash from rotting wood and concrete with melted windows and glass.

The people of America do not realize the catastrophe at hand.

It would be a surprise to all when they go outside to see the damage that has been done to the country and it will not be the end of it anytime soon.

The people are just unaware about everything but surely they believe their representatives and Senators in Congress are still alive along with the President and the Vice President of the United States of America but it will surely be a surprise when they find out that they are no longer alive in the great country of America.

It will be a surprise to all that have faced the test of time but they believe the allies will surely save them and liberate all from the common enemy of evil.

This could just get strange but people will soon find out about all that occurred in a devastating event.

As the day keeps on moving, January 1, 1943 is just a complete and utter disaster, and there are no signs of when the other allies will respond to the defeat of America.

Disaster will be the least of their worries as the people will have to face the harsh realities of National Socialism, fascism, Marxism, and communism, all in the name of the Axis Powers.

It would be the thing that shook the earth until there was no one standing anymore in the sense that everything was about to change for the betterment of society as a gratitude of how everything is supposed to be in the eyes of a mad man.

Something isn't just right and it will remain that way until a revelation reveals itself to society in the name of hope and change by the craziness of society.

That is the time it takes to understand that there is a new sense of taking on the enemy but the times have changed so there is just a case of abandonment from the allied forces.

The sense that people will now be free is just crazy because there is no truth to that.

Everything is just a game to play upon the innocent and that will always be the way it shall be in the name of society.

That time is now.

The disaster is now.

And it's just only beginning.

Everything will change but no one will know if it will change their habits of living in society.

No one actually knows but it is certain that there will be the changing of the guard.

It is not certain for anything and that is just the fact of life.

Anything could happen, bringing despair or happiness all at the same time, in order to startle and confuse the people about what is actually happening so that propaganda can be spread in order to make sure no one escapes the harsh truth of reality.

But it is a case of whether if it will ever happen or not because people are nervous in a time of war that makes no sense at all.

That is just the price that people must pay in order to sustain life because no one can know everything.

It is purely a figment of imagination that a person can survive a war of this shape and magnitude because in the end there is no hope but collateral damage in an age of uncertainty that has set its eyes to undermine civilization.

VIII

In the immediate aftermath of the January 1, 1943 the allied forces had a choice to make, to either fight and never surrender or to just surrender and wave the white flag of defeat by saying there is just no way to win the war that took everyone by storm by thinking that they had a chance to once again defeat the German state.

Surrounded on all sides there is no certainty about a decisive victory and it seems France and Britain have all but given up in a time of need, but they must have a chance to live on through the end of this war, because there might still be a chance to save the world.

That is just the act of courage that must persevere or else no one will ever have a chance in the existence of civilization again.

Time is short and this is no exception in a case of imagination.

On the morning of February 14, 1943 Britain and France join forces once again in order to try and defeat the Axis Powers knowing that they have one less ally to count on now.

It will take strength to get through this and only the weakest shall die in the name of foolishness and hooliganism due to a lack of candor and courage during the signs of the times.

The timing just couldn't be more than a coincidence but something was surely up with what could happen soon.

The timing is just impeccable because no one knows if a united Britain and France can actually defeat the combined forces of Italy, the Soviet Union, Japan, and Germany, unless they have some sort of secret weapon that no one else knows about.

That will be the day when all hell breaks loose in a matter of moments or in different stages to the extent that it will be hell of a situation to encounter on the streets and then something will decide the fate of the future of civilization.

Everything shall be at a loss for anyone that chooses that path of unorganized darkness to the extent that they shall face the consequences that will ultimately kill them in a matter of a few seconds.

Only hope will be waiting for the people that want to take a stand against this new regime.

The time to fight is upon society in order to fight back and it will be the ends of the earth until something brings forth peace and happiness to all of society.

Everything will be able to be peaceful and there shall be harmony for all to thrive in an environment that seems fruitful to the end of times in a sense that seems all too familiar.

It will only be a matter of time until the rise of anarchy and chaos begins and that will only bring destruction everywhere to all that are in the grasps of society. Nothing can escape anything and it will just be too late.

Britain has fallen as well as France, and it is only March of 1943, but there is nothing that can be done.

Long live chaos!

Long live destruction!

Long live National Socialism!

Long live Fascism!

Civilization faces the imminent wrath of a new totalitarian leadership at the control of the helm.

LONG LIVE HITLER!

LONG LIVE MUSSOLINI!

LONG LIVE STALIN!

SIEG HEIL!

SIEG HEIL!

SIEG HEIL!

EIGHT

I

April 19, 1943, recklessness and willful blindness plague the cities and towns of America with people taking to the streets and demanding answers from their elected representatives and government officials in order to see what is going on.

But something happens.

Shots are fired and no one knows who it was and where it came from and soon people start to panic and flee in a sea of confusion with nowhere to go.

They risk dying or saying here and getting to the bottom of the problem but that would just be catastrophic due to the very nature of an unknown situation.

People are going every which way and everything is just so chaotic. Confusion erupts so clear that no one knows what they are doing.

Screaming and shouting, that is just the very beginning of a situation spiraling out of control.

Suddenly, deafening noise can be heard by people everywhere, and it is only the beginning, as now more people are starting to scream and panic as everything continues in an unfamiliar way.

Tires screeching on the roads and streets as the people watch to see what's going on and there is nothing but contempt for the rule of law in a way that not one soul cares.

Police barreling down the streets to try and stop everything but it just looks like a trap.

The suddenness of people starting to rush towards each other as mayhem ensues the crowd to start something more than a fit of rage.

A show of hostility begins amongst the innocent and weak in a way that seems strange as people start a rush to judgment in a time of peril and uncertainty.

There is just something wrong here, something that seems to go against all of morality, but the mayhem just continues to strike everyone with a brief picture of what it might be like under a new leader and a new government.

But life is just as abysmal as it gets. Something is just about the silence of choice.

People watching from the sidelines as they try to grasp what they're seeing in a time of need and a time of crisis all to the point of wanting to know what is going on because there is just confusion everywhere because it is just crazy.

Then, things change for the worse, as people start pushing and shoving each other, in an attempt to show dissatisfaction and strength to the masses that are watching everything.

Crowds of people gather everywhere near other groups and all but leads to death.

All of a sudden, people start to fight against each other, trampling every person they encounter because of an unknown interest.

It is just to seek attention but there could be something more to it that just doesn't make sense.

Something is about to change and that could be a disaster waiting to happen.

The streets and roads have erupted in full anarchy, as the observers just watch in horror people pummeling and punching each other in a fight against their lives.

Protesters attacking each other about their civil rights and rioters breaking everything in a manner that is all too obvious, as there is no way of getting out of the way, with violence gradually taking a toll on the masses of the people.

Objects being thrown by the masses in the hopes it will lead to something great or at least the attention of the police.

Everything is just out of control.

Papers, pencils, pens, any ordinary things, are becoming projectiles against the innocent bystanders who are just watching all of this happening right in front of their eyes.

It's an all-out war against the innocent versus the aggressors of civil rights to gain and seek attention for their causes and it is just causing great harm as violence has now penetrated all walls of hope and change that once was possible.

A change in direction and a change in the atmosphere are happening just as it will only grow worse by the minute in a time of hostility and violence with full-on anarchy everything to the point of complete and utter destruction.

The world is watching and that is not a good thing, as people are just thinking to themselves about what is going on in the great and free society of America.

It would be news to them that America has fallen and there is no way out of this situation now.

What remains now is just a small train of thought of perseverance in a sign that demonstrates that the establishment will never give up.

It is about growth and that is just the tip of the iceberg.

Police running down the streets and roads as the violent rioters start to pick up speed with their projectiles of common everyday items but it is just getting to the tipping point of complete chaos, anarchy, and destruction with the added help of nonsensical violence that doesn't even make sense to the innocent bystanders.

Rioters lighting up garbage and recycle bins and then launching them throughout the streets in order to throw solidarity with their fight against the wrongs set forth by the establishment.

People are starting to get hurt and are trying to escape with possibly being hurt before they can even think about running away.

It's a race against time to see who will win and who will die but confusion has taken over everything in a matter of just under an hour.

The wrath has just begun and it won't be over until there is a consensus of people being arrested for trampling upon the civil rights and liberties of other innocent bystanders in a time that is not going to get any better in the near future.

That is just something to be put to the test as there is a precedent to be set amongst the masses.

It is all a hope to further the change of society and it is just that.

Crowds of people start to grow larger and larger as it is just now the rioters against the people that want to stop the violence, chaos, and anarchy before it leads to death and severe injuries.

There is no way of knowing about who will win but it soon might be revealed if there is no break in trying to calm both sides down.

That is just the understanding of the situation in the near crosshairs of both sides and it will cause more chaos and confusion for all in society to experience.

Nothing can just stop it as the chaos and anarchy is just growing by the minute. Soon it will all blow into an unstoppable mess that could have been prevented if people never got out of control to begin with but that is something that seems unviable now in the history of these mass riots.

Then it happens, rioters start smashing windows in, and they begin to destroy everything in sight they see as a problem for them that resembles hate and discrimination to the sense that it promotes a divide in society because of differing views.

Molotov cocktails start hurtling towards place of businesses and homes in an effort to demonstrate anger and dissatisfaction with the current climate at hand.

People start panicking and running away as they see the damage and turmoil at large from an uncontrolled crowd of reckless kids misbehaving in the streets all thanks to the adults outside who demonstrate that it's fine to commit crimes such as violence and arson in the streets and roads of the communities of cities and towns across all of America, but it is more than usual now as people don't want to listen.

The crowds of violent thugs just grow more and more violent as the day moves on and it is only the beginning of something raw with emotions.

One by one, rioters start to hurl projectiles at windows and storefronts once more.

It is just turning into a war zone that no one can escape its wrath.

It might all be coming to an end soon but no one will know until it's finally over and someone claims victory to which it shall be challenged.

And that will be the day but it will be at the start of something less optimistic.

More chaos ensues as the riots start growing more violent to the extent that it is now impossible to avoid being injured by shrapnel or from actual physical harm from an unhinged thug that wants to destroy everything in sight for their childish and selfish reasons.

It all boils down to one reason, in order to be united against the establishment by fighting them in a coup to overthrow the current municipal and state governments, just to show that they promote civil rights by claiming fascism and National Socialism are the ways of the future in a progressive society.

What a bunch of rubbish that is as they know they are fighting a fake war and yet they say they support civil rights in the guise of promoting fascism and National Socialism so that they can promote the propaganda of the Axis Powers in a time when no one hardly even knows of the defeat of the United States of America as well as the allied forces.

The situation won't get better any sooner and people will soon have to face the wrath of the harsh realities of their futures under a new form of government that undermines the values, beliefs, and views of society that America was founded upon.

That will be the time when no one will be able to escape persecution.

Shots fired, as the police try to get a handle of all the commotion, violence, and chaos going on in the streets and roads of their cities, and there are just constant attacks against everyone and everything.

Rioters, throwing any and all objects at the police while innocent bystanders are watching the carnage from the sidelines, and it all seems too familiar to people that fought in a war against a tyrant from the past.

Police dressed in riot gear as they try to catch any rioter staging attacks against anyone and anything in order to get a hold of the situation, and it just keeps picking up speed as the special forces of the police start to pounce on the people on the streets and roads trying to stop the violence, chaos, violence, and anarchy from happening in the very place they live and work in.

Grab after grab, pummel after pummel, the special forces of the police launch an all-out assault against all they could grab in a way to give them a taste of their own medicine.

Fights break out across everywhere and it is nothing but pure chaos as confusion weighs in against everything else in a time and place that seems to be divided amongst each other in the same way as there is hatred for freedom, liberty, and the pursuit of happiness in a free society such as America.

The whole thing is just ending in complete disaster as rioters and protesters both alike are facing the wrath of the special police forces in a time that makes sense because the Axis Powers recently defeated the allied forces in what was thought to be a war of tremendous victory for the allies because they had the better fire power of all.

Nothing could be further from the truth because the allies lost making it a victory for no one.

Surely there will be something better to do but it is just useless in the sense that many people have abandoned their homes and houses after they started to realize the catastrophic events of the war waged upon them by the Axis Powers.

There is no end in sight as the peculiarity of the mass attacks by the rioters and then the assault led by the special police forces begin to dwindle upon the populace.

Nothing like this has ever been seen like this in modern human history, as it is filled with chaos, anarchy, violence, as well as destruction in an effort to confront the establishment and to promote radical propaganda in order to spread a message of hate, racism, and discrimination in the hopes that it will lead to a better world that promotes fascism and National Socialism.

That is the way of the future and that is what they believe in so that can grab power from a very compromised and weak government in power. Everything is just a ruse and it will only continue until the people start to realize they have been duped from the beginning.

It is a losing argument and it shall remain that way forever in the hopes in that one day people could rise up and defeat the resistance.

Bright orange flames start to rise up from the streets and roads just as the special police forces pick up speed in their assault against the rioters and all the other protesters and innocent bystanders and it is only to get harder to take control of the situation.

The violence is only getting deadlier as no one is about to escape the consequences of war, and it is an all-out assault against the entire crowd, making it representative of each group present, because all are deemed responsible according to the special police forces.

It is all but a reality, as the flames spread and continue to grow, to the point that no one could claim innocence.

People dressed in protective gear try to observe and report back but they can't stand what is happening all around them. It just seems like a tragedy to all that are observing nearby or from above in the way that keeps on repeating forever and eternity.

Hooded with self-styled masks and holding shields, innocent civilians try to take advantage of the situation so they can possibly end the violence, chaos, anarchy, and destruction that are happening against everyone and everything.

Black smoke rises up and everything soon turns sour, as riots throw lighted matches everywhere, landing on innocent people and on vehicles to the dismay of everyone else, hoping to cause more chaos and destruction in the hopes it will get the attention of the special police forces.

It is just a game to all of them and it continues to be that way until someone stops them from the way of progress because the progress demanded by the rioters will just wreak havoc on everyone else. It is only the beginning of these events and they will soon sprout up everywhere in order to complete the transformation of a new America.

San Francisco, April 19, 1943, there is an uprising by members of the local resistance, in order to take down the innocent bystanders, and it is just past 0700 hours, as most people are just waking up to go to work, but they do not know what they are going to face as they soon exit the confines of their homes to head to work.

People overhear reports of shots being fired against a slew of traffic.

No one knew what was going on and it sounded like someone just invaded the coast for a reason or another in order to take control of the Bay so no one can escape the wrath of a deadly force set to begin in the next few hours of civilization.

The day was only going to get longer and longer as the people of the city will have to face something they have never faced before since a time of need for food and water.

It is only about to get crazier in this time-consuming situation of wanting to know what will happen to the rest of society when there might be no chance of survival and that is just the honest truth according to some people that seem to take the chance that it is not possible to stay behind when there is a constant threat of being attacked in the most sadistic way possible and then going against all odds by deeming everything inconvenient.

That is just awful to think about but when someone needs to fight against a lunatic fringe then there is no other thing to do but to face war at the knees.

Across the vicinity of the neighborhoods, people are seen rallying in hopes of getting more fighters to join the resistance in hopes of fighting for fascism, National Socialism, and communism, as a way to prepare for the new America once the takeover is complete, but the mystery shots seem to be something not yet known as nobody knew where they came from.

It could be something about nothing or maybe a bit sinister thinking on part of starting a false pretense to ignite a new war.

That wouldn't be the first time it happened but it wouldn't be the last, as the people are starting to throw a fit of rage now in an attempt to demand answers about what's going on with society in general.

An hour later, all hell breaks loose, as the threat of imminent warfare is now upon the people of San Francisco, by Imperial Japanese soldiers now just breaking the last lines of defense being protected by patriotic Americans standing on the front lines of the shore after they thought they had enough of just waiting off shore.

A fire fight ensued with soldiers firing heavy rounds of ammunition in every direction while also throwing grenades and launching lighted torches everywhere that resembles nothing out of the ordinary all in a manner that is about something more sinister.

But it only grows from there, as all patriotic Americans are either severely wounded or have died in battle trying to protect San Francisco Bay by making an attempt to prevent further hostilities of the San Francisco mainland from being controlled by Imperial Japanese soldiers.

It is just madness as now the Imperial Japanese soldiers officially breached the once protected shores of San Francisco and the Bay Area but it was a low and slow attack to get there just to escape the suspicion that there would be something happening soon.

Breaming with contempt, Imperial Japanese soldiers ram through the land firing at everything in sight, and they set their eyes on what looks to be the populace.

An all-out assault by land, sea, and air, as the soldiers begin their kamikaze attacks against innocent civilian targets by crashing planes at the highest rate possible because they want to send a message that no one can defeat crazy and suicidal Japanese Air Force pilots, to the extent that they are extremely on the fringe of war because of the timing of how to take control of society.

Complete and utter madness, as the first regiment of Japanese soldiers finally arrive in the metropolitan of San Francisco, and there is just no knowing what they will do, but instantly they start firing heavy gunfire in an attempt to silence everybody.

The land invasion has started and innocent people are being slaughtered like pigs in a blanket, led largely by the fringe soldiers of the Imperial Japanese Army, all in an attempt to take control of the city and government by making it hell for everyone to live and work, so no one will escape Japanese customs.

It was surely a surprise how the Japanese guided their warships in the night and day being undetected but it could just be they wanted to take their time by not being noticed in order to plan a well-crafted policy before they glided into the San Francisco Bay.

And indeed that is what they did by just making sure nothing bad will happen to their crew and soldiers, so they had a plan in the beginning, by carefully entering the Bay and then taking a chance to spot any Americans that dared to stop them.

There was almost a close call but it was stopped immediately in a matter of seconds when several Japanese soldiers launched a sneak attack from nowhere against anyone trying to do their job and protect America.

This wasn’t new but it has been done before but it is just a lesson to teach people about nothing.

And then it happened, the people of San Francisco found themselves in a perilous position of not knowing what their options were because they were so preoccupied about everything else and not protecting their lives in a matter of moments.

Just like that they were taken aback by the sheer strength of power by the Japanese, as it was a surprise to them, because they still did not know that the president, vice president, and all members of Congress died months before, so that will be news to them.

Soon enough, people were just running crazy in the streets and roads, trying to run as fast as they could before they could be hit by fire, and it was just like a wildfire with innocent civilians scrambling everywhere as Imperial Japanese soldiers fire heavy rounds of ammunition in all directions in a full all-out effort to commit as many casualties as possible.

It was always planned from the beginning but now there is nothing but a crazy spectacle of people running around in circles with no clue how to handle the situation during a very trying time.

Quickly, something ensues, as now people have just nowhere to go in the midst of a panic.

Protests break out forcing people to fend themselves all while trying to escape rampant gun fire from crazed and suicidal Imperial Japanese soldiers.

It was soon realized that nothing could stop this situation because it was just so impossible to get a handle on the situation, bringing the amount of casualties to an all-time high, if that is even possible to comprehend in such a society as America.

The carnage was pure and simple but it was just too early to tell, as people panicked everywhere not knowing how they could even escape the wrath of an unstoppable force of weapons and fire power from every direction.

Everything just amounted to an immediate loss of life as everyone stood in fear about their life ending all in an attempt to see if they are worthy.

Chaos soon breaks out as there is nothing but confusion everywhere to the point that it is impossible to tell what will happen next but that might soon end in case people try to acknowledge they will suddenly fight back in a time of need.

Everything could already be too late because it is, as there is just no stopping this spectacle of amazement that is taking on the city by storm and sheer force, to the extent that there shall be damage to nothing but the people, the buildings, and infrastructure.

It is all coming to an end but it won't end soon enough.

Full chaos completely takes over San Francisco as it has only been a matter of moments since the inception of the land invasion, but it is now worse off than ever before because of the calamity of the action being part of the hidden strategy.

People panicking, showing outright contempt and sound confusion, with nowhere to go but to hide, find themselves in a path that only offers destruction that is just continuing to grow in size.

Crowds are growing in number as the path to safety is dwindling, and people are starting to push and shove without realizing what they are even doing.

Chanting fills the streets and roads of the city as well as the neighboring communities and the neighborhoods, but this just creates more confusion in the sense that no one knows where to go.

There is just no stopping it, as just minutes later a riot breaks out after mysterious figures dressed in all black covered with masks start throwing objects everywhere.

Screaming for their lives, people now have to face additional danger, as the streets are filled with full-on chaos and now anarchy.

It is just complete war outside with full-on riots, chaos, anarchy, and protests on the streets and roads all across San Francisco, California, but the innocent civilians and all others faced the wrath of Imperial Japanese soldiers and the people that want to destroy everything, all the while facing Molotov cocktails, shrapnel, and projectiles from every direction.

Broken windows, shattered glass, and dust all plague the streets and roads, and now there is a sudden change with buildings burning and vehicles being turned over, demonstrating sheer acts of violence, but it is just all for a good cause they say.

It is inevitable that society will crash into the brink of extinction unless something is done to prevent that, but it is too soon to tell if anything will ever happen.

Everything is just collapsing around the people in all directions and that is a warning to the public not to get out of touch with the rest of the world because it might bring more disaster in a time of need and worry to the point that there is nothing that can be done to fix the threats of the world.

But it is just a case of smoke and mirrors because there is just this uncertainty about nothing but the case to live by every day of the year so it is utterly useless as the world watches about what to do next in this case of need and nonsense.

Something just doesn't make sense and it is all about the rest of the case of more irrelevance.

Everything just picks up speed with people attacking each other not knowing why they are attacking each other all the while facing the wrath of chaos, anarchy, riots, protests, and destruction on the streets and roads of all of San Francisco.

People are just screaming everywhere and then there are the crazed anarchists trying to destroy everything that America stood for in a time of freedom, liberty, and tranquility, so it remains to be seen what can be done in order to stop the crazy transformation of everything.

It is not too late to stop this but there is no one taking a risk to stand up to this chaos, anarchy, riots, protests, and destruction to people and property, as there are suicidal people lighting themselves on fire and then burning up like a bright burning candle to signal that they will sacrifice their life to show that they will take a stand to show solidarity with the armed resistance that supports the Japanese in order to make sure America dies in a fire with no customs or traditions that can be left.

There is nothing but debris lying on the ground with no one picking it up because of a lack of motivated people to make sure everything is clean, and yet it is just the same old motivation that can be used being demonstrated by the action of war on the streets and roads in San Francisco.

If only they can use that motivation for good but that will be a time when everything goes back to normal.

But everything just seems too powerless, as the Japanese are just getting inpatient, so they believe they are getting nowhere, and that needs to change now.

All of a sudden, several Japanese fighter planes intentionally crash into buildings, trees, and anything that can see, including people, and a spark instantly lights up, forcing the whole city to experience something very bad. And there are just more of these attacks one after another, until finally there is something new.

A sound is heard from above and instantly it falls to the ground creating a large and wide crater, and at the moment of impact everything just changes with a huge fume of smoke rising up in the form of a mushroom cloud with the appearance of bright red and orange flames everywhere, but now there is just fire spreading everywhere, to the point that everything is on fire and no one could save the day.

There is no word of any survivors but it could be a very slim chance that people could survive such a powerful blast of nuclear radiation. Everything just blew up in their faces with instant death everywhere, to the point that wooden and concrete buildings collapsed on the moment of impact.

It is such a travesty but innocent people just died not really knowing what comes next.

That is such a sad move but the Japanese are watching with fanfare from their ships, as they leave the San Francisco Bay just before the dropping of the atomic bomb.

And it was just like that the city of San Francisco faced a nuclear holocaust, to the point that all of the Imperial Japanese soldiers on land died at the moment of impact, making it their last move to sacrifice their lives to promote Japan in order to make sure no one but Japan controls San Francisco.

But there is just more of something that might arrive next.

Washington DC, New York City, April 19, 1943, there is a threat of something happening and the Eastern coast could be on the brink of collapse just as it is about to get crazy.

The time is 1100 hours Eastern time and ships have just been spotted off the Eastern coast, but the only people protecting the shores are innocent patriotic Americans, as much of the public still do not know that the president, vice president, and all members of Congress have been killed in such a terrible way.

And then it happens, as planes above can be heard dropping what seems to be bombs everywhere.

Slowly but surely the bombs land everywhere while innocent civilians are waiting below not expecting anything dangerous to happen to them, so they wouldn't expect a thing such as this.

There is nothing but collateral damage to the extent that several millions of innocent civilians in New York City alone faced the wrath of constant bombing by either being injured or faced imminent death by way of an explosion or shrapnel embedding itself within the skin of people all the while people in the nation's capital are suffering yet another setback from the buzzing warplanes above.

It could just be more collateral damage in order to stop everything and nothing is able to even create the attention that it once had.

Then it went all quiet, seemingly like the entire Eastern coast has been abandoned, all in an attempt to frighten people in an unpredictable manner of scare tactics just so no one will know when anything is going to take place.

Sirens blast throughout the five boroughs of New York City as well as the nation's capital warning of imminent impact of possible war and the threat of total destruction and annihilation of every major working part of a functioning city.

It should be clear now that America is under attack by a new threat after failing to win the war but most Americans don't know that yet due to a lack of strength and courage from within.

Something is just wrong with them but it just continues to get worse, as there is nothing that can be done to secure a future for the next generations.

All hope is lost and that is just so awful in a time of craziness.

People, running in circles and screaming for their lives, start to cause chaos and disruption throughout New York and DC, and it is just confusion all around, as nobody knows what's going on, except for the people above and off the Eastern coast.

There is just panic everywhere accounting for the most confusion that is seen and heard from all directions throughout the city of New York while DC is all quiet trying to have the courage to find a place to meet.

The threat of something more promising is going away with the type of series of events happening once yet again.

It is all more hope that there is a case of certainty throughout the public about nothing.

Nothing should hold it back and it will just be crazy if it didn't.

No one knows if they are going to die but they will just face the harsh realities of death after failing to realize the complexities of humanity not being exactly what they wanted.

That is just the case of life but it is just a distraction for the calamity that is happening all around New York and DC.

People start to rush the streets and roads of New York City as they have no idea where they are going.

They want to escape death but there might be no way out.

Quickly scouring to the closest exit possible out of the city, the people of New York face obstacles that force them to think about what to do next.

Rockets come hurtling down on the streets and roads as people flee in panic but not before tripping over sidewalks.

Deep craters, starting to appear with the abundance of nothing more to be done, as people are running and screaming everywhere, but it is just the start of a greater war.

Suddenly, there is a shift, and people do not know what to do.

There is now complete chaos in New York after a matter of mere moments and it was just too soon.

There is just too much screaming and shouting as no one knows what to do in a time of war.

Gaining crowds of people going in all directions trampling on each other while trying to escape, with chaos everywhere causing confusion for the masses, there is just screaming and shouting repeatedly.

With men in black masks dressed in disguised all to the point of concealing their true and only identity, start throwing Molotov cocktails everywhere, with projectiles flying throughout the streets and roads throughout New York City, and now there is complete anarchy with everyone participating in some sort of melee to target each other.

Gunfire from the sidelines and people being killed in plain sight, there is just something that must be certain, but there is just a sign of no return.

Crowds panicking and people joining in protests all the while rioters are trampling on businesses and preying on innocent Americans all because of no one in control.

People are just pushing and shoving with nothing to show for and now rioters are just burning everything in oblivion for the sole purpose of destruction.

Fire reigning from above and innocent people being killed, there is nothing that makes sense, it makes it all so obvious that the end is near and only destruction awaits civilians below.

Trees burning, the sidewalks cracking, and now tires screeching to make some noise for unruly hooligans that should be arrested, but it remains to be seen, as now rocks being thrown at local businesses and homes as well as vehicles, with people rioting everywhere, all the while as people are fighting each other in the streets and roads of New York City.

Vehicles being flipped over, people being constantly trampled upon, and now the sight that Nazi soldiers are entering the jurisdiction of the city to start a scene, there is just more ruckus here than ever before, but maybe order can be restored in order to create a more stable community atmosphere.

Rampant fire occurring everywhere, just as the Nazi soldiers line in formation, to kill all the instigators that started it, while everyone is trying to escape.

With Nazi firing squads everywhere there is not even a place to seek shelter, and now it is like a serial killer has plagued the city in a time to get the good guys and innocent people.

Nazi officers are everywhere and it is just more unpleasant than before and now it is a civil war amongst the masses of society, so no one is able to tell who's fighting who.

Destruction everywhere, with the city in full-blown chaos and anarchy with the added notion of riots and protests breaking out every minute of the hour, that is just nothing, and people being trampled upon while cars and buildings are being destroyed and broken into.

There is nothing that can be solved in order to create another crisis but this is a crisis of epic and new proportions.

People being shot at and now run over, the Nazi officers are now pouncing on the innocent civilians everywhere, grabbing and pummeling each person they can find, in order to launch a complete and utter assault on the masses, and with no way to protect themselves it is just a slaughter with flying projectiles everywhere and starting fires, there is nothing that remains except for rising smoke from bright red and orange flames, and now there seems to be ash and dust everywhere.

The sky is just filled with a thick layer of dense smoke, blocking the view of any clouds whatsoever, and it is just a toxic smell as people start to breathe it in, not realizing they have ingested carbon monoxide and other lethal substances along with ash and dirt from the combined debris.

Everything is just polluted in a mess that makes no sense at all but it is just chaos.

It makes it all terrible as people are inhaling the toxic material into their lungs, which ultimately will give them cancel if they are not careful, but the people could just die from smoke inhalation if they do not watch out where they are going.

And just like that an Italian flotilla started to fire at Galveston, Texas, in an attempt to show force and strength to the inhabitants residing miles away from the coastline.

Cannons firing like hell repeatedly all in a way that makes claim to the constant craziness of war, but it wasn't the end, as people living off the coast were wondering what was going on.

They could hear all the fire power coming their way and it was just like that when the first few cannon balls landed on the beach in which beachgoers felt puzzled that there seem to be a mysterious object that they thought were extinct.

They were just large black cannon balls filled with gun powder and weighed as if they were a bowling ball, and heavy indeed, but people were perplexed about how it came to be here, until they heard mortar fire near after spotting a flotilla of unidentified ships, and soon they ran away as fast as they could, before there was a land invasion.

Three hours later, the Italians set foot on dry land, bringing with them vast amounts of resources to invade all of Galveston, so it resembled a sort of mutiny, because the Italians wanted to take over Galveston.

And soon, people started kicking and screaming everywhere, as Italian naval officers started to shoot their high caliber weapons in all directions, making sure to hit anyone they wish, all in an attempt to just have fun.

There was panic and then there was chaos, as hundreds of people moved in opposite directions all at the same time making it difficult to get where they need to be.

There was just the epitome of drowning in the sense that innocent civilians were trampling upon each other because they were pushing and shoving and they were in such a rush that they didn't realize what they were doing.

This could all be some sort of punishment or it could be a sign that the end of the world is coming and no one could escape but no hard evidence existed either way, as it was a sort of conspiracy theory by the people because they didn't understand what was going on in the coastal city of their Galveston.

The people didn't want to take a chance and they decided to take a stand, well at least some of them, as the rest just fled and scattered to the other safer parts of the coastal city.

Trying to protect their city as much as they could, the brave warriors got anything they believed that could throw off the Italian naval officers, and it was just a crazy stunt, since some got sea shells, others retrieved guns, and many others just got every day ordinary objects, but it was unsure what their plan would be because they didn't have one, so they decided to make it up as they went along, which was just a bad strategy to begin with.

It could all boil down to one thing, safety, but they didn't know what they were getting into, as the Italians could easily outnumber the civilians.

So, with no plan in hand, they just went on their way to take back their city.

Ten minutes later, it was just chaos, as it looked like a tornado rolled into town and destroyed mostly everything in sight.

Trees were bent with branches broken and some were ablaze, with the sight of broken windows everywhere and nearly all fire hydrants gushing water, streets and sidewalks flooding and vehicles nearly floating away, and fire burning everywhere.

Thick white smoke rises up from bright dark red and orange flames and soon turns to gray and finally to black, all the while everything else is burning rapidly and there is no sign of stopping it as water is gushing out everywhere.

The complete coastal city of Galveston is just in shambles with dead people lying on the streets, glass and debris shattered everywhere, and with the constant burning of everything, all the while trees, windows, and buildings was all severely damaged.

It just devastated everything and everywhere, so there was really no chance of getting out alive, as the naval officers just advanced further into town.

This wouldn't be the last of it but it was only the beginning.

The time was now 1400 hours Eastern Time, and flotillas of ships were off the coasts of Hawaii, California, Alaska, Florida, Texas, New York, the Carolinas, Virginia, Washington DC, Louisiana, Georgia, Massachusetts, and all across the eastern, western, and gulf coasts of the United States of America.

With the Italians stationed off the coasts of Pensacola, Galveston, Grand Isle, Destin, Biloxi, South Padre Island, while Nazis were all along the Eastern coast, the Soviets stationed off the coasts of Anchorage, Quinhagak, Kipnuk, Scammon Bay, and all along the Gulf of Alaska, and the Japanese stationed at San Francisco, Santa Barbara, Long Beach, San Diego, Fort Bragg, all along the coasts of California, Washington, and Oregon, as well as surrounding all eight Hawaiian island, there was no way to stop the Axis Powers, as they were just everywhere.

Something would soon happen, but just like that, there was the sound of gun fire, missiles, and cannon balls coming straight at the United States of America in what seems to be a coordinated attack in order to further take control of a governmentless country.

The Axis Powers are finally ready to take down the once great empire of the United States of America in a great spectacle of an event that will leave people watching with amazement from around the world and a time of peace that will finally arrive to the support of the united people against a sign of hope and hate.

Soon, there won't be anything left, or if there is then there would only be ruin, while Middle America might turn into something new and remain unaffected by what has happened everywhere else.

That could be tragedy to all, as everyone else remains in the past while Middle America is trying to survive from constant threats by the resistance.

It is all important to stay focused on the real threat of disaster, the rise of totalitarianism, the rise of authoritarianism, the rise of military dictators, the rise of despots, the rise of anti-Semitic attacks by the fringe and the new government, the rise of the new America, and the rise of something that will target the fabric of what America stood for, all in an attempt to undermine history and to change it by forgetting what freedom and liberty stands for.

Everybody is on alert after sirens blasting an imminent threat of danger on sound systems all throughout the United States, making it so that the chance of survival has gone up significantly.

It is a warning to the people of America that they need to bunker down and hide somewhere safe if they want to live another day in the hopes they can see nature once again after the threat of danger has died down.

It will only be a matter of moments now until the threat of danger subsides and the people can venture out to see what they want to see again once more.

Long and wide bright flying objects started to appear overhead as the people started to look up only to realize they were under attack once more and there was probably no escape that could save them now considering how fast they were going.

At such speed they were just noisy, going twice as fast as the speed of sound, so it would be reasonable why people looked up when they heard something that resembled a sonic boom.

Everything was so quick and fast that there was no chance to escape the wrath of doom and gloom within a reasonable amount of time before the brink of collapse.

Something was just not going as what the people hoped for in the midst of a war.

There will be disaster after disaster and that is just the point of it to begin with.

With the impending doom of everything it just grows to show that no one can escape everything and so there was just the threat of what to do next in a time of nothingness.

All hope was loss as the threat of imminent explosions were now apparent, creating a new threat that will cause nuclear radiation for years to come.

That is the day when there will be vengeance for the things that were done to the innocent and then the counter-resistance will rise up from the ashes and dust of the past and start fighting once again to the point of new peace with the strength and courage that America once stood for during a beacon of new hope.

That is the day of happiness and that day is now.

II

Explosion after explosion with fire breaming from above shattering everything in sight and launching more by the minute, it is just something that is so spectacular.

A fire show that is, of shrapnel exploding everywhere, as a sign that it is just the beginning, from the midair to the ground, making sure there is nothing that can be done to stop this disaster from getting in the way of hope.

And then there was the fight of the century, with the last hope that nothing goes to waste, as missile after missile launching from warships off the several coasts, fire yet again, at the innocent civilians nearby, all as a way to send a message.

It was just the case to frighten the heck out of people so they will be scared.

Nothing would be better than killing a bunch of babies like these innocent civilians that are trying to escape because that is how they are acting like, babies, since they are screaming and crying and don't know how to act when they are being attacked.

They should be praying to God that nothing bad happens to them but they are just screaming and shouting like a bunch of children and babies, making it all bad for everyone in the end of something marvelous, thus resulting in the craziness and hysteria of the new revolution.

Fire lights up the skies from above, while missiles collide with bombs and other missiles, all at the same time when there are millions of people who are down below that do not know what is happening.

It is just pure chaos and panic down below, as there is nothing better to do, and there is no sign of it ending anytime soon.

People flee in horror as bombs land on buildings and missiles that crash land on the streets and roads from above, creating craters and causing mass destruction everywhere, for the purpose of intimidation and nothing more than that.

There is nothing but bright red flames of darkness anywhere people go, with a lack of certainty and a need of hope, it is all just a waste of time.

A hellhole of desire and adrenaline, in all the hopes it could lead to the creation of nothingness, but there is nothing but chaos in a time of need and quietness, as to all the people that demand it stop so that there will just be the same thing all over again.

Everything is on fire.

With broken windows, flipped vehicles, damaged homes, nonstop fires, and cracked sidewalks, nothing can be stopped now, as people are just throwing projectiles everywhere.

Suddenly, all hell broke loose, as a sole warplane dropped a fat and short bomb below, bringing a deep crater into existence stretching to the other part of the world during impact, as well as creating a large booming sound so deafening that it caused people to cover their ears, and creating the large mushroom cloud of doom when it was all over, forcing fire and fury to extend outwards everywhere in all directions.

The Soviets have struck Alaska with an atomic bomb so dangerous and powerful that it nearly killed all plants, wildlife, and people in a 50-mile radius, creating destruction everywhere and causing chaos for the people that heard the blast from a few miles away from the blast radius, but being that big and powerful it created mayhem and anarchy as survivors outside the 50-mile radius could feel the earth shaking beneath them.

It was the experience that no one would ever have to face but then it happened all again, as there was destruction everywhere, with buildings collapsed everywhere, which turned to dust and ash, as burning trees stood on all major intersections, and sidewalks and streets beginning to break apart, this was just a catastrophe that couldn't be forgotten.

The innocent people that all lost their lives shall be remembered but it might happen again, because relatives and family members that lived to tell the tale might rise up and demand change, causing the counter-resistance to stop the resistance from creating a new world order in a time of chaos and destruction everywhere, to the point that everything is necessary to live by, but it is just nothing other than life.

Thirty minutes past the hour and an unidentified warplane appeared over the bright blue skies of Houston, Texas, making it possible that it is only still the beginning.

A few seconds later, a noise is heard from above and a fat and short object can be seen falling to the ground below, all to the nervousness of the people of Texas, and it seems history is about to repeat itself yet again by the destruction of everything nearby, possibly causing chaos and anarchy on the streets and roads below, making it possible that there will be an uprising that is inevitable from the beginning.

All of a sudden, a large explosion is heard, forcing people to realize that they might die imminently, and on impact the creation of a large crater appeared directly in the ground, with the appearance of a huge mushroom cloud with thick gray and white smoke, all with the fire and fury of several thousand jet engines while lighting everything nearby on fire like a severe thunderstorm.

Literally, everything was on fire, and the heat from the flames could be felt from miles away, making it possible for anyone in Houston to feel some sort of radiation from nuclear elements.

It was another atomic bomb and it was twice the size as the one in Alaska, and this time the blast radius extended to 100 miles, while anyone outside of it could still feel the ground shake and tremble, forcing anyone within the 100 mile radius to die instantly or face excruciating injuries and severe burns.

Nothing could save them now, as it would just be a desperate attempt to further drown in a shambling republic, but people thought there was a way out of this danger, all to the shock that warnings were not always going to be made on the public alert system, so that created some sort of déjà vu and a kind of queasiness in the stomachs of most people paying attention to the news and who did not face a threat from nuclear fallout.

That is only the very beginning of what civilization will be like if there is anything left for people to do.

Just minutes from nuclear fallout in Texas, sirens started to alarm in Pensacola, Florida, indicating the threat of imminent danger, and people were warned to get inside and seek shelter before they die.

And then more sirens sounded in Mobile, Orange Beach, and Biloxi, as there were reports of some warplanes flying above that would soon drop unidentified objects across the Gulf Coast.

It would seem that the world might be coming to an end and the time to rise up is arriving in order to stop the imminent threat of something that could have drastic changes to life as they know it.

Something is just in the midst of that and that is not how it's supposed to be but there is just the case of nothing more apparent than civilian controls in charge of all of the country's operations because Congress and the president are nowhere to be found.

All in the face of nuclear radiation there is nothing that can be done to stop anything.

Minutes later, sirens are sounding the alarms all across the Gulf Coast of the United States of America, as unidentified planes can be seen from above, all moving mysteriously in a pattern that is too close to tell if they are the good guys or the bad guys.

And then, it happens, as the planes start dropping bombs below, but in a matter of seconds, large explosions can be heard, creating large craters on impact and the presence of large mushroom clouds with thick white and gray smoke surrounded by bright red and orange golden flames.

Everything within a 25-mile radius of any of the bombs were immediately killed or faced severe burns on impact, but the sheer amount of power caused by the impacts also caused buildings to fall to pieces, the ground to shake and tremble, causing cracks, and everything within the near vicinity to face destruction, as always in these turbulent explosions.

With the destruction of property, people, and infrastructure, there was no way of knowing how anyone could escape, but then it could be for the greater good, until it happens again.

Just a mere minute after the explosions all across the Northern Gulf coast of America, sirens started to sound in California, Washington, Oregon, and then all across the Eastern coast of the country, making it seem possible that this was now a coordinated attack.

From Jacksonville to Maine, it was certain that the Germans have made their plans clear to attack any place along the Eastern shores of the United States of America, as it was also clear that any place on the Western shores of America would be attacked by Imperial Japan.

The threat was clear but people just didn't know.

As the sirens started to sound planes started to appear above the Eastern and Western shores of America, and soon bombs dropped on several millions of innocent civilians below, causing people to face the wrath of death or severe injuries, as the impact of the bombs created large craters all throughout the coasts, along with large mushroom clouds appearing with the presence of white and gray smoke surrounded by rings of fire, causing severe damage and destruction to buildings and homes, and making the earth shake and tremble forcing cracks to appear, all the while not one person knew what was going to happen.

Millions of people have now died or were severely burned from the presence of nuclear radiation of several atomic bombs and this could only be the beginning or it could be the end of the bombs and the start of an invasion that has yet to officially begin.

It is only the creation of what will be the next to arrive as everything is a waiting game.

That is just how it seems and it is for that reason why nothing is ever normal now.

III

Two years from the first dropping of the atomic bomb, the date is now January 1, 1945, and the full land invasion has been completed, with all of America under the control of Germany on the Eastern Coast, Japan on the Pacific coast and Hawaii, the Soviet Union on Alaska, Italy on the Gulf Coast, and a demilitarized conflict-free zone in the middle of everything.

Laws have changed and the people are getting to everything after they realize life won't get any better.

The Axis Powers have finally gained full control of America but the Treaty of Succession 1945 established the new boundaries of America and made it clear that a conflict-free zone had to be established in order to have peace, and it was agreed upon that all of Wyoming, the Dakotas, Nebraska, Colorado, Kansas, Missouri, Iowa, Minnesota, Wisconsin, Illinois, Indiana, Montana, Michigan, Ohio, Kentucky, New Mexico, and Tennessee will all serve as a buffer for peace and tranquility.

Tanks were rolling out on the frontier and the people now had to listen to the new leaders of America.

There was now the threat of the counter-resistance trying to rise up and defeat the resistance.

It will give way to more chaos and violence while the minds of most people will be at the opposite ends of the spectrum, to the point that most people won't bother to get involved in the fight against power, freedom, and liberty, as well as the pursuit of happiness.

Ultimately, it will be a fight to the death in order to defeat each other and the opposing sides will face constant attacks from everywhere, forcing the counter-resistance to go underground in an attempt to continue everything.

Thus, belonging to the resistance will be considered lawful, while being part of the counter-resistance is unlawful, all because the latter is for the United States of America going back to the way she was before she was invaded, while the former is a by-product of the Axis Powers to help make sure the former greatness never sees the light of day anymore because that would be a threat to new America.

But all of that doesn't matter anymore, as the four nations will use their secret police to strike against the actions of the counter-resistance while the resistance will be a specially trained force to stop the counter-resistance from succeeding.

The Japanese have the Kempeitai and the Tokubetsu Kōtō Keisatsu, the Germans the Gestapo and the Sicherheitsdienst, the Italians the OVRA, and the Soviets the NKGB and the NKVD, in order to crush the opponents that seek the truth, but to also make sure propaganda is never threatened by the people that seek freedom, liberty, and the pursuit of happiness, all in the name of promoting a one-party state by instituting the values, beliefs, and views with those that align with the nations that invaded America and then became the successors by overthrowing the government.

This isn't anything new but it will keep the populace in control from trying to start a successful rising while any association with a movement that identifies with the counter-resistance shall be considered treason and a one-way ride to imprisonment for going against the state.

It will be threatening to anyone that opposes fascism and National Socialism, for the sole purpose of anything against the state, including the act of criticizing state policies and laws as well as the hierarchy, is illegal, as those actions go against the state.

Laws will be strictly enforced everywhere except for the conflict-free zone that separates the four powers because there is still a place in America that believes in freedom, liberty, and the pursuit of happiness, and that place is needed for tranquility and peace.

But the ultimate goal of the conflict-free zone is to maintain a zone where people can avoid constant conflicts and be free of the restrictions of everyday life faced by the people living in the four regions of occupied America and to make sure no one power attempts to take control of another part of America.

Thus, it will be used to maintain peace and security for all so conflicts shall be avoided, making it one of the most unpredictable places in the world, so it seems that Japan, Italy, the Soviet Union, and or Germany will never encroach upon each other, because that would violate the Treaty of Succession 1945.

And so America was divided into four sections and a fifth to make sure that there could be peace and stability amongst the four ruling powers in case something sinister happened but to also make sure there is no break out of war since the Axis Powers agreed to peace and harmony so that none of the people are threatened by neighboring forces.

It is supposed to be neighborly and friendship.

Yet people don't care about any of that.

They care about their lives and nothing else.

That is why the Treaty of Succession 1945 established the five regions of the Japanese Western Pacific States and Hawaii, the Reich States of America, the Gulf Fascist States, the Soviet territory of Alaska, as well as the conflict-free zone right in the middle of everything to promote and to maintain peace.

Germany took possession of Maine, New Hampshire, Massachusetts, New York, Pennsylvania, Maryland, Delaware, West Virginia, Virginia, South Carolina, North Carolina, Georgia, and the Eastern coast of the state of Florida.

Japan took possession of California, Oregon, Washington, Hawaii, Utah, Idaho, Nevada, and Arizona.

Italy took possession of Louisiana Oklahoma, Arkansas, Mississippi, Texas, and the Western coast and the panhandle of Florida.

The Soviet Union took possession of all of Alaska.

Every other state consisted of the conflict-free zone that created a buffer zone for peace designated under the Treaty of Succession 1945.

There was just one problem, the treatment of Americans.

Americans in the Japanese Western Pacific States and Hawaii were treated as third class citizens while everyone else there was treated with respect.

Americans in the Reich States of America were treated with respect but only the Nazi hierarchy was treated with the utmost respect, while any person associated with the counter-resistance was considered an enemy of the state and the Nazi Empire.

Americans in the Gulf Fascist States were treated as though they were second class citizens because promoting Italian heritage and unity was the only goal in mind and any American that said anything against celebrating the Italian heritage was thrown in jail as well as any American that decided to speak up against fascism in general and or joined the counter-resistance.

Americans in Alaska were treated as the enemies of the state if they didn't give up their land and property to the government, and so they would end up in jail and then their property and land would be forcibly taken from then which will then will be transferred to impoverished Soviets brought over from the Soviet Union to live off the stolen land and property that once was part of something glorious.

Nothing seemed like it was supposed to and if it seems crazy it wasn't because any American caught in the crosshairs of the counter-resistance shall automatically be considered a traitor and an enemy of the state and death shall be the punishment if caught and captured.

Time will only tell when something happens and it shall be near as the counter-resistance rises up from the ashes to stop the glorious spread of propaganda to promote fascism, National Socialism, and a one-party bent on influencing garbage.

RISE UP!

RISE UP!

RISE UP!

The resurrection of the counter-resistance is here.

LONG LIVE THE VICTORY WORLD FRONT!

NINE

I

October 1965, Katrina Maribelle rises up from the ashes of her home in the much affluent town of Winslow, South Dakota, a place that has all been too familiar for rural America, but is a place of hope change, and prosperity, as it all just seems the same but it is much different than that, being protected from the rest of the conflict-free zone, where everyone is still doing their normal thing of living their lives without any hesitation due to the just sheer luck of location.

However, the same can't be said for the rest of the conflict-free zone, as it is filled with carnage, lawlessness, constant violence, and trickery everywhere with everyone making their own laws.

There is just no respect anywhere except for Winslow.

Reports of the Victory World Front have emerged that they are about to plan something big that will get the attention of Nazi leaders in New York, the designated capital of the Reich States of America because it is the most populous city in all of America.

Katrina hears of the plan and goes to meet up with a local member of the Victory World Front to offer her assistance.

As has always been, Katrina is still and always remains a member of the Victory World Front.

But they continued to strike up a conversation concerning the strategy to stop the resistance from winning the war on humanity, all at a time of need and hope.

"Shall we get to business," asked the local area member?

"Sure, but we will need more than luck," said Katrina.

"Well, then we can use a plan that might turn back all of the events so the Axis Powers would have lost the war," said the local member.

"That will be fine; I like that idea; and we can surely make sure that the allies will win the war," said Katrina.

"This would obviously involve time travel, so at the most precise time someone will need to prevent Hitler, Mussolini, Japan, and Stalin from trying to win the war, but the secret police might attempt to stop us," said the local member.

"Yes, the secret police or the resistance, they might kill all of us or even take us hostage just to make us suffer, but I will be happy to volunteer myself to time travel, so when that plan is ready to be put into motion tell me where and what I need to do," said Katrina.

"Okay, that will be fine, but we might be here for a while just to cause chaos to the Axis Powers, and right now we are safer here than anyone else, so we will move cautiously," said the local member.

"Sure then, then what do you have in mind," asked Katrina?

"Well, since this needs to be carefully planned, we will need to make sure nothing gets out of hand, and since not many in the counter-resistance trusts us because of our money, we will have to do it alone with you and the other recruits and members from this town," said the local member.

"Why don't any of the members of the counter-resistance outside of Winslow trust us," asked Katrina?

"It could be that we are so wealthy and they are trying to get by, so they believe we could be colluding with the resistance by hiring them as our bodyguards and what not," said the local member.

"How do they even know of our community," asked Katrina?

"They see the upscale neighborhoods and schools as they pass through the interstate," said the local member.

"Do they know that the city center still has some old charm from like old western movies," asked Katrina?

"No, because most of them hardly ever come here to stay or visit, and so they have this image in their head that only rich people live here that do not agree with the buffer zone," said the local member.

"Well, are any of the other members or recruits here outsiders or are we actually all insiders," asked Katrina.

"All except for one are insiders, so we have you, me, and then five other people, one of which is from the small neighboring town of Knifeweed, South Dakota, which is another affluent place located five miles away from here," said the local member.

“Is there anything else that I should know,” asked Katrina?

“Not really, so if you don’t mind, then we can begin this meeting now, and since you decided to join, you will need to make sure you have a greater understanding of the plan, since not many people will want to join us from the counter-resistance,” said the local member.

“That sounds fine to me, so let’s begin then,” said Katrina.

“Perfect, so guys and gals of the united and unified counter-resistance of the Victory World Front, let’s convene this meeting so we can just go over it with everybody here,” said the local member.

Upon a table, the local member placed a map of an unknown era that seemed to have been tarnished with dust.

Something just didn’t feel right as though it was familiar.

But that could be anything or something other than hope in the midst of this crisis.

“Shall we begin,” asked the local member?

“I have no problem, if it’s fine with the rest of us present,” said Katrina.

“Okay, we are right here in Winslow where the red dot is, and we need to get to New York (the blue dot), San Francisco (the yellow dot), New Orleans (the orange dot), and the panhandle of Florida (the brown dot), but from there everything will be set into motion, so we are going to sabotage major plans from there.” said the local member.

“So, are there any questions,” asked the local member?

“No, okay then, so we can proceed with the plan,” said the local member.

The plan began with great fanfare, addressing the need that someone will travel back in time as well as going to all the major points of interests in the initial part of the plan.

“So, let’s get this over with, and going over who’s who and what we will do,” said the local member.

“Sounds fine to me,” said Katrina.

“Okay people, we have a new recruit to our team, but isn’t really that new, so she really isn’t a recruit and it isn’t really fair to say that, because she has always been a member of the Victory World Front, so please say a warm welcome to Katrina Maribelle, a member of this community of Winslow but from a different era, which is simply to say the 21st century,” said the local member.

“Hello all, my name is Katrina, and I will be working closely with all of you here, probably financing everything even though we have lots of money, but I will be the first to say that I will volunteer myself to time travel back to the time necessary,” said Katrina to everyone.

"Okay, since we got that out of the way, we can begin the plan, which might take approximately 2 years, and this will involve several distractions over that period," said the local member.

"What exactly will be the point of this," asked another member?

"To make sure that Hitler and his friends of the Axis Powers are defeated," said the local member.

"So we have outside contacts," asked Katrina?

"Yes, but we can address that later," said the local member.

"Okay, that is fine," said Katrina.

"Perfect, so this is how it will go down; we will do this all as a team so no one will get left behind; this is just necessary because if we stick as a group it will look less suspicious to the secret police; the last thing we would want is to get arrested, so we will blend in with the crowd in order to avoid any suspicions and detections by them, and then we will be in disguise just in case, for obvious reasons; we will travel as a group but at times we might split up for the purpose of not getting caught; on the way we might meet up with some contacts but don't expect them to work with them, as they tend to think of us as pawns because of our wealth; everybody needs to play their part in this mission and by doing so it will be less likely anyone will ever get caught, so we must be careful and vigilant, because anyone or anything could be a spy; this is why no one can let their guard down, and when we actually do commit to something we will have to go with it anyway, since an aborted mission will look suspicious to not only to the crowd but also to the secret police; everyone will be watching and that is why we must be careful, so we will have to wear the uniforms of the secret police and order organizations of the Axis Powers when it is necessary to do so; this is why the vehicle we will travel in will be all black, because the color black is usually associated with government agencies and power; this is a dangerous mission, so make sure nothing happens," said the local member.

With that it would only be a matter of time until everybody left the vicinity of their lair or whatever it shall be called.

Whether something happens or not it could be the end of the world as people know it.

That will be the day when all hell breaks loose with everything being at the forefront of chaos, anarchy, and violence, and when that happens there shall be a blight bringing a famine to all.

In that incidence there will be nothing left but a case to target the people of humanity and it remains to be seen what will even happen to the counter-resistance and the resistance.

The hope of humanity remains with the counter-resistance.

But the hope of maintaining the establishment remains with the resistance.

Only then could everyone be happy with nothing.

And then there should be something that remains with nobody except for everything.

Nothing remains with either group, so says anyone that cares, because no one actually cares about anything due to polarization of everything that is happening between civilization and society.

All remains a hoax until the people realize what is happening.

It must be quick and formal, quick and quiet, quick and cunning, but most of all, silent and trickery.

That is all that might remain but it will surely be at the forefront of nothing more than speculation.

The rise of the Victory World Front is only the beginning.

Only then will the Hällstadftß, a force only known to bring war and destruction everywhere with the added benefit of chaos, but with being the sole body of law and order to the Axis Powers in a time and need to protect the status quo of the establishment, so it is likely not a coincidence why they support corruption in order to engage in outlandish tactics that attempt to try and distort everything.

Unethical practices and doing the devil's work is nothing short of something evil because it is evil, as the Hällstadftß will try to get away with anything as they see fit.

They shall only bring chaos, anarchy, doom, and destruction, as they know nothing better, but the Hällstadftß just creates evidence as it sees fit, making sure to frame everything in its midst by trying to win at all costs in a time of need.

Everything the Hällstadftß does is part of an elaborate network of nothing that promotes safety and security, law and order, peace and strength, because it is all a façade and a hoax that is the front to turn people against other people, in a way that seems all too familiar in the name of those who shall not be spoken of.

The Hällstadftß is the true enemy of the people, by creating crazy and outlandish civil and criminal trials through misinformation and by making most of it up just to throw a curve ball at everyone so no one will ever find out the truth.

But it is just not over until they say it's over, by turning civil matters into criminal matters, by turning a hoax into a reality, by turning happiness into doom and gloom, by turning a future of happiness into dystopian chaos in the name of chivalry, and by making sure no one shall ever know about the plan being executed to conceal the real truth of the matter.

It has all been seen before but this will just be the beginning of the end for something so sinister that no one will ever understand the meaning and true purpose of what is about to go down but it is for that in which not a single person will feel safe only because of betrayal.

As they say, the Hällstadftß will claim they support the little people, the peasants and commoners, but in reality that support the people in power to grow the hierarchy, and to make sure the peasants and commoners are fighting against each other.

It is just a war to confuse everyone and everything by diverting the facts into a cleverly devised plan that attempts to upend society by making sure they control everything to make sure no one has the advantage but them in every aspect of civilization.

It will be the Victory World Front against the Hällstadftß but surely someone must win but people might have to entertain the notion of joining the enemy just to defeat them.

Until then, all hope is lost, and remains until humanity has ended.

II

A black sedan, long and stretched, rolls out of a secret cove, all in a manner that seems to take the center of attention, and it remains to be seen what the cost will be, as the people decide the fate of all humanity in a way of unknown and pure speculation, to the point that nothing is left unturned or else it shall be ruined, to the idea that chaos is information to the greater good of determining what is actually happening, and to the point that the enemy can actually be defeated by making sure that there is the will and the power of a counter-resistance that has the strength, courage, and ability of defeating the resistance, but for all of that comes a price that there must be bloodshed and war to the extent that chaos rises in favor of anarchy in order to provoke emotion and discord for the purpose of destruction knowing that it is the only plan that shall win.

With the elite group of people in an unidentified car, all that remains to be known is that San Francisco is on the horizon for everything to begin in the name of something unexpected and exciting.

A sudden acceleration all it takes as the car moves forward with ease and control outward of the event that seems all too crazy and kind of unheard of in the eyes of many that don’t want to get involve, and for the ever concept of fascism and National Socialism, there stands something to fight for in this new society.

Cruising along a highway that has seen better days of heavy traffic, Katrina and the rest of the members find it so intriguing and interesting about the damage that has been done, from cracks in the roads, to signs being out of place, from burned down buildings and their remains, along with empty cars and vehicles standing everywhere, there is nothing but a desolate wasteland of sand and clay everywhere hoping for another chance to repopulate all that is needed.

Nothing can be said.

Nothing can be understood.

Dry and barren, rife with debris anyone can imagine, decorated with the most awful smell or stench of a foul smelling odor, something that had the same consistency as sulfur, it all remains to be seen that something must have gone on here that destroyed the wildlife and plants that once inhabited this very region.

The very grasslands that once stood are no more.

Replaced with nothing but the dirt and soil and the sand brought by the natural heavy winds, all life looks to be burned to a pulp that seems to be reminiscent of bombs and missiles striking from above, and it so happens to be something of amusement and something of familiarity to the people that once called this place home to roaming pastures and grazing cows that had all the milk and beef in the land.

There was nothing but contempt, nothing but a place of abandonment in the sense that no one cared anymore, all the while people had to make a new choice of whether to live or die in terms of trying to just get by in the nick of time forever what reason.

It was humanity calling, as there remains some hope, from Katrina to the other members of the Victory World Front, the resistance wants to stop at nothing to silence anyone that stands in the way.

Nothing will stop the Hällstadftß from attacking the Victory World Front in a game of wits and targeted nuance, for all that remains is the same old tricks of the past in a time that is just the same as always from the end of the craziness of society, so all might be disappointed to say the least, but there remains the hope of a better future and that starts now as people are on the verge of changing everything.

Just as everything turns forward, the car keeps on moving, like it has to or else it will die, but it is just a thing of the past by not looking forward to what might come next.

Nothing can be certain but it is just a force of nature, from what is going on now, to the epitome of something uncertain, it all faces on the true goal of infighting for which an ultimately fight might occur sometime soon in the very near future or at least many people will die because that has already been seen.

Surely it will take time, but the vehicle will arrive when it does, but there is a certainty that there might be rest stops and other breaks, just due to the fact it is a 24-hour drive of nearly 1,600 miles, so there will just be a time of what to think, otherwise there will be no other stopping, except for dining in some discrete and unknown locations.

Crossing into the vicinity of unknown paradise with humanity still intact in certain places, there might be hope after all, as Katrina and the rest of the gang rolls into Wyoming to find nothing but glorious grasslands with sand and dirt still intact along with trees and shrubs while animals are still roaming everywhere in enclosed fields surrounded by nothing more than open pastures, but without anything new this is the last frontier that might have survived anything.

There are still some more miles to go but it will take more than a day in the prospects of trying to not settle in the midst of something uncertain that could drag out to nothing more than something sinister.

Across the Great Plains and past the Rocky Mountains, there is just wide open plains and plateaus that are all unaffected by the disaster caused by the atomic bombs, missiles, and other weapons fired upon the people by the Axis Powers, so it seems there is hope for all of humanity that will get to the bottom of something better.

Surely, that will take some time, as it will take the time to get to a new independence of a satisfying turn.

With a spectacular countryside in Middle America, the people are just a living testament that not everyone has given up, because they are the many members of the rural community that raise and farm food for much of the United States of America, from sugar beets to grain and from honeybees to cattle, there is just nothing standing in the way of future if this keeps up, as horses run loose everywhere.

It all seems to focus on something as hope runs dry to the point of no return in the aftermath of something sinister.

Halfway across Nevada, and there is nothing but devastation, as it gets closer to California, so there was an impact here by the bombing or by the missiles.

Flying birds circling everywhere resembling vultures or what seem to be very hungry and waiting for the first thing to die, there is just nothing but a dry and barren wasteland that is nothing but a desert filled with craters and cracks everywhere.

All in the name of the Axis Powers there is nothing good but to reign in everything.

The dryness is just ruining everything, with the air conditioning on full blast, due to the heat being so strong and high that no one can escape the wrath of the sun.

There is still nearly a half day of driving with stops along the way, but with nonstop driving, there is surely to be a sight set on the hope that it will be sooner than later, or else there will be nothing but a case of lacking time of an unknown anomaly of craziness.

Everything won't make sense but it is for that reason why there will never be the presumption of trying to complete the mission in a way that is up to the resistance.

Quickly and slowly, Katrina maneuvers the car as tightly as possible, grasping the wheel in order to avoid anything in the way.

Turtles and rabbits, roadrunners and coyotes, there is nothing that can actually be more peaceful with a lack of vehicular traffic on the nearly but cracked and broken roads connecting the Nevada deserts to the state of what seems to be California.

There is something but craziness in all of this.

As all of this unfolds, there is just something unknown.

Hope only remains if it is certain that people are defeated.

But that remains to be seen in the midst of something that is not too old but a lack of credit given to the heroes.

What lies ahead is mysterious.

But the certainty will only grow stronger as the time gets nearer.

The battle between good and evil gets closer and it all remains to be seen in the context of another.

It could be nothing sort of evil but there is just a case of something that is the opposite of what might happen, because that is just the true and actual feeling of the war that shall arrive shortly in a matter of time in the midst of the country.

Rocks and tumbleweeds, dust and dirt, sand blowing everywhere in all directions of the car, there is something that seems familiar in the life of a sandstorm that seeks to harm everything in sight.

And then, about eleven hours later, there was just applause, but only for a short time, as the group from Winslow saw the devastation caused by the Japanese in San Francisco.

Alas, it was now time to hide the vehicle in somewhere unknown circumstances.

In just a matter of minutes, the group went to a secret location off limits to most people, but not to the members of the Victory World Front and the people fighting for freedom.

III

Arriving in fashion, at an unidentified location, there seems to be a place of safety and security, as the group firmly finds a place to park the car in the midst of an unknown crisis, so it wouldn't be in the mind of what will be set across everything.

"Welcome to the Mission Bunker, where we shall stay until we need to leave, but no one knows about this but us, so it is sealed to the public, and no one will know anything," said the local member.

"What will we actually do here," asked Katrina?

"To plan and operate, to organize and help, but to also live and prosper, so nothing happens to us, but we will be out in the field shortly with no car or anything, except for weapons and other items of need," said the local member.

"How soon until we leave to go to the field," asked a member?

"It depends on the situation at hand, but soon, so we will go soon in the name of freedom, but first let's go to our living quarters," said the local member.

Walking down long and winding corridors in the deep of darkness with just an ample enough of light, with the natural limestone and sandstone walls reinforced with heavy-rated steel rods and beams, there is just this case of an ambivalent nature that is just in the interests of finding something better to do, and with the costs high and uncertain, there is still much thinking to do in the interests of the public.

Through narrow but winding hallways, it's sure as long as time had hoped for, but the natural lighting is seen as an ease of a relief for the few that walk through its areas for whatever reasons, all the while it ceases to amaze no one during the time of an uncertain future, and when it is complete for the season of picking, then the battle between the Victory World Front and the Hällstadftß will take place in an unprecedented manner because no one would expect when it will actually occur.

The dwindling light of hopelessness just fills up whatever is left of the country as a way to determine what needs to happen in the minds of most people.

As Katrina and the group pass through several hallways there is just a sign it could take longer to get to the lobby, to the point everything is getting closer and closer at each passing second, and to the sign that each step could be the death of something strange with the hope that no one will be ever able to live to tell the truth.

It only remains to say when it will all go down in the minds of the people that will be responsible for everything.

At long last, there is light at the end of the tunnel, as the floor turns to bright and glowing granite and marble tile, hoping to lively up the dullness, with a long desk expanding fifteen feet from one side of the room to the other in an abundance of glamour, it all seems fishy.

With lighted torches on the concrete walls reinforced with steel and masonry, there is something that is better, but the group comes to a complete halt in front of the lobby desk that has seen worse days.

From the top of the desk, there sits nothing but office supplies and some accessories out of place, but there are no keys in sight, unless they are surely hidden so no one can find them.

And then the local member goes behind the desk and pushes a button of some kind.

Up appears what resembles a thing of the future, a thing that seems out of place, and a thing that shouldn't be here, but it is here and the local member inputs information and up pops out a keycard one after the other in a way that seems possible but suspicious.

"Rick, Steve, you will take room 43L; Katrina and person from out of town, you will take room 50X, I will take room 62B; Aaron and Conrad, you will take room 48K; so since all of you have your assigned rooms you can go to them now and then have a look around, but first I would ask if there are any questions," said the local member.

"Why such strange room numbers," asked Steve?

"No idea, it's probably because the builder of this place was just a crazy and strange person that wanted to assign strange room numbers for the sole purpose of driving people crazy, or it could be for some other reason that might not make any sense at all," said the local member.

With that, there were no more questions.

"If you all follow me, I will take you to our rooms, so just follow my every footstep as we take the elevator to the fifth floor below this facility, because that is the location of the rooms according to the chart that I got from the desk," said the local member.

The elevator opened its wide yet tall doors, as the group entered to see what everything looks like, and it just takes a matter of seconds to arrive at the final destination.

"Follow the signs," said the local member.

Down the long winding hallways, Katrina and the other person continue to walk, only to find it is like an endless maze that is not going to see the light of day, until there is nowhere else to go, because there is just a sign of no hope.

And then the light appeared at the end of the tunnel, as a sign that read 50X appeared in front.

Grabbing the keycard, Katrina pushes it in, and turns the handle of door, opening to a wildly specular space filled with color and fancy living arrangements all for the luxury of rich and expensive taste.

The door closing behind them, it was just a kind of indulgence that sparked nothing that has been seen before.

There was just vivid bright colors everywhere, as the walls were just so beautiful that lined everything with natural light from the red and yellow paint that brings tranquility and peace everywhere to the point of complete and warranted seduction.

Everything was just so great, with wide open windows and the sea of hope that can be seen from everywhere, to the place that nothing is as it ever seems to be.

Walking forward, there is just the case of something that helps the mind to settle on something, for some unknown purposes.

It could be the drapes donning over the windows or the elaborate carpeting that seems so ornate and beautiful to the naked eye, but that is only the beginning of everything, as there is nothing more beautiful at what can be seen to the world of darkness.

The room was just so big that it was fit for a king or someone of very high importance, but there was just more, as a staircase appeared to the right of a door, and that could be an expansion of everything, making it so that this might be the largest room in existence, but to the left of the windows were a second set of doors that led to a corridor that further led to a bathroom and a kitchen along with a private spa and some other rooms that no one should care about.

Something just doesn't seem right.

There shouldn't be any windows anywhere unless they are painted to resemble something that looks real.

It could all be an illusion.

Or it could be something more sinister by playing a trick on the mind.

That could be it.

But there is just no other explanation about any of this.

It is pure coincidence about anything.

That is just the end of something that needs to be settled before any more information gets out of hand.

Nothing is that simple but it is just crazy.

There was nothing that can be said but it is surely a case of surprises to everyone else to the point that nothing can be seen in the eyes of the crazy and new world of destruction outside.

Just then, there is only quietness, as silence is everywhere.

Looking at everything now there is just complete conviction of what will happen next.

There is a pause in the air, as Katrina and the other person look at each other like they were mesmerized to see each other, be it by their looks or by their character, but it was like a game was being played on them by a new mysterious force.

Closely, they look at each other, and Katrina leans in closer, as her lips grow closer to his, all in a time of the unknown.

Both get closer and closer until their lips meet and then they kiss passionately to the point that seduction has set in for the purpose that it is all for the better.

It is now a passionate love affair as both wrestle each other to the bed and continue to rip off their clothes in the heat of passion caused by some type of unknown cause, but it will surely rattle anyone at the point of nothing more than an illicit affair frowned upon by everyone in society.

Pressure was increasing and soon it was just a spectacle for everyone to see, should any outsider decide to watch, as both lie completely naked in a large bed draped with a tall canopy, to the point that something is just crazy about nothing.

Caressing her thighs, as his fingers slid so ever lower down her body, it is a sensation of happiness; all with her legs being wide open for pleasure of something unknown.

She thrust her body on top of his and it took off from there as she moaned loudly and whimpered quietly, as she continued to try to climax to his body, while there was a sensation of pleasure and tingling across both of their bodies, in a way that seemed uniform.

Her tender yet sweet sexy body was all over him as both passionately kissed while they were rocking the bed.

There was a rush of adrenaline as the speed picked up and then it was like something spectacular.

The bed was moving like it was never before and there was surely a love affair going on but it remained to be seen in the light of day to the point of distinction.

Both flipped, and she was now on the bottom, and he thrusts himself inside her, penetrating her body and offering a sensation that has only been felt before a few times.

She grasps her lips as she moans lightly with the sensation of a shock and a pleasure of guilt.

As he is thrusting, her nipples are just rock hard, like they are ready to explode with leaking breastmilk, but everything is just too pleasurable to the point it is surely a positive sensation to the point of excitement for everyone to experience something new.

And they flip over again, where she is on top, and he is now on the bottom, with everything being a love affair, while leaning closely to his lips in order to kiss passionately, and with him sliding his fingers slowly down her chest, touching her breasts to feel the nice and young tender skin of her body, so it all seemed worthwhile.

Moving back and forth, while rocking the bed, there couldn't be any better thing to do, with all the rough and easy maneuvering of their bodies in unison, to the point it was about love.

There was just pleasure.

Stroking her body endlessly, he made it felt like something special, the thing that matters the most, but it was just discrete and hidden from the view.

No one saw this coming but it was just a beautiful experience of wonder.

They flipped again and again and it was not a cause of concern for something that never made sense at all and all because of something crazy like this ever before.

They tossed and turned like it was a wrestling match between some battles against who can be the best.

Her plumped lip and raised nipples, all felt the sensation of the thrust as she continued to ride him back and forth in compassion and passion, to the point of hope and dignity.

She felt the sensation ever so gradually and it continued to grow between them, leading to something that felt like a fantastic dream of hope and pleasure, making it so that it was nothing bad because it was just all too good to be true in the sense that something like this would always happen all because of happiness.

Their bodies finally collided, as they both felt a sensation of never-ending tingling, forcing the pressure out of every part of their body like a truly relaxing experience at the beach for all to watch when putting on some sunscreen to ward off the sun from burning the body to a crispness of bacon from all the heat on a hot and sunny day in paradise.

Their bodies climaxed together as both felt satisfied from pleasure and sensation of a deeply sensual experience.

They stop and he lies her head on his chest as he stokes her hair softly and mildly, all while falling asleep on each other, to the point that it is all to the point of comfort.

IV

Softly and slowly, they get up and walk to the bathroom, all while making sure everything is fine, to the point that it is, but in the mindset of what is to come next by trying to get on with the mission of how to solve the problem at hand.

The water is set to lukewarm, as both get in to rinse off from their sensual but beautiful experience.

Suds overflowing their bodies while water dripping down their body past their thighs, while caressing each other; it is just a display of passion and love for everything to see.

Embracing each other, they begin a passionate affair and love, as Katrina places her hand on the steamy clear shower door that begins to show evaporation, while he penetrates the inside of her body once more in a sense of pleasure and glamour in a leaning and bent over position with her legs spread wide and clear.

Faster and faster, the speed picks up, and she is just moaning to the sounds of joy, whether it is luck or just a coincidence, but pleasure is just a sign of love.

Climaxing together, they feel a sigh of relief, something that makes them happy, as Katrina gets on her knees and begins sucking in a back and forth motion, making it all so pleasurable to him, as it's just like a field of sunflowers and daisies to the point that there is excitement from a very old type of act that is always sensual and tingling by nature.

It is just so arousing that no one can stop as they feel the racing of their hearts pumping as more and more blood fill up their veins making it so that the experience becomes more gratifying.

Harder and faster, it is making it pleasurable to the maximum amount of potential, and the point of no return has arrived, making it so there is just no turning back now.

Katrina swallows, grasping her mouth, and then taking a big gulp before getting up.

They kiss again and rinse off to the point it is a tingling sensation all across their bodies.

Finished and done, they dress themselves, all the while putting on something sexy yet flirtatious after walking completely naked into a large and wide walk-in closet.

It is all simply a distraction to look at, as there is cause for alarm when no one is watching, as Katrina dresses in sexy yet sheer lace lingerie and something special in a gorgeous black dress not revealing any flaws of her body, while Eric wears something more glamourous that says sexy but too sophisticated in a pair of designer jeans and a shirt along with a dark and black leather biker jacket.

Some things are just the same as always but this is surely the first step of all straws in the way that it doesn't even make sense at all because of the way it sounds.

They depart the room and head to look around the Mission Bunker, all in a way that seems suspicious to no one but the rest of society and on the brink of hope.

The door shuts behind them and they think where to go and what to do before it is too late.

It is just curiosity that kills everything, as both discover a map of the facility and look for something that interests map.

They find the location of something that seems spectacular but also kind of daring, to the point that it will get them nowhere.

Ripping off their clothes as they run, they streak in the daylight from the natural lighting of the bunker, and there is little care in the world if for some reason they are spotted, because they just don't care if anyone sees them in the flesh.

Arriving at the elevator, they go to the sub-basement, where they arrive at a private grotto.

A bright light illuminates from the outside offering some fresh air to anyone that cares all the while offering a chance to see civilization and to see if there is anything that can offer relaxation.

There is just nothing but natural limestone surrounding everything in the distance, as they skinny dip all around natural lighting.

It is just fun for everything and for the world to watch as something is about to happen soon.

But that is just normal as usual in the prism of time.

Kissing and laughing they are just having a good time and it is meant to be that way, and it seems like paradise because everything is so close to the ocean that waves can be heard outside, linking something that need to check out for the better of time.

They get out of the pool and walk toward the light, as they can see nothing but beautiful golden sand everywhere in the near vicinity, with vibrant blue waves flowing with waves to palm trees and cabanas lining the shoreline everywhere.

This is the chance of the lifetime, as it is a private beach, and no one else knows about it.

Everything just feel so spectacular as they soon embrace and fall on top of each other, passionately kissing and engaging in wild beach sex for all to see, and it is just spectacular to witness while they have it all to themselves with no one watching

Two hours later they are just lying in the sand as they just wait to see what happens next.

It is nothing short of anything.

The view is just breathtaking with no clothes, no rules, and nothing to be followed.

With the wind flowing in their hair and all through their bodies, there is nothing but a sensation of a wonderful experience of getting sand in places that can never be imagined.

The fun is just beginning.

All just feels so wonderful with everything present that anyone could ever want.

Hungry, they decide to go find a locker room, and they put on some clothes that seem to represent battle ready armor, in the sense that it includes heavy-duty black trousers, heavy-duty military jackets, boots, a belt, panties for ladies, boxers for men, socks, a blouse for ladies, and dress shirts for men, all in an attempt to make sure everything is ready.

One by one, both put on their underwear, followed by their tops, then their trousers, the military jacket, the socks, and then their boots, all while not thinking of anything else.

There is just nothing to see better than all dressed in black while looking dapper in something sexy yet convincing to everyone else that no one is messing around.

No nametags needed and it is to be kept that way in order to not keep anyone from finding out anything.

That is how it is meant to be and it will remain for always and eternity in a way that is confusing to everyone as they world sees fit to strike the plan of the century.

They find an automated vending machine and it just spits out hot food in a matter of a few minutes.

Feeling content, they decide to leave the area and go back to their rooms for whatever is left to do and because they don't want to miss anything that will happen.

And then something bizarre just happens that doesn't seem like it should be happening.

Everything is about to get crazy.

Sirens are sounding everywhere, presenting a sign of an imminent threat to national security or to the world, that war might be inevitable and no one will be able to escape the wrath of anything.

It is just so deafening with it being nonstop and repetitive, but there is just so puzzling that no one is reacting to anything except for Katrina and Eric, so there is probably something up with what's happening outside of this bunker, and it might be a surprise to find out about anything.

Everything was just so sudden.

They didn't know how to react at first but it was just so crazy.

Stopping and thinking, they just remained calm, until they could find a way out.

Arriving at the main lobby, they found a note, indicating that there is danger ahead, as the Victory World Front and the Hällstadftß have started an all-out war against each other, after the Hällstadftß blew up and then razed a building belonging to the Victory World Front.

There was a warning of leaking gas everywhere and to put on and wear gas masks located behind the lobby desk.

Another warning appeared saying there is not enough time left and to leave as soon as possible before there is any more danger to innocent people that don't deserve to die.

Quickly thinking, Katrina and Eric look behind the lobby desk and find two objects that resemble black ski masks with two holes in the middle, one for the left eye and the other being for the right eye, while there is one more hole below it containing a filter and respirator in order to breathe better just in case.

So they put the masks over their heads and it fits perfectly with the rest of the black clad uniform, making it a match, while making it old school and obsolete for some familiar and strange reason, in the reason that there is better technology.

In fact, the two holes for the eyes had fog-proof lenses that made it easy to see, while the respirator and filter made it easy to breathe whenever a breath of air was made or whenever an odor was detected, so it was part of the feature that made it automatic.

But then they read the letter again and it told them to grab some black gloves located one shelf below, in which it will protect their hands from fire and any other dangerous substance, so they find the lower shelf and put on a pair of black gloves.

Still reading, they read that they are not still fully protected, as they are told to put on fire-proof protective gear over their clothes, gloves, and boots so they don't burn in a fire.

The note says to press a button underneath the desk of the desk and so they both feel for a button, and for once they feel something and press it as hard as they can, making sure it will help them to be fully protected from the elements.

Out of nowhere, they hear a noise, sounding close enough.

Behind them, a secret passageway opens, revealing some sort of secret room.

On the wall there are two hooks containing black body suits, one for Eric and the other for Katrina.

They unzip the protective body suits and then step inside and zip each other up, where it is tight-fitting but somewhat comfortable and warm inside due to special protective black aluminized material along with an added gel and rubber protection on the interior as well as on the exterior of the suit to provide for extreme heat and fire protection.

Heavily insulated, they have an added layer of protection, with another way to escape death.

Katrina and Eric read the note again, and it tells them to just walk forward, and the secret door will close behind them, and so they walk pass the hooks and straight towards endless darkness.

But then another siren sounds the alarm, indicating something bad.

It is a gas alert.

The secret door closes behind them, while the rest of the building fills with lethal gas that has never seen the likes of day.

Lighted torches soon appear on the sides of the natural limestone walls reinforced with concrete and steel, all to the added protection of some hidden feature.

There is an imminent war.

And it has just begun to settle in across the minds of many people making them feel nauseous and causing chaos.

The world could end soon but nothing is known.

It is all for a cause.

Katrina and Eric might be the last hope of saving the future from anarchy and destruction everywhere.

They find themselves stuck but they see a knob to the left and then turn it clockwise.

Nothing happens.

They see a button and push it.

A secret passageway opens.

They walk forward and can see they are not in the same building anymore.

It is now a secret passageway of natural and manmade tunnels with little light.

Lighted torches align the walls making it better to see.

And then there is a hard noise, something that looks to sound like it fell down.

They look behind and see nothing.

The secret door has shut itself behind them, trapping them or making it impossible to escape the same way they entered.

The two must find a way out but they don't know how to get out but to just move forward until it leads to the light at the end of the tunnel, making it possible to see where they are going.

Looking at the note, they are told to just move forward until they reach the end.

That is just simply vague to tell the truth.

But who cares?

Everything is a manner of life and death right now.

There is no way of knowing if anyone is alive in the Mission Bunker anymore so all hope seems lost.

What lies on the other side is just a mystery as they continue forward on the path.

Since they can't do anything else they just move forward.

Immediately, after they take their first step, the natural lighting from the limestone appears to illuminate everywhere, all in a way that makes sense of the darkness.

But there is no more light, with it disappearing after taking the second step, all to disappointment.

Only natural stone remain.

Katrina and Eric keep on moving making sure that nothing happens to them in the course of events.

Nothing but darkness until there is any more in what seems strange to the thing of the past, because it all happens for the same reason that belongs to nothing in the mind of a tunnel.

Deep within the confines of the underground, Katrina and Eric continue their descent or ascent to somewhere special, somewhere they might have been before, but there are no signs of claustrophobia, while there is just a quiet and pleasant noise of water droplets dripping down from above, all in a usual manner of constant repetition.

It could be that they are already deep beneath a large body of water with nowhere to escape, but as they continue, they see a sign saying that they are now 10,000 feet below sea level, indicating a rush of adrenaline for a very brief second as blood rushes to the veins for a chance to think about the possibilities.

And then, the smell of gas starts to appear, as they go deeper and deeper underground, smelling all the natural gases plus any other poison that seeps from the pollution above.

Everything just smells like rotten eggs, the type of stench only found in sewers and other places that are unknown.

Sewer gas, combined with methane and usually other gases such as hydrogen sulfide, which gives it an odor so awful that a person would run away.

The stench is so toxic it will just lead to pain and suffering but thankfully Katrina and Eric are safe from everything, as they go deeper and deeper underground until they arrive at a point of no return that guides them to the surface.

There will be no pain and suffering today.

No, because anyone in a protective suit will be safe from hazardous odors that might cause people to faint, causing it just to affect the dwelling of the natural limestone walls.

Suddenly, both Katrina and Eric stop, after seeing more writing on the walls.

Torches appear all around them attached to some base.

Both pick one up.

With a torch in hand they need to light it as it is only getting darker and darker in here.

More writing appears and it tells anyone to push a switch on the side and then scrape the wick of the torch on the limestone.

So they do exactly that and bright orange and red flames appear, causing heat to spread everywhere, all because of too much gas being in the air.

And then it just gets darker and darker as they go deeper into the tunnels of an unknown destination.

There could be secret passageways and then cracks in the bedrock, both of which could trigger the collapse of an already fragile yet unknown environment.

They move forward, being careful, as the only lighting is from the torches carrying by hand.

Several tunnels appear and it is a cause for confusion.

Going through the wrong one might trigger a tap door and no one would want that to happen.

Anything could happen now and it is decision time to decide what will happen next in what could become a very frightening situation that will lead to hope and change disappearing for humanity.

Someone must make a decision now?

Should they take the tunnel to the left, to the far left, to the right, to the far right, or in the center?

There is no way to know.

They could play it safe and go through different tunnels but that would be devastating if something bad happens to either of them, so they are just going to have to decide as a team.

Without hesitation, they look, and decide to take the middle tunnel in hopes it will lead them to the outside.

Trap doors could still appear anywhere, and the bedrock could just start to crack.

Embedded lights soon appear within the walls and ceiling of the tunnel, and it all seems like this was the safest choice to pick, but it is still so dark without anything near in sight.

It was just so creepy and dark because of the unknown.

Anything could happen in a matter of seconds.

At long last, there was finally some light, as the tunnel appeared to reflect the rays of natural sunlight.

After three long hours of walking through the middle tunnel, there was hope, and hope for everyone else.

They don't know where it will lead, but it was just chance by luck.

As they get closer and closer, they finally see land, and then it all leads to the outside world.

Katrina and Eric exit the tunnel, leading them to a lush tropical paradise somewhere unknown, until they see a sign indicating they are in the Yucatan Peninsula of Mexico on a crisp warm beach with calm waters near a Mexican beach resort.

It is far away from where they need to be but it is just by chance that they ended up here.

That is safety.

But they need to figure a way out before it all ends in disaster.

The world could be ending but it is not more than something that needs to happen in the nick of time to prevent a disaster.

They check in at the resort, all to the surprise that no one is even here, so it is just a sign something bad happened already.

Everything seems too empty and looks too suspicious.

Something isn't right, as they think to themselves just as they enter their room, a larger than life presidential suite with everything that can be imagined to the point of luxury.

And then it dawns on them.

They are the only ones to escape the Mission Bunker alive.

Everyone else died from poisoned gas spread from the air vents in their rooms.

The resistance has attacked and this is all a diversion.

It could be all over in a matter of moments.

But there is something more to find out.

Quickly, it will happen sooner or later.

The place just seems deserted with no one in sight so it is like the whole world has abandoned society.

Katrina and Eric find their room and it leads them to a surprise of a lifetime again in the apparent hope they will figure out why they are in some Mexican beach resort and how they ended up here anyway.

Sun rays are everywhere and the heat is getting to them.

They carefully unzip the fire protection suits off from each other's bodies so they won't burn up anytime soon.

Spotting some hooks in front of them, they hang them up so nothing gets dirty, because then it will become contaminated and nobody would want that to happen.

Thinking quickly, they look around, and feel as though the room is rather large, noticing an ocean view from a balcony enclosed with tall but elegant French door windows that has an ornate but beautiful design of what seems to be wonderful structure.

The bed is draped with a spectacular canopy all the while the ocean can be heard from below, to the point of seduction.

The glass windows are just amazing with the beach making a perfect fit.

To their right they see a door.

It opens.

A bathroom appears.

Full of gold and diamond encrusted, it is so large that it can be turned into a separate hotel room, with fine porcelain sinks and toilets along with a free standing tub, the floor is yet so elegant made of marble with hues of red, pink, black, white, and green interwined everywhere across all surfaces while gold lines the walls and diamonds are embedded throughout the towel bars and handles along with the knobs to show a sign of gold old-fashion quality of luxurious living.

Closing the door, they look to their left and see another door, not even knowing where it will lead.

They open it and see a gorgeous indoor spa where one can relax after a stressful day of hopelessness and torture to the extent that it will remove any bad thoughts or misgivings about life.

The floor is lined with high quality marble with low bamboo and cedar benches on opposite sides, with a small Roman bath in the middle of everything, a sauna to the right as indicated on the door, and a private shower room on the left indicated by another door.

Another door appears right in front of them, saying galley, so it must be some sort of private kitchen.

Going forward, they open it and see something just spectacular, from marble floors to granite counter tops, along with restaurant-style ovens built into the walls and surrounded by cabinets, to a flattop wood and coal burning stove, all in the name of being vintage and unique, with sinks as clean as they ever could be and fine white porcelain china.

Nothing seems right.

The layout of this room seems strange and just mysterious.

But it is a breath of fresh air to be finally inside of a safe building once again.

Exiting the kitchen, it is a time to relax and think about something less stressful, so they head to the sauna.

Nothing but black stone lines the wall everywhere, yet there are no towels in sight, but just some built-in benches to sit on along with the steam tank and cord that generates the heat and steam.

So they just check out the shower room, and find it to contain several towels, along with a few toilets, sinks, and a flat walk-in shower with no sign of a curtain anywhere as well as with an added feature that the entire floor is made out of vintage ceramic tile with a built-in drain.

With an open shower in mind everything is going to be more exciting in a spectacular but vibrant environment.

There is just something to think about as the sky is about to clear of clouds that are on the horizon.

Feeling tense and stressed out from walking underground and then somehow all the way to Mexico, Katrina and Eric undress and grab some towels for the sauna.

It feels just so relaxing to them, as the steam starts to flow out all around their bodies and through all orifices of their skin, as a way to weed out any toxins or poisons that might be harming harm.

But especially, it provides relaxation to the best amount possible, as the heat warms their bodies with the kind of heat needed for winter weather in a time of need and shelter.

Both are just sweating with joy as their pores start to open up with every ounce of steam that penetrates their bodies, all for a sign whatever they are facing will go away soon.

Katrina pulls the cord again and again with some notion it will help get rid of any particle of gas or dust stuck from the suit, as it seems to work in a matter of moments, and so this might cause something to overlook but it just feels necessary.

The heat is working.

The steam is draining out the toxins as they continue to sweat in a gorgeous sauna that is just of fine quality.

A few hours later, they get dressed.

Now, they must find a way to get back to civilization, before it's too late.

VI

Suddenly, a flashing bright light appears, and there is just the case for déjà vu all over again, as this sighting seems odd and strange because light does not appear out of nowhere unless it could be a trapped spirit, but it is just there, appearing out of nowhere, flashing or blinking, whatever people will call it, trying to seek some sort of attention, but this could be a sign that the times are changing and it is about to get messy because there is just a sign of uncertainty everywhere with no other people around, so there is a lack of important information to get to the bottom of this issue, making it difficult to comprehend in the minds of many.

The light is still flickering, like it is waiting for something or someone to enter it.

Curious, Katrina and Eric put on their black clad military gear with the exception of the fire suit, and they immediate jump into the bright white light that continues to flash.

No one knows where it will lead and no one cares but it is about to happen.

There is just something to counter with about nothing.

Time will just have to wait and that might be soon.

It is just something unusual.

But in just a matter of moments, they are spit out of time, entering into an unknown time that resembles desertion.

The year is 1945.

And war seems to be everywhere.

Destruction is everywhere, with buildings on fire and high-rises about to collapse under their weight from structural damage.

It is a scary but frightening scene, with nearly everything up in flames for unknown reasons.

High-rises are already tumbling down, with people screaming and shouting while they try to seek shelter or hide, in order to not die in a fiery death.

Ash and debris rain down on the streets and roads of a destroyed city landscape, as people watch in fear what is happening to their much beloved and sprawling civilization of progress, but it all remains that there isn't much time left to live, for the world is seen crumbling down as everyone is helpless in a time of need.

Katrina and Eric watch in dismay as everything starts to crumble down before them.

It is entirely chaos, as destruction just keeps on coming.

There is just the feeling everything is a war zone.

No one can escape.

But who would want to enter this dump of a place?

No one, as it is a disaster here in DC, with everything soon to be on fire.

The feeling seems mutual while it is actually catastrophic.

Buildings continue to crumble, as their foundations crack, and their support have been lost from destructive damage.

Death looms as everything gets worse.

People are everywhere, running and screaming, as they try to find a way out.

Many have already been crushed to death.

Some are trying to stay alive.

And the rest are having a tough time about how they can just run and hide in order to avoid imminent death.

There is nowhere to go.

Police are nowhere to be found.

Firefighters are missing from the scene.

No paramedics can be seen helping the deceased or injured.

A lack of emergency personnel is on the line of duty.

The people are just insane and do not know what to do but that is just chaos.

There is a new fear.

Innocent civilians are being trampled upon as the people are pushing and shoving each other in a violent manner making it impossible to escape any sort of injury.

Death and destruction are imminent but has already occurred.

Soon there will be nothing left to do.

Chaos will take over everyone and everything, but it already has, making it impossible to eliminate any doom and gloom from society in a time of peril and collapse.

Nothing is left but full-scale anarchy.

DC has been destroyed, as people start to protest in violence against each other.

Taking to the streets, they demand answers, with pitchforks and torches in hand, there is no sign that anyone will give up.

The sidewalks are full.

The streets are busy.

Violence and anarchy is everywhere, as there is nothing but chaos and destruction.

Residents are angry.

They have the right to be.

They are upset and frustrated about everything because no one is helping them.

It could all be a waste of time but no one is paying to attention to Katrina and Eric.

No one even notices anyone except themselves.

Everyone is just too preoccupied with what they are doing.

Molotov cocktails are being thrown everywhere.

Vehicles are on fire.

There is broken glass everywhere.

Streets are starting to crack, with sidewalks smashed in.

Trees are on fire while branches are falling off every second.

Leaves are up in flames and nothing can be stopped.

There is just something everywhere and soon it might all come to a screeching halt.

Something could happen soon and that might be a problem for the rest in the way of turmoil, as no one is known to anyone, because there is a lack of answers.

Anyone could be a spy within the group of rioters taking to the streets and that will be just defeating to say the least.

The Victory World Front could be embedded anywhere.

The Hällstadftß could have enemies within the groups.

Nothing will be off limits and that is such sorrow.

With pitchforks in hand and torches held high, they start to march against everything that America stood for.

They target everything in sight.

There is nowhere to hide, as people start to throw projectiles in the air trying to protest everything.

And then there was something that came crashing down, sounding like a supersonic fighter jet in the way that it just broke the sound barrier yet again.

People fled in panic, as they didn't know what was happening.

They just didn't know.

Was it a new threat?

Possibly, but it was an unexpected sign, making it unpredictable.

No one ever saw this coming and yet somehow this did happen in an unpredictable way.

Panic is just everywhere now.

There is more uncertainty than ever as the people suddenly erupt in turmoil from the possibility they might now suffer an imminent death for some unknown reason.

It could be a sign from above.

Or it could be a sign that someone else is under attack.

Another sonic boom is heard and it's just deafening in the sense that people are developing migraines from some unknown noise that is coming from an unidentified source.

The world could be crashing down.

But there is something else to this.

There is something else happening.

Still, everyone is just unaware, while Katrina and Eric are just looking and acting with glee.

Turmoil is just about to turn the tide with nothing being relevant ever more so relevant in this time of chaos or a form of uncivilized society that acts on a whim of nonsense.

All of a sudden, fire balls are seen flying through the skies, like they are coming from space.

People start to flee and panic again, as they now scream and shout to the top of their lungs, all in a sign that this is the end of the current world as they see it.

There is only destruction and it is looming wild from the chaos, the panic, the anarchy, and the violence.

Mayhem just sounded like it will be the best thing that will happen to anyone that's watching.

Katrina and Eric are standing still while everyone else has nothing better to do than panic, all in a time of uncertainty while sonic booms and fire balls are terrorizing DC.

The former capital is now under complete mayhem with nothing that can be done to stop it.

People are under attack and believe it is the apocalypse.

As the rest of the world watches in horror, there is just a sign of unity that hope shall arrive in time, with the added notion that this is only a dream and everything will go back to normal, unless someone somehow decides to interfere with everything else.

And then, it happened again.

Something just wasn't right but it happened again.

There was more uncertainty.

Out of nowhere, a cloud of darkness appeared, eliminating the hope that it was only a dream.

The sky turned pitch black.

All of DC was now under threat with the fear that a severe rainstorm was on the way.

Heavy winds start to appear and there is even more destruction.

It appears like something of the past, like a severe hurricane, just with no rain and thunder.

This could also be a twister.

But where's the funnel cloud?

A monsoon is possible and so is a typhoon.

Yet there is only heavy wind.

There are only pitch black clouds.

And there are only fireballs raining down from the skies above.

Something isn't right but everyone is just too busy running away from an imminent disaster.

Will it happen or will it not?

That is the question.

No one knows.

No one cares.

They just want to escape without dying, if possible.

But everything is collapsing around them with a new threat on the rise.

A bright orange cascade of smog suddenly without notice covers the dark pitch black clouds, all of a sign that something that there will be danger to be done.

People are fleeing like hell because they don't know what to expect.

It could all be a nightmare but it isn't

The panic and screaming continues, as Katrina and Eric just watch from the sidelines in the vicinity of a secluded area.

It's a good thing that both of them are wearing their gas masks or else they might face the same situation.

The sky turns to orange and people panic as it is a sign that people will inhale toxic elements.

No one wants to experience that but it will happen since they are always predictable in running away.

They are not thinking.

Something is just a pain but it isn't new, so that is the time it ceases to exist.

Suddenly people begin to choke and cough.

And then there is the fainting of many people.

Everything is crashing in around them but not before something dire is in the midst of something sinister.

All was too strange and it was just a fact of life something more could happen in a time of uncertainty with regards to everything else because that is just something about nothing.

It was like a sudden wreck, as something surely happened.

High-rises continue to collapse and now there was toxic air from some type of smog that has never been seen before.

Something did not feel right.

Everything went silent like people were expecting something more threatening.

Then it was made clear from the sight and sound from it.

A tsunami rolled down the streets and alleys of all of DC and they knew this was the end of the world.

This could be the end of their lives.

A few seconds later, lightning strikes the water, followed by fire balls of death, and then the inevitable sonic boom.

It was all there.

Katrina and Eric were watching the madness as it all happened, from the sidelines, out of harm's way.

Most of DC was now underground in water, making it hopeful that it will lead to something better.

Such a catastrophic event has never occurred before but maybe this is a sign from Mother Nature that the enemy has been defeated.

Incredibly, the immense pressure from the tsunami ripped open the high rises making them collapse upon impact, breaking the glass, and then drowning everyone in a matter of seconds.

That was just a disaster of epic proportions, making it impossible to determine the fatalities from a flash flood.

It was all over as the dead bodies flowed through the streets of DC and were taken to the river or any other bodies of water from a sense that was just catastrophic to civilization.

And then, a bright white light appeared, flashing like there was no tomorrow, indicating it was probably time to leave.

Katrina and Eric run towards it, disappearing like they were never there, just moments before it impacted the place where they were standing on top of the old Lincoln Memorial.

In a flash, they were gone, as if nothing ever existed for the time that they were here, all in a time of a notion that something major is about to happen for something not present.

Reality has set in, with the added awareness that nearly all people within DC have either drowned or are going to drown if they don't find a way out soon.

That is such a sad reality.

Within an instant, Katrina and Eric were spit out, taking them to a place of unknown certainty.

Allied forces were seen breaking the barriers set forth by the Axis Powers all in a matter of hours making sure they could defeat the type of obstacles that could blow everything up.

But the Atlantic Wall was no match for the Allied forces.

The allies broke through using brute force and strength.

The invasion of Normandy has begun and not one person expected that to happen.

It is a battle worth fighting for as there was just warfare in every direction.

Katrina and Eric disappeared and were nowhere to be found, just as something was going to go down in one of the greatest invasions of all times thanks to something unexpected.

A fight breaks out unexpectedly between the Victory World Front and the Hällstadftß, making it seem all too familiar as the Germans continue to fend off the allies, and for the time being there was just something for the thing to prosper.

It was the fight of the century but the Hällstadftß was just on the brink of defeat within the month.

At long last, the Victory World Front has defeated the Hällstadftß, but nothing is seen as normal ever again.

Something was just crazy about this.

The victory was short-lived and it was soon the beginning of the great day that the resistance was defeated.

Timing was just inevitable.

There was no sure way anyone would win but the Victory World Front did just that.

They defeated the Hällstadftß when no one else could.

Time was now on the side of the allies.

No one needed to do anything more, as everything was back on target for people to win once again.

The allies were victorious by finally winning in a time when no one else thought they could.

His plan worked and it was all thanks to Winston Churchill, who faced an uphill battle of trying to stop the allies.

It was a sign of hope, and everything was just back on track, helping the rest of society and civilization.

The allies finally celebrated their victory in Europe on May 8, 1945, with the defeat of the Nazi Reich, all in the name of strategy making it a sign of good hope.

On September 2, 1945, Japan finally surrenders, celebrating a victory for the people and society.

It was happiness for everyone, as it was clear the bad deeds have been erased.

Exactly on time, a bright white light appeared, transporting Katrina and Eric to a time of familiarity that is already racing for the status of a much heated debate.

The date is November 3, 2020.

Appearing in a field dressed in a trench coat is a young woman of elegance and glamor with a gorgeous body and thin physique waiting for the reason of hope, as the race was just called, with Donald Trump reelected as the 45th President of the United States of America.

Katrina was just waiting and wishing, as she smiled and winked just as she was leaving the vicinity of the White House, wishing his reelection well, making it all possible by setting up a course of events to win as if it was always certain.

She departs and goes to wherever needed next.

Everything is back to normal as if the things of the past never even happened.

Katrina knew of everything and was responsible for all.

She left the lawn smiling with a display of hope.

Wherever she will go, time will tell, making it a thing of the past.

No one ever saw her again.

Just like that she disappeared into thin air, like a ghost, making it seem Katrina Maribelle never existed.

The White House started to flow with applause.

It was just the beginning of a new and great revolution, making it all seem possible people was watching.

Everything was now back to normal.

It was as if nothing ever happened.

And just like that, everyone became illuminated with joy.

Hope and change has won again.

Katrina was just holding back while walking off to where she was needed next.

She smiles, as she waits what to do next.

www.ingramcontent.com/pod-product-compliance
Lightning Source LLC
Chambersburg PA
CBHW081128300726
48982CB00005B/885

* 9 7 8 0 9 9 8 4 3 1 1 8 5 *